Praise for The Ea

"A swoonworthy summer read with a hopeful lesson about how to move forward without fear." —*Kirkus Reviews*

"Readers looking for a gentle read about recovering from grief, buoyed by a community of welcoming new friends and new love, will find Snow's latest fits the bill." — *Library Journal*

"*As Much as I Ever Could* is a charming, fast-paced love story that will leave your heart full. Everyone needs a Memaw in their life, and everybody deserves a Jett to look at them the way he looks at his Cami. CJ's journey will make you laugh, cry, cringe and most of all, love. I'm so lucky to have been able to read this early. Brandy Snow is a talented author you'll want to add to your auto-buy list." — Deborah Crossland, YA author of *Within and Without* and *The Quiet Part Out Loud*

As Long as I Have You

Brandy Woods Snow

Sugah Publishing

Sugah Publishing | Fountain Inn, SC | www.sugahpublishing.com

Cover Design © 2022 by JRC Designs/Jena R Collins | www.jenarcollins.com

Farm Scene Scene Break Graphic "Designed by createvil / Freepik"

Wheat Chapter Graphic "Designed by macro vector / Freepik"

Publisher's Note: This is a work of fiction. Names, characters, places, and incidents are a product of the author's imagination. Locales and public names are sometimes used for atmospheric purposes. Any resemblance to actual people, living or dead, or to businesses, companies, events, institutions, or locales is completely coincidental.

As Long As I Have You | Brandy Woods Snow

A headstrong Appalachian girl, determined to save her family farm from foreclosure, takes on a lucrative internship at Johnson Farms where she competes for prize money and the heart of Farmer Johnson's son.

ISBN 978-1-7363019-4-4

ISBN e-book 978-1-7363019-5-1

❀ Created with Vellum

To Myself

It's been a hard two years, Brandy, but you pulled through. Learn to love yourself more and give yourself credit for being a boss. I'm proud of you, and I think it's time I finally told you so.

CHAPTER 1

Bo

My cap and gown sit in a puddle in the backseat while a dozen roses ride shotgun. The look on Laurel's face when she sees me standing on her doorstep is going to be priceless. No more boring fresh-off-the-farm Bo Johnson who never leaves Edisto. I have a year off between high school and whatever I decide to do for the rest of my life, and dammit, I'm going to start it off right by surprising my girl and defining this "thing" we've got going. It's been three years of long-distance, but this morning I graduated and she's graduating at the end of the month so there's no reason we can't come up with a better alternative. The endless texts, occasional phone calls, and one week every summer when her family makes the 415-mile journey south to visit her grandma for vacation just isn't enough. I need more, and I'm hoping she agrees.

Turn left onto Ashworth Avenue. Your destination is on the right.

I wait for a woman with a schnauzer on a leash to cross the street then follow the GPS's robotic commands, pulling to the curb in front of a tan two-story colonial with green shutters. A couple of stately maples stand guard on either side of the property line and a row of trees cross the back. I glance down at the photo on my phone—the one Laurel sent me of her standing out in front of the house, wearing a blue sleeveless dress before her family's Easter service at church. I run my thumb over the image. Yep, that's the house, all right. I'm here. And all it took me was seven hours in the car on I-95. Well, three years and seven hours to be exact.

I pop a mint in my mouth and grab the flowers from the seat beside me. My heart drums in my chest. Romantic gestures have never been my thing—that's totally my sister Gin's department —but now seems like the perfect time to start. I step out onto the asphalt and bump the door closed with my hip while running my fingers through my hair, trying to tame some of the wild curls that've surely gone astray from riding with the windows down.

I stoop slightly, catching a full body glimpse of myself in the reflection on my Bronco. Hair looks okay. My blue button-down shirt isn't too wrinkled from the long drive. Jeans are fine. Even put on my new boots, not the mud-stained ones I use in the field. I take in a deep breath, letting the oxygen wash over me in a calming wave.

Let's do this.

I trek up the cobblestone pathway. On the property's far edge, a handful of cars sit on the driveway that sweeps up the hill and around to the backyard. At least people are home.

In all my "seize the day" decisions, it never dawned on me to ensure she'd actually be here when I arrived. I did text her last night, casually asking about her weekend plans, and she'd responded with a bunch of snoozing-face emojis, saying she had a lot of studying to do.

I hope she won't mind a little diversion from hitting the books.

At the front door, I push the bell and step back, re-tucking my shirt. And wait.

When no sounds of footsteps approach the door, I lean in, getting a fractured view of the inside foyer through the cut glass pane. It's dark, quiet.

I step off the porch and walk toward the driveway. When I

round the front corner, peals of laughter and a mangle of voices emanate from the backyard. Makes sense. It's a nice evening with a warm breeze, the sun setting low in the sky. I'd probably be out here too.

A tall girl with blonde hair jogs toward a car with keys in her hand, doing a double take when she spots me.

"Hey," she says, coming to a halt but not stepping closer. She eyes the flowers in my hand, and I sheepishly drop them to my side, tucking them behind me. "Can I help you?"

"Oh, hi... um, I was looking for Laurel?"

"Cool, a delivery," she says and I don't correct her. The girl thumbs over her shoulder. "Laurel's in the back, at the gazebo, I think." I nod and give her a smile, which she returns and dangles the keys in the air. "I'm on a pizza run. See you."

She ducks into a gray Honda, does a three-point turn, then shuttles away. Well at least Laurel's mystery friend didn't think I looked too conspicuous. That's a good thing.

I walk toward the backyard and stop at the corner, concealing myself behind a large bush, hung heavy with white blossoms. At least thirty people mill around, some sitting around a fire pit, some standing and talking with drinks in hand, others sitting solo and staring at their phones. The gazebo—a large, square structure with ferns hanging from every archway—sits in the middle of the yard. It appears empty until a smidgen of dark hair pops up from behind a pillow on the settee that faces away from me. I can't see her face but I know it's her. She's wearing her hair piled up on her head like she always does.

I'm about to step out from my hiding place when a guy with orangey-red hair wearing a striped polo and khaki shorts steps up into the gazebo, two drinks in hand. As he sets them both on the side table, Laurel stands up and walks behind him, wrapping her arms around his waist.

My stomach twists and the cheeseburger I grabbed while on the road a few hours ago gurgles inside, threatening to resurrect itself.

What the hell is going on?

He pulls her around in front of him and leans down to press his lips into hers. She reciprocates, her hands running up and down his back, before they both sink onto the settee, disappearing from sight.

I freeze, my muscles refusing to budge, my lungs screeching in pain like I've just taken a direct hit with a basketball to the chest. There has to be an explanation... right? But I'm pretty sure I saw their lips touching and their bodies smooshed together so there's really no explanation that classifies that as "just friends."

A tingling chill filters down through my limbs as if I'm standing in a freezer despite the May humidity saturating the air, a flood of memories flashing forward in my brain. What about those nights on the beach when we talked about our future?

What about all the texts when she called me her Bo-Bear and said she missed me?

What about three damn years?

The ice in my veins turns to fire. Red hot pokers stabbing my flesh.

I tuck the flowers under my arm and pull my phone from my pocket.

<Me>: *Hey*

Across the yard, under the gazebo, a brown head pops up from the settee. She leans over the metal arm, shielding her phone with her body.

I guess dude doesn't know about me either.

My phone buzzes in my hand.

<Laurel>: *Hey Bo-Bear!*

The guy gets up, pointing toward the house, then leans down to kiss Laurel again before heading inside. When their lips touch, the churning in my guts accelerates.

Calling me Bo-Bear and kissing another guy all in the space of a single breath? What happened to the Laurel I knew?

Correction. Thought I knew.

<Me>: *What's up?*

<Laurel>: *Nothing much, just missing you sooooooooooo much!*

My back teeth grind together. Really Miss-Ten-Os? You miss me that much? It's hard to tell.

I stretch my neck from side to side, the vertebrae popping like a fistful of bubble wrap.

<Me>: *So, are you studying?*

Okay, this is her last chance to come clean. Lie or tell the truth—it's her call now.

<Laurel>: *Yep. LOTS of exams coming up.*

<Me>: *Oh yeah? What are you studying?*

<Laurel>: *History*

Appropriate. I hope she enjoys studying history because that's exactly what we are. Starting now.

I step out from behind the bush and walk halfway across the yard, stopping several feet from the gazebo, and stand directly behind her.

<Me>: *From where I was standing a minute ago, I would've assumed it was anatomy.*

Her phone dings. She looks down then springs forward on the settee. I send the second text immediately.

<Me>: *Or does he not have anything worth taking a closer look at?*

Laurel jumps to her feet and spins around, her eyes landing on mine. She gasps, wrapping her hand around her throat, as the color drains from her cheeks.

"Bo?" she asks, her voice wavering. "Wha—what are y—you doing here?" She steps off the gazebo and walks toward me, hesitant, cautious, like the yard is full of unseen land mines. She threads her arms over her chest, glancing from side to side.

Too late to hide now, Laurel.

I shrug. "Well, I graduated this morning—thanks for asking about that, by the way—and I decided that the first day of the beginning of my adult life was so important that I wanted to share it with someone I care about." I bite my bottom lip as the ugly realization bubbles up. "I just never expected this would be the day I found out she doesn't give two shits about me."

Laurel steps closer, and every muscle in my body goes rigid. "You *really* should have called first," she whispers.

I chomp my teeth together so hard I'm afraid the enamel will crack. I've caught her red-handed in lies, and she thinks I should've called first? "That's what you have to say to me? I should've called first?" My voice comes out louder than intended, and a few kids across the yard look up. Laurel's face blushes bright pink.

"Bo... I..." She glances over her shoulders and then back at me, her eyes drifting to the flowers in my hand. Her mouth softens, bottom lip quivering. "Are those for me?"

"Were—*were*—for you. Now they're compost." I throw the bouquet on the grass and grind the toe of my boot into the buds. The petals crumple under the force, turning to a fuchsia paste that stains the leather.

"What's going on? Who's this?" Red-head Guy rushes toward us, glancing between me and Laurel. He glares down at the pile of broken flowers on the ground. "Did you seriously just bring my girlfriend flowers?"

"If I'd known she was your girlfriend, then I sure as hell wouldn't be here." I set my gaze on him, reaching my hand up to stroke the stubble on my chin. "By the way, how long have y'all been going out?"

Laurel grabs his arm and shakes her head, as if trying to convince him not to talk with me. His frown deepens as he pulls from her grasp. "Five years almost. Since before freshman year."

Oh my dear God. She made *me* the other guy.

Not once had she ever mentioned a boyfriend back home in Virginia. In fact, she relished telling me about how she was the "nerd" and the "homebody" who was more worried about grades than parties and popularity.

Guess she forgot to add "liar" to that resume.

"Well for three of those, she's been lying to you and me

both." I turn away from the supposed boyfriend, ignoring his dropped jaw and wide eyes as the realization washes over him, and demand Laurel's attention. Her eyes drift to mine and she swallows hard when I say, "I can't believe you'd do this."

"Wait! You've been cheating on me?" the dude yells, shoving me sideways. I stumble and regain my footing as he stabs a finger in my direction, his lip snarled as he eyes me up and down. "With him? Some hick in work boots?"

In a quick beat, all the solidarity I feel for the guy evaporates. I summon the advice Dad always gave me when dealing with dumbasses. Never throw the first punch. A true man of integrity and maturity uses his words, not his fists. Still, I'm sort of hoping this ginger jackass takes a shot because then jaw-jacking him would be totally justified. I'll take my hick boots over his thigh-high khaki shorts any day.

"No, Sammy, just chill." She grabs his arm and pulls him toward her, away from me, and whispers, "I don't know why he's here."

The flames burst out of my veins and rage in my ears. "That's interesting, Laurel, since I literally just told you why I am here a minute ago."

Sammy plows to a stop and wrenches from her grip. "Who is he?"

The backyard goes quiet, and a circle begins to form around us, everyone holding up their cell phones so as not to miss a minute of this epic meltdown. The anxious stares cut through the three of us like laser beams and I suddenly feel like one of those stupid guys on that trashy talk show who's just found out his girl is a big, fat cheat. So, who's going to be the one to take off their shoe and hurl it at someone's head first?

Laurel shrugs and stares at the grass. "He's some dude I met at the beach three years ago."

My brain blows a gasket. Steam has to be spiraling out of my ears at this point. *Three years ago.* Like we haven't had a very real relationship in the time since. Like I'm some weirdo sniffing her trail like a lost puppy, and she's the innocent bystander.

"Are you kidding me? You make it seem like I'm some stalker that has been following you around for years. We text every day! Why don't you tell them that?" I hold up my phone and swipe open the text messages, tapping her name. A million texts populate the screen, and I pan it around for the crowd to see. When I circle back to Laurel, her doe-eyed stare drops to her shoes. "Show them your phone!"

Then it dawns on me. What will that achieve besides proving my point? I don't know these people. I don't even know Laurel. And I don't care what any of them think about me. The only thing I want is distance between me and this shitshow. And to get the hell out of Virginia.

I shake my head and turn on my heels, shoving through the wall of bodies congregated around us. As I reach the side of the house, my feet pick up speed. My bronco waits at the curb like a beacon. A life preserver. The quicker I can get there, the quicker I can get away from this nightmare.

"Bo! Wait!"

The grass crunches behind me. The Bronco is within arm's reach. I should get in and never look back. I should, but I don't.

Even though my head and my feet scream at me to run, my heart demands answers.

I step out onto the asphalt and turn around. It's like being fully off her property gives me the right to stand my ground against her excuses. "What do you want?" I snap.

She steps to the edge of the grass and reaches out to stroke my cheek, the same way she always had on the beach as we'd watched the tide roll in.

I shudder, wiping the memory from my thoughts, and take a step back. "Why, Laurel? I just can't wrap my head around the fact that you're the same girl I know from Edisto. The one who texts me just to chat. I trusted you but now this? This is what you think of me? I'm just some random guy from the beach?"

Tears stream down her cheeks, creating puddles of black under her lashes. "Bo... I can explain. Really—"

"Laurel!" Sammy stands in the driveway, hands on his hips and frown on his face.

Laurel glances over her shoulder and then back at me. She wrings her hands. "I just...can we meet up somewhere tomorrow and talk?"

Tomorrow? I get pushed back in favor of the scowling boyfriend? Nope.

"I won't be here." I straighten my spine and pull my keys from my pocket, backpedaling toward my door. "This 'random guy' from South Carolina is going back home where he belongs. And don't worry—I'm most definitely not stalking you or whatever the excuse is you're feeding your boyfriend. In fact, just to ensure there's absolutely no more confusion..." I pull up her contact information on my phone then plunge my finger onto the delete option. "Lose my name and my number because I just lost yours."

"Bo, please!" Her voice echoes down the deserted street, but I ignore it, ducking into the Bronco and slamming the door behind me. Laurel darts into the road and pounds on my window with her fists. "Please don't walk away. I'm so confused. Those weeks at Edisto were the best I've ever had, but..."

I roll the window down two inches. Limited contact. "But what? You already had a boyfriend at home, and I meant nothing. It was just a game!"

She glances back up at the driveway as if determining what she should or shouldn't say. Sammy is already gone, so she takes a deep breath and begins. "It was never a game. I would've come home that first summer and broke up with him, if you..."

"If I what?"

"If you weren't so far away. But the long distance is hard. Not seeing you. Not being there with you. It's not the same over texts."

I roll my eyes. "I was in the same long-distance situation, and

I never had a girl tucked away somewhere you knew nothing about."

She presses her palms against my window, her fingers curling over the top rim. "I'm sorry. I'm so sorry!"

I roll my eyes. "Yeah, me too. I'm sorry for ever being stupid enough to believe any of this was real."

"Please, just give me some time to figure out—"

"Take all the time you need, but do it for that other dude's sake, not mine, because this"—I swish my finger between the two of us—"is no longer my concern."

"Bo..." she whimpers, releasing her grip on the glass then pulling her hands to her mouth.

A lump rises in my throat. I can't allow her to play on my sympathies. She's been a cheater for three years. She blatantly lied to me over text not ten minutes ago. Games. All games!

"Go back and study your history book, Laurel. You might want to pay close attention to that last chapter—the one where I walk out of your life forever. We're done." I roll up my window and motion her to move away from the vehicle.

She staggers backward as I crank up and peel away from the curb, tires squealing. I don't look back because as much as I want to hate her, I can't.

Because my feelings were always real even if hers weren't.

I shove them away and merge onto the road that leads to the highway. And home.

CHAPTER 2

Jordan

I stand outside the kitchen door, pressing myself into the wall and eavesdropping on the conversation. The nuttiness of my grandma's dark roast wafts into the hallway, and the pop-pop-pop of bacon grease creates a baseline rhythm to the melody of their happy voices.

"Easy on the gravy, Pa. Remember what the doctor said." Mama's sing-song voice makes her concern come across as a friendly warning instead of a stern instruction. A tried-and-true Daddy's girl, she always treats Grandpa with kid gloves.

I can't begin to imagine what that must be like—to be a daddy's girl, that is.

My mother's cowboy boots clack against the heart-of-pine floors. I can always tell her mood by the staccato of the heel beats across the wood planks. When she's happy, they tap lightly in little bursts, almost as if she's skipping. When she's tired or upset, the footsteps drag in the slightest way, the boot bottoms sliding along with a gravelly slur. Then there are the times she's barreled in so fast that I've worried her feet were going to surge straight through the floor to the underpinning below. Only one time had those heavy steps been about me, but once was enough.

No, today she's in a good mood, and considering I'm getting

ready to leave home in a couple hours, I'm not sure whether I should be happy or offended. I shake my head. No, that's silly. Of course, she'll miss me—I know that—but she's excited for me too. This summer could have major implications for our struggling family farm, but it's more than that. Mama's on me constantly to go "find my life" somewhere beyond here, but I'm no fool. She's hoping this summer brings more than just some grant money.

I hate to tell her but that country-mile-wide stubborn streak she boasts was passed straight to me somewhere in the DNA coding, and the only thing I'm interested in is doing right by my family and getting the hell back home where I belong.

Metal chair legs scrape across the wood as Grandpa's deep voice grumbles, "The doctor ain't worth the paper his phony degree is printed on. Too many years of trans fats, my foot! Too many years of listening to that kook, that's what!"

"Too many years of eating Ma's cooking," Mama says with a laugh, her signature soprano lilt an opposing force to Grandpa's gruffness.

"You saying my cookin' ain't good?" Grandma fires back with feigned shock, and I can almost imagine her standing in front of her stovetop, turning meat in the cast-iron skillet with one hand and the other propped on her hip.

"I'm saying your cooking is *too* good." Mama laughs again, a gentle, rolling one that seeps into my bones.

I close my eyes, soaking it in, relishing the sound. By the end of today, there'll be 400 miles between us for the next twelve weeks. I mean, we can do phone calls or video chats but until technology comes up with a way to encapsulate this smell, this place—this feeling—and transport it via radio waves... well, it just won't be the same.

Not to mention the fact that in my entire twenty years, I've never spent a night outside of this Appalachian county.

When I open my eyes, a whirl of activity draws my attention to the opposite wall where Grandma keeps all of our important family moments in rustic frames Grandpa fashioned from grayed barnwood. In the reflection on the glass of one picture frame—the one that holds the photo of the five of us standing in front of the Wright Family Farm sign—I catch a glimpse of the scene inside the room. Grandpa sits at the head of the table, sneaking crumbles of bacon off the paper towel-lined plate every time Grandma turns her back.

His recent heart issues, including one dramatic episode that sent him to the local ER with sirens blazing, turned out to be some massive warning flags, and Dr. Mattison insisted we swap out the fresh pork products for turkey bacon and some faux sausage links. Grandpa wasn't having it and so after a highly emotional debate, they reached a suitable compromise: Grandma would keep cooking the good stuff and Grandpa would agree to eat only two slices.

So far, Grandma is the only one holding up her end of the bargain.

She opens the oven door, bending down to grab a pan of biscuits, then slides them off into a basket. She carries them over to the table and plops them in the center, side-eyeing Grandpa as he snatches a steaming one off the pile.

"I learned to cook from my mama who learned from her mama," Grandma says. "A good roux, some bacon grease, and a skillet of sawmill gravy—now that'll get you somewhere."

Mama slides out a chair and sinks into it. "It'll get you somewhere, all right. The ER." She darts her eyes in Grandpa's direction and wags her finger. "Remember?"

He answers with a harrumph, and I plaster my hand over my mouth, trying to stifle the giggles.

Grandma slumps in her seat, picking up her coffee mug before stopping to ask, "Where's Jordan? Call that youngin' down here to get some breakfast before she hits the road. We don't know when she'll get another home-cooked meal like this one."

"Oh Ma, I'm sure they eat just fine down on Edisto Island.

And please, let's avoid saying anything negative to her this morning. Jordan's scared enough as it is and she's already homesick without even leaving the driveway yet."

There it is. The concocted image I've been trying to purge from my thoughts all morning. The one where I pull out and leave them all in my rearview. Tears well up in my lower lashes, and I try blinking them away, but nothing eases the million knots in my stomach that feel as if Grandma's taken her knitting needles to my intestines.

"Jordan Sassafras Wright!" Mama yells. "Get your butt down here and eat some breakfast while it's hot!"

I slip off the wall and ease backward down the hall before responding, "Coming!" No need having them realize I've been spying this entire time. I grab my suitcase from where I'd left it at the bottom of the stairs and lug it into the kitchen with me as all eyes turn in my direction. Grandma's lips draw down at the corners and she covers her face with a paper napkin so I won't see.

But I do anyway and have to fight back my own quivering chin as I take my seat at the table. A humid breeze blows in through the screen door, the May air already heavy like a blanket. My grandparents don't believe in spending money on nonessentials, and air conditioning is one of those luxury items that doesn't suit our homespun lifestyle. That's the best I could derive from Grandpa's rambling protest each time it was brought up. The one time when I was about twelve and asked why we never got it, Grandma just smiled and asked why would God make trees and cool breezes and lift the mountains halfway up to heaven if He wasn't providing his own version of A/C? Surely that was better than store-bought air.

After that, I pretty much shut up about it. Who could argue against a grandma with God in her corner?

Across the table, my eyes land on the empty highchair. "Where's Weston?"

Mom chews her biscuit and blackberry jam, then licks her

teeth before responding. "Little booger got up with me to feed the chickens and now he's tuckered out again. He's in his playpen in the den."

I laugh. There's nothing cuter than watching his tiny legs toddle out to the henhouse and peer in the little door. "He loves those damn chickens."

She wipes a dribble of jam from her lip with a napkin and pauses, staring at me. "He's a farm boy. It's in his blood."

Across the table, Grandpa fidgets in his chair and slams an open palm on the table, rattling the salt and pepper shakers. "Let's just hope that by the time he's grown there's still a farm here for him. If that bank has its way—"

"Pa, let's not rehash that this morning," Mama interjects, holding up her hand like a stop sign and shooting him a sharp glance. "We have until September, and we'll find a solution. We always do."

A deafening silence descends on us, the only sound a shrill tinkle of Grandma's windchimes and the squeaking of the rocking chair against the porch floor as the wind pushes it back and forth. A solution. We have just a few months to come up with $35,000 or the bank can foreclose on our farm, our home. And I am the only hope at this point. They haven't said it in so many words, but I know it.

Grandma plops a biscuit in front of me and ladles on a heap of sawmill gravy. It creeps down over the sides and puddles on the plate. "Eat," she says, nodding her head toward the food. I pick up my fork and sliver off a chunk, stuffing it in my mouth. Everyone knows better than to argue with Grandma. "You want some coffee?" she asks, scooting back in her chair.

"I'll get it, Grandma. You've been on your feet all morning. Take a rest." I stand up and walk to the coffee percolator and pour myself a cup. As I reach for the sugar, something in the yard catches my attention. A large shadow on the ground. I lean forward, pressing my nose to the window above the sink. Mabel, our heifer, stands under the oak, munching grass from the yard.

"Shit! The cow's out again!" I holler, running for the door.

Mama jumps up, flinging her napkin on the table. "Right behind you!"

So much for a calm good-bye breakfast.

Clink. The metal gate clicks shut, penning Mabel back into her pasture. And all it took was a half-hour of wrangling a stubborn cow and re-nailing a broken fence board. Mama and I walk side by side back toward our farmhouse. The mid-morning sun now hangs higher overhead, casting lemony light over the white wood exterior and the worn black shingles. The paint peels in several places and the third step on the side porch is rotted clean through.

Mama grabs my hands and threads her fingers with mine. "What are you thinking, Sassy?"

Most people believe her nickname for me is a statement about my general attitude, but it's not. Sassy is short for Sassafras, my middle name. The name I share with South Carolina's tallest peak. *Because I stand strong, tall, and proud—a natural force of nature.* That's what Mama says anyway. But if that's true, then why does my heart feel like it's buried somewhere out there in the lowest valley?

"How can I leave you with all this?" I ask, panning my hand around us. "And taking care of a rambunctious Weston and the grandparents on top of that?"

She nudges her shoulder into mine and rolls her eyes. "You act like I haven't done this before."

"Well yeah, but Grandpa was a lot younger and healthier back then. Now it's going to be all on you."

"Don't worry about me. I'm tough as nails." She smiles. "Something I like to think I passed on to you."

"I know, but—"

She presses a finger to my lips. "Now hush, Sassy. You're

doing this. End of discussion." She lowers the tailgate on Grandpa's old Ford truck and hops up on it, patting the open space
beside her. "Let's just take a minute to soak this in. Your view is
going to be quite a bit different for a while."

I hoist myself on the tailgate and lay my head on her shoulder, staring out over the rolling hills. She wraps her arm around
me and just like that, I'm six years old and she's calming my fears
about the first day of public school. Only this time, I'm technically an adult on the outside, even if the insides don't feel so
mature and independent at the moment.

In the field, a lonesome call floats up from the wildflowers.
Bobwhite. Bobwhite. I smile. Something about the quail—or the
Bob White bird as I called them as a child—feels like home.
Familiar. Cozy. A real connection to our piece of Carolina clay. It
was the sound that'd soothed me when I hid out in the shed on
the day the closest-thing-I'd-ever-known-to-a-father walked out
of our lives. It was the sound that reassured me on the afternoon
I sat out in the tall grass and contemplated how to tell Mama
that I was sixteen and pregnant. It's the same sound now,
calming me in the few moments before I'll step out on my own
for the first time ever.

"I'm gonna miss this," I whisper out into the breeze.

"They do have birds in the Lowcountry, you know." She
tightens her grip on my shoulders, giving me a squeeze. "And
cows. And deer. And farms twenty times bigger than this one.
And a big ol' ocean, so blue you can't tell where it ends and the
sky begins. It just sort of fades off in the distance."

Mama has never spoken of the ocean before. She never really
speaks of her past at all. It's like after she'd had me, all of that
evaporated and she was left with only her immediate surround-
ings. "Sounds like you've been there before?"

"Just once... but that's a story for a different day." She
unwinds her arm from me, pivots on the tailgate, and tips my
chin up to meet her gaze. "Today, Sassy, is all about you. And
your adventures. And your future."

"Some adventure," I snort. "A summer spent farming. And my future is here. You know that, Mama."

"First of all, futures are subject to change. Second of all, you're going to be in a brand-new place with brand-new people. Live a little. Do your job, but don't forget to sprinkle some fun in there too. You never know where a little adventure is lurking."

I pull my phone from my pocket, open the itinerary saved in my emails, and thumb down the list. "Report to Johnson Farms main office by 5 p.m. today to sign in, and I start bright and early Monday morning."

"So?"

"Just checking to make sure I was correct. Absolutely no mention of adventures or fun."

Mama rolls her eyes, her dishwater blonde curls bobbing around her. "Your head is harder than week-old cornbread left out on the counter."

I laugh and slide off the tailgate, turning back to her with a smirk. "I know. I get it from my mama."

"Moo-moo!" Weston yells, pointing toward Mabel who's wondered up closer to the house again, though thankfully still in her fence.

I squeeze him against me, his chubby hands kneading into my arms. My stomach drops. "I don't know if I can do this." A rush of electricity sizzles under my skin, and my throat tightens, my heart drumming in my ears as the tears flow. "He's so little. He's going to wonder why I just up and left him, and—"

Mama steps closer and uses her thumbs to wipe away the wetness from my lashes. "No, he's not. Because you're gonna talk to him every day and I'm going to take so many pictures and send you that your phone'll blow up." She says the last part in baby-talk, tickling Weston's tummy, and he squeals. "Really, now is the perfect time because he *is* so young. He won't even remember this time apart in years to come, but he will remember whether or not his Mama was happy and fulfilled." She grabs my chin, using her fingers to prod each side of my mouth higher. "Weston wants his mama to be happy."

I don't utter the words that swim in my head—that she never applied that logic to her own situation. I grab her hand, squeezing it tight in mine, and reframe my words into a message she might be willing to hear. "I'm sure he'd want his Mimi to be happy too."

"Probably so, but we're not talking about me right now." She smirks and arches an eyebrow. "And who says I ain't happy? You ever heard tell of that old saying that whatever you see in someone is just a mirror reflecting back on you?"

"You're impossible."

"I know. It's my God-given talent. That and producing a damn beautiful, smart kid. Here..." She reaches down and grabs a woven picnic basket and holds it out. "Your grandma packed you up a few snacks for the road."

I take it, and my arm screams under the heft. "Grandma does know that they have food at the coast?"

"She's skeptical." Weston holds out his hands toward Mama, and she gladly pulls him into her arms as she ticks her head toward the basket. "I tucked you a little something in there too. It's in a plastic baggie in the zippered pouch."

I hoist the basket higher in my arms, fiddling with the latch.

"No! Don't look now. Later," Mama says, and for the first time, I see the mistiness in her own eyes and the slight quiver of her chin.

"Mysterious," I tease, trying to diffuse the emotional tension swirling between us like a tornado.

She clears her throat, blinking away the tears. "We gotta do something to keep things interesting around these parts."

I nod and glance down at my phone. 10:15 a.m. The jumping off point. "Looks like it's that time," I whisper, stepping closer and wrapping my arms around both of them. "I love you, Westie.

Love you, Mama." As we stand there, the knot recaptures my throat, and I have to swallow it down. Maybe this whole thing isn't such a good idea. "Really, if you need me to stay then—"

"Go!" Mama kisses my cheek and then pulls away, physically inserting distance between us. Like she knows I'm not strong enough to take those first steps without a little push. Like that baby bird leaving its nest. "Call me when you get there."

I spin on my heels and barrel toward my Jeep. The door weighs a million pounds as I swing it open and heave the picnic basket into the passenger seat, then take my place behind the wheel. When the engine roars to life, I slip it into gear and press the gas. My breath comes out in heavy spurts as I death-grip the wheel.

I don't want to look back—don't want to risk falling apart—but I can't help myself.

At the end of the dirt driveway, I hit the brakes before turning out onto the main road and glance up at the rearview mirror. Mama and Weston stand in a haze of dust as she gently sways him back and forth on her hip. I take a mental screenshot. When the days get long and my heart gets heavy, this is what I'll remember. They are my reason.

I turn right, gravel spitting off my tires as they hit the asphalt, and head east.

CHAPTER 3

Bo

The market's parking lot is empty. Thank God.

I dart in on two wheels, zoom around the building, and deliberately park in the sunny patch between the shade awnings, letting the blistering rays pour over me. I'm already in Hell—might as well embrace the full experience.

I sit a minute, stifling the ache in my guts that could only be the aftermath of a good old-fashioned heart stomping coupled with the extra-large, all-meat pizza I tried to wash it away with in my motel room last night. Death by greasy cheese, pepperoni, sausage, three crappy hours of sleep in a roach motel, and then an eight-hour drive. Yet here I am.

Still here. Still rejected. Still pissed.

My stomach gripes, and I wrap my arms around myself, squeezing to suppress the urge to vomit. If I don't get out and walk, I just might ruin the refurbished interior of my Bronco. No girl is worth that shit.

I open the door and slide out onto the gravel, pulling my phone from my pocket. Three new messages. Laurel. Laurel. Laurel. *Delete. Delete. Delete.*

So not interested in hearing more lackluster explanations.

I shove open the screen door into the market's back room

where the farm workers unload produce from stacked crates, barely raising their eyes from their work as I barrel through. At the entrance of the main store, I hide behind a display of pork rinds and scan the floor. My sister Gin stands behind the cash register, leaning over the counter on her elbows. Her eyes glue to the pages of her latest romance book as she sighs and fiddles with her heart-shaped earring.

I shake my head. She can be that moth, and she can have that flame. Mine turned out to be one of those electric bug whackers that left me no better than a crispy-fried clump on the porch floor.

Another soft gasp from Gin. The rustle of a page turning.

Yeah. No freaking way I'm in the mood for that.

I slip from the wall and pad stealthily along the perimeter of the shop, using the display crates and tables as camouflage. All I want is an ice-cold Cheerwine from the refrigerator case and zero talk about my failed love life or the imaginary ones in Gin's stories. Is that too much to ask?

I pause behind a large stack of peaches, just a couple feet from my destination, and peek at Gin, still buried nose-deep in her book. A sudden gust of wind blows in off the marsh, whipping through the wooden-slatted walls and open-air entrance, sending the bottle cap wind chimes swirling in the rafters. A stack of flyers on the counter spirals off, fluttering to the ground behind the register.

Gin slides off her stool and disappears behind the counter, grumbling as she gathers the fly-away papers. I take the opportunity to lean forward, ease open the fridge door, and pull a bottle from the rack. The door slips from my grip and slams shut, the glass bottles rattling against each other. I duck back behind the produce table, the toe of my boot snagging the leg. The wooden crate teeters on top; a few peaches roll off and land on the packed-dirt floor with a thud.

Shit. These damn new boots I'd put on for *her* sake. Of course they'd cause me more trouble than they're worth.

I drop to my knees, pulling up the hem of my shirt and dropping in pieces of fruit, one by one.

"Bo?"

A pair of sandals step beside the last errant peach. Shit. I want to snatch the fruit and smash it until its stupid pit pops out of the mush in my fist. But I don't. It's not the peach's fault. I grab it and stand up, plopping it on the top of the mound as I begin to unload the others, intentionally ignoring Gin's squinted eyes.

"Bo!" she tries again, this time with no implied question mark. More like a warning. "What are you doing here?"

"I'm not here. You never saw me." I brush off my shirt then twiddle my fingers in her face. "I'm just a figment of your imagination."

She rolls her eyes and throws her arm in front of me, blocking my attempted quick exit. "I don't think so. Now tell me why you're here."

"I work here, don't I?" I turn on my heel and take off up the next aisle, the back screen door in my sights.

Gin's sandals flap against her feet as she hurries behind me. "You're supposed to be in Virginia... visiting Laur—"

"Stop!" I holler, my voice rousing a heron standing at the edge of the tidal flats outside our market. His wings make a whooshing sound as he takes flight. I whirl around to stare at Gin, who nearly faceplants into my chest. "Do not mention the L-word ever again."

Her eyes widen and she mouths *oh-kay* in silence. "So..."

"And no—before you ask—I do *not* want to talk about it."

A sly grin spreads across her face. "Sure you do."

"Gin," I say, wagging my finger in her face, "I'm warning you."

She holds up both hands, feigning innocence. But I know better.

"Okay, okay. You don't have to tell me anything. I can always give Mom a call instead." Her hand creeps down to her pocket and pulls out her cell phone. "This is right up her alley. You know she—"

"You wouldn't!" I fire back, reaching out to swipe Gin's phone from her grip, but she dodges me. Dirty game, pulling the mom card, because we both know how that'll end. Our mom, a family therapist, believes in discussing feelings "in the open" while ignoring any and all personal boundaries. The topic of my train-wreck love life would be the perfect appetizer for our communal family think-tank at the dining room table tonight. I huff out a loud breath, sneering at Gin. "Fine. Whatever. Can we at least go over there and sit down?" I nod my head toward the stools behind the counter, and Gin leads the way with me trailing behind.

She perches on the metal stool, kicking her legs against the bottom rung, and threads her arms over her chest. I lean against the one across from her, twist off the cap of my drink, and take a long pull. The fizzy soda burns my throat, though not as much as the thought of repeating the stupid Laurel story.

"Well?" Gin goads.

"Well... Laur—*she* was 'busy' when I got to Virginia." I frame my words with air quotes.

"Busy? With what?" Gin frowns, her thick eyebrows scrunching together.

"With who," I correct her.

She pulls her hand over her open mouth, eyes saucering. "You mean... another boyfriend?"

"*The* boyfriend. He predates me. Turns out *I'm* the other guy."

"That heifer!" Gin's cheeks blaze as she slams her fist down on the counter. The jars of saltwater taffy rattle against the top. She takes a deep breath and blows it out, retraining her eyes on me. "I'm sorry. Keep going."

My heart thumping, I dive in, repainting the scene in real time: me hiding behind the bush, Laurel's lying texts, our confrontation. Gin slides to the edge of her stool, gnawing her thumbnail.

"Wait," she says, reaching out to grab my arm. "Everyone was gathered in a circle watching this go down?" I nod, and she shrieks, fanning herself with her hand. "OMG, I'm dying of second-hand embarrassment."

I cut my eyes at her before finishing my Cliff's Notes version of events.

"And you just left her there, standing in the street?" She shakes her head, licking her tongue across her teeth. "I hope she choked on your exhaust."

"Gin!"

"Well, I do," Gin says, her face staunch and matter-of-fact. "I never liked her."

"Now you tell me," I grumble.

"I try not to stick my nose—"

I interrupt her with a loud snort. If there's one talent Gin has perfected in her seventeen years on Earth, it's planting her nose in everyone else's business. I slide off my stool and walk to the back window, craning my neck to get a better look at the afternoon sky.

"What are you doing?" Gin asks.

I stride back to her, crouching to look her dead in the eyes. "Looking for that God-strike-me-dead-if-I'm-lying lightening you always hear about."

"Shut up." She rolls her eyes and turns back to the counter, picking up her book again. "Actually, your story reminds me a lot of this one I'm reading. The main guy gets his heart broken by a total you-know-what, and just when he's given up on love, here comes—"

I snatch the book from her hand and thump it hard. "I am *not* one of the hopeless, helpless characters in this drivel you read."

"Don't you dare! My books are not drivel... they are detailed studies in human emotions!" Her face turns all moony, eyes far off and fixed on the corner of the room. "The frailty of our defenses when our person walks through the door and we just know that we've found them! It's the most human and realistic experience of our existence because it's love, and love—"

"Love sucks." I drop the book on the counter, the thud waking Gin from her romance-induced stupor. She glares at me as I continue. "Love gets your brain all foggy and stupid and makes you a fool and just when you can't sink any lower, love takes its foot and shoves it square up your—"

"Bo!" Gin slaps her hand over my mouth, stifling my words. Her face softens, and she drops her fingers. "Look, Laurel wasn't your person, but I could've told you that years ago." She pauses, biting her bottom lip. Gin usually doesn't think twice about sharing her insight.

I fold my arms in front of me. "Say what you need to say. You're not going to hurt my feelings."

Gin sighs. "She never posted any photos of y'all on her social media. Not once in three whole summers! And half the times you wanted to video chat she was conveniently at a 'friend's house'. I mean, did she ever stay at home? And she was too quiet when we all hung out, like she honestly couldn't wait to get away from us. Oh, and she had beady eyes. You never trust someone with beady eyes, all rat-like."

"And you learned this from your romance novels?"

"No, I learned that from good ol' observation and gut instinct." She picks up her book from the counter and wields it like a weapon. "What I've learned from my novels is that there is a Miss Right out there. You just haven't found her yet."

"She'll be pretty damn hard to find if I ain't looking, so there's that." I grab the book from her hand and toss it on the shelf under the counter. "I'm done with love or lust or whatever that shit was with Lau—her."

"You know what Dad says: 'Don't let one rotten fruit spoil the bunch.'" She walks over to a seagrass basket of strawberries on the display table and plucks one off the pile. "You throw out the fuzzy one. Not the entire basket."

"Insightful." I walk over and sink my teeth into the berry, the sweet juice dribbling down my chin. Gin grimaces and drops the green stem to the floor. "In fact," I say after I finish chewing, "you and Dad should write a book about finding romance in the farmer's market."

She wipes her hand across her pink T-shirt, leaving a wet smear. "Good idea. And quit being a jerk to me because you're nursing a broken heart. You should be grateful. The trash took itself out."

Well, she's not wrong about that. I head toward the back room.

"Where are you going?" she asks.

I turn back to look at her, face fallen, mouth downturned, and it dawns on me that, sure, she's a nosy little sister but she's *my* nosy little sister, and all she really wants is for me to be happy. And to know *all* the things. But still.

"I'm going to help unload some of these trucks, and you..." I say, taking her shoulders and maneuvering her around, "you are going to drop all of this and pay attention to that customer who just drove up." I point toward the parking lot where a brown Jeep Wrangler pulls into a front spot. Gin gives me a thumbs up and ducks behind the counter.

In the back room, I grab a wheelbarrow and steer it to the nearest truck, lower the tailgate, and begin filling it with cantaloupes. The main rush of visitors to the island should arrive like clockwork over the next couple hours. Though the official summer rush won't start until Memorial Day weekend, the middle weeks of May are always busier than normal with a ton of senior citizens and families with non-school-age kids trying to beat the crowds.

Gin's laugh echoes from the other room and another voice— a much softer one—accompanies it. She loves the newcomers and the crowds. So many new people to chat with. So many new stories to discover. I prefer the less hectic, slower paced seasons and gladly volunteer to work the farm in the summer, filling my hot days with riding tractors over open, lonely fields rather than traipsing around the loud beach crowds.

A lingering thought of Laurel creeps in and circles my brain like a fish in a bowl. She had been the bright spot in my summer. The one thing I'd looked forward to.

I shake the thought away. There'll be none of that this summer. I want to forget all about Laurel and anything else to do with so-called love.

Instead, I'll focus on the farm and assisting with Dad's new internship program because I literally have no time left to figure out what it is I want to do with my life. High school is over and Dad doesn't hide the fact he wants me at the farm but the question remains: do I want to be at the farm?

I don't know, but what I do know is that there's only one way to find out.

"Hey Bo!" Gin calls from her position at the counter. "Is today the check-in for the summertime grant program?"

Really? It's not enough for her to ask me a gazillion questions, but now she has some sort of direct link to my inner thoughts? Wouldn't put it past her.

I slam the tailgate and lift the wheelbarrow, pushing it into the main market space, then park it at the corner near the register. "Yep. At 5 p.m."

"Didn't you tell me the names of the interns? I can't remember." She cocks her head to the side and bats her eyelashes.

Oh no she doesn't. The incoming interns are here to work on the farm—not serve as potential boyfriend material to make her go swoony-eyed all summer. "These guys might be fresh meat to you but they're here to work and compete for the grant money."

I step behind her and ramble in the box under the counter, producing a plain cardboard placard and a permanent marker. **Fresh-Picked Cantaloupes. $3/each or 2 for $5**

"They don't have time for love and all that." I pick up the

sign and place it in front of the cantaloupes. "And who can blame them? It's more trouble than it's worth."

"Not this again." Gin props her fists on her hips. She's pretending to be mad, but there's something—a sly glint—in her eyes that gives her away. What's the end game here? "Just tell me their names," she demands.

"Christopher Carlson. You remember him from the home-school group, like two years ago? He's a little older than me. Black hair, kind of short, drove that red truck."

"Oh yeah, I remember him now." She twirls a lock of hair around her finger. Yep, definitely plotting.

"He's a damn good farmhand. And the other one is some guy from the upstate—Jordan Something-or-other, I think—but I don't know him."

"Correction. Some girl named Jordan." The voice is a soft alto with a hint of feminine Southern twang. When I turn around, she's standing behind me, a girl about my age with tanned skin and hair that looks as if she'd been riding with her windows down.

"You're Jordan?" I stammer. My jaw drops. This is totally not who I expected.

Gin leans across the counter, hand clamped over her mouth as she giggles between her fingers. "Plot twist."

Jordan laughs and reaches beside me, handing a five-dollar bill to Gin but never taking her eyes off me. "Don't look so shocked. Girls are farmers too."

She sticks her hand out and I take it in mine, shaking hello. Her grip is solid, firm, and full of authority. Unlike most of the girls who spend their summers in Edisto, she has trimmed, rounded nails and none of those mega-stabby acrylic ones. "I'm sorry if I offended you. I know several female farmers, it's just I didn't expect... um, the paperwork didn't say... Jordan is just one of those names, so I didn't know."

"Don't worry. I'm not easily offended." She smiles, her thick lips a natural cherry color, and a wisp of sun-streaked hair, loos-

ened from her ponytail, falls over one ice-blue eye. A trail of
freckles smatters the bridge of her nose. There's something both
sweet and hearty about her; she reminds me of graham crackers.

"Here you go," Gin says, handing the change to Jordan. She
quickly pockets it in her cut-off shorts. Gin pops the top off a
glass Cheerwine bottle and slides it forward on the counter. At
least the girl has good taste in soda. But as Jordan steps forward
to grab the drink, her hip grazes the edge of the overloaded
wheelbarrow, and the cantaloupes topple forward. We both
spring to action, grabbing them before they hit the ground.

I stand up, holding two of them against me; Jordan has one.
She runs her fingers over the textured rind and then fixes her
gaze on me, snickering. "Nice melons," she says.

My mouth moves quicker than my brain functions. "Yours
too," I say, nodding to the cantaloupe in her grip... the one she
has pressed to her chest.

Oh shit. Why did I just say that? My cheeks flame, and I
pray that the dirt floor will open up into a marshy sink hole and
sweep me away. Jordan presses her lips into a flat line,
suppressing her giggles.

Gin steps around the counter and pulls the cantaloupe from
Jordan's grip, placing it on top of the pile. She turns back with a
gigantic grin. "I'm so sorry. Where are my manners? You two
haven't been properly introduced. Jordan, this is my brother Bo
Johnson. He's helping out with the summer grant program." She
pauses, turning her focus on me, then winks. "And Bo, this is
Jordan Wright. You can call her Miss Wright."

CHAPTER 4

Jordan

Poor guy. I could fry an egg on his face. And the fact that his sister is profusely enjoying his humiliation isn't helping. These two are definitely not what I expected from Farmer Johnson's kids. Somehow, I didn't think they'd be this down to earth.

The fire in Bo's cheeks disperses, turning to pinkish swirls before fading into his tanned skin. He gives the two cantaloupes to Gin who arranges them on top of the pile by the counter. When she's done, she hands me my drink, and I take a long pull, enjoying the rush of sweet-hot fizz against my tongue. Sodas are another one of those luxuries Grandma insists we can do without.

"Are you excited to be a part of Dad's inaugural grant program?" Gin asks, breaking the awkward silence.

Mouth full of soda, I nod while swallowing and then say, "Definitely." I glance over at Bo, his bewildered expression now melted into a pair of blue eyes, soft and relaxed. They fix on mine. "Will we get to work together this summer?"

He clears his throat. "I'm not sure how he's arranging things but there are two interns and two intern leaders. I don't know if he'll pair us up or what."

"Cool. Maybe we'll get buddied up." I take another swig,

wondering about the other leader. Another someone like Gin or Bo with their friendly personalities and there's really no bad outcome. "What about the other intern leader?"

Gin rolls her eyes and smirks. "That would be our cousin Brice, the male chauvinist, thinks-he-walks-on-water, total jerk, dirtbag."

Bo opens his mouth as if he's about to dispute Gin's tirade but stops before any words come out, then turns to me with a shrug. "What she said."

My stomach sinks to my toes. Oh great. This could be the biggest break of my future career and succeeding is a hundred-percent necessary to save our farm. I can't be derailed by anyone or anything, especially a total jerk, dirtbag, whatever-else-she-called-him.

"If he's so bad, then why is he a part of it?" I ask.

"Because, even though the farm belongs to our father, it was started by our great-grandfather whose dearest wish was for it to be a family-run business." Gin rolls her eyes, shaking her head. "Southern roots, southern blood. You know how that goes."

"Well, this Brice sure sounds like a peach."

"Yeah, a rotten one." Gin laughs, settling back onto her stool. "Anyway, I think dad should've turned the internship into a reality TV show. Then there could be cameras and lights and juicy drama to, you know, perk things up a bit."

"No," Bo and I say in unison. He looks at me, a grin nudging up one side of his mouth and revealing a dimple in his cheek.

"I like to work out in the field to escape. Get in my own brain for a while." Bo crosses his arms into an X. "No drama, no people, and definitely no cameras."

"Right?" I take another swig of my drink. "And those reality shows are not really about work. They're about stirring up drama and exposing secrets for the sake of sensationalism. No thank you. Just teach me how to make my own farm profitable and let my sleeping dogs lie."

"Sleeping dogs?" Gin tilts her head, eyes scrunched.

The "sleeping dogs" saying is Mama's favorite; she often hurls it at me when I'm asking too much about her past or why she never settled down. Her dogs must be in a coma.

"It means secrets, skeletons in the closet. Best not to disturb those."

"I'm too young to have skeletons in my closet." Gin giggles. Naiveté at its finest. I want to grab her shoulders and tell her that she's not too young. That I was just her age when Weston came along and forever changed my life. That all it takes is one smooth-talking guy with a handsome face to create a distraction that knocks you off course. I want to tell her but I don't, because people aren't always so understanding about young mothers, and I'd rather not give anyone the opportunity to tarnish my chances of winning this grant money. I can't and I won't.

Bo reaches over the counter and produces a paperback with two people snuggled on the front. "Gin's biggest secret is she's addicted to these ridiculous romance stories that are completely, totally, and disgustingly unrealistic."

Gin grabs the book from his clutches and pulls it to her chest, glaring at him. "Ignore my brother. He's recently discovered his long-distance girlfriend was a total cheater and liar so now he's anti-love." She turns her gaze on me, oblivious to Bo's drastic flinch at hearing her revelation, and cheerily continues. "I bet you can appreciate a good love story, right Jordan?"

"Maybe once upon a time." I smirk. "And that is exactly why I quit reading about once-upon-a-times."

She buries her head in her hands in dramatic fashion, mumbling through her fingers, "Not you too. I can't take another cynic."

"I'm not a cynic. I'm a realist. I don't *not* believe in love, just that it's really hard to find." Gin's sapphire eyes find mine, a gleam of hope returning. Man, give this girl an inch and she's going to take a mile. I glance down at my watch. "And speaking of hard to find... I'm supposed to check in with your dad by five. Can anyone point me in the right direction?"

Bo nods and motions for me to follow him to the open-air entrance. I trail behind, unable to keep my gaze from drifting to the way his jeans hug his thighs as he walks. As soon as the thought rears its head, I shuffle it away. It's like Mama's wide-eyed optimism is puppeteering my brain from afar, and I have to cut those strings and focus on the real purpose of this summer.

He points out to the road. "Take a right onto this main highway and about a quarter-mile down, you're gonna see—"

"Why don't you just show her, Bo? It'd be so much easier." Gin steps behind us with a smirk. Yep, and just like that, she's back to her shenanigans, though she does make a valid point.

"That might be best... if you don't mind, that is," I say. "I did get lost a few times on my way down here."

Bo, red-faced again, motions for me to lead the way. I shuffle past him, kicking up a swirl of sand that snakes its way into my shoes. It's different than the red mud back home. This scratches like sandpaper grit.

Gin runs up and grab my arm, and Bo strides past me. I turn to look at her, beaming and giddy. "Can I show you around tomorrow? I want to take you to the beach and the pier and all the cool places."

I nod, smiling. I might as well get to know this place and with Gin, at least I'll have an enthusiastic tour guide.

"Promise?" she asks.

"Swear."

She shoots me a thumbs-up and runs back into the store, and I head to the parking lot.

When I get to the Jeep, Bo stoops near the front, checking out the grill. "Jeep Renegade," he says, running his fingers over the hood. A lump rises in my throat when they smooth past the brown chipped paint and the peeling orange striped decals. She's been around the block but she's still going strong. Someone with the Johnson's resources, though, probably has a brand-new, fully-loaded ride. Nothing old and seasoned like mine. He lets out a low whistle. "A '79?"

"A '78 actually."

He steps back, an approving smile stretched across his face. "I have a '73 Bronco. They don't make 'em like ours anymore."

I bite my bottom lip. Huh. Misjudged that one.

He swings open the door and confronts the oversized picnic basket in the passenger seat.

"Sorry about that," I say and motion toward the backseat. "You can toss it in the rear."

He picks it up then presses his nose to the wicker side, inhaling the mesquite and molasses aroma I'd enjoyed the entire drive down. "What is that? It smells so good."

"My grandma's barbecue pulled pork. She makes her own sauce—secret recipe—and the meat is freshly smoked." He opens the wooden top, peering down into the basket filled with sandwiches, wrapped individually in tinfoil. An invisible cloud of spicy sweetness rolls out, filling up the Jeep. "Grab one. Give it a try."

He shakes his head. "I don't want to eat your food."

"There's enough in there for, like, five people." I nod toward the basket, and he pulls out a sandwich then carefully peels back the wrapper as he slides into the seat, buckling himself in with one hand while maneuvering the sandwich to his mouth with the other.

I back out of my parking space and pull up to the main road. Bo points right and then shoves the sandwich back to his open mouth; one-third disappears in an instant. The tires hum against the asphalt, salty breezes floating in around us as he stuffs his face. Three more bites, and it's nothing more than an empty wrapper. He licks saucy drippings from the foil then wads it up and slides it into the white plastic trash bag hanging from my stick shift.

"Your grandma's cooking is phenomenal!"

I laugh. Her barbecue has won more county fair blue ribbons than I can count. She keeps them in her junk drawer in the kitchen pantry. "Between you and me, I believe she thinks I won't have access to a decent home-cooked meal down here so she's got me stocked."

Bo stares at me, wiping his mouth with the back of his wrist. "Come on, you're in the fresh seafood capital now. My best friend Jett's family has shrimp boats that go out every morning and come back in brimming with all the fresh local seafood you could ever want. And who doesn't love fresh shrimp?"

I raise my hand tentatively.

Bo does a double-take. "What? You don't like shrimp?"

I shrug. "I don't know, actually. I've never had it."

"You've *never* had shrimp?" His jaw drops open, eyes wide. He turns sideways in his seat, back against the passenger door. "Crab?"

I shake my head.

"Scallops?"

Again, nope.

"Never?"

"Not once."

"Fish?"

"Trout. And catfish. And striped bass." Grandpa does love a good fish fry, though I think he likes spending all day on the banks catching them best of all. "That's what we can get in the streams near our house. I've never been to the beach before now."

He laughs under his breath, leaning back against the seat. "Wow. You've got a lot of new experiences headed your way this summer."

Up ahead, the moss-laden oaks give way to large flats, expansive fields of green sprouts in endless rows. Large center-pivot sprinkler irrigation systems spray water down onto the plants from above, the long mechanical arms of the machines bigger than any farm equipment I've ever seen. Grandpa would have no idea what to do with all of this.

"Turn here." Bo points to a white metal sign with JOHNSON FARMS HEADQUARTERS in blue block lettering beside a gravel road splitting the fields. Rocks ping against the bottom of the Jeep as we creep down the path at a snail's pace. I can't stop looking at the stalks of early corn, already knee high, and remember being a little girl running through our own field, letting the leathery leaves brush against my skin.

"Wow. This is huge."

"This is just a small piece of the farm. There's plenty more to see." He turns to stare at me as I scan the fields, taking it all in. "You look—I don't know—overwhelmed. Internship jitters kicking in?"

"Maybe. It's just... our farm is small. Teensy, really," I say, pinching my fingers together. "And my grandparents are simple people. They wouldn't know what to do with all of this."

Around another bend, the road opens up into a large clearing with a white wood-paneled farmhouse with black shutters and a wrap-around front porch. Behind it, a single oak, sprawling branches laden with moss, stands proud. An old tire swing sways in the breeze. My heart warms in my chest.

"It's a house."

"It's my great grandparents' old house. Now it's the main office." He points toward a patch of gravel on the right and I pull in line with a group of parked trucks. "Dad's cousin, Patrick—that's Brice's dad—is the COO, and he wants to tear it down and build a new facility but my dad is sentimental. He says the concept of the farm started at that kitchen table and that's where it should stay."

"I like your dad's way of thinking." We get out, walk to the front porch, and climb the front steps as I run my fingers over the wooden rails. "And I love this house. It reminds me of home."

Just as Bo reaches for the front door knob, a flurry of heated voices rises from the other side, one much louder than the other. He stops, leaning in close as the words bleed through the walls.

"You know it's the right thing to do, Clay." The gruff voice pauses and a loud bang, like a fist coming down on a table, rattles the windowpanes. "You're allowed to play whatever ruse you want to in your own home, but not here at the farm. This is *our* legacy, not just yours, and you know it."

Bo sighs and rolls his eyes. "Sorry about this. Sounds like Patrick is up to his usual antics. Just one of the fringe benefits of working with family." He opens the door slowly, sticking his head in through the crack. "Dad! You here?"

The voices cease, and after a moment of silence, a response echoes up the main hallway. "I'm in the office. Come on back."

Bo pushes the door open wider and steps back, allowing me to enter. He closes it behind us and leads me down the hall to a large room in the back that looks like it was once a living room. A faded sofa sits against the far wall with an overweight man perched on the rolled arm, his arms crossed in front of him. All the hair missing from the top of his head seems to have found its way to his unruly goatee. When we walk in, he doesn't speak, only grunts and looks out the window. Behind the wooden desk, a stocky man with a five-o'clock shadow pushes back in his chair and stands up, brows furrowed.

"What are you doing here? I wasn't expecting you back until tomorrow evening."

Bo darts his eyes uneasily between the two of us and I suddenly remember Gin mentioned something about a recent heartbreak. "Change of plans."

His curt response resonates with the man who I recognize as Clayton Johnson from the farm's website. He pinches his lips together and nods, shifting his gaze to me. The wrinkles in his forehead deepen as he stares as if trying to place me from somewhere.

"Who do you have with you?"

Oh crap, why am I sitting here like a lump? This is no way to make a good first impression.

"I'm so sorry," I say, edging past Bo with my hand outstretched. "I'm Jordan Wright, one of the summer interns."

He opens his mouth in a silent "ah!" and offers a warm smile. "Of course you are. My apologies—I just have a lot on my plate this afternoon." He walks to a file tray on his desk and shuffles through a pile of folders, pulling one from the stack. "I see you've already met my son, Bo. He's one of the intern leaders. The other is his cousin Brice, but he won't be here until tomorrow."

"Yes sir, Bo and Gin already—" I almost say *warned* me but think twice and recalibrate my words— "told me."

"Ah, you've met Gin too. You must've stopped in at the market. I have no doubt that she has already commandeered your free time in some capacity."

I laugh, nodding. "She's taking me out bright and early tomorrow to show me around Edisto."

"That girl is a one-person welcome wagon." His smile widens to show two rows of pearly whites, but what I notice most is the glint in his eye when he talks about his daughter. A look of pride. A look of intimately knowing and understanding his kid. A look of love. My stomach twists again, but I shove the sensation down. There'll be no moving forward if I keep getting caught up in the past.

Mr. Johnson hands me the manilla folder, brimming with printouts and pamphlets. "Here is the information about how this summer will work and any paperwork you need to fill out. Read through it by Monday, let me know if you have any questions, and..." He steps behind his desk and slides open the drawer, producing a set of keys. "You'll be staying out on the beach side of the island, in the guest apartment behind our home. So if you need anything at all, we'll be close. You should have everything you need but I'm sure between my wife and Gin, you'll be invited over for plenty of family dinners and there's also a pool you're welcome to use anytime."

Living oceanside with a pool and a complete nuclear family. This is the kind of stuff I've only seen in my dreams. My heart butterflies against my ribs. "Wow. It all sounds amazing, and I just want to say thank you again, Mr. Johnson, for this opportunity."

"Call me Clay," he says, darting his eyes uneasily at Patrick who's still sulking like a toddler on the sofa and refusing to even look in our direction. I guess Brice's apple didn't fall far from his father's tree. He drapes his arms over both our shoulders and turns us toward the door. "I'll walk you kids out."

Silence envelops us down the hallway, not breaking until the front door slams shut behind us and we step out into the freedom of the front porch.

"Who pissed in his cornflakes?" Bo grimaces, rolling his eyes.

"It's always something." Clay smiles and scans the parking area. "Where's your Bronco?"

"Over at the market. I rode with Jordan to help her find the place."

"Why don't you accompany her to the house, and I'll just drive the Bronco home this evening when I go get Gin?" Clay sticks out his hand in my direction, and I take it. The hard callouses scrape my palm as he pumps it up and down. "Nice to meet you, Jordan. I look forward to working with you this summer." I nod and smile, turning to leave, but Clay grabs Bo's elbow and keeps him from following. "Hey son, are you okay?"

"Yeah, I'm good."

His voice wavers a bit, and I'm sure Bo's in no mood to discuss a failed love life in front of me, so I walk on and get in the Jeep, slamming the door behind me. In the side mirror, though, I catch a glimpse of Clay grabbing Bo, pulling him close into a hug. It's sweet. Touching. Everything I'd ever wanted and never gotten.

Bo jogs to the passenger side and slides into the seat beside me. "Sorry about that. My dad still suffers under the idea that I'm twelve."

I smile, cranking the engine. It roars to life, drowning out my own pity party. "I think it's nice. He loves you. It shows."

"Yeah, he does," Bo says, and I can't help noticing the new

calmness softening his features. Clay's fatherly advice seems to have proven the perfect medicine. Mama has always done that for me. A picture of her holding Weston on the gravel drive kicks up in my memory, and I swallow the hard knot in my throat.

We crawl over the bumpy drive to the main entrance. Bo points right, and we pull out onto the two-lane road, picking up speed as we maneuver through the intermittent tidal flats and canopies of twisted oaks laden with moss. I crank my window down, letting the briny breeze flow in and lift the wily tendrils of hair that have come loose from my ponytail. Beside me, Bo rests his head against the seat, eyes closed so that his long lashes skim the top of his cheeks. His strong, angular jaw is more relaxed now than when we first met, and I like the way the dark hair on his arm prickles as the beachy air swirls around us.

I redirect my gaze to the road, which curves sharply to the right, and the trees give way to a flat expanse of grayish-brown mud that hugs each side. And up ahead, just beyond a sandy dune and stand of wispy sea oats, a vast horizon of blue, speckled like diamonds by the sun's rays.

I gasp and pull off on the shoulder by the Piggly Wiggly. "Oh my gosh! It's like nothing I've ever seen before."

Bo rouses beside me, grasping the dash, and leans forward, peering up at the grocery sign. "What? They don't have grocery stores where you live?"

I deadpan and he snickers in response. "Not the Pig. The ocean," I say, panning my hand toward the windshield. "Mama was right."

I glance at Bo who arches an eyebrow into his forehead. "About?"

"You really can't tell where it ends and the sky begins." I bite my bottom lip, staring out at the waves crashing to shore, the white caps dotting their approach, and the dark blue that is only a shade or two lighter than the clear atmosphere above it. Bo laughs, shaking his head, and I side-eye him. "Don't laugh at me because you think I sound stupid."

"I don't. I think I'm stupid." He plunges his pointer finger to his chest, eyes pinched together as he stares out at the Atlantic. "I've lived here my whole life. I don't even pay attention to it anymore, but you make it seem special."

Something about it feels sad. Not a day passes that I don't sit out in the valley at home and marvel at the rolling mountaintops and the wildflowers dancing in the thinner air. Another pang of homesickness ignites in my stomach, but I squash it by focusing on the scene before me now, the beauty of my new home for the summer. "Sometimes it just takes a fresh perspective to remind us of what we do have."

Bo's jaw clenches and releases again, and he swallows hard a few times before reaching for the door handle. He ticks his head toward the beach, a grin crimping his lips at the corners. "You want to go stick your toes in?"

Nothing would be more exciting than running across the dunes and discovering the blend of sand and salt water between my toes. To stand at the edge of the continent and look out on a great unknown.

"Yes... but I can't. Not yet." I purse my lips, shelving my enthusiasm. "I promised Gin I'd wait for her."

"It's going to be a long summer if you give in to my sister's every whim." Bo wags his finger at me, then contemplates something, chewing the inside of his cheek. "She doesn't have to know. We could always just..."

He drives a hard bargain. One I'm almost tempted to take.

"But I would know. I can't break my promise." Bo's face falls, his smile disappearing. That's when a new idea strikes me. "You could come with us tomorrow, though."

He darts his eyes at me, lips flatlined. "Sightseeing with my sister? That's going to take a lot of arm twisting."

I grin and grab his arm, giving it a playful squeeze. My heart skips a beat as my fingers wrap around the solid girth of his biceps. It's been a long time since I've touched a guy, especially one as cute as Bo, and a small butterfly pitter-patters in my stomach.

He looks down at his arm, staring, as if he can detect my racing pulse through the skin contact. I blush and loosen my grip, grabbing hold of my gear shifter and pulling away from the curb. We really don't know each other so touching him might have been a misstep. My cheeks flush.

As we turn onto the oceanside highway, he laughs and shakes his head, staring out the window before turning back to me. "Okay, I'll consider it."

The guesthouse is small, but oh-so-large. Quiet and empty. So unlike home. I stand in the middle of the open living area and close my eyes, perking my ears to listen for something—anything —reminiscent of home. No cows bellowing, no Mama laughing at one of Grandpa's jokes, no metallic clink of utensils as Grandma makes a poundcake, no Weston giggling over the chickens.

Just quiet.

Loneliness.

A sharp pang tears through my heart, my breaths shortening to quick puffs as I grind my teeth, willing my nerves to settle. How will I ever get through this? I don't know if I can.

I don't know if I'm strong enough.

I open my eyes and scan the very beige, very beachy-yet-elegant room. Professionally decorated—it had to be. Shag rugs, bronzed floor tiles, rolled arm matching couch and chairs, and the only knick-knacks (that's what Grandma calls them) in sight are decorative slabs of driftwood mounted on the wall and conch shell bookends. The scant personalized additions are two framed photographs on the far wall, one of a girl with long blond locks holding a sand pail and the other a dark-haired boy sitting in the surf. Exuberant smiles mark both of their faces. Bo's babyish curls remind me of Weston's own chocolate ones, and I imagine bringing him here, letting him splash in the ocean until both of our noses are slightly sunburnt. The thought incites another barrage of firecrackers inside my body and a new, bigger knot ties itself into my esophagus.

No. I have to keep myself busy, my thoughts focused on something else, or I'll get back in that Jeep and go home right now.

My gaze falls to the picnic basket on the kitchen counter. I should put the remaining sandwiches in the fridge before they spoil. I walk over and lift the lid. The corner of a clear plastic bag sticks out from the flat pocket in the back. I pull it out, finding Mama's scrawl across the folded paper inside: **Mama's Words of Wisdom (Travel Edition)**

A laugh escapes my throat. The woman thinks of everything.

I pull it out and unfold it, reading the bolded caption at the top and the short note beneath it.

When You Get There

Stop crying this minute, young lady! There will be none of that this summer! Don't think of this as the first night of your internship—think of this as the first night of a terrific adventure. No worrying about us as we're all fine here. Now's the time to focus on you. Remember what our fabulous, iconic Dolly said about wildflowers and how they can grow anywhere. You are my wildflower so grow, girl, grow!

Love, Mama

Classic Mama, relaying all the life advice she's gleaned over the years as Dolly Parton's number one fan.

"For you I will, Mama," I whisper into the quiet. "And for Weston."

I spend the next several hours unpacking my things and getting situated in my new home-away-from-home before curling up in my bedroom armchair to call her. As expected, after I chatted to Weston and sent him a million blow-kisses, Mama got back on the line to grill me on the drive down, if I'd met the family, how'd I liked Mr. Johnson since I'd be working for him for the foreseeable future, if I'd eaten, if I'd cried, and if I'd met any cute guys already.

The drive was easy. The family—including Mr. Johnson, I mean, Clay—are great. I've eaten enough barbecue to win my own blue ribbon in the pig parade. My tears are stubborn customers but I've got them under control. And no, Mama, I'm not here for cute boys.

But cute boys make things so much more fun! That's what she tacks on with a chuckle before telling me good night and hanging up.

Okay, Mama, I think, but a smile lingers on my lips. She's always a warm blanket for my anxiety. A few minutes hearing her chipper voice and my heart's fuel tank is filled once again. I shake my head and lean down to grab the charger for my phone when a muffled voice from outside floats in through the opened window. I pull back the cotton sheer and peer out into the Johnson's backyard as a shape emerges from the darkness of the covered patio and walks poolside, into the spotlight of the full moon overhead.

Bo runs a hand through his hair, splaying curls left and right, as a voice emanates from the phone in his other hand.

"So from graduation to Dumpsville, population y-o-u in a day's time? Dude, that might be the saddest shit I've ever heard. What now?"

The voice echoes crystal-clear through the night air, carried directly to my ears via the humid breeze blowing in off the beach. His accent is as Southern as Bo's, though he talks much faster, and I have to concentrate to differentiate each word.

Bo blows out a loud breath before responding, "What else? Work. Dad's new internship program kicks off Monday and I'm helping."

"At least it's almost vacation season so in a couple weeks,

there's going to be loads of new girls on the island." He sing-songs the "new girls" part as if dangling a carrot under Bo's nose. A carrot that the quirked eyebrow on his face says he's not apt to chase.

"Hold up, Jett! I thought you always said vacation girls were too much work for one week a year?"

"And I was right, wasn't I? Laurel was way more trouble than you needed, but that's because you tried to take a one-week-per-year-kind-of-girl and make her into a full-time girlfriend when what you need is easy, uncomplicated fun. No strings."

Maybe I shouldn't be eavesdropping on their private conversation. Bo made it perfectly clear earlier in the market that he was in no mood to advertise his recent heartbreak, and he'd probably be mortified of my listening in now. Still... something in me pricks my need to know more. A radar signal of sorts to get a little insight into the spurned male mindset. My own feelings of rejection and distrust of the opposite sex I knew all too well, but it's always seemed to me they have no remorse, no conscience screaming in their heads. Maybe even no heart. My grandpa has been the only one in my entire life to challenge that ever-growing theory.

"Not exactly my style," Bo mumbles, pacing by the row of loungers. "I'm looking for more commitment, not less."

My breath catches in my throat. Now this is a new development. A guy willing to actually commit? And a cute one at that? I press my nose to the screen for a better look.

"And your current M.O. is working for you?" the Jett guy snorts. "Look, you don't always have to be the serious, sensitive one. You just graduated. Live a little."

Bo shakes his head. "I don't know. How does that even work?"

"See? You're already overthinking it. If it takes too much brain power then it ain't easy and uncomplicated. Just let it be."

"I think I might be better off alone." Bo's low, monotone

response tells me exactly what I've begun to suspect. He's just like me. Hurt, tired, and over it. Preach, brother.

"Now where's the fun in that?"

Jett's jovial tone only increases, as if he can single-handedly convince Bo that the answer to his problem is no more complicated than sliding right into another dead-end situation. Immediately my mind puts together one of those analogies like they include on the SATs. Jett is to Bo what my mama is to me. Pushers. Instigators. Won't-leave-well-enough-aloners.

"Where's the fun in any of it? It's just too much stress and misunderstandings and freaking lies."

"Dude, you hooked up with the wrong girl. It happens. But the right one is out there. Until then, just have a fun, no-strings, no-expectations summer. You owe it to yourself."

No strings. Yeah, right. Like that exists. Everything—I repeat, everything—is full of strings. Like a giant relationship marionette.

I readjust in my seat, the charger cord wrapping around my ankle and sending my phone flying to the ground with a thud and shaking the lamp on the table. It bumps into the window sill with a loud thump. I slump behind the tall back of the chair and crane my neck to get a good view of Bo's reflection in the glass of the other closed window. For a moment, he looks up, eyes squinting, as if trying to detect my presence but then turns back to stare at the water when I remain hidden.

"So?" Jett goads.

"We'll see. That's all I can promise."

While they say their good-byes, I creep my hand over to turn out the light, bathing my room in darkness. It only serves to intensify the moonlight, which gives Bo an amber glow as he stands there. He tosses his phone onto a lounger and steps to the pool's edge, staring into the depths as if the answers will reveal themselves in crystal ball fashion across the surface.

"To hell with it," Bo mumbles and hooks his thumbs into the hem of his T-shirt, yanking it over his head. The moon's reflection on the water freckles his body with diamonds of light, and my eyes linger on the squared muscles of his chest and abs. His boots land with a *thud* on the concrete surround, and in another quick motion, his jeans crumple to the ground. He steps out of them, leaving them in a puddle, revealing a black pair of boxer briefs that hug his butt and thighs. One, two, three steps and he plunges headfirst into the deep-end, not fully resurfacing right away but moving like a shadow just below the surface to the steps on the shallow end. A few bubbles breach the surface before the wet curls, now plastered to his head, follow.

Bo sits on the steps, letting his head drop backward to rest on the edge. This should've been one of the most memorable weekends of his life, not some over-dramatic heartbreaking shit-show. Maybe his friend offered some good advice. Maybe he does just need an anything-goes summer.

Then again, maybe so do I.

CHAPTER 5

Bo

Gin informed me last night that's there some stupid formula about break-ups she read about in a magazine. Apparently, you divide the time you were together in half and that gives you how long it's going to take to get over the failed relationship. Three years divided by half is one-point-five years.

Eh, no. Especially considering how much better I was already feeling 24 hours in.

That's when Gin politely reminded me that my so-called relationship had really only consisted of one week for three years spent in the same zip code because texting doesn't count. So, 21 days cut in half would give me 11 days max to get the hell over it.

I roll over in my bed and stare up at the ceiling fan, circling slowly. What Laurel did was crap, but in some weird, oxymoronic twist of fate, the ache of missing her is only a blip on the register. The anger is still here full force, but a new wave of something—relief maybe—is filtering in. It's hard to feel a sense of loss for something you never really had in the first place, and I'm pretty sure the only reason I feel anything at all is because I'm mourning the loss of what I'd hoped to have—something Laurel was never capable of giving me.

An actual partner. A long-haul type of girl to ride out life with me.

A true love.

My stomach lurches as the thought crosses my mind, and I'm positive I'm about to wretch my guts out. Not because of the break-up but because another realization strikes me: I sound exactly like one of those dopey saps in Gin's romance books. Oh dear Lord, when did I turn into some pile of mush looking for true love?

Jett. And CJ. And their whirlwind, dramatic, all-encompassing, made-for-TV-movie love. I saw it and I wanted it, and that shit messed me up for good. I mean if Jett can find it, then surely I can too?

A quick glance at my watch—4:36 a.m.—and not a wink of sleep in sight. My body must've depleted its need earlier in the evening when Gin helped me sneak up to my room, avoiding Mom in the kitchen with her hundreds of questions. Gin was only helpful because she already knows the scoop and wouldn't have been nearly so compliant if I'd been holding out. She did me a solid by helping me escape the third degree and lock myself up here, safely away from scrutiny, for the duration of the night. It's deferral at best, because Mom will be lurking today, angling for the perfect time to pounce.

I throw back my covers and pad to the door, cracking it just a bit to get a decent view of the hallway. Dark, quiet. Just the way I like it. I pull on a pair of shorts and grab a t-shirt slung over the back of my chair and slip out into the hall and down the stairs without so much as creaking one floorboard.

Undoing the deadbolt, I ease the front door open, escaping onto the porch. A cool breeze blows in from the ocean, rustling the palm fronds and tousling the monogrammed flag mounted on the post. I sit on the top step staring down to ground level and the precise row of conch shells Gin has collected over the years and made into some sort of edging around the base of the palmetto tree beside our driveway. At the end of our road, just beyond the sandy dunes of the beach access, waves tumble to shore, giving the morning a thunderous, rumbling backdrop against the pitch-black sky, freckled by a million pinpricks of light. Something about the shore at this time of day feels so solitary, almost like existing in a vacuum or one of those snow globes. Like you're isolated from the world and everything in it. I inhale the briny air, letting it filter down, down, down. Erasing, expunging. I close my eyes, losing track of time, letting my mind go blank, feeling the wind across my face.

"What are you doing up?"

The voice startles me, and I glance up at Dad, whose face hovers above mine as he eyes me up and down.

"Couldn't sleep."

He nods and steps beside me, taking a seat on the wooden step. "Don't suppose it has something to do with why you're back home from Virginia already?"

I sigh. His prying won't be nearly as intense as mom's forthcoming interrogation, but my parents share everything. In his ears and right out his mouth to Mom. "I don't really want to talk about it because then you'll tell Mom and it'll be a big thing and then we'll have to do one of her 'feelings inventories.'"

I love my mom. I do. I just hate how she's always digging around in my head.

Some things a person wants to keep to themselves once in a while, but everyone knows that a shrink and a mother are two of the biggest know-it-alls on the planet. Combine them together and... I shudder.

Dad waves his hand in the air, shaking his head. "Nope. I'm leaving that up to you as to how you handle this with your mother. She kept trying to wait up for you last night but you somehow evaded her. I don't think you'll be so lucky today." He tucks his bottom lip between his teeth. When I don't say anything, he nudges me with his elbow. "But really, right now it's just us—man to man—if you need to talk."

"Don't you need to get to the farm?"

"The farm can wait a minute. You're more important."

I know he means it. If anyone could be the poster boy for unconditional love of family, it'd be him. He can tell I'm not my usual self, and it's not fair to worry him. But the thought of relaying the break-up in detail again—reliving that humiliation—gripes my stomach. I suck in a deep breath and blow it out.

"Laurel has another boyfriend. I found out when I walked up on them together." I shrug. "Guess my surprise visit backfired."

"Ouch." Dad grimaces as if he's somehow tapped into the physical and emotional pain of that moment in replay. "I'm sorry. I can't believe she was cheating on you."

"Oh no. It's worse." I roll my eyes, threading my arms over my chest. "She was using me to cheat. I'm the other guy."

Dad's mouth drops as he stares at me, unblinking, as if the news is registering at a snail's-pace. Probably because he's now imagining in full detail the forthcoming Mom Interrogation in his head. "Wo-ow." He draws out the o for a solid ten seconds. "Your mother's gonna shit a gold brick when she hears this."

"Precisely why I've been avoiding her."

"Well, kiddo, time's running out. Tonight is her Sunday Share family dinner and guess who's topic numero uno?" He pokes his finger into my chest, a raised eyebrow and knowing expression conveying the message loud and clear. "And heads up, she invited Jordan too. Poor girl hasn't a clue what she's in for."

Terrific. If my humiliation isn't enough to fulfill the family psychological vultures, then we might as well share every tiny facet of that wonderment with the new girl in town. I mean, why keep things like total humiliation a private matter? Just lay it on the table like a big roasted turkey and let everyone dig in. I mean, obviously what I really need is everyone's opinions because they make things so much better. I shake my head. Very possibly Jordan and I could be working together this summer, and it would've been nice for her to think me a normal, non-loser for at least the first week.

A memory of Jordan and I walking into the farm office pops in my head and with it, an overheard conversation.

"Speaking of Jordan," I say, turning on the step to face Dad head-on, "when I brought her by the farm yesterday, I couldn't help overhearing the argument between you and Patrick. About you owing him something?"

Dad clenches his jaw in and out several times, something I've seen him do when trying to maintain his temper. He rarely loses control. "Patrick believes that he and Brice should be the legal owners of the farm. Not me."

Of course he does. Douchebag and Douchebag the Sequel feel like the world owes them everything on a silver platter while never lifting an actual finger to do any legitimate work. "But grandpa got the farm from his father, and when he retired, he left it to you. It's all legal."

"Yes, but your grandfather was the younger of the two original brothers. The older one—Patrick's dad—walked away from it all, got married, and moved north. It was when Patrick got older that he moved back down and wanted to be a part of things, but by then, Grandpa had already inherited the farm from your great grandfather. He gave Patrick a role in operations to honor great-grandpa's wish that this be a family-run affair. It's the same commitment I abide by too. It's why Patrick and Brice have significant roles in the company despite their bad dispositions." Bad is a complete understatement. Dad blows out a loud breath and diverts his gaze out across the yard. "However, Patrick thinks that since he never got a say in the inheritance and that since he's the oldest son of the original oldest son that it naturally follows that he should be the sole inheritor and after him, Brice."

A fire ignites in my belly. "They really think you're just going to hand things over to them?"

"They wish, but..." Dad stops, biting his top lip between his teeth. His leg jackhammers on the step.

"What?"

He turns back to me, his eyes dark, intense. A little moisture gathers in the corners. "I am getting to that point in life, Bo, when I need to start thinking about the future... and how I need to prepare the farm to keep going well into the next generation."

Oh.

The weight of the implication falls on me like a ton of bricks. The hardest part of leaping into adulthood is making life-changing decisions and picking out your "path" long before you've even really lived. And it doesn't help that the options always come with some expectations, whether parents mean to force them or not. The farm—well, I know the farm—and I'd be happy to carry on the family traditions, but is it really what I want to do forever?

I don't know.

"And you're waiting on me?"

Dad reaches out, grabbing both of my arms and leveling his eyes with mine. His grasp is firm but not hard, more "I've got your back" than "do it my way."

"Son, I'm never going to put pressure on you to follow in my footsteps. You just graduated high school. You're on the cusp of the rest of your life, and I know you said you needed time to figure out your direction. I understand that completely, and I don't want the farm to be a burden or an obligation to you." He gives me a tight-lipped smile and drops his hands into his lap. "I'm hopeful this internship will give you a taste of what it's like to do this full time, and maybe by the end of summer, you'll have a better idea of where you're heading. If it's the farm, great, but if it's not, then I need to seriously weigh the options."

His face betrays him. The desperate wish he has for me to come alongside him at the farm is evident, despite his valiant attempts to disguise it. When it comes to dads, he's the gold standard, and I want to make him happy. But I want to make me happy too. "I don't want to disappoint you, Dad. Ever."

"You never will. I only want the best for you. You're happy, then I'm happy." He scoots closer and leans forward, wrapping me in a bear hug. That's when he whispers in my ear, "Now as for your immediate future, I have it on good authority that your mother is sleeping in but that her alarm is set for 9 a.m. You might want to make yourself scarce before then."

I nod, understanding completely. "Point taken."

The beginning tinges of sunlight filter through Gin's blinds, shooting rainbow flashes across her comforter. At 7 a.m., the two-hour window to Mom's alarm has entered the countdown stages and I'd rather not be around in case she wakes up early. I place the tray of vanilla coffees and the bag of cream cheese Danish on her dresser and walk over to nudge her shoulder. Gin grunts and rolls over away from me. Oh no she doesn't. We have an ever-narrowing opportunity to get dressed, go get Jordan, and get the hell off of this property before Mom wakes up with a mission to obtain the 411 I'd kept under wraps last night.

"Gin!" I hiss, leaning down to her ear, as I shake her again. "Time to get up!"

"Go away," she mumbles, tugging the covers over her head so only a blonde tuft remains visible.

Fine. I'll just resort to some Gin-specific warfare.

I sprint to her window, which overlooks the guest apartment, and pretend to flick my fingers between two of the slats in the blinds. "There goes Jordan to the beach. I guess she got tired of waiting on us. Now you'll never be able to—"

"Wait!" Gin throws the covers back, bounding straight from the bed as if she's had a direct injection of adrenaline. She leaps off the side and beelines for the window, yanking the blind's cord to get an unobstructed view, then squints, nose pressed to the pane.

"But I don't see—" I laugh as she sweeps a fierce gaze in my direction. "You lied, you little—"

"I had to!" Holding my hands up in protest—or maybe

protection—I backpedal a few steps. "I'm a desperate guy trying to avoid our mother, remember? You promised you'd help me, but you wouldn't get up."

"Well, I'm up now." She sticks her tongue out at me while twisting her hair into a ponytail. "And I did help you avoid Mom last night, but today you're on your own. I have plans."

"Yeah, well, I have plans too. The same plans as you."

She picks up a brush off the dresser and runs it through her ponytail with a side-eye glare. "You're going with us today?"

"It would appear so."

"Why?" She squats down in front of her dresser, rifling through a pile of clothes to produce a swimsuit, a pair of jean shorts, and a purple T-shirt, which she tosses on the bed. I offer her my hand then pull her to standing.

"Because Jordan asked me to."

"Oh she did, did she?" Gin waggles her eyebrows and licks her tongue across her top lip. The words come out super slow and sultry, and it isn't hard to guess where this is going.

"Would you stop?" I ask, removing one of the vanilla lattes from the carrier and handing it to her.

She blows across the sip hole, sending spirals of steam out from her cup. "Can't you just admit that you think she's pretty?"

"What part of our conversation yesterday confused you? I'm done with relationships." If I'm not mistaken, I made it pretty clear where I stood with this. Jumping into a relationship—especially with a girl I don't know from Adam—would be insanity. Like sticking your burned finger back on the eye of the stove just to make sure it really is hot. Better to just bandage it up and not make the same mistake twice. "Besides, I don't even know Jordan."

"First of all, I didn't ask you to marry her. I simply asked if you thought she was pretty. You're getting awfully defensive over an innocent question."

"That's because I understand with you, it's never innocent."

Never. EVER. Gin has spent so much time with Miss Bessie

next door that she's become her meddlesome, teenage clone never leaving well enough alone.

"Look, I talked to CJ last night about your... predicament... and we both think it might be good for you to cut loose for a change."

It's always nice to hear your friends have been discussing your failed love conquests behind your back without even consulting you. Everyone's got an opinion on the subject. Everyone should be running advice columns on their local social media neighborhood boards. Everyone should just butt out already.

I roll my eyes at Gin and she shrugs. "You tried so hard to make something work with Laurel and it blew up in your face. Why not just have fun?"

I glance at my watch. Another ten minutes ticked away.

"I'll try, but talking to Mom would be anything but fun so can we please hurry up and get out of here?"

She picks up the remaining coffees and, after snagging herself a pastry, hands them and the rolled bag to me. "I'll be ready in five. In the meantime, why don't you head on over to Jordan's?" When I start to protest, she quietens me with a conspiratorial grin. "The quicker she gets her breakfast, the quicker she eats, the quicker we leave before you-know-who wakes up. Just saying."

I groan and tiptoe out into the hallway. Relentless.

"What is this?" Gin stands beside the table in the guest apartment where Jordan and I are sitting and finishing off our lattes. Her eyes and nose pinch together and she pans her hand up and down beside Jordan.

Doe-eyed, Jordan glances from Gin to me and then down at herself. She pinches the coral fabric of her tank top in her fingers, holding it out and inspecting it. "My clothes?" she stammers. "What's wrong with them?"

"There's nothing wrong with them. You're just not wearing your bathing suit. You know, so we can go to the beach and get in the ocean later."

"Oh!" Jordan laughs, relaxing back against her chair. "I don't own a bathing suit. I just wear my cutoffs."

Gin stops, mouth hanging open as she stares at Jordan while blinking rapidly. I've seen that look. I know that look. Jordan has just walked straight into a Gin Trap. My sister turns to me with a maniacal smile, and I half expect to see her eyes begin swirling in her head from the current excitement blowing the circuit board in her brain.

"Okay, change of plans. *First*, we're going to the surf shop and *then* we're going sightseeing and to the beach." She turns back to Jordan, rubbing her palms together. "You, my dear, are getting your first bikini."

Ten minutes later, we're standing in front of the latest swimwear fashions that the Surfin' Safari shop has to offer while Gin scrutinizes the selections and Jordan cowers behind her.

"Look at this one!" Gin plucks a royal blue bikini from the wall rack and presses it against Jordan. The top is nothing more than two triangles and some string. "Bo, don't you think this would look so good on her?" Gin glances back at me with a wink. "You know, Bo's favorite color is blue."

Flames lick my cheeks. If Gin doesn't shut up, I swear I'm going to lose my shit in the middle of this store.

"What about this one?" Jordan pulls a conservative black one-piece from the rack and holds it out, scrutinizing the V-neck. It's the same style Mom wears. Better to keep my mouth shut about that, but my disappointment aches inside just a little. I mean, I'm not buying into Gin's fix-ups but I wouldn't hate seeing Jordan in that two-piece.

Gin's face scrunches into a full-face frown. "No! You're twenty with a smokin' body. You don't wear pilgrim couture!" She rips the ugly suit from Jordan's fingers and slams it back on the rack, then shoves the tiny two-piece into her grip instead. "Trust me."

"Famous last words," I mumble in a warning to Jordan as she disappears behind the curtain of the dressing stall, looking as if she anticipates meeting a firing squad on the other side. Gin loops her arm in mine and tugs me toward the souvenirs counter in search of the perfect "welcome present" to present to Jordan. As she fumbles through keychains, bumper stickers, and shot glasses, a slight movement in the round security mirror in the corner of the store grabs my attention.

A miniature reflection of Jordan peers out from behind the curtain and then darts to the three-way, full-length mirror beside the dressing rooms. She steps up on the platform and turns from side to side, getting a 360-degree view of the itsy-bitsy bikini.

Props to my sister. It is the perfect fit and the perfect color for her skin tone, and the side ties rest high up on her hip, making her legs look a mile long. Her body isn't spaghetti-noodle thin and flat like Laurel's but curvy in all the right places. I swallow hard. If the store owners had her model that thing in the front window, they'd sell out in a few minutes.

A burning sensation pricks the hair on my neck and I glance sideways at Gin, whose narrowed eyes flick between me and the mirror I'd been staring at. A cock-sided grin pulls her lips up to the side. "I told her to trust me. Was I right or what?" She turns back to the rotating display, plucking an Edisto Beach key chain in the shape of a Loggerhead sea turtle off the rack. "I think this—"

A long, low whistle echoes across the shop and I dart my eyes to the mirror again, catching a glimpse of a large male figure walking toward Jordan. She steps off the platform backwards, nearly colliding with the mirror, and wrenches an arm over her chest.

Gin tosses the keychain on the counter and tells the cashier she'll be back then grabs my arm, hauling me toward the dressing area. The closer we get, the more familiar the perpetrator looks.

"Dang girl," he drawls. "You don't have to try so hard. You already got my attention."

That voice. I know that voice. My blood boils, and my feet quicken their pace.

"Excuse me?" Jordan narrows her eyes, her mouth deepening into a frown.

He laughs and props against a table of folded t-shirts. "Now don't play coy. I can tell when a girl's trying to put on a show for me. I'm just letting you know that I'm looking... and liking."

Jordan rolls her eyes, stabbing her finger in the air. "And I'm letting you know that—"

"Brice! What is your deal?" Gin runs behind him and shoves him hard. He stumbles forward but grabs hold of the table, correcting himself.

He whirls around to face us, eyes fiery, as he runs his hands over his plaid shirt sleeves, straightening them. "Damn, Gin. Can you be any more of an idiot?"

"Can *you?*" She plants one hand on her hip and points the other toward Jordan. "You think you might start off this summer program *without* harassing one of our interns?"

His mouth drops open as he swivels his head back toward Jordan, who grabs a bright orange beach towel and holds it in front of her. "Interns? You're definitely not Christopher, so are you..." He slits his eyes. "You're Jordan?"

"Yeah. That's me." Jordan glances between us as she utters a monotone response.

"Well, isn't this an interesting little turn of events?" Brice laughs and runs his tongue over his teeth as he steps sideways and cranes his neck to see around Jordan's towel. She grimaces and tugs it even closer as he grins, saying, "I might not hate this stupid idea of Clay's half as much if I get to look at you all day."

Gin finagles herself between Brice and Jordan, holding out her arms to block his view. "You're a pig."

Brice bends down to Gin's eye level, a sleazy expression on

his face and he uses his finger to push up the end of his nose. "Oink, oink, baby."

Jerk.

I step behind him and spread my arms out, creating a safe escape for Jordan between Gin and the dressing room. Jordan scoots toward the dressing area, her back pressed against the wall, and pauses only a moment in front of me to whisper, "Thanks, Bo."

I smile and nod, and as she ducks into the tiny room, we both grab the curtain to pull it closed, our fingers grazing against the heavy fabric. An electric tingle pulses under my skin and I quickly let go, turning back to face Brice.

"You're a liability to Johnson Farms. And if you hate working at the farm so much, then why are you even here?"

Brice slits his eyes, the skin wrinkling around them as he cocks his head. "Why are you?"

I step forward, bowing my chest. "Because my dad wants me there."

"Does he now? Does he *really?*"

I grind my teeth together, stepping forward once again, until our chests are only millimeters apart. "Because *I* belong there."

"We'll see about that." He smirks and thumps my shoulder before turning on his heels. "Tell Jordan that I look forward to tomorrow. I'll be happy to show her how to work all of my equipment."

In a few quick strides, he spans the store and pushes through the glass door, the seashell chimes tinkling as the door swings closed behind him.

Gin folds her arms over her chest. "I hate him."

"I hate him more," I say.

"I hate him most." The curtain flies open and Jordan steps out, fully clothed, with the bikini in hand. "And his equipment."

CHAPTER 6

Jordan

I stand in a towel, staring into my closet, the wet ends of my hair dripping down my shoulders. What does someone wear to a family dinner when you don't really know the family? I haven't even met Mrs. Johnson yet though I can't imagine she'd be anything but awesome considering the kids she raised.

I glance over at the tiny blue bikini hanging from the hook on the bathroom wall, shaking my head over the fact that Gin actually talked me into it. That thing made my underwear look modest in comparison, but there was something about the way it made me feel, like I was bold and free or something. And the fact that I caught Bo staring at me a few times didn't hurt either.

His sideways glances and quick grins weren't sleazy and leering like Brice's but more—I don't know—appreciative or something. And it's been a long time since I've felt appreciated by a guy.

My phone buzzes on the dresser and I grab it, swiping across the screen.

<Mama>: *Sightseeing today, right? How do you like Edisto?*

Mom's first text of the day at nearly 5 p.m.? What a measure in self-restraint. Up until yesterday, we'd spent all of my twenty years joined at the hip, and while she reiterated that she wanted me to gain some personal space and perspective over the summer, I'd figured that still included a near constant flow of communication. A vision of her sitting on her tailgate and staring at her phone, waiting on my reply, forms in my brain, and I laugh to myself, opening up the text box. Might as well end her impatient suffering.

<Me>: *Hey Mama! Yep. Saw the entire island, including the pier, the marina, and the surf shop. Gin made me buy a bikini.*

<Mama>: *A bikini, huh? Send me a pic later. Did you get in the ocean?*

<Me>: *Yes! It was amazing, though no one warned me about undertow and how the sand just disappears below your feet. I tripped and fell in. Soooooo embarrassing!*

<Mama>: *Too bad you didn't get a pic of that! LOL*

<Me>: *Gee, thanks, Mama. :P I mean, don't worry or anything. I didn't drown. Bo pulled me out.*

<Mama>: *Bo, huh? The Johnson's son? Is he cute?*

<Me>: *Mama...*

<Mama>: *Just asking! Relax already!*

<Me>: *I am relaxed. Well except for picking out an outfit for tonight. The Johnsons invited me to dinner.*

<Mama>: *That's nice of them. Wear your peach sleeveless with the sheer overlay. It suits your complexion.*

I fumble through the hangers in the closet, locating the exact shirt, pull it out, and hold it against me. Perfect.

<Me>: *Good idea! Thanks. I'll call you afterwards and maybe we can tuck Westie in together?*

<Mama>: *OK. Have fun. Love you.*

I toss my phone on the bed and examine the peach blouse against me in front of the full-length mirror. The plastic hanger wobbles in my trembling fingers. It's a simple dinner, yes, but it's dinner with the head of Johnson Farms AKA my boss for the summer. The one man who could single-handedly hold the key to the future of Wright Family Farm—or its downfall. I have to impress him. I need that grant money to satisfy our liens so we can actually focus on moving forward and not treading water, praying to keep our heads above the waves. If we don't get it, our farm will undoubtedly be swept away in the undertow of all our financial burdens and that would kill my grandparents. And Mama. And me.

I pull my shoulders back and lift my chin. I've got this.

Mrs. Johnson—Claire, I remind myself, remembering that she told me to call her by her first name—forks the last sliver of her roast beef, pushing it around on the plate to soak up the remaining gravy before slipping it into her mouth. The conversation, now oddly quiet, had been easy during dinner. No one prying into my personal life beyond the general questions, only laughing and talking about the day's experiences on our Getting to Know Edisto tour.

But as she chews the last morsel and pulls a napkin to her mouth, Clay clears his throat, and Bo and Gin exchange glances. My anxiety skyrockets, the mood at the table turning ominous. Like a grenade on the brink of explosion. And the way they're all eyeing each other leads me to believe I'm the only one in the dark here.

My stomach clenches, and I'm glad I went easy on the beef.

Claire drops her napkin, smacking her lips and pushing them into a wide grin. "I think it's probably a good idea to have a little Sunday Share time. There have been some pretty big things happen this week and it's nice to have a little time to vent, chat, discuss."

A Sunday Share time? What is this?

Gin and Bo emit simultaneous groans, sliding down in their chairs. Bo glances up at me from under the fingers he's visored against his forehead, and my heart pounds in my ears, sending a warm flush up my neck. I finger the neckline of my blouse, hoping the redness in my skin doesn't peek out from behind the fabric.

"Mom, you're scaring our guest," Bo mumbles, voice monotone.

Claire's smile grows wider as she shakes her head. "Nonsense. Therapy isn't scary work. It's healing work. This isn't a forum of judgement. This is a place to be heard, to ask for opinions, to have healthy discussion. There's nothing you can say that's wrong. It's about how you're feeling and knowing how best to deal with those feelings." She pauses, her gaze roaming the table. When no one speaks, she goads us further. "Would anyone like to go first?"

Oh my dear Lord. Do we all have to talk about our issues—including me? Don't guests get a free pass or something? I swallow hard, my insides knitted into a tight ball. Gin taps her fingers on the table, drawing my attention.

"Mom's a family therapist. She works mostly from her home office and conducts her therapy sessions via the internet because work is slow here on the island." She looks over at Claire, lips pinched. "People come here to escape their problems, not rehash them."

"Also, she doesn't adhere to personal boundaries," Bo says, shoving his fork into a leftover carrot on his plate. The metal hits against the stoneware with a grating shriek. I take it he's not a fan of these sharing times.

"Thank you both so much for that wonderful—even if inac-curate—explanation."

Claire doesn't look like the stereotypical therapist, except for the tortoise-frame glasses she pulls from a leather pouch and perches on the bridge of her nose. Her dark hair, curly like Bo's, fans out like black flames from her head, and she has a few small but visible tattoos peeking out from the collar of her V-neck T-shirt. Her boyfriend jeans are rolled at the bottoms with large, frayed tears across the front that show her tanned skin. She's sort of EMO, punk rock, naughty therapist except she never speaks above a low, melodic tone and she has weird obsessions like collecting porcelain bells from all the places she visits and keeps them on display throughout the house.

The silence covers the table like a weighted blanket—one getting heavier by the second.

Finally, she relaxes in her chair and says, "Fine, I'll go first. I want to say that I'm happy you're here for the summer, Jordan. I know you were probably expecting just a lot of time on the farm but the farm is built around our family, and you should consider yourself a part of this family while you're here. Our home is your home. We've put you in the guest apartment so you can have your privacy when you need it, but please know that these doors are always unlocked and open to you, whether you need a bite to eat or just want to hang out with us." She angles her head, pushing one shoulder up to her ear, as she beams at me from the end of the table. "Especially Gin because I know she's thrilled to have another girl her age around here."

"Thanks," I offer, my heightened nerves making my voice quiver. I take a deep breath and compose myself. "I really appreciate everything your family is doing for me. And for this internship position."

I take the opportunity to throw in a smile and nod to Clay, reiterating my gratitude and commitment to the summer internship. My breathing deepens, my heart slowing to an easy, natural rhythm. All that fuss for that? Why was a simple welcome making everyone so up in arms?

"Great speech, Mom," Bo says, sliding back his chair and tossing his napkin on the table.

Claire's smile evaporates as she snaps her fingers and jabs one toward the ground. "Why are you getting up? We're not done here yet."

Bo freezes mid-stride and closes his eyes, pressing his lips together in a firm line. The breath pushes out of him like a deflating balloon, his shoulders drooping as he reclaims his seat.

Gin giggles out loud and Clay tucks a grin away behind a clenched fist he presses to his mouth.

Uh oh. This must be the real sharing part of the evening...

"Now Bo..." Claire's voice turns to honey once again. "Would you like to fill us in on any new developments with you?"

He doesn't look up, only stares at his plate. "I'd rather not."

"Bo, we are a family who talks things out."

"Yeah, while we die of absolute embarrassment," he says, massaging his temples.

Claire lets out a sharp exhale and trains her gaze on me. "Jordan, if any of this is uncomfortable to you, then I'll let you make the decision on whether you'd like to go or stay. While this is a family issue, I'd love to have you here to have a voice at the table because this summer, you are family. And sometimes," she continues, a new edge coloring her tone as she turns to Bo, "it's wise to gather as many good opinions as we can."

Bo looks up at me through his long fringe of dark eyelashes, his cheeks red and splotchy. "Feel free to go."

"Jordan?" Claire asks.

Gin leans toward me and whispers, "I think you should stay."

Bo clenches his jaw and shoots her a death glare, which only increases her giggling.

Decisions, decisions.

I purse my lips as I study both of them—Gin nodding, a wicked grin plastered on her face, and a somber Bo who keeps ticking his head toward the door.

"I think I'll stay."

Gin shoots me a thumbs-up as Bo issues me a pained grin and shakes his head, mouthing "I owe you one."

Claire ignores them, clasping her hands together in front of her chest. "Perfect. To give you a little background, Laurel..."

"Laurel is the witch you heard us talking about in the market," Gin butts in. "She's some goody-two-shoes chick Bo 'dated' for three years, and by dated, I mean they hung out for one week a year when her family came down here to visit her grandma and then barely ever talked again."

"That's not exactly accurate." Bo folds his arms and leans back in his chair.

"Oh I'm sorry, you're right. Bo would call her and send her text messages all the time, and more often than not, she ignored them or waited hours to respond with some cockamamie excuse." Gin clicks her tongue. "But now it's become oh-so-clear what her hang up was really about."

Bo reaches over and pats Gin on the shoulder. "Thanks for that wonderful and unbiased synopsis. Very helpful."

My mind reels. At the market, Gin mentioned a recent break-up with a liar and a cheat, but who in her right mind would treat Bo in such a way? I mean, I've only just met him but so far, he's been one of the nicest and most genuine guys I've ever met.

"Um... what exactly became clear?" I ask. Bo darts his eyes across the table and I shrug. "I have to know the full story before I render an opinion."

"Well, he showed up to her house in Virginia with flowers and where was she? Canoodling in the backyard with her boyfriend of five years!" Gin holds up a hand with all five fingers splayed wide. "That's right, she'd already been dating the guy for two years before she even met Bo!"

Claire gasps, covering her mouth with one palm as she clamps the other over her throat, and Bo slides lower in his seat. "She made you the other guy? That's... reprehensible... and I'm sorry."

Bo's frown deepens as he pinches the embroidered edge of the tablecloth. The little bit of amusement I'd shared with Gin in taunting him dries up because I know all too well the sting of rejection. The pain that sears your heart when everything you thought you knew turns out to be lies. I stretch my foot under the table and nudge his leg. He looks up at me, and I mouth "You okay?"

He smiles and nods before looking back down.

Gin, however, doesn't relent. "Now we know why she was throwing all that shade. Bo should have listened to me when I warned him about her."

Claire straightens her glasses on her nose. "It isn't very helpful to lambast people with what they should have done. Instead, we should empathize, offer support, and gently point out some missed warning flags that can be helpful next time."

"Next time?" The words tumble out of Bo's mouth as an automatic response. He snorts and picks at a hangnail. "There ain't gonna be a next time."

"Of course there will." Clay leans forward, elbows on the table, finally contributing to the melee.

I'm pretty sure he means it as a show of support but Bo only deadpans.

"No, there won't be. I let my guard down, I 'made myself vulnerable' like Mom tells us, and I got shit on." He picks up his knife this time, twiddling it in his fingers, and I wonder if he's just fidgeting or currently planning a murder. It's hard to tell from the look on his face. "You can't trust people. They tell you one thing to make you stay just so they can leave you in the long run. Nope, if it ain't easy and convenient, I don't want it."

"Bo, this is a very unhealthy way to look at this. Jordan?"

My heart drops to my toes. Is it my turn for the emotional guillotine or is she asking for my input? I turn my head in her direction without establishing full eye contact. "Ma'am?"

"You and Bo are about the same age. Do you to care to weigh in here with any words of wisdom?"

Heck to the no. Times two. I'm the last person to give useful, unbiased advice on this subject. "Um, I think maybe I should stay out of it."

"No, please." She taps her knuckles on the table and out of sheer instinct I look over at her. Our eyes lock. Damn. She smiles and circles her hand, goading me on. "Your opinion is valid and welcomed."

Valid, yes. Welcomed? Probably not by anyone except Bo at this moment.

I sigh. She asked for it. "Well, I pretty much agree with Bo. People lead you on, use you, and then dump you. Who wants to sign up for more of that?"

"Thank you!" Bo shouts, standing up and raising his arms in the air. "She gets it!"

Claire purses her lips, tilting her head to one side. Her eyes burn holes through me. "It seems we may have two broken hearts sitting at this table." I drop my head and stare at my hands folded in my lap as she continues, "But you know what Miss Bessie next door says: 'heartaches are healed by the sea.'"

I gnaw the inside of my cheek. I never considered myself to have a broken heart. Isn't that for moony-eyed people suffering from unrequited love or something like that? There's definitely no pining away for Weston's biological father or any other guy for that matter. Still, maybe a broken heart doesn't have to be romantic. Maybe it can happen in a lot of different ways.

"Clay, are you going to say anything into this?" She turns toward him, pleading, as she pans her hand in our direction.

He laughs, rubbing his chin. "Nope. Sometimes I think it's best to let nature run its course and not force everyone to have a conversation about it." Claire opens her mouth but he holds up a finger, keeping her protests at bay. "I know, honey. But you're a therapist—you get people to talk for a living; I'm a farmer, and we generally prefer the solitude with just our own thoughts. If anything will help these two, it's some long hours in the field." He grins and gives a quick wink to me and Bo. "Speaking of which, the morning starts early so..."

Clay pushes back from the table, taking the napkin from his lap and laying it across his plate. When he stands and holds out his hand to Claire, she slips hers into his with a defeated smile.

"Y'all win. Enough of my interrogation." As everyone begins to disperse, she can't help adding in one last plea. "If anyone needs to talk, though, I'm here."

I slide my chair under the table and put my dishes on the rolling cart by the wall. The look on her face gets me; it's like going to the animal shelter and finding that one puppy desperate for a home. It dawns on me that she's not trying to be intrusive, just helpful. Therapy is more than a profession to her. She obviously wants to ensure everyone's living their best life.

She just gets a little overzealous in the process.

I walk over to her as she watches with eager eyes. "Thanks, Claire—for dinner and the offer. I might just take you up on it."

A new power grin spreads her lips, revealing two rows of white teeth. "We're so happy to have you with us this summer. And I'm here if you need anything at all. Just holler." She wraps her arms around me, squeezing tight, and a lump knots my throat as an ache for my own mama and Weston flares. Maybe Claire can be a soft spot for me here in Edisto.

Afterwards, I walk to the double French doors that lead out onto the patio and the walkway to the guest apartment. Gin leans against the wall beside them and grabs the knob when I go to leave.

"I had so many hopes for you, Jordan," she says, shaking her head. "And then you gotta go and do me that way."

"Oh Gin, you'll be okay."

She purses her lips, faking a pout, but releases the knob.

I open the door and step out into the breezy salt air. "Goodnight. See you tomorrow."

She sighs. "See you tomorrow... traitor."

I laugh to myself as the door clicks shut behind me. Above, the moon glows bright, casting golden light across the patio and pool, and I stop a minute closing my eyes and listening to the wind rustle the palm fronds and the roar of the waves coming ashore.

"Well now the secret's out. My family is certifiable."

I startle as Bo's voice breaks in from somewhere behind me. Whirling around, I find him sitting on the edge of a lounger, elbows propped on his knees.

"No they're not. They're great. Very open... but great."

He ticks his head toward the open space beside him, and I walk over and sit down. My arm rubs against his, and chill bumps spill down my skin in response to the friction. The musk of his cologne swirls around us, warm and earthy like him.

"Your mom? Does she do that? Force you to talk when you don't want to?"

I laugh. "No, no, no. My mom is the queen of holding it all in and driving on strong." And crying into her pillow at night, but I obviously don't add in that part. "She *is* pretty good at writing letters with her words of wisdom for me to read. I think it's easier for her just to make her point and not have to discuss it."

"Can she teach my mom her ways?"

"Maybe they can teach each other. Somewhere between the two extremes, there has to be a good middle ground, right?"

"One could only hope." He runs a hand through his hair, tousling his dark curls. "Hey, thanks for standing up for me back there."

"For what it's worth, I understand what you're going through, and I'm really sorry. It sucks."

He's quiet for a moment then turns to me. Our eyes lock as he searches mine, almost looking for understanding, solidarity. "You were cheated on too?"

"Cheated on. Lied to. Rejected." I count off each offense on my fingers, making sure to leave out a few key ones like 'abandoned while pregnant.' That one's really no one's business at this point.

His eyes widen. "Recently?"

"No, it's been a while. The sting goes away eventually, but it's hard to trust again. Hard to put yourself out there. But you will. When the time is right." I glance down at my phone, surprised to see I'm already ten minutes late in calling Mama to talk to Weston before bed. "And speaking of the right time, I need to get my butt in the bed. Morning comes early, and it's a big day."

"Yep. Nervous?"

A total wreck. "Nervous-excited. But it's going to be a great summer. I can feel it."

Bo stands up and extends a hand. I slip mine in his and he pulls me to standing. The warmth of his skin sliding against mine spreads up my arm in a fiery rush. The chill bumps reappear until he withdraws his fingers from mine.

"Sounds good," he says, turning to go back in the house but not before he tacks on, "I think we both deserve it."

CHAPTER 7

Bo

D^{*ing.*}

A notification chimes on my phone, and it buzzes against the wooden conference room table. I lean forward, my chair squeaking in the silence of the room. I like to come in here sometimes and sit and get a feel for the place. Or try to, at least. The tractors, the dirt—that I get. The office, the politics, the corporate red tape—that not so much. Will something resonate by summer's end?

I swipe my finger over the screen and read the notice of an unknown number from a wish-I-didn't-know person. I can erase the girl from my phone but I can't erase the recognition of a Virginia-based area code from my brain.

I click open the message.

Talk to me. Please call. I miss you.

I roll my eyes. The chances of her actually missing me are probably even smaller than the likelihood of my answering this message... or the fifty before it. I won't spend another minute as her puppet.

Delete. Again. I thought she'd get the hint by now.

Three summers spent waiting on one week that only meant something to me. No more.

The door swings open and Brice struts in, chest bowed, chin to the sky in his usual conceited way. He fixes his snarky glare on me, as if I piss him off by just sitting here, and kicks the door shut. It slams in the frame, shaking the walls of the boardroom.

"What's up, Bo-sephus?" He reaches across the table and ruffles my hair as I duck out of his reach. "What are you doing here? Isn't this where the big kids hang out? Last time I checked there's no kiddie table in the boardroom. Or is it 'bring your rugrat to work day' and Clay got stuck with you?"

Brice steps to the head of the table and plops in dad's chair, propping his feet on the edge.

I steel my jaw, teeth clenched tight. I know Dad preaches family connection but the only connecting I'd like to do with this jerk is my fist to his big fat mouth.

"I'm an intern leader this summer, but you know that. You just want to be a..."

The words die on my tongue. Probably better to keep it to myself. For dad's sake, at least.

"Finish that thought. I dare ya." He tips up his chin, taunting me.

I clamp my jaw shut. If my back teeth could talk, they'd be begging for mercy right about now.

Finally, I mutter, "I wouldn't get too comfortable in that seat if I were you."

Brice spins a pencil between two fingers. "Why? It'll be mine one day. We both know who has the brains and gumption to run this operation... and who doesn't." My mouth drops open as he narrows his gaze on me. "Don't look so shocked. Everybody knows it. Everybody talks about it. I'm just the only one with enough guts to say it to your face."

Voices echo in the hallway, and I swallow down rage, burying it somewhere behind my ribs. The pressure threatens to blow me apart from the inside out.

Dad opens the door and walks in with Patrick in tow, discussing something about planting schedules, but they freeze when seeing us at the table. The hostility hangs in the air like a brick wall, and it's as if they've both just walked face-first into it.

Patrick shuffles to his usual chair at the conference table, and Dad walks to his, stopping in front of its occupied place. He swats Brice's feet with the manilla folder and notepad in his hand, a hard *thwack* breaking the silence.

"How 'bout a little respect for the furniture?" When Brice doesn't immediately budge, Dad grabs his feet and yanks them down. The chair sways sideways and nearly dumps Brice in the floor before he regains his balance. Damn. Can't say I wouldn't have laughed about seeing him faceplant on the floor like the slug he is.

Brice jumps up with a huff, bucking his chest nearly squared with Dad's.

"Why? It's a hundred years old, like this house and all the equipment."

Dad cocks his head to one side. "Excuse me?"

"Come on, Clay," he says, brushing past Dad and walking to an open chair beside Patrick and across from me. "When are we finally going to raze this decrepit place and build a real head-quarters? How are we ever going to grow with this old house being the face of Johnson Farms?"

Dad tosses his folders and paperwork on the table and sits down in the vacated chair. "We're growing just fine, Brice." Patrick side-eyes his son and they both shake their heads. Dad jams his finger onto the tabletop. "There wouldn't even be a farm if it wasn't for this old house and for the people who lived here who had a dream. It might do you both some good to remember what the word family means."

Patrick sits forward in his chair, his smirk morphing into a hard sneer. "Family? That only means something when it's conve-nient, right?"

"I'm going to pretend you didn't say that." The muscle in Dad's jaw flexes in and out as he stretches his neck from side to side then grabs a pen and flips to a new page on his notepad.

"Now, before our interns get here in a few minutes, do we have anything to discuss? Any business opportunities or ideas?" When no one says a word, his attention focuses on me, the corners of his eyes upturned. Hopeful. Encouraging. "Bo?"

My heart drums in triple time. No one mentioned coming prepared with business ideas. Suddenly I feel like that kid in English class who didn't read the assignment when the teacher announces a pop quiz. I swallow hard, everyone's eyes like burning lasers on my face, and shake my head.

"Shocker," Brice whispers and jabs Patrick in the ribs. Dad pretends not to notice, but he tucks his top lip between his teeth and bites down. There goes his jaw muscle again. *Clench clench clench.* My stomach fills with lead; I hate disappointing him.

Brice clears his throat, tapping his fingers on the table. "Last quarter I sent you some information on hemp farming. Any progress?"

Dad nods, opening one of the folders, and thumbs through some papers. "Yes, that was a great idea, but we can't just jump headfirst into a new—"

"Are you hell-bent on shooting down the boy's idea?" Patrick blurts out, his eyebrows stitched together and cheeks flushed.

"Maybe if you'd let me finish?" Dad fixes his eyes on Patrick, engaging in an intense stare-down that lasts for what seems like minutes. The tick-tock of the clock on the wall marks every passing second like a cannon shot before Dad sucks in a deep breath and continues. "I think it's a great idea. But there are feasibility studies to be done, governmental regulations to consider, upfront costs, and—"

Brice slams a closed fist on his knee. "We need to get off our asses and act! That's how we make a name for ourselves."

"We already have a name—Johnson." Dad leans forward, enunciating the syllables of our name so hard his lips curl. "It's family, blood."

"Well, mostly," Brice mumbles, biting curved impressions

into the side of the pencil in his hand. If Dad hears his backtalk, he doesn't react but goes back to shuffling papers.

"We'll also need to research land or any potential farms going on the market."

"Already got one in mind. In Goose Creek. Family farm, 100 acres, been in their family since the 1800s." Brice sits back, tucking the pencil behind his ear, and folds his arms across his chest.

Dad's slitted eyes go round as he strokes his chin. "Looking to sale? Or perhaps we could discuss partnering—"

"Partnering?" Brice spits out the word as if it's poison on his tongue. "They're in hock up to their eyeballs. Late by like fifty grand on two mortgages. We don't have to partner or even negotiate. We have the money, and the money is power. I say we go straight to the bank, buy it out from under them, and get those eviction notices rolling."

Disgust splatters Dad's face, and a flame ignites inside me. Brice gloats from his side of the table with his yes-man of a father backing up every word he utters while my dad—the good one, the honorable one—sits there alone. No, I won't let him face these bullies by himself. "That is *not* the way Johnson Farms does business!" I yell. The force of the words spewing from me shoot me to my feet. These jerks will not ruin the legacy my dad has fought to instill in this farm. In our name.

"Maybe not you, but it's the way I do business." Brice stands and we lock eyes across the table. "As a matter of fact—"

Three quick raps on the door stop the conversation. It opens a sliver and Doniella, our farm manager, pokes her head around the side. "Are you guys ready for..." She darts her eyes between me and Brice then over to Dad. He stop-signs his hand, and we both sit down, letting the matter drop, though the tension hovers over us like a storm cloud.

Dad composes himself then smiles toward the door. "Please come in, Doniella! You have our interns, I see. Welcome,

Jordan... Christopher." He nods to each as they enter and motions for them to sit down at the far end of the table.

Doniella slides into the empty chair beside mine, leaning in to whisper, "What did we just walk in on?"

"Just another Johnson disagreement."

"Let me guess. Brice thinks he's an actual human and you were telling him he's no better than that chicken shit we spread on the fields?"

I laugh. "Pretty much."

Doniella should know better than anyone. She started working on the farm over a decade ago, right after she finished her two-year degree. Her family had been here for generations on end, her mother serving as one of the homeschool co-op's teachers and her grandmother running the local Gullah tours on the island. Born and raised on Edisto, she has an undying love for our coastal lands that Dad knew would be the basis for the perfect farm manager. If anything happens on Johnson Farms, Doniella knows about it.

And she loathes Brice with the fires of a thousand hells.

"This is why we need you here, Bo. Your family has worked so hard... those two will ruin it for sure." She reaches over and grabs my hand, squeezing it in her calloused fingers.

Dad stands up at the head of the table, a huge smile spreading his lips. "We are so happy to have you two participate in the first annual Johnson Farms summer internship program. It is my fervent hope that you both will have a summer full of learning and hands-on experience that will take you even further in your own agricultural careers." He pans his hands across the table, one in my direction, the other in Brice's. "Our two intern leaders for this summer will be Bo Johnson, my son, and Brice Johnson, my cousin Patrick's son. Hopefully you've had a chance to see them and chat, but if not, I'm going to give them the floor to tell you each a little bit more about themselves. Pay attention to what resonates with what they say—one of you will have the opportunity to select who you will be working with this summer."

Jordan and Christopher let out a collective gasp, exchanging glances. Brice and I do likewise. This is a twist Dad kept all to himself.

He retakes his seat and nods, deferring to us. Brice's top lip curls into an evil smirk and he motions toward me to go first.

Doubtful that's a show of goodwill, but I stand up anyway, shoving my fists deep into my pockets and smile at Christopher and Jordan. Christopher ticks up his chin, expressionless, but Jordan smiles back. A small one that barely parts her lips. She fiddles with a leather cuff bracelet on her wrist, and I wonder if her anxiety is skyrocketing like mine.

"Um, hey y'all... I'm Bo. I'm here because—"

"Because my daddy made me!" Brice says, puckering his lips and talking in a whiny baby voice, but quickly shuts up when Dad slams his fist on the table.

I take a deep breath, continuing, "This farm belongs to my family, so I've been lucky enough to grow up around here. I... um... just graduated from high school, and I'm anxious to get my hands dirty and sort of... find my place... in all this. I hope to learn a lot this summer along with you, so pick me if you want a partner to dig in with." I catch myself making a digging motion with my hands as if I'm holding an imaginary shovel and quickly squash it. Lame.

I sink back onto my chair and stare at the brown woodgrain of the table.

Across from me, Brice stands up, straightening the black visor on his head. His spine lengthens tall, sturdy. "While he's digging..." Brice mimics my stupid shoveling motion, then pulls his thumbs to his chest. "I'll be winning, so pick me if that grant money actually means something to you."

Flames lick my face, the heat spreading to my ears. I took zero shots at him. Of course he'd start out his speech by eviscerating me in front of everyone—the interns, Patrick, Dad. I side-eye him, sitting like a statue in the head chair, a sympathetic gaze leveled on me. But while his eyes are soft, his fist clenches the pen in his hand so tight, the plastic makes a slight crunching sound.

Patrick laughs under his breath but switches to pretending to clear his throat when Dad turns to glare at him.

Brice smirks again and continues, "Unlike my cousin here who's on some mission of self-discovery at your expense, I already know who I am and where I'm going. I just finished my junior year at college, double-majoring in Agriculture and Business Management. I've worked in almost every aspect of this particular farm and completed hands-on training on others during my coursework. I am well-connected with the farming community both locally and regionally, and everyone knows that in business, it's not just what you know but *who* you know. And I know a lot of people."

Silence envelops the room as Brice retakes his seat, reclining back with one leg crossed over the other. I lift my eyes, finding his squarely fixed on me. He forms the letter "L" with his right hand, holding it against his chest and mouthing "loser." Every muscle in my body clenches tight and my nostrils flare.

I hate him.

And I'm mad at myself for being so unsure. So unsettled.

"Now, you're probably all wondering how these pairings will be handled. That's where this comes in." Dad breaks the awkward tension, holding up the manilla folder. "This is your first challenge, due to Doniella by seven o'clock tonight. We need to work harder and smarter on gaining attention for our brand on social media. As our world goes increasingly virtual, our farm will also need to stoke this presence. You will create a social media ad for Johnson Farms that will appeal to this online demographic. Doniella will post both ads on our page, open up a secret poll, and gather votes until noon tomorrow. Whoever's post receives the most votes will be our winner. The winner will select which of these two they will work with over the next few months of the internship." He hands each intern an instructional paper from the folder. "Good luck."

Dad nods toward Patrick and Doniella, and they get up to follow him out. Before she leaves, Doniella leans over and hugs me tight, asking, "Want me to run Brice over with the tractor?"

"Maybe later? I'll be your alibi."

"Cool," she laughs with a wink then walks out.

I walk over and lean against the wall, pretending to thumb through my phone but straining to listen in on Jordan and Christopher's conversation. They sit elbow to elbow, their heads bowed together as they whisper, and a trill of jealousy slivers through me.

"This is going to be a breeze." Christopher brags. "I was a social media influencer for a local men's boutique in high school, and I took a comp-sci class where I learned how to create those cool flashing graphics. What about you?"

Jordan fingers tremble around the paper. "To tell you the truth, I'm sort of lost. I've never really done social media before."

"Bummer." Christopher shrugs and immediately begins talking about the grant money when a hard grip circles my bicep and pulls me backwards.

"I seriously hope you're not interested in her," Brice says, eyeing Jordan. "Face it, Bo. If she wins the challenge, she's picking me. But even if she loses and just wants some... company... for the summer, she'll still pick me." He licks his lips and stares at her like a lion casing an antelope at the watering hole.

I jerk my arm from his clutches. "Jordan's a nice girl. She wouldn't want someone like you."

"And who would she want? Someone like *you*?" He furrows his eyebrows and stabs a finger into my chest. "You know, if this whole farming thing doesn't work out for you, maybe you'd have a decent future in fantasy writing."

CHAPTER 8

Jordan

What would you use the money for, Jordan?
Christopher had a million ideas of how to use the
grant money, and then my stomach churned when he turned to
me and asked about my plans. I'm pretty sure I mumbled something about new tractors or something to get him off my back,
while our hometown banker, the one who I'd concocted into
some sort of mean-looking Monopoly guy with moneybags in
hand, haunted my thoughts. I couldn't bring myself to enunciate
what I was really thinking.

The grant money could save my family's farm from foreclosure. It still wouldn't be enough to clear all the debt, but it'd buy
us time—time to figure a way out of this mess. I don't want to
tell anyone the truth, to see that gross look of pity and disgust
floating in their eyeballs. Christopher's knowing the depth of my
desperation could only give him an advantage at this point, and I
can't be giving stuff away.

I slip the keys from the ignition and throw my head back
against the seat's headrest. The first challenge of the summer,
due in—I glance at my phone—four teeny-tiny hours and not
one ounce of inspiration.

I don't know social media. I don't do social media. Mama

hates it, the grandparents don't even know what it is, I certainly don't want Weston's bio dad slinking around any facet of my life, and who the hell even has time anyway?

My mind flashes to a cocky Christopher who eagerly bragged about all of his online experience.

I was a social media influencer for a local boutique and I took classes in web design. I know exactly what to do!

Yeah, well, bite me, Christopher.

Ugh. Never have I wanted to punch someone so hard. It's not like he even needs the money—well, not in the same way I do. His parents have plenty of cash to spot him what he needs to start his venture. We literally have nothing. Less than nothing. Like thirty-something-thousand less than nothing.

No. I will not descend into a useless pity party. One thing I learned from Mama early on is that the world will kick you when you're down and it's your job to come back swinging. A Wright doesn't go down without a fight.

I stare up into the rearview mirror, deepening my frown. Trying to perfect that Rocky-esque mentality. Nope, it needs to be meaner, more determined. It needs—

"Jordan! What are you doing?" Her cheery voice followed by a rapid knocking on my window startles me from practicing my facial expressions. I glance over at Gin, standing outside my door, gigantic grin spread across her face as she waves with one hand and cradles a large wooden crate against her chest with the other. The crate itself nearly dwarfs her petite frame, and for a minute, I'm afraid it'll topple her over.

I throw open the door and slide out quickly, grabbing one side of it. "Let me help."

"Thanks!" Her voice drips with sunshine as she takes off walking across the lawn and I scramble to keep up.

"Where are we going?" I ask, glancing over my shoulder at the Johnson's place.

"Oh! We're going to Miss Bessie's house next door. Mom and

Dad always send her fresh produce once a week. You haven't met her yet, but you're going to love her!"

I groan internally. Someone named Miss Bessie sounds like a person down for some long-winded conversation, and today I have zero time for that. "I'll help you carry this up the stairs but I might have to get acquainted with her another day. I just had my first project assigned and it's due by 7 p.m. tonight."

"Is it the social media post where it comes down to the popular vote?"

I nod. How did she know about it already?

"That was the idea I submitted to Dad when he was planning everything. Great challenge, huh?"

It was her idea? Man, you screwed me Gin.

"Not so much for me. Christopher has worked as an influencer before. Me? I don't even have one social media account. I have no clue where to start."

"Then we're going to the right place! Miss Bessie will have some ideas for sure, and they'll be good ones. Wait and see." Gin shoots me a conspiratorial grin and ticks her head toward the house next door.

Am I missing something? An older grandma lady with cutting-edge ideas? The dots aren't connecting.

We stop at the bottom of the steps and coordinate our feet to ensure no one trips. Step-step, stop. Step-step, stop. Step-step, stop. Times another ten or so. By the time we reach the landing, Gin and I are both huffing and puffing, trying to calm our racing hearts. She reaches out and pushes the doorbell. A deep chime sounds from within followed by footsteps.

The door swings open to reveal a short, older lady—maybe in her late 60s—with a chic short-and-spiky haircut, rouge-y cheeks, and rounded, sparkling eyes. The deep V-neck of her black shirt exposes a line of cleavage that jiggles when she leans forward to peer in the crate.

"This looks wonderful. Your parents are the cat's pajamas! Come on in... you know where to put it!" She steps back, allowing Gin and I to waddle through, then shuts the door and trails behind us.

I no sooner lug my end of the crate onto the countertop than she's a foot from my face. Her breath smells of cinnamon and something else. Something a bit tangy. Liquor maybe? I glance around, locating a highball glass on the kitchen table. One melting piece of ice remains in the bottom.

"And you are?"

"I... um... I'm Jordan."

Gin laughs and steps beside me, wrapping her arm around my shoulder. "Jordan is here for the summer, living in our guest apartment. She's interning at the farm, but she's originally from the Upstate."

"Ah! A little bit of new blood around here—I like it!" Miss Bessie claps her hands, eyeing me up and down, then helicopters her finger. "Turn around, youngin', and let me look at you." Um, awkward, but I do it anyway while trying to catch Gin's line of vision. When I do, she grins and giggles. Is this part of the Edisto Welcome Wagon treatment? When I complete a full rotation, Miss Bessie clicks her tongue and cups my chin in her hand. "You are a beauty! I am so looking forward to getting to know you." And as quickly as she inspects me, she turns her attention to the crate on the counter and shuffles over to it, standing on her tiptoes to peer in and rifle through the contents. "Now, let's see what we got here."

Gin leans in, whispering in my ear, "She's a little in your face but you'll never meet anyone with a bigger heart. She might annoy you, she might embarrass you, but she'll always have your back."

Miss Bessie pulls out a bright red strawberry and presses it to her tongue, closing her lips around it. In one swoop, the fruit disappears, leaving only the green stem pinched between her fingers. "Have a seat you two," she says as she chews, nodding toward the barstools at the island.

We obey without protest, and as soon as she's situated, Gin blurts out, "Jordan has a conundrum and maybe you can help."

"A conundrum, huh?" Miss Bessie darts her eyes between the two of us, hitching one hand on her hip. "Already? You just got into town!" She leans forward on the island, propped on her elbows. "Is it a boy?"

"No." The response rolls off my tongue before I can stop it.

"Well, good then. If it's not about a boy, then the solution should be simple. Lay it on me."

I sigh and relay the details of the challenge to Miss Bessie, who narrows her eyes, listening without ever diverting her stare. She nods from time to time and chews her lip as if concocting a suitable plan. I'm almost sure that at any moment I could peek into her ear canals and see the cogs churning.

When I finish, she stands up straight and gnaws her thumbnail. Silent. Plotting.

"Maybe we could peruse some of my romance books?" Gin suggests.

I shake my head. "We're not going to find the answer in your romance book."

Miss Bessie wags her finger at the two of us. "I don't know about that. There is some truth to that old saying about how sex sells."

Sex sells? Nope. This line of thought needs to be squashed. Like now.

"I'm not sure what you're implying but—"

"Just hear me out, okay?" She walks over to the counter and opens up a cardboard box, rambling inside. She pulls out a square piece of painted metal, whisks off the Styrofoam peanuts, and holds it up. "Take a look at this sign my granddaughter CJ just sent me. She's off at some racing tours this summer with her boyfriend, Jett, but she always finds time to think about her ol' Memaw."

Jett. Where had I heard that name before? Oh yeah, Bo's conversation at the pool.

His best friend.

Stop, Jordan. Focus. Only three-and-a-half hours left now.

I survey the metal sign. A mermaid in shimmering purple and turquoise sits on a dock in front of a glowing sunset, martini in hand. In large white lettering across the top, *Chasing Tail and Raising Hell.*

"A perfect addition to your collection," Gin says, giggling. Collection? My eyes dart around the room and land on a hand-painted wooden board that spans the space above the double windows over her sink.

No Bitchin' in My Kitchen.

Gin leans in close to my ear. "There's more. Check the foyer on our way out."

Miss Bessie turns around from the far wall where she's been trying out potential homes for her new sign and lays it on the counter. "See, people like things that are funny and just a smidge naughty. It's human nature. Your ad has to have that to win." She begins unpacking the produce from the box, laying ears of corn, cucumbers, strawberries and cantaloupes on the counter.

"I've got it!" Gin squeals, sliding off her stool and then jumping up and down. "And it comes straight from real-life experience. Remember when we all first met on Saturday at the market? The cantaloupes?" She picks up the two fruits and holds them to her chest with a broad smile.

"What cantaloupes?" Miss Bessie asks, eyes sparkling like firecrackers. Gin launches into a retelling of that first meeting in the market by the cantaloupe stand and the fire in Bo's cheeks when he stuck his foot in his mouth.

"So, the boy thinks you have nice melons, huh?" Miss Bessie walks over and jabs me in the ribs with her elbow. "That boy *is* a looker!"

Gin's face sours. "Gross."

"I know!" Miss Bessie grabs the cantaloupes from Gin and holds them against her chest with deep bedroom eyes. She lowers her voice to a sultry whisper, saying, "You're gonna love our melons!"

Gin pipes in, "Fresh, sweet, and juicy!"

Fire flushes my cheeks. No way in hell can I stand around on camera with two melons pressed to my chest, using the word juicy. Just no.

"You two are trouble, that's what. I cannot do something like this!" I scramble to my feet, crossing my arms in front of me like a barrier. "Your dad will see it!"

Gin waves me off. "Dad's not judging it, the followers are. Besides, he's a businessman. He's going to look at the bottom line." She grabs my wrist and shoots me a matter-of-fact look. "And don't you want to win this? It would be a really great advantage in pursuit of that grant money."

The money. That's the main objective here and not my personal pride. I told Mama I'd find a way to erase our problems. No matter what.

Dear God, I'm going to regret this.

"Okay then. You're hired. Show me what to do."

Gin and Miss Bessie share wicked grins, rubbing their hands together, and suddenly I wonder if I've just made a deal with the devil... and her Memaw.

A cool breeze wafting in off the ocean bristles the hair on my arms as I sliver another piece of strawberry cheesecake and spear it into my mouth. Since Claire had found a new recipe online for the "creamiest cheesecake ever" and had just brought home a carton of the season's best strawberries, those two coinciding twists of fate ended up in dessert. She invited me for a slice with the family on the patio after dinner. Earlier, I'd nuked a bean burrito and ate it on a paper towel at the apartment. Claire made it perfectly clear that I was welcome anytime for supper but Mama always told me that it was better not to impose. Besides, I needed a minute to myself after the utter humiliation of that photoshoot earlier.

"Jordan, how did the first challenge go? You get your ad to Doniella so she could upload it on the site?" Clay wipes his mouth with a napkin while awaiting my response.

An instant heat flushes my skin. "It went... well. All submitted. Good to go." I shoot him an awkward thumbs-up—why I don't know—and immediately wonder if it'd be feasible to jab it backward into my eye.

Quit bumbling already, Jordan. Geez.

If he notices, he plays it off well. "I'm really excited to take a look, see what you came up with." He glances at the silver watch on his wrist. "When is it being posted again?"

"The post goes live in a couple minutes," Gin pipes up. "Doniella is keeping the poll private so we won't know the winner until tomorrow's meeting." She eyes me, chewing the end of a strawberry on her fork. "But I know it'll be Jordan. Hers is *muah*," she says, doing a chef's kiss in the air.

"You've seen it already. Why am I not surprised?" Claire laughs and nudges her shoulder into Clay's. "Between you and Bessie next door, we don't need a newspaper or residents' webpage. You two know everything, sometimes before it ever happens!"

Bo, who's been sitting quietly while shoving his face, scrapes the remaining crumbs off his plate and into his open mouth. He licks the fork and sits the plate on the table then looks over at me. "What was the inspiration behind your ad?"

Gin snorts, but I stop her with a sharp glance. She presses her lips together, so tight they disappear, as she stifles the urge to spill the details.

"Um, the produce. I helped Gin carry a crate of produce over to Miss Bessie's this afternoon, and it all looked so good... what can I say?"

Muffled giggles emanate from Gin, who now has her face

squeezed into the crook of her elbow. For the love of all things holy, shut up.

Bo cocks his head to the side, staring in her direction. "All right. I know this reaction. What am I missing? You two are leaving something out."

Gin folds her arms across her chest. "Let's just say that Jordan brought her own unique... body of knowledge... to the assignment. No one will ever look at fruits and veggies the same."

He glowers in her direction, brows knitted as if trying to unravel the clues. To my side, Clay and Claire have the same puzzled expressions splashed on their faces.

Gin could have just let it go, not make a big deal about it. But no. This clandestine clue dropping has only piqued everyone's interest. My stomach churns and I lay my fork on my plate. Maybe it won't be as embarrassing as I think; I did always have a knack for jumping to catastrophic scenarios. Maybe everyone will enjoy this little tease and then simply forget about—

Ding! Ding! Ding! Ding!

A quartet of cell phone notifications pepper the evening air. All four Johnsons pick up their respective phones and thumb across the screens. The realization hits me as a hot stream of bile rises to my throat.

The Johnson Farms social media challenge post just went live. And they're all looking at it right now.

Oh shit.

I gaze up into the darkening sky praying there's a pelican on this island big enough to swoop down, pick me up, and deposit me somewhere out there in the middle of the ocean. Why did I let them talk me into this ridiculous plan? The first tiny bit of anxiety about this internship rears its head and I fold like a lawn chair, giving in to the cheap and tawdry.

Clay chokes on a bite of cheesecake, and Claire wops him on the back until he quits coughing. Gin is weirdly quiet, staring at her screen with a satisfied quirk of her upper lip, and Bo stares at his, mouth hanging open. Screwing up the nerve, I pick up my own phone and open up the site to Christopher's professionally-perfected ad, complete with flashing graphics, adjacent to my Daisy Mae-style sexy fruit flyer. I can't believe they talked me into those cut-off shorts and my bikini top. All I see is a crap-ton of my bare skin and a pair of well-placed melon boobs.

"Well..." Claire is the first to speak, a definite note of hesitancy in her tone. "Your ad sure does... make a statement?" I don't miss the weird question mark hiding in her intonation.

I pocket my phone and clamp my hand over my face. "I literally cannot show my face at this table," I groan. "I was blinded by the fact that I wanted to win the challenge and I was coerced."

Gin sighs. "It wasn't coercion... it was inspired assistance."

"From who?" Clay asks.

I side-eye Gin from between my fingers. She plunges her thumb to her chest. "From me... and Miss Bessie."

The rest of the Johnsons nod their heads, letting out a collective *oh!*

"When Jordan and I went over there, we told her about the challenge and it sort of went from there," Gin explains. "It started with Miss Bessie's new sign and then I brought up how Bo told Jordan she had nice melons and..."

Claire gasps, jerking her head toward Bo. "You said what?"

I slink further down in my chair, wishing the shifting sand below the concrete pavers would open up and suck me in.

For the first time since it went live, Bo drops the phone from his line of vision and instead directs his gaze at Gin, slack-jawed. "Woah! When did I say—"

"In the market Saturday." Cool, calm, collected. Her matter-of-fact retort cuts through Bo's argument. "Jordan said the cantaloupes were nice and you said 'so are yours' while you were staring at her chest."

What's even worse is that while she's saying the 'staring at her chest' part, Gin swipes her hand in the air in an imaginary line that extends from Bo's face to my chest.

Bo's face floods crimson and he, too, sinks in his chair. If we keep this up, he and I will end up under this table together. But I'm sure Gin would find a way to spin that too.

"Gin, maybe you and Bessie should have let Jordan pursue her own ideas for this project instead of pushing her into something she's so obviously uncomfortable with," Claire says, adjusting her glasses on her nose as she glares over them. I'm assuming this is her own form of mild chastisement. But I can't let her take the fall. She pushed, but I signed on. I agreed.

"Please don't be upset with Gin. She did make her case, but I agreed to do this. No one forced me. I wanted to win, so I took a risk."

Correction, I need to win so I caved in desperation.

"I appreciate your honesty." Claire reaches over and pats my hand. "Now let me be honest. There's nothing wrong with this photo, nothing you should be ashamed of. It's cute, it's funny, and you look beautiful in it. No one could call this distasteful when you can flip on the TV and see things twenty times worse." She looks back down at her phone once more. "Actually, it makes me want a slice of cantaloupe. Maybe I should cut one and put it in the fridge?" she asks Clay with a wink.

Clay nods with an eager smile and then lays his phone on the table facing me. He points to the like/share buttons at the bottom of the post. "The point of this challenge was to draw attention. Mission accomplished."

I lean forward, getting a closer look at the numbers. Forty-two likes already. No, 55. No, 78. The numbers roll by, faster and faster. I stare up at him, wide-eyed. "You mean...?"

"This post could go viral. Not too shabby."

Just as my mortified heart notes a slight tremble of joy, it's dashed once more by an icy tidal wave brought on by one word.

Viral.

A vision of mama, sitting down with her morning coffee, thumbing through her emails and messages from neighbors, only to find a suggestive ad splashed with her daughter's melons? What if Weston saw?

"Going viral would be awesome!" Gin shouts, clapping her hands.

I drop my head. "Not if my mama sees. She'll kill me."

Gin laughs, squeezing her hands in front of her chest, mouthing the word "cantaloupes" in Bo's direction. Clay pins her with a hard glare and she immediately shuts her mouth as Bo slides even further in his chair.

"You had a job to do, and you got it done. She'll understand." Clay says, standing up and walking behind Bo's chair. He grips his son's shoulders and looks down at him. "We parents have ways to get past when our kids do—or say—things we might not exactly approve of."

I gulp hard, shaking my head. "You don't know my mama."

Claire scoots her chair closer to me, the metal legs grating over the pavers, then wraps an arm around my shoulders. "You're being too hard on yourself. The only thing I've learned about you from that photo is that you are one hundred percent dedicated to being successful in this internship, and that," she says grabbing my chin and turning my face toward hers, "is something to be proud of. I'm a mom, too, and I know these things." She winks, tugging me into her in a side hug, then stands up from the table. "Clay, want to help me get these dishes to the kitchen?"

He nods and gathers the dessert plates and forks into an organized stack and trails her into the house.

For a moment the three of us sit in silence, Bo and I avoiding eye contact and Gin flipping her gaze back and forth between the two of us. When no one responds, she slides her chair back and jumps to her feet. "You two seriously need to lighten up. Jordan, your ad is awesome and I guarantee you're going to win over—" She stares again at her phone. "—over whatever that lame crap is that Christopher submitted. And Bo, you should be happy too. If Jordan wins, maybe she'll throw the dog a bone and select you as her intern partner." She blows out a loud breath and stomps toward the house, pausing behind his chair to wallop him in the back of the head. "If you play your cards right, that is."

Once she disappears through the French doors, I muster up the courage to speak first. Throughout the entire process, I only worried about my embarrassment. I never stopped to consider how Bo might be mortified that his words could've been used against him for my gain.

"I'm sorry if that whole thing embarrassed you. For what it's worth, I know that's not what you meant about the cantaloupes in the market. I just—"

"Thanks, but I'm good. Really. And this isn't about me. It's about you and your future. You needed to do something to help you win." He slides his phone across the table and points to the like/share stats, still ticking up at lightning speed. "From the looks of it, people are responding."

Yeah, but there's no telling which post is getting the votes. The votes are what count, not the likes. "What if they're responding to Christopher's?"

Bo shakes his head. "Not likely. I know which one my eyes go to."

The way he looks down at my picture when he says it sends electricity zapping through my body, like my veins are an inner network of fire. I swallow hard.

I want to win tomorrow, but if I do, then I have to make a decision. A wise one. The best one. Brice is a total jerk, but he has the education and the connections. He has a track record. Working with him would be torture, but could it be more profitable in the long run? Then Bo. What I wouldn't give to spend the summer working with him, so mild-mannered and supportive. But he doesn't have Brice's connections or experience. Can he really teach me what I need to know to take back to our farm? Can he and I pull out a win in the end for the money? And then there's something else...

Like the way my heart flip-flops when he turns his gaze on me. Or the tingle in my skin when we accidently touch. Or the way my mind keeps imagining him—no. I can't get sidetracked like this when so much is at stake. And God knows my mind would be going a hundred miles a minute in so many directions working side by side with him. But then again, would I regret not taking that chance?

Too many ifs. So many emotions. I can't think clearly, and I need to know what's in this for Bo. Is there anything on the line for him or is this just a summer job?

"Can I ask you a question?"

Bo pockets his phone and shrugs. "Sure."

"What's your goal for this summer internship? Like personally?"

He rubs his fingers back and forth across his forehead. For a minute he stares off into the distance, pensive, before turning his gaze on me. "Personally... I need to find direction. Dad needs to start planning for the future, and I need to discover whether I am—or want to be—the right fit for the farm. Whatever that decision may be, it has to be good for me, but it also has to be good for the farm. Whether my future's there or not, I love that land and what we do. It's... family."

A warmth spreads over me. His words speak to my heart, telling me the exact thing I didn't even know I needed to hear. Bo and I are walking the same path, on the same journey to find ourselves and secure our families' futures. He understands the weight on my shoulders more than anyone else.

"I know exactly how you feel about needing to find direction and help your family."

He presses his lips into a flat line and nods. "I thought you might."

"And as for the question of whether or not you want to work on the farm, there'll be a moment when you know, when it becomes clear."

"You had that moment?"

Purpose found me and set my course the moment Weston

came into the world. "Where the farm's concerned, at least. The rest of my life... well, that's still pretty muddy."

"Tell me about it." Bo laughs and stands up, swiping a few dessert crumbs from his lap. From across the table, he connects in an intense eye contact. "Good luck, tomorrow. I hope things turn out the way you want them to."

I smile, unable to get any words out of my brain and onto my tongue. Chills filter down my spine, despite the humid evening, as I sit alone at the table and watch him walk into the house. Five minutes ago, I was worried about winning and shouldering the burden of solidifying my future. Now, the fear of not winning scratches inside because for one of the first times in my life, the best choice is clear.

Every nerve ending in my body crackles like lit fireworks. Christopher sits beside me in the main office's boardroom, swiveling back and forth in the chair like he hasn't a care in the world, laughing, joking, making small talk about the internship. I'm not listening, only nodding and throwing in an occasional *mm-hm* to satisfy his need for an echo chamber. Across the room, Bo sits in a high-back chair in the corner, his leg jackhammering so hard it rattles the dry-erase markers on the whiteboard's ledge. In the opposite corner, Brice props himself on a file cabinet and stares in my direction. I shift in my own seat under his leering looks, which gain new life each time he stares down at his phone and then back at me. A few times he winks and ticks up his chin. Gross.

I drop my shoulders, straighten my spine, and stare back, unwilling to succumb to his intimidation. My ad was for my benefit, not his.

A stir of voices, a door opening, and a group of people walk in. Clay leads the way, followed closely by Doniella, Patrick, and Gin. Clay waves a sealed envelope in the air. "The results of our first challenge! Right now, only Doniella knows the winner. Are the rest of you ready to find out?"

Everyone claps and I finally catch Gin's gaze, sending her telepathic messages for some kind of hint. She only shrugs.

Crap. Of all times for her to *not* know something.

"Here we go." Clay rips open the envelope and Doniella clicks her tongue in a drumroll. "The final tally..."

Please let me win, God. Please.

"Christopher with 576 votes."

Crap, that's a ton of votes. My stomach knots.

"And Jordan with..."

My heart squeezes; my breathing halts. Silence grips the room.

"2,384 votes. Jordan wins!"

I won? A million butterflies bounce around my stomach. I won!

Another round of applause breaks out and people congratulate me but the words blur into white noise. The internal screaming drowns it out until one voice breaks through.

"Jordan!" I look over to Gin, who shoots me two thumbs up, a gigantic grin splashed over her face. Gosh, she's a pain sometimes, but I could've never done this without her.

Clay raps on the wooden table and waves his hands, demanding everyone's attention. "As the winner of the challenge, Jordan, you get to choose—"

"I choose Bo."

Silence once again grips the room as all eyes turn on Bo. He looks up, wide-eyed, and plunges a finger to his chest. I nod, mouthing the word *you*.

A blush filters into his cheeks as he says, "I'm in."

Clay pans his hand toward Bo. "Well, there you have it."

"What do you mean 'there you have it?'" Brice yells, stomping around the table and jabbing a finger in my direction. "This girl is stupid! Any idiot can see that I'm the better choice."

He glances over his shoulder, leveling his slitted gaze on Bo. "By a longshot!"

Clay blows out a breath and rolls his eyes. "Brice, you must understand that your perspective is not Jordan's perspective... or anyone else's here, save Patrick's, for that matter." He walks beside me, placing a firm hand on my shoulder. "She made her choice. Bo will be Jordan's internship leader this summer. You will work with Christopher."

Ignoring Clay, Brice walks to my chair, leans down and puts a hand on each chair arm, pinning me back. He hovers in my face, his breath reeking of whatever he had for lunch. Something garlicky. "I thought you wanted to win? Isn't that why you got naked for your ad?"

He wobbles his head when saying the word naked, and a fire ignites in my belly. I've spent my life surrounded by worthless men, and I'll be damned if I'll sit here and be denigrated by a jackass who could be their leader.

I muster all my strength and spring to my feet, so hard and so fast that I physically push Brice backwards. As he steadies himself, I push up on my tiptoes, angling my face toward his, saying through gritted teeth, "I did *not* get naked. You're just pissed because someone finally told you you're second place at best."

He smirks. "We'll see who's second place by the end of summer. At least my intern has some real potential. My expertise would be lost on someone of your caliber." He cups both hands and brings them to his chest, mocking me. "Now we know where all your brains are—in your melons."

Brice pushes past me and grabs Christopher by the arm, yanking him up from the chair, and they march out the door, Patrick run-waddling behind. In the silence of the boardroom, the rest of us exchange a knowing glance and then all burst into laughter.

CHAPTER 9

Bo

Tee-totally floored. I didn't see it coming. And I don't think I'll ever forget that expression seared on Brice's face, all red and squinty. For a moment, I half expected smoke to come boiling out of his ears like one of those cartoon characters.

Outside, an engine revs, vibrating the walls, and I walk to the window and peer out to the parking area where Patrick and Christopher scramble into the cab of Brice's truck. No sooner does the door close than he throws it in drive, spitting gravel out in all directions, and disappears in a cloud of dust.

I shake my head. All because he didn't get picked first. Poor Brice-y always having to have his way.

"Hey partner." Jordan steps beside me and cocks her head to one side, following my gaze through the window at the lingering haze. "I don't think he's too happy with me."

I turn to face her, leaning against the wall. "He's an over-grown toddler."

Jordan smirks and wags her finger in my face. "Oh no, give toddlers some credit. That's a straight-up man-baby."

No argument there. God knows we've all seen these sorts of tantrums before, from him and Patrick. He gets it honestly. "Everyone expected the challenge winner to choose him. So..." I zero my eyes on hers, searching them for answers. "Why did you choose me?"

She doesn't flinch. "Because I wanted to."

Okay, decisive, direct, but there has to be an actual reason. I know this opportunity means a lot to her so this couldn't have been a fly-by-night decision. "I get that I'm the lesser qualified of the two choices you had, but—"

"You're the only one who feels that way, Bo." She shakes her head, eyes soft at the corners. "After we talked last night, I knew exactly who my choice would be. I have no regrets." She pokes her finger onto my chest with each word of her last sentence.

"But he's Mr. Double-Major, contacts galore—"

She snorts. "From my experience, people who love talking about how great they are rarely live up to the hype."

Jordan curls her finger, motioning for me to follow her. We walk down the hall and out the front door. When it clicks shut behind us, Jordan stops and turns back to me, grabbing my hand. A trill of flutters dances up my arm.

"I heard everything Brice had to say. But I also heard everything you didn't say." Her words are like a microscope, honing in on my innermost thoughts. I drop my head, trying to evade her knowing stare, but she squeezes my hand, a silent command to listen. "This summer is for your family and the land. I like that you're willing to learn and be open to the experiences. I like the fact you don't feel that you have nothing left to learn. I need someone to grow and discover with, not someone to bark orders and stare at my butt like I'm a piece of fruit from the market."

She lifts up her other hand, a set of keys dangling in the air. Keys to the four-wheeler.

"Where'd you get those?"

"Your dad. He thinks we should get started on our orientation."

Dad did say it was my responsibility this week to show her around the farm's buildings and locations.

I grin. "Then what are we waiting for?"

She unfolds the fingers on my hand she's holding and plants the keys onto the palm. "Just make sure you find some good mud holes along the way."

She laughs and darts off the porch toward the ATV parked under the large oak. I run after her, thanking God for all my good luck, even if the job is intimidating. Jordan could've picked Brice, and I would've been here with Christopher.

I slide onto the seat of the four-wheeler and Jordan climbs on behind me, looping her arms around my waist. I close my eyes, relishing the feel of the breeze across my face and the warmth of Jordan's body through my T-shirt. No way I'd want to be here with Christopher. Nope.

The engine rumbles to life, but before I shift in gear, I lean back, yelling over my shoulder, "You do realize you pretty much just declared war on Brice, right? I would've been disappointed if you hadn't picked me, but I wouldn't retaliate. He will. And we need to be prepared for whatever he might do."

She flips her hair over her shoulder and pushes closer in behind me, her lips grazing my ear. "I'm not afraid of Brice."

I towel off the drips of water dotting my shoulder, trickled down from my still-wet hair. A hot shower was just what I needed to scrub off the caked-on mud pies. Shortly into our orientation, Jordan asked to drive and then she purposefully sought out ever brown puddle she could find and barreled through it at top speed. We ended up taking a dirt bath from the spray coming off the tires, as if she locked on each puddle as a target.

It was freaking awesome.

My phone buzzes on my dresser, and I reach over, silencing it, without looking at the screen. I know who it is. The same person who's been calling me every ten minutes for the past two days.

Who knows what this onslaught of calls is about? I don't

know, and quite frankly, I don't care. I haven't talked to her since that day on her front lawn when I told her that we were done. I said it, and I meant it.

I open the bottom drawer, grabbing a pair of swim trunks, and then pull them on. I'm rubbing sunblock on my nose when a series of knocks sound on my bedroom door before it swings open. Jett strolls in, towel draped around his shoulders, and flops on my bed, leaning back into the pillows and crossing his arms behind his head. "What's up?"

"Y'all are actually on time?" I laugh, picking up my phone and pretending to check the clock. "CJ is seriously rubbing off on you."

Before he can respond, my phone buzzes in my hand, the same number popping up for the millionth time today. I silence it and tuck it into the waistband of my trunks. Jett shrugs. "Go ahead and take your call. I don't mind."

"No one I need to talk to. Some out-of-town area code."

"Probably a telemarketer trying to sell you a pair of these awesome swim trunks." He stretches out the material of his shorts so I can get a closer look. Black material with orange flames and little floating circles filled with pictures of—I squint, leaning closer—his headshot?

Only Jett would buy these God-awful things. "Those are heinous. You're the only person I know who'd walk around with pictures of your face on your butt."

He slides off the bed, swiveling a full 360-degrees. "These are awesome! I get to sit on me all day long."

I shake my head and grab the towel from my desk chair, throwing it across my shoulder. I wish my bank account was the size of Jett's ego. Then I wouldn't have to worry about what to do the rest of my life. I could just sit back and live a life of leisure somewhere.

As if tapping into his Best Friend ESP, Jett nudges my shoulder. "How are things at the farm? You still trying to figure out what you want to do?"

I shrug. Too soon to tell. The past week, especially my time with Jordan on the farm, has been fun. But it's just a week. A blip on the radar of life. And those moments of fun have been interrupted frequently by outbursts of the general shittiness that is Brice and Patrick. If taking on Dad's farm life means dealing with them the rest of mine, that's definitely what I'd call a con on my list.

"I know of an opportunity coming in the fall working on a pit crew for an up-and-coming racer. Great management group. I mean, if you're interested or decide the farm's not for you. In the meantime, I have a couple races this summer where I'm gonna need some help in the pits. You could work, get some cash, build up your experience."

Working in Jett's pit crew is nothing new. I did it most of my high school years, and even when I wasn't, we were always working under the hoods of our cars. He tried to recruit me into racing years ago but being in the limelight was never my forte. I'd much rather be supporting from the sidelines without all the eyes on me. The idea of working in the racing industry had never been something to consider before, but it might be a good option if this whole farming thing doesn't work out.

"Sure," I say. "Just let me know."

Jett nods and walks to my window, looking out over the pool area. His head jerks to attention and he pops two fingers between the blinds and pushes them apart, leaning closer to the glass pane. His mouth drops open. "Woah, mama. Is that your intern partner?"

I peer through the window to the patio below where Jordan has just pulled into the driveway and is getting out of her Jeep.

"Yeah. That's Jordan."

Gin wastes no time dragging her over to CJ for introductions. I smile, watching Gin's and CJ's eyes sweeping up and down Jordan who obviously hasn't made it to a shower yet. Her T-shirt and cutoffs are caked in mud along with her arms, legs, and face. It's even drying in chunky knots in her hair.

Despite all that, her beauty shines through. It somehow finds a way to radiate off of her.

My phone, still stashed in the waistband of my shorts, buzzes again, and I silence it. Again. Although this time, I'm grateful for the interruption because I can already guess where Jett's mind is going—on a one-way racetrack showdown to Let's Play Matchmaker.

Apparently, the brief disruption doesn't pump the brakes.

"Jordan as in 'my pal, Jordan' or Jordan as in..." Jett trills his tongue and quirks an eyebrow.

I deadpan. Sometimes he's as bad as Gin. "We work together."

"Do you play together too?"

I roll my eyes and step past him, checking my hair in the dresser mirror one last time before we go down to meet the girls at the pool.

In the reflection, my eyes meet Jett's and he spreads his arms wide, palms up. "Just saying, maybe she could be the new Laurel."

Hell no. Rule one: no more Laurels. Ever. Rule two: we don't talk about Laurel. Ever.

I spin around, pinning him with a hard glare. "Jordan is the anti-Laurel. That's what I like best about her. And secondly, forget that name you just uttered, and maybe I won't have to hurt you." I grind one fist into the other palm, steeling my jaw, trying my best to look fierce.

Jett smirks and flicks his finger between the two of us. "If my memory serves, we agreed that you needed a fun, no-strings kind of summer."

"I think you agreed. I didn't say one way or the other."

He steps forward and grabs my shoulders, connecting eye to eye. "You're here. She's here. Y'all are together every day. She's living in your freaking backyard. I mean... come on. If this isn't the universe dropping a clue right in your lap then—"

"Stop! I'm not chasing Jordan." I push his hands off and point to the door, reminding him this day is about hanging out at the pool and not giving me some third-degree.

He trudges to the door then turns around with an evil glint sparking in his eye. "But you want to." Jett laughs, swirling his towel between two hands, then snaps it against my thigh. The sound echoes so loud, his mouth drops into an "o" and he takes off down the stairs with me hot on his heels.

The three girls are standing poolside when Jett and I walk out, though Gin and CJ have visibly backed away from Jordan, inserting a bit of distance between them and the smelly farm mud still clinging to her. CJ commandeers their attention, talking about her and Jett's latest trip and a killer piece of chocolate cake she nabbed from a restaurant on the road. Only Jordan peeks up as we arrive, shooting me a quick smile and a twiddle of her fingers in hello, before turning back to the conversation.

I smile and return her wave, but by the time I turn around, Jett plunges his elbow into my ribs. "I saw that," he whispers.

I ignore him, crank open the umbrella, and set my phone on the table underneath it. Jett slouches in a chair, spritzing himself with coconut-scented tanning oil, when my phone buzzes again, rattling against the glass top. He stops and eagle eyes it before turning to me, mouth downturned. "Who the hell keeps calling you?"

I pretend to ignore him instead of opening up any line of discussion that could lead back to the L-person who shall remain nameless.

Wrong move. Jett blows out a deep breath and reaches for my phone.

"No! Don't answer it," I whisper-yell, slamming my hand over the phone, blocking him. "It's Laurel. She keeps calling but I'm not answering. I'm done with her."

He smirks. "Then maybe you should pick up the phone and make that clear."

"I'm not sure how much plainer I can say it. I told her we're done and I meant it. She'll quit calling. Eventually."

God, I hope so. At this point, I'm about to drown the damn thing in the pool.

Jett shrugs and goes back to his tanning oil. I walk over to the girls, and after a quick hug from CJ, I grab Jordan's elbow and lead her away from the pack.

"No time for a shower yet, I see." I pluck a clod of mud from her hair and drop it to the ground.

"How'd you guess?" She rolls her eyes then fixes them on something over my shoulder, studying intently. "So that's your best friend Jett? CJ's boyfriend, right?"

"The one and only. I'll be happy to introduce you but... maybe we ought to get you cleaned up first?"

"And what's so wrong with me?" Jordan lifts her arms, circling in front of me, then pulls her arm to her nose, taking a long sniff. She grimaces. "Never mind. I smell awful. No wonder Gin and CJ both kept backing away while we were talking."

I lean in and take a whiff of the moist, earthy aroma emanating from her. "You totally stink," I say, pinching my nostrils with one hand and waving the other in front of my face.

"Oh yeah?" A twinkle dances in her eyes as she levels them on mine and pulls a runny chunk from her shirt and smooshes it onto my chest with a giggle. "Now so do you."

I thump the clod from my chest; it splatters on the concrete pavers. "I've already showered.

"Guess you'll have to take another."

It feels like a challenge. A fun one.

"Oh really?" I arch my eyebrow and slink sideways toward our outdoor shower and the hose coiled to the side of the wooden door. Jordan trains her gaze on me when I swing open the stall and turn on the faucet. As the rubber hose expands with surging water, I grab it and twist the nozzle, shooting a stream directly at her. "You first!"

She squeals and blocks her face with her hands. The water soaks her, mud spiraling off in all directions as she rushes toward me. Her wet T-shirt and shorts meld to her curves, becoming a second skin, and I can't keep my eyes from wandering up and down her body.

When Jordan finally reaches me, her giggles fill the air as her hands cover mine, wrenching around my fingers, fighting for control. She manages to push the nozzle toward the sky, sending a torrent of water that rains down on both of us. Our eyes meet and suddenly, the droplets seem to fall in slow motion, wrapping us, nearly nose-to-nose, in a quiet cocoon. Jordan's lips curl up at the corners, puckering slightly at the center. A ruddy trail trickles down her temple and onto her cheek, and I loosen my grip on the hose, reaching up to wipe it away with my thumb.

That's the precise moment I feel their eyes on us.

I twist the nozzle and the water slows to a fast drip before drying up completely. Gin and CJ lean in, whispering behind their palms, but Jett stands closer, my phone focused on me and Jordan.

"Are you videoing us?" I ask, running a hand through my hair and slicking it back from my face.

Jett smiles. "Nope. Just solving your little problem." He licks his lips and presses a button on the screen, reversing the camera back to him. With a smug wave, he silently mouths, "Bye Laurel."

I drop the hose and run toward him, grabbing for my phone. So much for my plan to lay low and hope Laurel disappears from my call log. "Dude! You didn't."

"Yes, I did." He hands it over. "Now maybe you can focus more on..." He glances up at Jordan then lowers his voice so that it's barely audible. "...her."

As if picking up on the awkward moment, Gin grabs CJ's hand and drags her over to Jordan saying something about going upstairs to put on their swimsuits. All three girls dart up the steps to Jordan's apartment and disappear inside.

Jett grabs my shoulders and pulls my focus back to him. "Seriously, what *was* that?" He swipes his nails across his bicep and then blows on them. "It was hot."

I shrug it off, but a tingly sensation sweeps through me. It had been too easy to get lost in the moment. In her.

Jett laughs as he iterates the same thoughts running through my own brain. He nudges me with his elbow. "You're sure there's not a little something-something you should tell me about?"

I shake my head. "Nothing at all."

"Not yet." He throws his arm over my shoulder, wrapping me in a headlock, then ruffles my wet curls with his knuckles. "But you want there to be."

CHAPTER 10

Jordan

The briny air whips through the cab of the farm truck as we cruise down a two-lane road, heading back onto the island. The low hum of the local country music station barely sounds above the whistling wind, but Bo still manages to keep time with his thumbs thumping the steering wheel.

This past week and through the next, Clay needs one team to concentrate on the fields and the other on the market. Brice immediately claimed the market assignment, which required strategizing on how to increase visibility and traffic, because of the upcoming Memorial Day weekend. The weekend when summer tourist season finally re-opens the island to its usual visitors. The rush of out-of-towners is straight up Brice's alley. He longs for swarms of people basking in his supposed greatness.

Neither Bo or I had protested, only exchanged silent gazes in the boardroom as Brice made his case. He could've saved the argument for another day; tending the fields for two weeks, us alone working hand-to-dirt, is what we both prefer. Our tenure in the market would come soon enough, but surviving the rush of Memorial Day vacationers wouldn't be it.

Instead, we'd spent the entire week traipsing through rows of knee-high corn stalks, sweet potato plants, and peanut bushes, taking soil samples and checking growth. Today, we loaded in the truck and drove an hour and a half to Hampton County and several hundred acres of golden stalks of Johnson Farm's winter wheat crop swaying in the breeze, nearly ready for next month's harvest. Next week, we begin readying the dirt for the planting of soybeans and sorghum.

I close my eyes and relax my head against the leather seat. With all the hours in the fields this week, working shoulder to shoulder, Bo and I found plenty of time to talk about nothing in particular. I now know that macaroni and cheese is his favorite comfort food, the scar on his left leg is from a go-cart accident when he was eight and had to be stitched, and during the summer, he volunteers for "hatchling duty" with the local Loggerhead turtle association.

Thinking of Bo with one of those teeny baby turtles melts my heart a little.

The shriek of small children's voices draws my attention, and I swivel my head to gaze out the passenger window at a modest two-story home where a group of kids splash each other in a large pool, sprays of water glistening in the sunlight as they fly through the air.

My mind wanders back to last weekend and my own poolside incident. The one that Bo, in all our many conversations, has yet to bring up. But then again neither have I. Like it's taboo or something. Every time I walk past and see the hose coiled there by the outside shower stall on my way to the guest house, I replay it again and again, seeing it in real-time as if I've time-traveled back and am hovering outside my body.

I grab the brim of my baseball cap and yank it down over my eyes, sinking back in my seat once more. The warm wind caressing my arms and the monotonous taps of Bo's fingers on the wheel lull me into a half-sleep that's suddenly interrupted when Bo's agitated voice breaks the calm.

"What in the—" The truck swerves right so fast my seat belt

pinches my chest, and I open my eyes, pulling the cap off my head.

The market is full. Like no available parking, lined-out-the-door craziness. Cars edge the shoulders of each side of the road, and the crowds spill out across the open grass beside the wooden building. Bo maneuvers through the cars and people to the back where the workers park underneath a stand of large oaks.

When he cuts the engine, he pulls the key from the ignition and turns on the bench seat to face me.

"How in the hell did Brice pull this off?"

I slouch down to get another look at the crowded market in my side mirror. This is all Brice's doing? Today kicks off the start of Memorial Day weekend so I expected an influx of customers and island visitors. "This isn't typical for a holiday weekend?"

Bo shakes his head, eyes slitted. His easy smile from earlier fades to a tight-lipped line. "Not by a longshot. It's easily double what we'd normally see."

"Whatever he did, it worked. Somehow, he sweet-talked these people into coming."

"What? With his winning personality?" Bo snorts and throws open his door, sliding out onto the sand below. He slams it hard, shaking the entire truck, before he leans his head back in the open window. "No... something's off."

I swallow hard. Bo despises Brice, so much he can't see how this could be legit. Brice is a jerk to everyone at the farm, but I've known people like Brice before. They treat those closest to them with sour lemons but pour honey on everyone else. Besides, he has an ax to grind—he said so himself—after I dared to pick Bo as my partner. Bo himself warned that Brice would be gunning for me, so is this really a surprise?

Bo stands at the tailgate, waiting, so I get out of the truck and follow him in through the market's back door. No sooner do we make it halfway through the stockroom than we hear Brice's voice booming over the murmuring crowd. Pausing at the door, Bo and I stand side by side, surveying the scene. People pack the small space like sardines, milling around, talking, laughing. The fruits and vegetables remain neatly stacked in their assigned spaces, but along the far edge, the refrigerator cases with the bottled sodas are blown out.

A college-age guy in a T-shirt and jeans opens one of the doors, rambles through the few remaining drinks, then turns and nudges Brice. He snaps his fingers in the air, mouthing something to Gin, who scowls and rolls her eyes. She trudges from behind the counter, heading in our direction, when her eyes land on us.

She shrugs, throwing her hands in the air. "What is going on? The produce hasn't had to be restocked all day—I've literally sold none—but I've had to refill the drinks and snacks, like, fifty times. What gives?"

Bo steps forward beside her, pulling his fist to his mouth and gnawing his knuckle. "We knew Brice would do anything to draw a crowd this weekend. He wants to win this leg of the internship challenges. And there are bodies in here, for sure, but this is not our usual clientele."

"Right? Where are the families? The retirees? These are all our age, and they're just sort of hanging out, like this is a pub or something."

From across the room, Brice fixes his gaze on us with a satisfied grin before pulling his fist, thumb out, to his mouth and ticking his head back, a silent signal for Gin to get moving on her task.

Gin huffs out a loud breath, mumbles something about breaking Brice's fingers off his body before the day's end, and plods to the back.

A young guy jogs up to me, pushing in so close he physically knocks Bo out of the way. Bo grimaces as the guy pushes the shaggy blond hair from his eyes. "Hey, can I take a selfie with you?"

"With me?" I point to myself, and the mystery guy grins wide, nodding. Weird. The last thing I want to do is smoosh myself beside this sweaty guy I don't know for some random photo, but technically, he's a customer of the market. The Johnson Farm's market. My current boss. So do I really have an option here? I step beside the guy but push my elbow out to insert some space between us. He holds out his phone, centers us on the screen, and *snap!* He checks the picture then trots off, not even bothering to say thank you.

As he leaves, something printed on the sleeve of his shirt grabs my attention. A string of symbols and letters. Is that Greek? I search the room, the other guys... Oh.

Gin returns, pushing a rolling cart brimming with bottled sodas and bags of chips. She stops to say something to Bo, but I step in between the two of them. "Hey guys, is Brice part of a fraternity?"

"Yeah, he's a member of—" Bo stops talking as his eyes fix on the very things I'd just noticed. Three Greek letters. Stitched on polos. And visors. Keychains, koozies, and car decals. Even in ink on their tanned skin. "Sneaky jerk. These are his frat brothers."

Gin's mouth drops open as she scans the market. "Typical Brice. All show and no substance."

Suddenly another guy with long brown hair pulled back in a man-bun butts into the conversation. He flicks his sunglasses down on his nose, looking at me above the rim. "Selfie?"

I blow out a loud breath and look into his outstretched camera. He snaps the picture, but as he turns to walk away, I grab his elbow, drawing him back in. "Can I ask why everyone is so interested in taking photos of me?"

"You're kidding, right? You're half the reason we're here!"

Both Bo and Gin's eyebrows furrow together as their gaze treks between me and the frat guy. I stop-sign my hand in his face. "I'm confused. I thought Brice was the reason you're here."

"Brice is our frat president so pretty much what he says goes. He needed us here, and here we are." No wonder his ego is so inflated. I guess if Brice said to jump off a bridge, then they'd all plummet into the Intercoastal Waterway too. The guy pulls a folded piece of paper from his pocket and hands it to me. "But he did promise us that we might catch a glimpse of the Melon Girl, and here you are."

Hold up... Melon Girl? I unfold the piece of paper and stare down at a photocopied version of my cantaloupe-wielding social media post with Brice's handwriting on the bottom.

I need your help, brothers! Mandatory meet-up at Johnson Farms Market on Edisto Island this Saturday, 2-5 p.m. You just might catch a glimpse of those melons!

My cheeks turn to fire as the realization sinks in—these guys aren't looking at me, they're looking at my chest. I wad the paper into a ball, crushing it in my fist as I thread my arms in front of me.

"He lured all of his fraternity brothers here by using you as bait." Bo's voice is razor-sharp as he stubs the toe of his boot into the dirt floor. His jaw flexes in and out.

Across the market, Brice makes eye contact and gives me a little wave, a wicked smirk on his face. *Well-played, jerk, but we'll see who comes out on top at the end.* I square my shoulders and narrow my eyes, refusing to be the first to look away, mentally transmitting the message: *You don't intimidate me.*

He steels his jaw and reaches up, tipping his visor, before returning to his cronies.

Bo growls under his breath. "Just when I think he can't get any lower. Wait until I tell Dad about—"

"No." I grab his arm and squeeze it. "We're not playing into his hands. You already said Brice would be gunning for me. And we can't forget that Christopher is most likely innocent in this. He didn't pick Brice, but now he's stuck with him."

"Yeah, but these numbers are skewed and Dad will consider this a success when he's making the final decision with the management team over who wins the internship money."

Bo's seething intensifies, and I realize he has just as much on the line this summer as I do. Brice isn't getting the better of us. We can beat him. We will beat him.

"Then we'll do better on our turn," I say. "Let's get together one night at my place to plan."

Bo looks up at me under a long fringe of dark lashes and nods his head.

I'm just tossing a bag of extra-butter popcorn into the microwave when he knocks on the door. I jog across the den and swing it open.

"Hey! Come on in."

Bo grins, holding up a couple bags of chips, but stops abruptly, his hand frozen in mid-air as he scrunches up his nose and examines me. "Woah, someone forgot to apply sunscreen."

I bring my fingers to the bridge of my nose then yank them away again when the reddened skin screams at my touch. Gin had asked me to spend the day with her at the beach. We baked underneath the scorching sun, Gin talking non-stop, for hours, only getting up every now and then to run out in the waves for a refresher. Apparently, my attempts to re-apply sunscreen were spotty at best.

Bo steps in and tosses the bags on the coffee table then strides over to me. He tips my chin down, examining the burnt skin. "Is this the only place?"

"No. There's also a weird patch between my shoulders. I guess I couldn't quite reach that spot." I turn around, swiping my hair into a makeshift ponytail and holding it up to show him the skin exposed by my camisole.

Bo lets out a loud whistle and then grimaces. "Does it hurt?"

"No. It feels quite lovely, thank you."

"Go sit down. I have something to help."

He walks to the kitchen window and snaps a long stalk off the aloe plant on the sill, then grabs a saucer, a knife, a fork, and a plastic container and walks over to take a seat on the couch beside me. With the knife, he trims off the outer spines of the aloe and then slices the long leaf into smaller sections, then puts all of them except one in the container and seals it. He slices the remaining one down the middle and runs the fork across the gelled insides.

"Now, we just need to rub this on." He grabs one half, sweeps my hair to the side, and smears it across the burnt patch on my back. The aloe feels a bit slimy at first but then radiates a pleasant coolness that takes the edge off the soreness. "Instant relief, right?"

"So this is why your mom keeps these plants all over y'all's house and out here too?"

"Yeah, this stuff is a miracle cure for bites and burns. Plus, it's one of the few houseplants Mom doesn't seem to be able to kill." He discards the spent plant rind and grabs the other half. "Now face me."

I pivot on the couch, and Bo inches closer, applying the aloe strip like a bandage to my nose. He mashes down, pushing the balm out onto my skin but keeps his touch light. When it's spent, he peels off the remaining piece and lays it on the plate, then uses his thumbs to spread the gel over the burn, blowing softly on it. Chill bumps prickle down my arms, and I lift my eyes to meet his—deep, intense, and connected. In a blink, we're back by the pool last weekend, the same weird fluttering birthing in my chest. His lips pucker and relax each time he blows across my skin. Hypnotic.

And so inconvenient. And stupid.

We're here to work on the project. For the internship. For the money I need to win.

"So..." I say, jumping to my feet, flustered. "Should we get to work? Oh yeah, I made popcorn. Let me get the popcorn and drinks. I should get those." I sprint to the kitchen before Bo can respond and yank open the fridge door, hiding my face behind it as I reach for the Cokes. Good Lord could I be any more spastic?

I grab two bottles and set them on the island before pulling the now-barely-warm bag from the microwave.

"Is it hot in here?" Bo stands up, fanning the front of his shirt. Red swirls dot his cheeks. He points to the double windows behind the sofa. "Care if I open these?"

I shake my head and carry the snacks and drinks to the table then settle in on the couch. Once the windows are secured, Bo sits beside me and grabs a drink, twisting off the cap and taking a long pull.

"How 'bout some music?" I ask, opening the app on my phone and clicking on my "favorites" folder. Music is good. A little something to ease the awkward silences and take the edge off. It seems to work as Bo begins brainstorming ideas for our market project, tossing out ideas like social media campaigns and raffle tickets for a big-ticket giveaway. We discuss for nearly an hour, never landing on anything that seems good enough to upstage Brice.

My phone, lying on the couch cushion between us, vibrates, and the screen lights up with the first part of a message. One I don't want Bo—or anyone else down here—to see right now.

Weston misses you. He says he loves...

I grab the phone and wrench it to my face, angling it away from Bo's eyes, which had briefly settled on the screen and lifted curiously as I snatched the phone away.

He stares at me with rounded eyes. "Everything okay?"

"Yeah, just my mama," I reply, taking a moment to read the rest of the message. *He says he loves you.* My heart flip-flops just thinking of his chubby cheeks and all their squishiness as he says the words. *Wub ew, Ma-ma.* I needed to hear it, especially after hearing him cry for me earlier on the phone. Nothing pinches my soul more than hearing my baby sobbing for me when I can't be there to rock him to sleep.

I set the phone face down on the table just as one of my favorite folksy tunes comes on. At the first twangy trill of the banjo, I close my eyes and lay back against the couch, soaking up the cool night breeze dancing in through the curtains.

"Something about this moment feels like home," I mumble.

"What exactly?" Bo asks.

"The air, the music, the lingering smell of popcorn butter and salt. All that's missing are the calls of the Bobwhites and I'd be there. I think I miss those most." I open my eyes and shift in my seat, facing him. "It reminds me of the annual county fair."

I tell him about the banjo pickers and the old man who plays the fiddle, the sweet crunch of fresh-from-the-grease funnel cakes, the buzz of the lights on the kiddie carousel, and the colorful patchwork quilts on display for the blue-ribbon prize. As I continue talking, Bo scrunches his nose, staring down at his lap.

"A couple years ago, Grandma sold her barbecue at—"

"That's it!" Bo snaps his fingers, jumping to his feet. "We can use the idea of your fair to create our own event at the market. Live music, food trucks, vendors, and of course, all our produce on display. We'll double the numbers Brice brought in and actually sell our produce too."

A piece of home coming to life here on Edisto? I can think of no better meshing of the two worlds.

I stand up and, without thinking, wrap Bo in a massive hug. "I love this idea! We're going to blow Brice out of the water!"

After a moment, he circles his arms around my waist, squeezing me closer as he lowers his lips to my ear and says, "Well, we do make a pretty good team."

CHAPTER 11

Bo

Doniella's gaze lifts from her conversation with Luis and Hector as I walk into the barn. All three wear a tight-lipped expression and hooded eyes, a sign that they're discussing something more than a farm manager's daily assignments for the farmhands. And by the way Doniella shifts her eyes back to her shoes and takes a deep breath, I suspect the subject of their group chat is me.

I wave a quick hello and stalk to the opposite side, immediately beginning to sift through bags of fertilizer. For each five, I make a tally mark on the inventory sheet. We're so behind on prepping the fields for our first-of-June planting that Dad pulled Brice and Christopher from market duty to help me and Jordan in the fields. Awesome. Like one big happy family.

One bag shifts, sliding off the stack, so I grab it and toss it back on top. That's 47. Then 48, 49, 50. When I stop to mark the next group on my sheet, the rustle of footsteps across the wooden floor draws my attention. I glance over my shoulder at Doniella, who leans against the stall's doorframe. She scowls, creating a few deep lines above her nose.

"Morning," I say, but before I can reach for another bag, she grabs my elbow, stopping me.

"Brice was here earlier." She hisses the "c" in Brice's name. The pronunciation is spot-on, definitely pointing to his snake-in-the-grass ways.

I smirk. "That explains the look on your face."

She doesn't crack a smile. "We're worried." I set my paperwork on the wooden ledge and pull off my work gloves, throwing them on top. Sweat drips down my forehead so I wipe it away with my forearm as she continues, wringing her hands. "He was bragging about crushing you in this internship challenge, and... we saw the numbers from their market event. They were good. Really good."

Not this. Doniella of all people should know that information from Brice shouldn't be trusted. Ever. I sigh. "They're heavily inflated, like his ego."

I reach for my gloves but Doniella steps forward, blocking me with her arm. Storm clouds roll across her eyes.

"Brice isn't playing around. He's determined to win. He's determined to take over this farm." Each time she says "determined," she stabs her finger at the ground. "It's time to realize that your decisions affect more than just you. They affect me, Luis, Hector and the other workers on this farm. If you go, then so do we."

I balk. Brice and Patrick's little coup attempts piss me off, but what can I do to stop them? No one listens to an insignificant newbie like me, and the fact that Doniella is this stirred up only proves Brice's tactics are working, undermining Dad's company already. How does this burden belong on my shoulders and no one else's? I didn't take Doniella to be one for guilt trips, especially before 9 AM.

"No pressure," I mumble, pushing past her to grab my gloves and inventory sheet. I'll finish later when my work day isn't served with a side of shame.

Doniella steps to the middle of the stall's doorway, blocking my escape. "We're not pressuring you, just being honest. I've had plenty of opportunities to go elsewhere, but I love it here. I love your family and the culture your dad has created." She stares at the floor, shaking her head. "If Brice takes over, everything will change... and not for the better. All your dad's hard work will—"

"No!" I snap, halting her line of thought. No more guilt. No more imagining the worst. No more decisions on my shoulders right now. "Johnson Farms is safe. Dad will keep it that way."

Doniella bites her bottom lip, stepping sideways to let me pass. "You need to find your fire, Bo." I stop in my tracks, looking back at her over my shoulder. Her eyes, softer now, plead with me to hear her words. "You belong here. We know it, your dad knows it. Now you just need to know it."

If only it could be that easy. But things always look easier from the outside. No one understands the thousand-pound weight they're throwing on my shoulders. Bo can do it. Bo can run the farm one day. Bo can save the day.

Only, I *am* Bo, and I definitely don't feel like any kind of a savior. More of a fraud, if I'm honest with myself. But they can't understand the tornado swirling inside me. No one can.

I stomp out of the barn and into the blaring sunlight. The point of this summer internship was to find myself, to determine if I had a place here at the farm. If. But how can I really get in tune with my own wants with everyone else pushing theirs on me? I grit my teeth and grind my fingers into my palms, pushing back a flood of anxiety. It surfaces anyway as a low, thundering growl that I give in to, letting it rip through me like a war cry.

That's when she clears her throat. I whirl around and find Jordan, back against the barn wall, waiting on me. She fingers the edge of her white tank top as she taps the toe of her boot against the rough wood.

When our eyes connect, hers soften at the corners, and she presses her lips together as if waiting on my next outburst. When I don't move, she pushes off the wall and walks over, her thumbs in the pockets of her ripped jeans. My stomach crimps.

This internship means everything to her, and I'm failing to be the leader she needs.

And she trusted me to help her win. Why I don't know.

"You heard?" I ask, voice trembling.

"Yeah."

"And do you agree? I have no fire?" I swallow hard, waiting for her to spew the truth. She should've picked Brice. I shouldn't even be here. But she doesn't.

"I wouldn't say that." She smiles and takes my hand, pulling me behind her to the farm truck parked at the corner of the barn. Her skin, moist with humidity, slides against mine with a growing heat. She hoists herself onto the lowered tailgate and pats the open spot beside her. I take a seat, the limited space just enough for the two of us. Our bodies smoosh together, from thighs to shoulders. A few wisps of hair, loose from her ponytail, swirl in the breeze.

Jordan turns and stares at me, her gaze penetrating the surface and examining me to my core. I squirm under her scrutiny, afraid of what connections are linking together in her brain at this very moment. Judging me. Exposing me.

"I think you're unsure—maybe even a little insecure—about your place in life. You have a lot of family pressures weighing on you. I know how that feels." She cocks her head to one side with an empathetic grin, her eyelashes fluttering in double time. "It blurs the line between understanding who you are as a person versus who you are as a member of the family. Do you want something or do they want it? Can you really do what they're asking or will you never live up to expectations?"

Just when I think I have this girl figured out, she goes and blows my mind again. She does understand what this feels like. She gets it. She gets *me*. She might be the only one.

Jordan grabs my hand. "If you're having trouble figuring out the 'what' that inspires you, then try focusing on the 'who.' *Who* are you fighting for? Your dad, Gin, Doniella."

Jordan's right. I have to fight. For the farm workers. For me. For Dad. Because even if this life doesn't pan out for me, I won't let Brice ruin everything Dad has worked for. He has given me so much that he didn't have to, and I owe him this much.

And I'll do it for someone else. Someone Jordan left out.

"And you," I say, squeezing her fingers. "I'll fight for—"

Across the field, a loud string of expletives rings out. Jordan's eyes saucer as she rips her hand from mine and slides off the tailgate, standing on tiptoes to look out across the fresh-plowed dirt. I stand up on the tailgate for a better view and spot Brice and Christopher on the far edge standing beside a tractor. Brice paces back and forth, his phone pressed to his ear while swinging the other arm in the air. I can only imagine what the person on the other end of that line is having to endure.

I jump down, nodding to Jordan, and we bolt through the crumbly dirt to the stalled tractor. Christopher waves, but Brice, preoccupied with kicking the tire over and over, doesn't notice us approach.

"What's wrong?" I ask.

Brice whirls around, lurching forward in my face. "There's a big hunting party coming to town tomorrow evening and we have to get these bags of deer corn hauled out to the shed pronto so we can finish spreading fertilizer in the fields. But your dad won't buy new equipment for the farm and we're forced to deal with this old, broken-down shit."

I fold my arms over my chest. "It wasn't broke until you started messing with it. Maybe user error?"

Fire ignites in Brice's eyes and his nostrils flare as he leans in closer, nose to nose. What's he going to do—hit me? I stand taller, refusing to back down. Jordan just reminded me of all the reasons not to.

"This tractor is less than five years old. We have equipment on our farm that's over 50 years old," Jordan says, inserting herself between us. She pans her hand at the tractor. "This is a top-of-the-line model, so I hardly think it's defective. What's the issue?"

"What do you care?" Brice glares at Jordan, looking her up and down, his lip curled in disgust. "I've already called Clay and he's on his way. He needs to scrap this junk heap and buy a new one."

Jordan sighs. "You don't just throw something away if you have a problem with it. Ninety percent of the time it's an easy fix."

Brice turns his back on the conversation, pouting, when Christopher volunteers, "The loader won't work."

Jordan walks over and discusses the issue with Christopher while I watch. Her self-confidence seeps out of every pore as she nods, assessing the situation. I wouldn't even know where to begin. Mechanical troubleshooting is something I know nothing about, but Jordan's confident smile when she stoops to the ground and begins fiddling under the front of the tractor tells me she's not intimidated.

Brice casts a side-eyed glare in their direction before sprinting over, shouting at Jordan's feet, which stick out from the side. "What are you doing? That ain't going to help shit."

"So, we have a loader problem?" Dad's voice catches us all off guard, and we jump. He approaches from behind us, eyes pinched in concern.

Brice loses no time, clomping to his side, hands on hip. "We have a shitty equipment problem, Clay. You need to buy new."

"Do you know how much that costs? If we can call a repairman, we will."

Jordan stretches out a hand, finger extended, from beneath the tractor, and yells, "Give me one minute and you won't have to call anyone."

"She's gonna hurt herself under there and then the farm's gonna be liable." Brice points an accusatory finger in Jordan's direction. When Dad refuses to react, Brice shakes his head, grumbling under his breath. "Maybe that's her plan—get screwed up and sue us for all our money."

Dad balks at one particular word in Brice's rant. One word that says so much about his lofty expectations of his place on the farm. "*Our* money?"

"*Johnson* money." Brice spits out the words with a cutting glance in my direction.

Jordan slides out from underneath the tractor, wiping greasy handprints onto her jeans, and nods at Christopher. "Give her a try."

Christopher turns the key and the tractor rumbles to life. I hold my breath as he reaches for the control stick. In one quick motion, the loader moves up and down without a hitch.

"On this model, the hoses are notorious for coming loose from the coupler. Especially this bottom one here." Jordan points to some miscellaneous hoses connecting the tractor and loader. Brice stares at her as if she's speaking a foreign language. For someone so "schooled" in agriculture, he's oblivious to everything except the business aspects.

Jordan continues, "When that happens, the hydraulic oil can't go through and your loader has no power. If it happens again, make sure the oil is cool and give that joystick valve a finagle to clear out the pressure on the lines, check all the hoses to make sure they're properly seated and voila." She struts toward Brice with a satisfied smirk, poking her finger to his chest. "Super easy and my fix was free. That's a lot better than a new $75,000 tractor."

Dad claps his hands and walks over to Jordan, throwing an arm around her shoulder. "Brilliant! That fix saved us a hell of a lot of money over Brice's suggestion." Dad shoots us a thumbs-up with a lopsided grin. "More than triple what was brought in on the market event."

Brice's mouth drops open, his face blank as he registers the remark.

I snort. Seeing Jordan challenge him head-on is the highlight of my day. Seeing Brice's face when Dad blows his farce of an event out of the water tickles me. But when Brice huffs out a loud breath and clamps his jaw shut in a sneer at Jordan, a gnawing sinks its teeth into my stomach.

This won't go unpunished. Brice will see it as another strike against Jordan, and she'll be squarely in his sights more than ever before. He's out for blood, and it's my job to ensure he keeps his distance.

Brice jumps on the tractor's side step and commands Christopher to roll out. Dad waves good-bye and heads to his truck, and Jordan and I amble back toward the barn.

"How'd you learn to do that?" I ask.

She shrugs. "Being broke has its advantages."

The sand shifts under my feet as I meander along the shore, watching the last slivers of sunlight melt into the horizon while running Jordan's words from earlier in endless loops through my head. She thinks I'm unsure and insecure. I never really considered myself either of those things until all of this mess with Laurel. The break-up has affected me in ways I never imagined, making me suddenly second guess every decision, every thought that enters my brain. If she could fool me so completely, I must've missed something right under my nose.

How could I have been so duped?

My toe stubs against a curved clam shell, and I reach down, pick it up, and chuck it into the surf. It plinks in the water, bobbing in the ripples, before sinking from sight. Immediately, from the same area, a large fish jumps, it's body flapping in the air before plunging back below the surface.

Jordan is nothing like Laurel. She doesn't giggle and tell me the things she thinks I want to hear. She makes eye contact and tells me the truth, even when it isn't easy. That takes guts. Just like when she's stood up to Brice time and again. And when she gave me the best advice of anyone: it's okay to not know what I want right now. Right now, I'm muddling through but that's okay. Focusing on the things that matter, the people that matter, will get me through.

I shake my head. Just a year older than me but so determined —she knows where she's going and what she wants from life. And here I am, clueless and aimless, flopping around like that stupid fish.

Up on the pier, the lights from inside the dive bar shine out on the sand, striping the dark with amber rays. The live band strikes up a soulful number, one that reminds me of Jordan's favorite song she played for me at her place. I step into the darkest corner under the pier, shuffling over to the wooden post decorated with carved names. I inscribed my name back when I was 13 and officially became a teenager on the island. I run my fingers over the markings, the once-sharp cuts now softened, rounded with age. Off to the side I find CJ's name still fresh and deep, having been tagged only a year ago when she moved here and first got involved with Jett. It's tradition—those who live and love Edisto leave their mark on this place and, therefore, should commemorate it on this living record.

Jordan's name should be here now too. I switch on my phone's flashlight and scan the post, locating a small bare spot near the bottom corner of my autograph. I slide my pocketknife out, unfold it, and scratch JORDAN into the wooden flesh. Perfect. She's made her mark on me, and now, on Edisto.

It's just a small gesture, though, and I wish there was some way to repay her for the trust and belief she's put in me. For reminding me about what really counts. For kicking my butt when I need it.

Above, the twang of a banjo floats through the night air, and a thought strikes me. Jordan's doing this internship for her family's farm, her home. A home she obviously misses. Every time she mentions it, the tears well in her lashes and her bottom lip trembles. Maybe she needs a reminder herself. A piece of home in Edisto.

I swipe my phone, opening the browser. After a quick search, I find the page of the local band Jordan loves. A few taps, a quick explanation, and go.

Message Sent.

CHAPTER 12

Jordan

The mid-afternoon sun glints across the glass panels of the greenhouse. Sweat droplets gather on my forehead as I connect the hoses to the spigot. Sundays are generally left as personal time but once a month, it's my turn to tend Clay's most special plants in the smallest greenhouse at the far edge of the fields behind the office. It houses his hybrids and experiments—the plants he cross-pollinates from two different varieties, trying to produce a more perfect version of tomatoes, peas, and peppers.

I adjust the nozzle setting and pull the trigger, releasing a gentle shower of water over the plants. This sort of duty is fine by me, a solitary moment to unwind on the farm with nothing but the thirsty plants to keep me company.

Today, though, a million troubling thoughts parade through my brain here in the solitude. I need to get more vendors lined up for our market event at the end of the month. Three isn't going to cut it. And has Bo held up his end of the bargain and reached out to entertainment? There's been no updates. Mental note to check in with him tonight at the Johnson's Sunday Share.

Ugh. Sunday Share. My stomach gripes. What fresh hell awaits this time? A blush rises to my cheeks just thinking of it.

And then there's Brice. Bo has warned me about retaliation, and I've been noticing how Brice's eyes follow me whenever we're in the same vicinity. He's definitely plotting something. But what?

And Weston. God, I miss my little guy. My heart goes all squishy each time his face pops into my daydreams, and I have to think of something else. Because if I don't, I'll pack up and go home to be with him. But I can't, because I'm doing this for him.

I sigh. So much for peace and solitude.

With my free hand, I pull my earbuds from my pocket and slide them into place then tap a few buttons on my phone. A stream of upbeat music replaces the silence, and my body reacts, shoulders dipping and hips sliding side to side with the rhythm. In a second, my worries evaporate. No internship pressure. No family debt. No uncertain future. It's only me, the seedlings, and the music. I slip into the beat, in sync.

When the chorus starts, I pull the back of the nozzle to my lips, using it as a microphone as I belt out the words. Moving down each row of plants, I keep watering and singing and dancing. Who knows? Maybe a little singing will help these babies grow big and strong. I remember some kid in middle school doing a science fair project about that once and proving that—

Tap. Tap. Tap.

On my shoulder.

What—? I whirl around, taking the hose with me. The spray hits the intruder in the face.

My brain, nosediving off the sudden rush, finally begins registering that the face belongs to... Bo.

I let go of the trigger, the arc of water diminishing to nothing. Bo stands, mouth agape, as rivers run down his face, his shirt, his arms. His thick curls matte to the sides of his head. I swallow hard, yanking my earbuds from my ears.

"I am so sorry," I say, eyeing him up and down. "I didn't hear—"

He throws up his hand, stopping me. "No, I'm sorry. I didn't mean to scare you."

Our eyes lock, and we burst into laughter.

"You're soaked," I say through giggles, squeezing the hem of his T-shirt, which releases a flood of water.

Bo smirks. "No big deal. I'll dry." He grabs one sleeve, sliding his arm from the hole, and then the other before pulling the fabric over his head. It peels off of him like a second skin, leaving a glistening trail across his squared chest. He bends forward, raking his fingers through the curls, scrunching the excess water from them. They unfurl into a wiry halo.

As he flips his head back and returns to standing, the light catches his chest and abs, highlighting the ripples of muscle below his tanned skin. My heart drums against my ribs, blocking my lungs from fully inhaling. He reaches out a hand, gripping my shoulder. I lift my gaze to the place where his fingers mold into my bare skin then follow them up to his face.

"Are you okay? You seem a little... shaken." His lips pinch and straighten as he enunciates each word, and it's the first time I notice the deep bow in his top lip and how the bottom one is just a bit thicker. Shaken doesn't begin to cover it when I think about—

No. Stop it, Jordan. This is the dangerous kind of thinking that gets you in trouble and makes you lose focus.

I turn away, pretending to lean over a few of the seedlings and check their leaves. "I'm fine. Why are you here anyway?"

"I may have some exciting news about our market event," he teases, leaning against the table beside me. He pulls the hose from my hand and fiddles with the nozzle.

"What?" I ask, looking over at him. We need some good news on that front.

He shakes his head with a sly grin, tsk-tsking me. "Chores, then chat." He stands up and pulls the trigger, sending a stream of water in my direction. I scream and run behind another table, but not before the water splashes my shirt and face. "But first, payback."

As I squeeze my ponytail, Bo laughs and calls a truce, and for the next hour, we take turns watering the plants. And I do my best to keep my gaze from falling to his exposed chest, but my eyes keep betraying the stern warnings from my brain.

When we're finished, I disconnect the hose and wind it around the holder on the wall while Bo takes a seat on one of the large overturned buckets near the door. The curiosity has been killing me, but no matter how many times I've asked, Bo just smiles and tells me to wait. Now that the chores are through, I'm demanding he keeps his promise to tell all.

I walk to him, wiping my hands on my cutoff shorts. "What's the big news?"

He crosses his arms over his chest with a satisfied smirk. "I booked the entertainment. A live band."

I pump my fist in the air, a flood of relief washing over me. One more piece in place. "Who'd you get?"

He smiles and stands up, his bowed chest once again dangerously close to my face.

Focus, Jordan.

Bo pulls his phone from his back pocket, swipes open an email message, and hands it to me. "Read this."

Bo, We're honored to hear your friend is one of our biggest fans. We love supporting homegrown businesses, and we happen to be available on your requested date. Let's talk details on Monday.

When I see the signature, my mouth drops open. Bo got the band from my hometown? But how did he—oh yeah, the other night at my place. We listened to their music while we planned.

And he paid attention. He remembered.

"I can't believe you did this. This is... this..." I stumble over my words, swallowing back a swirl of emotions.

"This is my way of thanking you for the kick-in-my-ass pep talk the other day. I wanted you to have a piece of home down here."

The dam breaks, the emotions rolling out of me in a mixed bag of happy giggles, tears, and gasps. Bo gets me like no one else ever has. I lunge forward, wrapping my arms around his back in a hard bear hug. He hesitates a moment then wraps his arms around me, pulling me closer. I close my eyes, feeling each contour of my body aligning with his, and for a minute, I don't stop those dangerous thoughts from creeping in. I sink into him like a memory foam mattress.

"Ahem."

My heart jumps to my throat as I backpedal at lightning speed from Bo's arms. Brice stands in the doorway, arms folded over his chest and sporting a Cheshire Cat grin. "What's going on here?"

Bo narrows his eyes and flexes his jaw. "Not that it's any of your business, Jordan and I are finishing our tasks."

"And that requires your hands on her ass?"

"My hands were *not* on her ass," Bo retorts in a tone with a bite of its own.

Oh. Disappointment trickles down my spine like ice. I shake it away, letting the sensation turn into something hotter, fiery. Especially as Brice struts in my direction.

"I like the way you tackle your task list." He tucks his lips in and nods, reaching out to stroke my hair. I dodge his attempt. "I might need some help tomorrow. I'll be much more fun to 'work' with." He laughs, framing his innuendo in air quotes.

"Back off," Bo growls advancing toward him, but I extend my arm, stopping him in his tracks. I got this.

I step forward, slapping on my best Southern Passive-Aggression. "Oh Brice. How soon you forget." I let my words drip out like honey and hold up my fingers to mirror his air quotes. "But I had a chance to 'work' with you, and I turned it down."

A shadow crawls over his face, wiping the egotistical sneer from his mouth. Maybe I should quit, not poke the bear, but I can't contain the next words.

"I turned *you* down." They spill off my tongue with so much hate, it surprises even me.

He doesn't say anything at first, only stands there, grinding his teeth, as he studies me like a specimen in a laboratory. Brice pivots on his heel and stomps to the door, throwing it open, but before he walks out, he stops and glances over his shoulder.

"It's not a good idea to play around in here. These are Clay's prized plants, and he'll be seriously pissed if you screw them up."

The metal door slams shut, and Bo steps beside me. "Maybe we should've left the hose out. If anyone needs a good assault to the face, it's him."

"Oh no. He's not cool enough to hang with us." I laugh, giving Bo a playful shove. "Tag. You're it," I whisper and dart out of his reach, running through the rows of plants with him hot on my heels.

I pause by the door, checking my reflection in the mirror and smoothing the frizzies from my hair. After finishing my work, I came back and took a long shower, keeping the water the same temperature as Antarctica, trying to ice out the fleeting thoughts of Bo still lurking in my brain. Then I smudged on enough mascara to bring life to my eyes before standing in front of the closet for an eternity, sniffing out the perfect outfit. Perfect for what I don't know.

This is the first Sunday Share since a month ago when Bo's love life was filleted on the dinner table and I somehow got dragged into the fray. I swipe on a thick coat of gloss, smacking my lips in the mirror. Tonight, I'm laying low if any drama ensues.

A stream of laughter floats in through my screen and I peer out, spotting the Johnsons milling around the patio. Clay flips burgers on the grill as it puffs white smoke into the air while Claire pours sweet tea into glasses with little lemons painted on the side. Gin and Bo relax in the loungers, thumbing through their phones.

What happened to the formal family dinner? Not that I'm complaining about a laidback cookout.

I step out onto the porch, easing the door shut behind me, and head down the steps, only making it halfway before Claire spots me and yells, "Jordan! Come join us, honey!"

Bo lifts his eyes, meeting mine, a small smile warming his face. I blush and descend the last few steps, fiddling with my hair, smoothing my white shorts, adjusting the spaghetti strap of my turquoise tank. Gin leans forward, elbows on knees, casting glances between me and Bo.

He doesn't notice because he's still watching me, and I suddenly wish I'd given more effort to my hair and makeup. Claire steps into my line of vision, the oversized sleeves of her silky cardigan billowing out in the breeze as she hands me a glass of sweet tea. Though her complexion is darker and her style more eccentric, she often reminds me of Mama.

And I'm grateful.

"No Sunday Share?" I ask, sipping my tea.

"Al-fresco Sunday Share." She laughs, panning her hand around the patio, then stops, narrowing her eyes. "Unless you have something serious you need to talk about?"

"No, I'm good." I blurt it out, waving my hands in front of me. Both Gin and Bo snicker, but Claire doesn't seem to notice. A huge grin retakes her face, and with a wink, she saunters off to serve the food.

After a nice supper and light-hearted conversation, the empty plates and dishes are loaded on the rolling cart and Claire motions toward chairs circled around the fire pit. Clay stokes a small flame with pieces of kindling, a few wisps of smoke curling into the darkening sky.

I sit in the Adirondack chair opposite Clay's, and Bo takes the one beside mine. He scoots it closer and leans in, our arms lightly brushing, our fingers a whisper apart. My pinky twitches. If I just move it a hair to the right, it'll join his.

"Much easier Sunday dinner this go-round, right?" Bo's breath tickles my ear as he whispers. A million pinpricks scatter down my neck.

I turn my head to reply but have to fight for breath when I find my face just inches from his. The words turn to verbal mush on my tongue. Did he always have the little brown mole at the corner of his lip? No, focus. I swallow the knot in my throat. "Almost erased the trauma of last time," I quip, hoping the words coming out of my mouth actually make sense. My brain is jumbled.

Bo laughs, but doesn't pull away immediately. We're frozen in place, until Gin slides into the chair on my other side with a loud groan. The bubble bursts and Bo slouches back in his chair and I shift toward Gin.

She grimaces, rubbing her stomach. "Ugh. I ate way too much."

I'm not surprised. For such a petite girl, she can sure pack away the food. Across the fire, Claire takes her seat, and Clay pulls something onto his lap. I strain my eyes to see through the flames.

"You play guitar?" I ask.

"Since I was a teenager."

His fingers strum the chords and a familiar melody drifts up into the night and as if by instinct, I begin to hum along with the tune.

I stop when Gin's eyes sear holes through me. "You know Dad's music?"

"It's Dolly Parton. Of course I know it." A wave of homesickness grips me, and my bottom lip trembles. Mama always said bedtime wasn't complete without a proper send-off from Dolly. She said her music could make anything better. "My mama used to sing this to me as a lullaby. She called me her wildflower." My voice cracks, and Claire glances up. She's a bloodhound when it comes to emotional crisis.

"Don't say?" Clay cocks his head to the side with a smile. "I actually learned to play this song—and just about every other Dolly one—for a girl I once knew."

Gin's mouth drops open as she sits forward in her hair. "Oooh, Mom! Are you really gonna sit there and let him talk about an ex-girlfriend?"

"She was never my girlfriend, thank you very much. She was a friend I met during my own internship when I was just about Bo's age. *Before* I met your mom." He lifts his fingers from the strings just long enough to reach over and squeeze Claire's hand. They exchange smiles and, for a brief moment, slip into their own world. I wish Mama had that kind of love. I hope she'll find it one day.

I hope I will too.

Clay returns to strumming. "We used to do bonfires on the marsh and sing songs and roast marshmallows as a group. I'd just started playing so I took requests, and sure enough, when it came to her it was always a Dolly song."

Claire holds up a finger. "She is one of the greatest recording artists ever."

Gin pulls her legs up into her seat, hugging them tight. "So, what happened to your friend?"

Clay's lips pinch tight, the corners of his eyes sinking. "Last time I saw her was the end of our internship and she was planning to head to Nashville and follow in Dolly's footsteps."

"I guess she didn't make it or we'd know who she was by now," Gin says.

He nods. "I guess so."

Nashville dreams are nothing new to me. I think every Southern country-music-loving woman harbors some fantasy of heading to Tennessee for their big shot. Personally, the thought of singing professionally doesn't appeal to me, but Mama always thought I should try. She's dedicated her life to pushing me to find myself outside of the farm, even though she needs me there. Secretly, I believe she's afraid I'll end up like her. "My mama used to say I should go to Nashville and sing."

"You sing?" Claire clasps her hands together at her chest, beaming in my direction.

"Hell yeah, she sings. I heard her earlier today." Bo's voice booms with pride as he gives me a wink.

Oh my God. That wink.

Current status: melting into a puddle.

Heat rushes to my cheeks. "I sing a little but just..." I pause, holding back the words from rolling off my tongue. *Just to Weston.* "Just around the house."

"Well keep it up," Claire says with a thumbs-up. "Artistic expression is good for the soul."

The twang of the strings gets louder, and Clay clears his throat. "I sure would love some accompaniment tonight. I'll strum, you sing. What d'you say?"

Sing in front of everyone? My stomach clenches. "I don't know..."

"Do it! Do it!" Gin chants, pounding her fists on the chair's arms.

"Um..." I hesitate, racking my brain for a way out of the request. That's when his pinky grazes mine. I stare down at my hand, unmoving, but not his. His creeps even closer, imperceptible to anyone else in the circle, until his finger loops over mine, interlocking them. I side-eye Bo but he stares straight ahead, pretending as if he didn't just touch me—on purpose. Butterflies swarm inside as I mumble, "Okay, sure." He doesn't pull away, but his lips betray his stony façade when they curl up at the corner.

It's too dangerous that this boy can sway my resolve with such a simple gesture. But I'm discovering I have a taste for his type of danger.

The first chords dance through the air, and I inhale before launching into the song. I close my eyes, blocking out everything except the memories of me rocking Weston on the front porch while singing this very tune. His little body warming my arms. Soft puffs of his milky breath on my neck. The fresh smell of his lotion after a bath. For a moment in my mind, I hold Weston again and sing him to sleep, praying that somewhere 400 miles north of here, he cosmically feels my presence.

On the last note, I open my eyes, releasing the daydream, and find everyone staring in my direction. Claire beams, an angelic smile on her lips. "What a beautiful song for your mama to sing to you. She sounds like good people."

I beam, nodding. "She's the best." I hope one day Weston will feel the same about me.

Clay begins strumming another song when a shrill tone splits the night air. He jumps to his feet, tugging his phone from his jeans' pocket. The screen illuminates Clay's face, which pinches in concern as his eyes rove the notification. He looks up at us through the dark shadows.

"It's the greenhouse alarm. Weren't y'all there today?"

My heart hammers my ribcage. Why would the alarm be going off? That greenhouse is Clay's favorite project, and now there's something wrong on the exact day I'm responsible for it?

No, there can't be. I checked the lock. Didn't I? I clearly remember the sliding the key in the slot... or was that when I was unlocking it? Oh my God.

Bo stands up, his fingers slipping from mine. "Everything was secured when we left."

Clay shoves his phone in his pocket and hands his guitar to Claire. "Maybe it's a false alarm. I'll be back." His nonchalance does little to disguise the rising panic lacing his voice. His tone is at least a few notes higher than normal, words slurring together as they spill out in high speed. The thick-soled bottoms of his boots thump against the pavers as he hurries to his truck.

"I'm going with you!" Bo yells, running after him.

I follow, sprinting to catch up. "Me too!"

We scramble into the truck, and Clay peels out of the drive, kicking up a cloud of sand and gravel, as we speed toward the main road. The trip to the office takes ten minutes on a sunny day in light traffic; Tonight, Clay makes it in five. No one utters a word the entire trip, but the cab is loud. The whir of the tires, spinning so fast I'm not sure they're even touching the road. The *tap-tap-tap* of Clay's fingers nervously thumping the wheel. The *clack-clack-clack* of Bo's thumbnail between his teeth. And my heart, jackhammering faster and harder than the roaring diesel engine.

As we turn on the path leading out to the main office, the noise stops, and I wonder if everyone is holding their breath like me. Clay pulls up to the greenhouse, the headlights shining on the wide-open door. Several large deer, obviously spooked by the engine, bolt from inside and scatter toward the wood line.

"Oh my God," Clay mumbles, slamming the truck in park and lumbering out the door. He runs toward the entrance, stopping at the threshold to pick up a few broken, half-chewed stems. After examining them, he hurls the pieces to the ground and runs his fingers through his hair, letting his hand linger at the back of his neck as he stares into the greenhouse's interior.

Clay's hard work, his research, his hybrid seedlings—gone. And it's all my fault. An unsettling sensation sweeps over me, one that feels as if the ground rips from my feet. Like I'm falling and flying in one swoop. Like energy builds behind the confines of my skin and threatens to blow me to smithereens.

Clay won't forgive me for this. My bags are as good as packed.

The other truck door swings open, and Bo grabs my hand, pulling me from the seat. A breeze off the open marsh snaps me back to the present as we run to the greenhouse and Clay who stands frozen, staring inside at tables and floors littered with sprigs of greenery and piles of soil. The place has morphed into a five-star garden bar for the Lowcountry deer.

Bo reaches for the door handle. It twists easily in his hand. Unlocked. And the one thing we all learned in orientation is that this door had to be locked because it doesn't latch properly without something holding it in place.

"Dad, we locked the door. We double-checked it. There's no way that—"

Clay silences him with an upheld hand. Bo's head drops as fast as my heart sinks to my toes. Did we secure it? Did we double-check? I think we did, but I can't be sure... I was too distracted. Too interested in fantasizing about a guy and studying the curves of his body more than taking care of something entrusted to me. I didn't stay focused. I didn't keep my end game in sight. I let my heart and mind lollygag off like some dish and spoon nursery rhyme. And my family will pay the price if he dismisses me from this internship.

Clay sweeps a light across the room's darkest corners then steps inside.

Crunch. Crunch-crunch-crunch.

He redirects his flashlight at the floor, where a handful of rounded objects catch the light. Those weren't there earlier. He stoops and picks up a few pieces in his palm, examining them, before he looks up at us with furrowed brows.

"Deer corn?"

Bo twists his head in my direction, our eyes connecting through the dim light. One person hauls the deer corn around here. And he was also sneaking around this greenhouse this afternoon.

"Brice," we utter in unison.

My mind recalls his last words about the plants as he huffed off after I insulted him.

He'll be seriously pissed if you screw them up.

Brice did this—his retaliation—intending to pin the damages on my negligence. Except in true Brice fashion, his devious plan comes up short because he fails to clean up after himself. Lack of follow-through is definitely his Achilles Heel. All show, no substance yet again.

No matter his short-comings, the plants are still in tatters.

"I'm gonna kick his ass—and maybe Patrick's, too, just for procreating that jerk," Clay growls, grinding the dried kernels in his fist.

"Me first," Bo adds, stepping to his dad's side. The gnarled expressions on their faces look one step away from grabbing lanterns and pitchforks.

But I can't let them do it. I can't let this feud keep stewing.

"Please, don't." I step in front of them, holding out my arms. "I'll stay and clean this up. Most of the affected plants can be salvaged. I'll get them back in the dirt."

They glance at each other and then back at me. Clay cocks his head to the side as if trying to make sense of my request. "Why?"

"Because maybe if he thinks he got away with it, he'll finally leave me alone and drop this stupid vendetta."

Bo grunts. "That's what you said about his fake market numbers."

"Yeah, but then I humiliated him out by the tractor, remember? That upped the ante."

Clay bites his lip but nods, stepping forward and patting my shoulder. "You're not cleaning this up alone. I'll go get my tools."

At least he understands. As Clay steps out, I look over at Bo's steeled jaw. He, however, does not.

I walk over to him, but he refuses to make eye contact. "Why are you protecting him?" he asks, barely moving his lips to speak. It's as if he opens his mouth any wider, the rage will spew all over.

I grab his arms and pivot him to facing me. "I'm not protecting *him*. I'm protecting *us*." The corners of his mouth soften, almost upturn, when I say "us" but immediately return to a pinched line.

"Brice won't quit. This will only give him more confidence to try something else." He stomps around me, heading toward the door, but stops to shoot me one last glance. "Next time will be worse."

If this is what Bo calls worse then I'll take it. Five whole days and not one peep from Brice. No side-eyed glares. No crazy mishaps. Nothing. As a matter of fact, if it wasn't for Christopher stopping by for a daily hello and shoot-the-breeze session, I wouldn't even know Brice is on the farm grounds. He never joins the conversation, only sits in the truck, letting the engine idle and shooting me satisfied sneers, while Christopher and I chat.

I knew I was right. Letting the pig think he bested me is working miracles for my stress levels. I could get used to a Brice-free workplace.

Bo, however, remains standoffish. Not mean or anything, but distant. No matter how many times I explain my stance, he refuses to understand me, always coming back with more what-ifs and what's-nexts. A shame, too, because our afternoon in the greenhouse had been nice.

Very nice.

I close my eyes, letting the gentle breeze ripple over me and carry in the memory of us squirting each other with the hose. The way we laughed. The way his soaked shirt peeled off his toned body.

My heart somersaults in my chest, and I snap my eyes open, forcing the daydreams to a hard stop. Maybe that day had been *too* nice. Since then, the memories come back more frequently at random times during the day when I look over at Bo hoisting a bag of fertilizer or climbing onto the tractor in those ripped jeans.

One minute Bo's asking me a question, and as I study the movement of his lips—*blink!*—I'm back in the greenhouse wishing I was the drop of water rolling down his—

Dear God. I have to quit this nonsense. Did the deer-fueled, near disaster teach me nothing? I'm here to work. To win. Get a grip.

In my peripheral vision, I spot Bo trudge into the barn where I'm working, but I don't turn around. I wait.

"Hey, can I talk to you for a minute?" His voice is serious, pensive, and this is the first time all week the conversation alludes to something more personal than professional. After the Great Deer Fiasco and my pleas to spare myself via sparing Brice, Bo's chip on his shoulder had reared its head through terse, unadorned job duty descriptions during the workday and his acute avoidance of me when off farm grounds. Now, though, sounds different.

I prop my rake against the barn wall and walk over to the haybale where he's taken a seat. "What's up?"

"Don't go to the bonfire tonight."

My shoulders drop as the request registers in my brain. Johnson Farms is hosting a small bonfire on the beach for the farm workers this evening. Nothing fancy, according to Doniella, just hot dogs and fixings. Bo and I need to be there to maintain our image for the internship. Winning will be about more than just the work; it's about bringing the whole package. And how will it look for me to be MIA from a planned function? Besides, I'd been hoping that maybe outside the farm and the Johnson house, Bo would finally let down his guard again. Maybe even have a little fun cozying up beside a fire with the ocean waves roaring in the background. With me.

Only he doesn't want me there.

I squint my eyes. "Why?"

He blows out a loud breath, looking up at me, those sapphire blue eyes stormy under his dark lashes. "I'd already committed to working the pits for Jett's race tonight, so I'll be out of town."

Well, there goes those silly fantasies of the two of us. Bummer, but why should I stay at home because he won't be there? I'm a big girl. Besides, we have a competition to think about, and one of us needs to be in the know on everything happening around here. One of us must attend.

"And?" I roll my hand in the air, urging him to continue his line of thought. How does his absence determine my plans for the night?

"I can't go." Bo knifes his hand in the air with each word, eyes bulging as if he's explaining a simple concept I'm not able to grasp. I understand what he's saying; I just don't understand how it affects me.

"All the more reason for me to go then. Our team needs representation there. It *is* a company bonfire."

Bo jumps to his feet, rubbing his palm back and forth on his forehead. Why do I suddenly feel like a kindergartner about to get in trouble with the teacher?

"A bonfire put on by Patrick and Brice. Dad won't even be there. He, Mom, and Gin are having dinner out with the grand-parents." Bo crosses his arms over his chest, shaking his head. "I just don't think it's smart."

I clamp my lips for a moment, stifling my words until I can formulate them into a respectful, understanding, yet firm response. Of course Bo is worried about me stepping straight into a lion's den. Brice and Patrick have proven their characters time and again. But we can't back down every time they rear their heads or respond from intimidation. Mama always told me that the worst thing you could do to someone was ignore them because people behaving badly only do it for the attention. If you don't give them the payoff, they look for it elsewhere. Besides, there are too many other great people at Johnson Farms to throw the entire function out the door for a few bad apples. "Doniella will be there. And Christopher. And a lot of the other workers. I trust them."

"Yeah, but I don't trust Brice."

I grab Bo's hand and squeeze it in mine. It's the first time we've touched since the Johnson's firepit, and a shiver runs through me. "Then trust me. I'm not stupid enough to fall for any of Brice's ploys."

Bo bites his lip and reaches up, cupping my chin. "I don't

think you're stupid." He stoops down to eye-level. "I just think you underestimate him."

His words light the fuse on a stick of dynamite inside me— one that explodes with years of pent-up rage over "well-intentioned" guys barking orders but never taking the time to do meaningful things, like, I don't know, stick around for two seconds afterwards. The fire rushes to my cheeks, my nostrils flaring as I say through gritted teeth, "And I think you underestimate *me*. That's really something you should quit doing, Bo Johnson."

I pivot on my boot heels, grab the rake, and stomp out of the barn before the sins of the guys in my past come back to haunt Bo and his big mouth.

CHAPTER 13

Bo

Everyone gathers in the boardroom, ready for our weekly meeting. Well, everyone except one. The chair beside me sits vacant.

"We're only waiting on Jordan?" Dad glances at his watch, eyebrows furrowed. "She's usually right on time. Anyone seen her this morning?"

I shrug, pointing toward the front of the office. "No, but her Jeep is outside so she must be around here somewhere."

Typically, I'd invite Jordan to ride in with me on a Saturday morning, but I hadn't been home last night or this morning. Jett had asked me several months ago to work in the pits for one of his local races. The cash for one night's work was hard to beat, and now that he had several racing managers interested in seeing what I could do, I needed all the exposure I could get. No point in slamming doors I might want to keep opened in the future. Since it was well after midnight when we got back to the island, Jett and I had just crashed in the apartment at their private racing facility.

An awkward silence descends on the room as Brice and Christopher exchange glances. Christopher's wide-eyed shiftiness, however, vibes much differently than Brice's curled-lip sneer.

"She's probably somewhere sleeping off last night." Brice tips his head back and pulls his thumb to his mouth as if chugging an imaginary beer. Dad narrows his eyes, his lips bowing into a deep frown, and then glances over at me as if I have some magical explanation when I didn't even go to that stupid bonfire. But one thing I do know is that Jordan isn't some party girl drunk.

"Nice try, Brice, but Jordan doesn't drink. She told me so out of her own mouth."

"That wasn't what she was saying last night." He laughs, socking Christopher in the arm. "More like, can I get another? Times four!"

The door squeaks open a sliver, and Doniella peeks around the edge. When we lock eyes, she wiggles her fingers, motioning me out into the hall. No smile creases her lips. In fact, her jaw is stone. I jump to my feet and dart out of the room. She grabs me by the elbow and drags me to the far corner, away from any prying ears in the boardroom.

"Apparently, last night one of our interns was being instructed by their leader to keep taking Jordan cups of 'Island Punch' or whatever the hell they were calling it." She smirks and rolls her eyes. "I'll let you guess which leader that was."

Oh God. Jordan's body would never be able to handle that toxic bullshit concoction of Brice's. And he had to have known that.

"Why is he such a reckless dipshit?" I growl through gritted teeth.

"If I had to guess? Two reasons. One, he's still mad she chose you and not him. And two, he's a filthy horn-ball trying to get her drunk and alone. 'Cause he knows no sober girl would look at him!"

The mere mention of him making moves on Jordan and my stomach twists as if I'd just drunk a frosty glass of soured milk. "Did he...? I mean, he wouldn't..."

The words refuse to form on my tongue. Brice's self-indulged behavior is his hallmark, but surely even a prick like him wouldn't touch her... wouldn't put his hands on her... wouldn't take advantage... Right? In a flash, the soured milk morphs into red-hot fire.

"I found him last night sitting next to her with his arm around her shoulders and she wasn't actively kicking his gross ass so I knew something was going on. She despises him, you know. When I got closer, the alcohol was saturating the air before I even saw her bloodshot eyes." Doniella swallows hard, a sympathetic expression writing itself on her face. "She was wasted."

I step forward, grabbing Doniella's shoulders, giving them a shake. Begging. Pleading. "What did he do to her? Where is she now?"

Doniella lifts her hand to my face, stroking my cheek. "Don't worry, Bo. I wasn't about to leave her with that jackass. I hauled her butt up, put her in my truck and dropped her off at your place. Even helped her walk up the stairs to her apartment. No way in hell was I leaving her alone and unprotected with Brice."

I grab her hand and squeeze it tight. "Thank God you intervened." A twinge of relief, short-lived, shatters with a new parade of what-ifs. What if Doniella hadn't been there? What if Brice had gotten his way? What if...

My throat tightens at the thought of a different outcome.

I stomp down the hall and shove the door open, so hard it slams against the wall behind it. Everyone jumps in their chairs and turns their eyes on me. I ball my fists, willing them to stay at my side and not go swinging with all the force I can muster into that dirtbag's chin. "Dad, I'm going home to find Jordan. Some jackass was forcing alcohol on her last night and she got sick." With the word jackass, I train my gaze on Brice, gritting my teeth.

He smiles and tugs at the collar of his shirt then leans back, crossing one leg over the other. Relaxed. Confident. Unfeeling.

"Don't look over here. No one forced anything on her. She couldn't get enough of the Island Punch. It was her own doing."

Dad blows out a loud breath, his jaw steeled, as he steeples his hands in front of his face. "What exactly is in that 'Island Punch'?"

"Pineapple, peach, cantaloupe, watermelon..." he pauses, lowering his voice, "and a shit-ton of grain alcohol."

Every muscle in my body goes rigid. This sick bastard thinks it's funny. Like it's okay to play with people's lives as if they're no more than pawns in his own personal Game of Life. Jordan may be sick, she may be in danger, she may have—I shudder—but hey! If Brice wants it, Brice gets it.

I stab my finger in his direction. "But you conveniently left that part out when you were sending Christopher here to supply her with cup after cup, right?"

"Quit complaining!" Brice stands up, bowing his chest, and extends his fist then slowly unfolds his fingers as he says, "Your little mountain rose opened up like a bright blossom just as soon as that alcohol put her prudishness in check." He thumps me on the forehead. "Maybe you should take a note, little cousin. It's obvious you're after her ass but she's never gonna give you what you want. Not unless you liquor her up first."

"You stupid son-of-a-bitch!" My vision goes red, and I lunge at him, my fists no longer willing to take orders on behavior. They want action.

Brice ducks my first swing and just as I take my next shot, a pair of hands grips Brice's shoulders and pulls him backward out of reach. Dad steps in, grabbing my arms, holding me in place.

"Bo, stop! I'll handle this. You go check on Jordan. And you..." he pauses and glares over his shoulder at Brice, "...get in my office. Now!"

With one last glare into his beady eyes, I leave Brice standing in the boardroom pouting, Patrick massaging his shoulders and placating him like the infant he is, and race out the door for my Bronco. No doubt that so-called punch could be near-lethal in large amounts, especially for a girl who'd never been one to drink. A shiver runs down my spine.

The engine roars to life and I peel out of the parking lot toward home, repeatedly dialing her number. But Jordan doesn't answer any of the times I try. Straight to voicemail.

I pound my fists on the steering wheel. Reckless maniac. Brice waltzes onto the farm after being gone for months, thinking he's so much smarter and savvier than the rest of us because he's been off at some university getting his hifalutin degree and engaging in God-knows-what kind of behavior with that group of frat-boy cronies that follow him around. Too bad they don't have courses on how not to be an incredibly irresponsible jackass. He'd probably fail out anyway.

Over the tidal flats, the briny breeze whipping across my face, I stomp the gas harder. Who knows what condition Jordan's in at the moment? The best-case scenario is a monster hangover; the worst...ugh. I shake the thoughts and images from my head.

I turn onto our road, the loose gravel spitting up and clanging against the underbody of my Bronco, before turning into the drive and throwing it in park. The door to the guest quarters is ajar—I can see it from my seat—and my stomach knots.

I jump out and sprint toward the door, pausing just outside. "Jordan? You okay?"

Silence, then a muted mumbling.

I push open the door and slip inside, scanning the room, catching sight of her bare foot protruding from behind the couch. She groans again, and the toes curl as if she's in pain. I dart toward her, her body coming into view, sprawled out face down on the rug, a vomit-filled trashcan beside her.

Her shirt, splattered with reddish swirls, lies in a crumpled heap beyond the trashcan. A sour, boozy stench hangs in the air. Sinking to my knees, I brush away a few strands of hair that stick to the side of her face. Her nose and lips crush hard into the carpet and one eye, barely visible, blinks under a long fringe of lashes.

"What happened?" Her voice is raspy like she has a throat full of sandpaper.

"You had a little too much to drink last night. You're going to be okay."

"Uh-uh," she mumbles. "I only had punch." She tries to push herself up on her elbows but fails, toppling back hard on the floor.

"Brice's Island Punch is pure, high-octane grain alcohol." I get to my feet and hook my hands under her armpits, pulling her up to standing, then guide her to the couch.

Her feet stumble across the carpet before she sinks into the cushions and pushes her fingertips into her temples. "Does the spinning ever go away? Or the pounding?"

"Eventually." I slide the elastic band off her wrist, finger-comb her tangled hair into a bundle and wrap the band around it twice.

"How do you know how to put up a girl's hair?" She looks up at me with a slight grin as she runs her fingers down the length of her ponytail. They stop abruptly when meeting her naked collarbone, her eyes saucering before dropping to her exposed bra. "Oh my God! Where's my shirt?"

My gaze drops to her chest and a quick peek of her lace-edged bra before her arms criss-cross over the top. I turn my head and reach out, grabbing the blanket from the arm of the couch and hand it to her. She tugs it over her shoulders.

"Looks like your shirt was another of last night's casualties. Why don't we get you to your room, find you another shirt, and get you settled in bed?"

Jordan shakes her head. "I can't go to bed. It's light outside and we have to be at work in..." She stares down at her watch, squinching and then widening her eyes at the numbers. "Oh shit! We're late!" She springs to her feet, still clutching the blanket around her, but her body betrays her, her legs like wobbly Jell-o. She falls back to the cushions.

"You get a day off, farm girl."

"I can't take a random day off!" she wails. "Your dad is going to fire me."

"You don't fire people from internships."

"No, you just tell them to go home, and I *can't* go home. I *have* to get that grant money. I have to."

A sense of desperation I've never noticed before rings through her words, but before I can contemplate it much, I notice a few fat tears trickling down Jordan's cheek.

"Look, Dad knows where you are and what happened. We figured it out. That's why I'm here."

A low, guttural groan escapes Jordan's grimacing lips. "Your dad knows I'm hungover?"

"Dad knows you were tricked into drinking too much. He knows you were set up."

Jordan drops her face to her hands, shaking her head. "I'm so sorry."

"Hey," I say, pulling down her hands and tipping up her chin to look at me. "Don't apologize for being innocent. You didn't do this, Jordan. My asshole cousin did. Now let's get you to your bed so you can recuperate."

I slip one arm under her thighs and one around her back, lifting her off the couch. She loops her arm around my neck and nestles her head into my chest. My heart drums against my ribs, so hard I'm positive it has to be vibrating against her cheek. I tug her closer as she groans into my shirt. Her body feels no heavier than the bags of fertilizer I was just loading on the truck this morning.

The bedroom door isn't fully closed so I kick the edge with my boot, swinging it wide, and carry her to the bed. Once seated upright against the headboard, I fluff a pillow and slide it behind her. She stares, almost dazed for a moment, eyes not focusing, as her head bobs in tiny revolutions like the neck muscles can't find stability.

"Is the room supposed to still be spinning?" She mumbles then smacks her lips, sticking out her tongue. "And why is my mouth so dry?" She attempts to readjust on the mattress but winces, crinkling her nose. "And I'm sore... like I ran a marathon!"

"Lesson one: hangovers suck." I muffle a laugh, clearly remembering my own first after-party experience, scraping myself off the carpet in Jett's family room after one of his blowout yearly parties a few years ago. It was my first and last attempt at a keg stand. "You're sore from your body rejecting and pushing out what appears to be the contents of your last five meals."

She groans again, louder this time, and pulls her hands over her face. "Oh my God, you saw that."

"I've seen worse. Trust me." Jordan doesn't look convinced, but she's still too preoccupied with rolling her tongue against the inside of her cheeks. "And you're dizzy and parched because alcohol dehydrates you, so after we get you settled, we have to get you hydrated. It'll help. Again, trust me."

Her mouth finally stills as she pulls the blanket tighter around her shoulders and looks up at me with watery eyes. "I do trust you."

Our eyes lock for the briefest moment, and the air turns to a ton of bricks. "Where do you keep your t-shirts?" I ask, breaking the tension.

She points to the white-washed credenza on the opposite wall. "Middle drawer."

I slide it open and pull a folded pink shirt from the top and toss it on the bed. "While you put that on, I'm going to the kitchen to grab a few things." I leave, pulling the door closed partway behind me to give her some privacy, then walk to the kitchen. In the small island cabinet, I locate a breakfast-in-bed tray and sit it on the countertop. Now for the rest. I create a quick checklist of items in my head: something for sustenance, something for a headache, something for hydration. The pantry has few items on the shelves—how often does this girl buy groceries?—but I find just enough to constitute a decent hangover cure.

I load the tray and carry it back to her room, knocking before entering to make sure she's dressed.

"Come in," she mutters, her voice still like sandpaper.

I nudge open the door and my eyes land on Jordan in her fresh T-shirt laid back on the pillows, hair falling over her shoulders. She's run a brush through it and rubbed on a little Chapstick. Her lips glisten with the slightest sheen, crimping upwards in the tiny smile when she sees me.

Quit staring at her lips, Bo.

"Here's everything you need to feel better. One of those canned coffee drinks you love, a few water bottles, a sleeve of saltines, and two aspirin." I balance the tray with one hand and fold down the little legs with the other, then place it on the bed in front of Jordan. She reaches for the water and twists it open, swallowing a long pull. I grab the remote from her nightside table, click on the television, then lay the remote beside her tray. The screen flickers on to some flashy game show with loud buzzers galore, and Jordan immediately taps the volume-down button several times. "Watch some TV, get some sleep, get hydrated, and relax. I'll be back to check on you later."

"Yes sir." She attempts to raise her hand to her brow to give me a salute but grimaces when the memory of last night once again pinches her muscles. I nod and turn on my heels to leave, but stop in the doorway when she calls out, "Hey Bo..." I glance over my shoulder. "Thanks."

I nod and walk out.

Jordan sits in my passenger seat, holding tight to the arm rest as we bump and rattle down the narrow, packed-sand road. I ease off the gas when she grimaces, her stomach probably still tender from last night's alcohol. I glance over at her, face relaxed once again, as she leans back against the headrest, looking up through the open top at the canopy of oak branches and moss shading our drive. The slivers of sunlight cutting through the leaves freckle her face in patches of light and dark, and underneath, her cheeks tinge pink, a positive change from this morning's pallor.

Maybe she's still not a hundred percent, but she's getting there. No thanks to Brice and his idiocy.

As if on cue, Jordan turns to me with a serious expression. "I just wanted to say that you were right about Brice. I should've listened—"

I hold up my hand stopping her. "I'm just glad you're okay." And there's something else I need to address. Something I want her to understand. "And I didn't mean to bark orders and try to control you. I just care about..." The word *you* dances on my tongue but fear strikes it down, substituting in a safer response. "Your safety."

She nods, a new softness in her face. "Thanks for everything. I'm glad I picked you... you know, to be my partner this summer."

She's glad she picked me even when I'd been so sure she'd come to regret it. A tingly warmth filters down through my body, but I just smile and say, "Me too."

The road narrows as we approach the welcome kiosk, and Jordan sticks her head out of the window, squinting at the sign. "Botany Bay Preserve and Wildlife Management," she reads aloud. "What is this place?"

"Just what the sign says." I brake gently, turning onto the six-mile scenic loop. "Probably one of the last few undisturbed coastal areas. Now you can see what the land is really like, without all the development getting in the way."

We ride the first few miles in silence as Jordan peers out her window, the windshield, the open top, and even my window after half-crawling over the console. She points out decrepit remains of old plantations and open expanses of sunflowers not yet gone to bloom. With a satisfied smile, she finally relaxes back in her seat. "It's like a forest of oaks and loblolly pines... but at the beach. It reminds me a lot of home actually. I wasn't expecting this."

"That's sort of the point of us being here." She folds her arms over her chest and shoots me a thoughtful gaze, like she's waiting on me to expand further. "I thought that after a rough start to the day that a taste of home might be the best medicine for your hangover."

"You've just been full of remedies today." She grins, shaking her head. "I don't see how you and Brice are even related. To be cousins, y'all are nothing alike."

"That is the best compliment I've ever received." I give her a wink and pull over onto a sandy patch off the roadside near a thick stand of moss-laden trees at the marsh's edge. I unclasp my seatbelt and jump out of the Bronco, jogging around to Jordan's side. "We have arrived," I say, opening her door and holding it wide.

She slides out onto the sandy ground and takes a 360-degree scan of the area. "Why are we stopping here?"

"Showing you will be better than telling you." I step to the front of the Bronco and climb up on the hood, letting my feet rest on the bumper. Jordan follows, and I extend my hand, helping her up beside me. When she opens her mouth, I pull a finger to my lips. "Shhh. Listen."

"I don't hear—" A soft call from the tall grass stops her, and she grabs my arm, eyes saucered. "Is that a—"

"A bobwhite."

She gasps and draws her hand to her mouth, leaving the other one on me. The warmth of her skin radiates through the muscle and burrows into my bones. "But how did you know?"

"You mentioned it one time, how much they comforted you."

She turns to face me, her eyes watery but her lips just a bit turned up at the corners. One of those weird expressions when you don't know if the person is going to hug you or cry buckets. Grandma used to call it a sad-happy.

Jordan cocks her head to one side. "And you remembered?"

"Well yeah, it seemed important to you so..." She doesn't move an inch, just sits there as if frozen in place staring at me. A slight panic rises in my chest. What is this expression on her face? Does she think I'm a nice guy or some super-awkward, stalker-y sap? Fire rushes to my face. "What? You think I'm a marshmallow, right?"

"No, not a marshmallow." She giggles and nudges my ribs with her elbow. "More like a cinnamon roll."

My eyebrows pinch together. Pretty sure I've never heard that term before. "A what?"

"A cinnamon roll is someone who is pure and good. Genuine."

Okay, it's a compliment. A renewed sense of calm washes over me. "I'm not sure I deserve all that, but I'll take it."

Jordan wags her head, rolling her eyes. "Oh believe me, after some of the people I've met, you absolutely deserve it. And..."

She stops mid-sentence, biting her top lip between her teeth, and turns away to stare out over the marsh.

I push my shoulder against hers, but she doesn't look back. "What were you going to say?"

"I better not."

"Come on."

Jordan twists the leather cuff on her wrist and blows out a loud breath as if there's a hot debate unfolding inside her brain. She finally blurts out, "That Laurel girl is a total idiot. They don't make 'em much better than you, Bo."

My breath catches. A slow tingle burns down my body, but before I can respond, she plants her hands on the hood of the Bronco and leans back, eyes closed, like a turtle sunning itself.

The bobwhites continue a birdsong harmony in the background. "I could listen to that sound all day."

"Why do you like it so much?"

Jordan opens her eyes and shoots me a sideways glance. "It reminds me of the best of home. And the sound? It starts off a little forlorn but that lilt on the second half sounds like hope and joy." As if on cue, the bird calls again and Jordan smiles wide, tapping her finger in front of her ear. "See? Listen for it," she whispers, hunching forward as she waits for the inevitable next notes.

Bob-White!

She dips her hand on the first syllable and then trills her fingers on the second.

I shake my head. Only this girl could make something as simple as a quail's call feel like a work of musical genius. "I like how you see the world."

"Correction," she says, laughing. "You like how I see nature. My opinion of the world is a bit more cynical." She hops down from the hood and steps to the edge of the path where an old, twisty oak bends its arms to the ground. Her fingers trace the rough bark ribboning the trunk. "Seriously though, my family and the land are so important to me. That's why I have to be successful here. I have to find a way to save our farm."

She turns back to me, a plea, a cry for help, budding in her eyes. Jordan's not here for just some run-of-the-mill opportunities or first-hand learning. She said "save." She has to *save* her family's farm. And she needs my help.

I run my hand down the back of my neck, rubbing away the onslaught of sweat induced by the heat and the sudden realization of Jordan's burden. "How bad are things, if you don't mind me asking?"

"I don't mind telling you. You, I trust." She trudges over and stands in front of me at the Bronco's front fender. Her eyes are watery again, but this time no hints of happiness peek through. Just sadness. And worry. She blows out a loud breath, wringing her hands. "The bank is threatening to foreclose... by September. Between drowning in a perpetual state of debt and Grandpa's declining health, my mom's working herself to death and me..." she pauses, her shoulders slumping, "...sometimes I think I'm just causing more trouble than I'm worth."

My breath stalls in my ribcage. Foreclosure. This is not a small-potatoes problem; it's a life-altering one. They could lose everything. And soon. And the cherry on top is Jordan's blaming herself.

I jump down and pull her hand into mine, squeezing it. "Johnson Farms is huge and we have resources. Let us help you."

She shakes her head, mouth pinched in a firm line. "I don't want anyone else knowing about how much trouble we're in. And we don't want charity. It's a pride thing, and maybe that's stupid, but pride is about the only thing we have left at this point."

Jordan's mentioned time and again that her grandparents are simple, proud people. No doubt the thought of the everyone knowing their troubles would cut to the bone. Still, no one should shoulder that much weight alone. "No, I get it, but please let *me* help you then. We're already working together on your internship, so let's really dig in and put together some possibilities. Maybe something will work. Maybe we can come up with a really great plan and the bank will renegotiate."

There has to be a way.

Jordan forces a closed-lipped smile but lets it dissolve quickly as she stares at her shoes. She swallows hard, rubbing her throat as if deliberately trying to push the emotions back down inside her. A breeze dances in from the marsh, splaying a few tendrils of hair across Jordan's face. Without thinking, I brush them away, my fingertips skimming the soft skin of her cheek. She shivers, a flood of chill bumps spilling down her arms.

Did I do that? No, probably just the wind. Right?

But secretly, I want to have that effect on her. I should be thinking about the business aspects of this, but knowing Jordan —being here with her—makes it more personal than ever.

"Maybe it's time to take a few risks and see what happens?" I suggest.

She jerks her head up, locking her blue eyes on mine, this mission gaining legs in our connection. The possibilities blooming. She nods. "Yeah. Maybe it is."

CHAPTER 14

Jordan

B o and I stand in front of the office computer, watching the green swirling mass on the screen and the hundred red lines spewing out to the left with forecasted tracks. In the center of the mass, cloaked in red and yellow, spins a thick cloud wall surrounding a well-defined patch of blue ocean.

I search Bo's face for any signs of worry, but he's perfectly calm despite the fact that the weather has to be perfect for our First Annual Johnson Farms Mingling at the Market. The vendor list filled, the food trucks scheduled, the entertainment arranged, and now a monsoon is headed our way, creeping across the Atlantic like an angry-eyed monster with its sights set on us. I wouldn't put it past Brice to have contacted some kind of marsh witch to conjure up a natural disaster just in time to shit all over our plans.

I stare again at the screen, the movement barely discernible. How fast do these things move anyway?

Spring and summertime storms I'm familiar with. This thing, not so much. Sure, I'd heard the local weatherman back home talk about hurricanes making landfall on the coast but all we ever got was a decent, steady rain and maybe a gust or two.

"Is that thing going to screw up our market event?"

"No way," he says, leaning forward in the chair, pressing his finger to the patch of green and then swiping it along the path of the majority of the squiggly projection lines. "This shows the hurricane moving more North than West, so it'll probably just skirt us as it moves up the coastline. It'll be out of here by Sunday, and that gives us five whole days to prepare for next weekend." The wheels on the chair squeak as he stands up and walks behind me, kneading his fingers into my shoulders, massaging the tight muscles. He leans in to my ear, so close his hot breath slides down my neck. "Relax."

I turn to face him, our chests grazing, and pink swirls color Bo's cheeks. "I make no promises," I say with a giggle. He opens his mouth to rebuttal, but the door swings wide as Gin walks in, creating our own proverbial parting of the Red Sea. Bo rushes to the file cabinets on the wall, and I, back to the computer screen.

"Am I interrupting something?" Gin smirks, casting suspicious glances between us.

I suck in a deep breath, willing it to slow my heart. If my voice wavers one iota, Gin will be all over it like white on rice. "Just a lesson on hurricane preparedness." Her face falls, obviously disappointed to have walked in on nothing more than a weather report. I glance over my shoulder at Bo, who's rifling through the file cabinet. "So, what do we do on the farm while it's 'skirting' us?"

"Not much to do except wait it out." He pulls a manilla folder from the drawer and holds it in the air. "The hard part comes today and tomorrow while we weatherproof this place."

I walk over and take it from him, then open the flap to two detailed pages of checklist items. The first few I read aloud.

- *Install windbreaks around greenhouses.*
- *Secure greenhouse vents and shutters around fans.*
- *Move all R&D seedlings to secure container storage.*
- *Apply fabric covers to burgeoning crops.*
- *Nail plywood over main office windows.*

- *Secure all equipment.*

Page two continues with another equally long list.

I point at the folder. "All of this for some puny 'skirting'?"

As if on cue, Gin pops her head in between us, a huge grin on her face. "A lot of work now for a lot of fun tomorrow night."

"Fun?" I search her expression for any clues. Gin's concept of fun could mean anything. And I do mean *anything*. What exactly could be fun about a hurricane?

She pushes Bo backward, demanding my full attention. "Well... since we can't work on Saturday because it'll be nasty weather and I just heard from CJ and Jett that they'll be in town tomorrow morning and staying for an entire week, I just think it's the perfect time."

Bo leans around her, grabbing her shoulder. "Perfect time for what?"

"A hurricane-inspired sleepover party in our upstairs rec room." Gin beams, holding up her hands like she just got nominated for an Academy Award. "CJ, Jett, you—" She points at me. "You—" She points at Bo. "And me." She plunges her finger to her own chest.

She bites her bottom lip, awaiting our response. Typically, I'm not a party-it-up kinda girl, but I do like everyone on that guest list. And I really don't want to be alone in my first hurricane, especially if the power goes out. And it does involve sleeping over at the Johnson's where Bo will be there, maybe in pajamas, or even... shirtless again.

Suddenly any semblance of normal breathing becomes elusive. I lift my eyes to Bo's, which glow with a mischievous glint.

"Sounds good to me," he says, never peeling his gaze from mine. "Safety in numbers and all things considered."

I inhale, letting the air stabilize my voice. "How could I say no?"

Gin squeals, clapping her hands as she jumps up and down.

I'm walking out of my door, overnight bag in tow, when my phone dings. I dart down the steps and across to the patio, dodging the raindrops to the Johnson's covered porch before sliding my phone from my pocket.

<Mama>: *Is it raining yet? Are you safe?*

<Me>: *Off and on since this morning. Main stuff moving in tonight. I'm fine. Headed to a thing at the Johnsons*

<Mama>: *What kind of thing?*

<Me>: *A spend-the-night hurricane party*

<Mama>: *With Bo?*

<Me>: *Bo and Gin and some others.*

<Mama>: *But he'll be there...*

<Me>: *Stop it!*

<Mama>: *Why? You already admitted you liked him. It is okay to be excited about a boy, Sassy.*

I sigh. In a moment of pure weakness, I'd confessed to Mama on one of our nightly calls that I thought Bo was one of the greatest guys I'd ever met. I even told her about the shirtless karaoke thing in the greenhouse. An eavesdropper would've thought I'd called to tell her I struck gold or something with the way she howled into the phone as I described him peeling off his wet T-shirt. Maybe I should have kept that part to myself because all it did was turn her into an incorrigible pain in the butt. And when it comes to her dreams of my confessing my feelings for Bo to his face, she just won't take no for an answer.

Sometimes having a mama I can tell everything to is a blessing. Sometimes, a burden. Or a curse. I'm still deciding.

<Me>: *I do like him. Bo's great, but the timing isn't right. He's six weeks out from a bad breakup and I'm... complicated. You know that. I also have this thing outweighing everything... called an internship. Maybe you forgot about that.*

<Mama>: *No, but you also have something called a life... maybe YOU forgot about that.*

Touché, Mama. Before I can contrive a clever response, she cuts the conversation mid-stream. Her way of telling me to shut up and go enjoy myself.

<Mama>: *Night, Sassy. I'll kiss Weston for you. Enjoy your evening.*

I shove my phone into my back pocket and enter the Johnson's house through the French door. Claire waves to me from the kitchen as I make my way to the back staircase and jog up to where the others are waiting.

Gin greets me by the door with a hug, pulling me inside to say hello to everyone. A new face in the crowd—one I've never seen before—stands out. Gin introduces him as Buck, Jett's brother and one of her best friends. Apparently, he lives in Beaufort, but Jett picked him up for the occasion. CJ trots over and also wraps me in a hug, launching into a million questions about the internship and how it's going. Bo and Jett sit on the couch, battling it out on some video game.

Clay knocks on the door and hands Gin multiple boxes of pizza, which she lays on the table amidst her feast of chips, cookies, and candy. My stomach growls looking at it. Everyone gathers around, heaping their plates with food, and for the next few hours, we stuff our faces, watch movies, and play cards to the incessant drumming of hard rain on the roof and the occasional whistle of winds through the palms.

When Jett wins his third hand of Rummy in a row, CJ throws down her cards, sticking her tongue out at him. "Now what? Something besides cards."

"Another movie?" Gin offers, but everyone groans at the idea.

"Oh, I know!" Buck takes a seat at the game table and lays his phone on top, tapping a few buttons. He pulls up an account on social media with a collection of shared videos. "Have y'all seen that guy who posts videos of people's public breakups? It's freaking hilarious!"

We all gather around, leaning over Buck's shoulder to get a better view. Bo stands beside me, his arm nonchalantly draped over my shoulder making it hard to focus on the screen.

The first one shows a girl and a guy in the middle of a screaming match in what looks like a high school cafeteria. Lots of interesting name-calling and a few handfuls of chicken nuggets used as assault missiles. Apparently, he's been cheating with a girl on the soccer team but tries to deny it. That is until her best friend comes running in from the side and hurls a soccer ball square into his crotch. Each one of the guys in the room gasps audibly and grimaces as if the ball has somehow cut through time and space to tag each one of them in their privates.

"That's just wrong!" Jett yells while the rest of us laugh.

Buck swipes up, the next video populating the screen.

The couple remains hidden behind a sea of bodies that have flanked them on both sides. The guy filming must be pretty short because he keeps jumping to try and get a better view but all he's successful in capturing are the backs of some bystanders' heads, the loud music playing on a speaker, and the tip-top of the couple's hair. She has a brown messy bun, and he has dark curls. I squint for a closer look. Dark curls that look just like... I side-eye Bo. Oh my God. My stomach relocates to my feet.

Bo's face blanches a pale white, the muscles in his neck constricting. Is this him and Laurel? No, it couldn't be.

Could it?

His arm slides off my shoulder, and I glance down at his hands, now balled into fists. His breathing stagnates, as if he's trying to hold it all in, and he tucks his bottom lip between his teeth. He looks over at me, head cocked to one side. I reach out to touch his elbow but he shirks the contact. His eyes saucer, black pupils overtaking the sapphire blue.

Oh shit. Does he know that I know?

The girl's voice on the video breaks through the background noise. *You really should have called first.*

The words break the dam Bo's struggling to hold back. He shoves between Jett and Buck, hitting the "x" button and sending the phone back to its home screen. "Why don't y'all watch something useful instead of this shit?" The edge in his voice catches the room off guard, and around the table, mouths drop open. Even-keel Bo throwing a tantrum is a rare occurrence. And from the confused expressions on everyone's faces, no one understands the root of it.

But I do.

Bo glances around, a deep scowl etched on his face, before he turns and stomps out into the hallway. Two seconds later, his bedroom door slams shut.

Stunned, no one utters a word or even moves. They stare at each other, the cogs in their minds running at full steam and producing no logical explanation.

Finally, Buck speaks up. "Geez, what's his deal?" He shakes his head, looking at Gin for an explanation. She shrugs, shaking her head.

I lean in, whispering in case Bo can still hear us. "I think it might be too soon... you know, to laugh about people's public break-ups?" I emphasize the last two words, nodding my head as I say them.

CJ gasps and clamps her hand over her mouth, speaking from between her fingers, "It didn't even occur to me. It's been over a month and he never mentions it. I guess we all thought he was over it. Should we go talk to him?"

I shake my head. "From what I can tell, he's over *her*, just not the feeling of betrayal. Watching some random breakups probably inflamed that wound a little." I make sure to throw the word *random* in there so no one goes back to the video and connects any dots that Bo so obviously wants disconnected. It's the least I can do in the moment to protect him. "I think maybe we should just give him a minute to himself."

"Jordan's right. In the meantime, how about a game of pool? Girls versus guys?" Gin, infusing her tone with more upbeat positivity than usual, sweeps her arms, directing everyone to the pool table. Everyone except me. As she gathers the others, she steps beside me, locking eyes, ensuring I know what to do.

I give her a slight nod. Of course, I'm going to check on him. He just needs a moment to decompress first.

"Next game for me," I say with a wink. "I'm just going to text my mama and give her a storm update. Let her know we're all okay and didn't blow away in the hurricane so far."

Gin shoots me a grateful smile and then flits to the pool table, announcing the rules for the game. In a heartbeat, everyone is back to laughing and talking. Crisis diverted.

I retreat to the far corner of the room and sit down in a bean bag chair, my back to the wall. From here, no one has a clear view of my phone screen. I plug in my earbuds and insert them in my ears. Remembering the poster's online handle, I type it in to the app and wait for the videos to load. Within seconds, thumbnails populate the space, and I scroll down, finding the right one.

A quick glance up to make sure no one's spying on me, then press play.

It begins with a flurry of movement—someone running to the scene of the conflict. My heart accelerates as if I'm the one in chase. It drums in my chest, and a pang of guilt runs through me. Bo obviously didn't want anyone witnessing this nightmare, but another part of me has to watch it. I want to understand it. Understand him. And I have to know if there's any chance he might still have feelings for her. He says not, but I have to know for sure.

For five minutes, I watch the scene unfold, never fully glimpsing a full-on, discernible view of Bo's face. Laurel remains concealed, too, except for a pluff of brown hair knotted on her head. The big red-headed guy—the one I assume is the boyfriend—is visible, especially as he enunciates an infuriating jab that shoots hot fingers of fire through me. *Some hick in work boots.*

I shudder. Stupid jerk. Bo is ten times better than this guy will ever be.

That's when Laurel's voice chimes in, insinuating she doesn't know why Bo's standing there. At her feet, a crumpled bouquet of roses lay in a heap. After Bo traveled all that way, the only thing she can do is pretend to barely know him? I grind my teeth. Can you hate someone you don't even know? Because this girl...

A few more heated words—hard to hear over the loud music playing in the background—before a figure breaks free from the crowd, disappearing around the corner of the house, and the video cuts.

I yank the earbuds from my ears and lean my head against the wall. My insides ache for Bo. For the way his heart was trampled. For the way he was blindsided. It wasn't so many years ago, I stood in front of my very own liar as he flippantly told me there'd been nothing between us, despite the very obvious evidence growing inside me at the time. Bo had hoped what he had with Laurel was love, the same way I'd hoped love was what tied me to Weston's father. But it wasn't love, not on either count. That sort of manipulation drags your self-esteem through the ditch.

While everyone else smack-talks each other about the ongoing pool game, I stand up and pad to the door. When I'm positive no one's looking, I slip out and down the hall to his room, letting their laughter fade behind me. His closed door separates us, sequestering him alone with his pain, but I know from experience that being alone can lie to you as well. Tell you that you deserve what fate dished out. Tell you that you aren't worthy and never will be.

And I won't let Bo wallow in those lies. I lift my hand to the door and knock softly. A low grunt emanates from the other side, but he doesn't tell me to come in or go away. I'll consider that grunt an invitation, so I twist the knob and ease the door open, peering through the crack.

Bo lies on his bed, arms crossed behind his head, as he stares at the ceiling. No lights are on, but the constant flashes of lightning outside the window brighten the room. His face is stoic, hard, and it's almost as if his mood feeds the rumbling thunder shaking the house.

When he doesn't yell at me to leave, I slip through the opening and shut the door behind me. He keeps his eyes on the ceiling as I lay down beside him on the bed. For several minutes, neither of us utters a word. We lay there, side by side, in silence.

Finally, I roll onto my side, propping my arm underneath my head. "Are you okay?"

Without looking at me, he asks, "How did you know?"

So he *did* realize I'd figured it out. I hesitate, trying to frame my answer in such a way that doesn't make me sound like a stalker. I knew it was him because I'm used to watching him lately. Watching his reactions. Bo wears his emotions scrawled across his face like a badge. "I was watching you. Your face. Your eyes. And the way you tuck in your bottom lip a little. You do that when you're angry."

His lips curl into a faint smile before it fades again. "Do the others know?"

"No."

He pivots his head toward me, eyes slitted. "You didn't tell them?"

I shake my head. "After you walked out, I smoothed it over by reminding them that the topic of breakups might be a sensitive subject and to drop it. But none of them know that they were watching *your* breakup."

"Thanks," he mumbles before looking back at the ceiling. "I'm an idiot. You know that, right?" Bo unlaces his fingers from behind his head and balls his fists, pressing both onto his forehead. "Here I am preaching to you about not getting tricked by Brice when I'm the King of Being Duped. And now we have video evidence to prove it." He pulls his hands down, resting them on his chest, as he grumbles, "As if I need a reminder."

"Screw that video. And that dumb girl. And all those stupid people. And those roses you ground into dirt."

He lifts his head up, turning toward me. "Roses?"

Oops.

"You watched the entire video." It isn't a question. He drops his head back to the pillow with a loud exhale. "Why?"

"I don't know. I just had to... I wanted to understand you better."

His biceps flex in and out, pulsing under the fabric sleeves of his T-shirt. "And what did you learn? I'm a pathetic loser? A hick in work boots?"

He spits out the word *hick* as if it tastes like sour lemons, and hearing him repeat the slur socks me in the gut. Bo is not going to put on that insult and wear it around like reality. I won't let him.

"First of all, that hick in work boots comment came from a guy wearing loafers and khaki shorts. His opinion shall not be considered in our world. Agreed?" I hold out my hand, asking for a handshake. Bo snorts but slides his hand into mine, pumping it up and down. "Secondly, and most importantly, you are not a loser in that video. That girl? She's the loser. If I had you, there's no way in hell—"

Shut up, Jordan!

My stupid tongue just took off on a tangent of its own, talking about *if I had him*. A lump knits itself into my throat. Maybe he didn't hear me. Maybe—

"Finish that sentence."

His lip twitches as he closes his eyes then pushes up on the bed, readjusting onto his side. Facing me. He lies on his pillow and I lie on mine, our bodies mirroring each other's.

My thoughts jumble when his eyes fix on me. I shouldn't have blurted that out. I have to be more careful. "What sentence?" I shrug one shoulder, playing it off.

But he's not letting me off that easy. "You said, 'If I had you, there's no way in hell...'" he repeats, a smile turning up the corners of his lips. "Finish your thought."

"There's no way in hell I'd treat you like the 'other' guy when you deserve to be an 'only.'" Chill bumps shoot down my arms, prickling the skin. "You would be the only guy for me."

Our eyes lock, an intensity building in the connection—one that rivals the electrical energy streaking the night sky outside. He leans toward me. I close the gap further, my lips burning like fire. The same fire licking every inch of my body. As if I'm combustible. My ragged breaths claw at my lungs, but just as our lips hover only inches apart, Bo stops, shaking his head, snapping himself out of whatever trance had gripped us. He flops onto his back, and I blow out a loud breath, viscerally feeling the gut punch.

I have to get out of here. Bo and I are intern partners and that's what we need to stay. Like I told Mama earlier—the timing is bad. And I can't keep putting myself in these positions. Because I want him to kiss me. I want his arms around me. I want to know what his body feels like up close.

But that could ruin everything. And Bo knows it too. That's why he just squashed whatever this was.

I take a deep breath, steeling my insides, and scoot off the side of the bed, straightening my blouse. Bo props up on one elbow, watching me walk to the door.

"I... um... I'm gonna get back to the party now." I open the door, stepping out into the hallway, but lean back in when I remember what I'd meant to tell him earlier. Something that might give him a bit of peace. "I reported that video for a copyright infringement. There was music playing in the background—the full length of one song—which is a total violation of community standards. They've already taken it down."

I give him a wink before heading down the hall. Bo will join us when he's ready. He has to do it on his time, and I won't push.

CHAPTER 15

Bo

Five hundred people mill around the market, filling their canvas totes with Johnson Farms produce, browsing the crafters' fares, and ordering dinner from one of our many food vendors.

Earlier, I'd even hauled Jordan over to the Ramsey's food truck to buy her a basket of fried shrimp—her first—and held one up to her lips. She hesitated, but when she looked up at me with wide eyes and I told her to trust me, she opened her mouth and took a bite. Her tongue accidentally brushed my finger in the process, and I required a few moments to come down off that high.

Dad hasn't given us his official review but he's walking around here like that crazy, toothy grinning emoticon. So many people showed up that he had to request special permission from the two local churches to utilize their parking spaces.

I close my eyes, inhaling the scent of spicy crab boil, and listen to the happy symphony of voices. We could say our first annual Mingling at the Market is proving more successful than Brice's bribed crowds but that wouldn't be accurate. We didn't just beat him—we creamed him. We wiped the floor with his fake ass. The only minor glitch all day was a frantic mom missing her kid, but that quickly cleared when Jordan dropped everything and joined the search, finding him salivating by the cotton candy and shaved ice trailer.

I hold up my phone, snapping a panoramic photo of the scene. We did it. We pulled off a major hit. She and I made this happen.

Overall, today's been perfect. The vibe, the weather, the entertainment. And her.

She's perfect.

I crane my neck to the left and right, searching the crowd. Jordan wondered off about twenty minutes ago, at one point chatting with the band but then gone again when I found the opportunity to sneak another glimpse.

"Who are you looking for?" Gin sing-songs as she walks beside me.

Always with a bloodhound-sniffing-out-a-trail angle. "No one," I lie, avoiding her prying eyes. "I'm just taking in this awesome turnout."

"It's amazing..." Gin's voice trails off but the air is thick with humidity and her unspoken inferences. I hold my breath, waiting for her to hit me with the rest of it. Like that moment in a terrible storm when the lightning flashes and there's a brief lull before the booming thunder shakes the house. She digs her elbow into my ribs, saying, "You and Jordan are quite the couple."

I deadpan, refusing to take her bait. "Only we're not a couple."

"Maybe not yet." She waggles her eyebrows, a new glint dancing in her eyes.

"I agree with her." CJ walks beside Gin, linking arms with her. A united front. Surprise, surprise.

"When do you not?"

"Come on. When are you going to ask her out already?" CJ

flits her eyelashes and nods eagerly. "I really like her. Much better than... that other one. And you two did look pretty cozy last weekend after you came back in to the party."

"I'm *not* going to ask her out. We're intern partners. It would complicate things." It's not a lie. Jordan and I dating would definitely complicate things, though I wouldn't mind taking the chance if I thought she'd be interested. There's definitely been moments of... something... between us, but for all I know it's just Jordan being nice. And I don't want to misread things. Lord knows I did that with Laurel and that ended in total catastrophe. The fear of repeating that scenario binds my tongue from confessing my growing feelings for Jordan. I just wish it would halt the endless parade of what-ifs in my brain that thrive on fruitless hopes. Jordan is focused on her farm. Not me. "We're just friends," I mumble.

Gin and CJ look at each other, clucking in unison, "Denial!"

The screech of the microphone in the speakers catches everyone's attention and offers me a much-needed reprieve from the girls' goading. The band's lead singer drags a wooden stool closer to it and settles in, clearing his throat. "I want to thank you lovely folks for coming out to support us here tonight and Johnson Farms who provided us with this wonderful venue. How about a round of applause for our co-hosts this evening, Bo Johnson and Jordan Wright?" He lays his instrument in his lap and claps loud in the microphone. It thunders over the crowd. "Jordan, where are you?" He visors his hand over his eyes and searches the sea of faces. I follow his path, hoping to spot the same one he's looking for. He pauses at the left-side center of the stage and smiles, wagging his finger in her direction. "We have a few more songs to play tonight, but this next one goes out especially to Jordan, who is an Appalachian girl herself and whose grandfather is also a banjo picker like me. I hope this gives you a little piece of home on this Lowcountry evening."

I side-step a few feet and catch sight of her through a small gap in the audience. Jordan presses her fingers to her lips then sends a kiss flying through midair toward the band. The drummer counts them off, and as the first peals from the banjo and guitar harmonize in the evening air, Jordan closes her eyes, swaying back and forth to the rhythm while keeping the beat by tapping her hand against her leg. A breeze floats in off the marsh and lifts a few tendrils of her hair, making them dance in perfect sync. Lightning bugs spark around her—little flashes of light— silhouetting her form against the dusk. The pink tank top accentuates her curves as she moves, flowing like waves over her body, and her cut-off jean shorts kiss the top of her thighs, exposing an expanse of tan skin that stretches down for what seems like miles to her bare feet. Jordan's always been pretty, but tonight, lost in herself and the music, a new softness shines through the tough exterior.

And it's beautiful.

"Bo?"

I snap out of my own thoughts and turn to look at three pairs of eyes glowering in my direction. "What?"

"What do you mean what?" Gin demands, hands on her hips. "Go ask her to dance. You know you want to."

I shake my head. "I don't dance. It's not my thing."

"It's not that hard." CJ says, patting the underside of my chin. "But I think you might find it easier to do if you pick your jaw up off the ground first."

Jett, who's snuck up behind me, reaches around and swipes his finger across my lips. "Or at least clean up the puddle of drool."

The three of them crack up and share conspiratorial grins. A group of comedians, I see. "She seems to be enjoying it without me."

"If you don't move fast, she's about to be enjoying it with *him*." Gin points to the far edge of the field where a guy about our age is marching toward the stage, eyes fixed on Jordan. Gin shoves me and I stumble forward on my boots. "Get the lead out already!"

Flames lick my belly. Over my dead body. Who does this guy think he is? She's way out of his league, and Jordan would never dance with him. Would she?

I dart toward the stage, pretending not to hear Gin's squeals echoing behind me, and keep my eyes on the approaching guy, who's maneuvering through the camp chairs, target locked. Not today you don't, random dude. I quicken my pace, my feet barely making contact with the grass, and cut him off at the pass. He glares at me as I take the lead and stop just inches behind her, trying desperately to catch my breath and not huff and puff all over her like a perv.

She hears me anyway and glances over her shoulder, a huge smile spreading her lips. "Hey Bo!"

I will never understand how I am able to elicit that sort of response from someone like her.

"Hey," I stutter, still trying to tame my heavy breathing while also managing to get enough oxygen to my brain to ensure it can come up with some non-idiotic conversation. "This is a great song."

Awkward.

She nods. "One of my favorites."

Oh God. Why is this so hard? My tongue feels like a hundred-pound dumbbell. *Just do it*, I scream inside my own head.

"Um... would you... maybe... like to dance?" My voice shakes, breaking and cracking like a middle schooler.

Jordan's mouth drops open and she leans back as if I've just delivered shocking news. "You dance?"

"No, not usually, but I'm making an exception tonight."

"Well, if you're making an exception for me, then how could I say no? I'd love to."

She takes my outstretched hand and twirls herself into my

arms and then out again. Panic floods through me. I don't know any steps. What do I do next?

Jordan giggles and steps in, capturing my other hand, and waves my arms around. "Don't worry. There aren't any specific moves. Just let yourself loose and feel the music. Let it become like a second pulse to take you where it will." She sways back and forth a few times then spins around, pressing her back into my chest. She leans over her shoulder and whispers, "Just have fun."

I can do that, no problem. Just having my hands on her skin, the humidity thick around us, has already launched me somewhere up in the troposphere. I press myself against her, taking cues from her movement, the friction between us a steady fire. She throws her head back, laughing, eyes closed and the widest grin spreading her lips. Pure joy. I grab her hand, spin her out and back into me. She rolls her shoulders, fluidly as if waltzing on the sound waves themselves, as she sings along, her alto voice blending with the music. She circles me, lost in the tune, while I cling to her and wait impatiently for the sweet moments when she spins a little faster and her tank top flails out just enough to give me a peek of her tanned stomach.

As the last notes echo and the crowd claps, she begins to slip her hand from mine. Immediately feeling the loss, the emptiness in my palm, I clamp down, catching her fingers in my grip. She turns, her eyes fixing on mine then traveling down to our joined hands and back again.

"Care to make it two?" Everything hinges on the next word from her mouth, like the planet is hanging in a weird state of balance, ready to spin off at any moment, but before she can speak, the band starts again—a slow, folksy tune brimming with acoustic guitar. The kind of song that only feels right when the bodies dancing push out all the discernible space between them.

And she's still holding my hand; she hasn't let go. My heart somersaults in my chest.

The edges of her mouth turn up in the slightest way as she steps closer, directing my arms to her waist. A protest swells inside when she moves her fingers from mine but dissipates when she loops both arms around my neck. Oh yeah, this is much better.

The waning slivers of sunlight fading on the horizon lay our shadows on the ground beside us, long and lean and so close they appear as one. My other hand finds her hip and tugs her to me as the tempo builds in the first words streaming through the speakers. She responds, deepening her embrace, leaning into me, her chest pressed to mine. Our lips hover mere centimeters apart, but neither of us closes the gap.

Are we afraid to open up to each other? Reluctant to cross those boundaries established by the internship? Scared to trust? I don't know, but at this moment I hate all of those reasons that keep my lips from touching hers.

The crowd noise fades, the faces and bodies surrounding us assimilating into the background, and it becomes the two of us —me and Jordan—alone in the field. The breeze kicks up again, lifting her hair around us like a curtain, the peachy scent of her shampoo perfuming the air. I close my eyes and inhale, breathing her in.

She slides her cheek beside mine, skin to skin, and her breath, now just a bit ragged, tickles against my collarbone, shooting chills down my spine and awakening every part of me. I wallow in the sensation as Jordan runs her fingers up my neck, twining them in my curls, the intimate touching setting off explosions in even the remotest parts of my body. I slide my hands to her back, dipping my fingertips under the edge of her flowy tank top, tracing circles onto her silken skin, moist from the humidity. A small sigh escapes her lips as her back arches ever so slightly. I gasp at the visceral response rocketing through me, the one encouraging me to hug her tighter, pull her closer. Not close enough.

We fit together, every crest and valley, and as the music trills over a few bass notes, so do we, swaying in unison, and I pray that every verse lasts longer than the one before. That they never stop.

With one hand still tangled in my curls, Jordan trails her other fingers down the side of my neck, the urgent thumping of my pulse rising up to meet her touch. She pauses there a moment then uses her nails to trace my jawline, to the chin and back again, sometimes extending beyond and letting them whisper against my cheek.

As the chorus rises, so does my courage. I want to know the taste of her lip gloss. I need to know it. To know her. I tilt my head, letting the weight of it meet her palm, and lick my lips. I'm going to do it. I'm going to kiss—

"Can I cut in?"

The crowd comes back in a flash, loud and intruding. Jordan backpedals out of my arms, a rush of hot air slicing us apart like a knife, though our fingers remain interlaced. My eyes spring open and I look down at the violent tugging coming from my hip.

The little boy Jordan helped earlier stands at my feet, finger looped in my pocket, yanking hard.

"I'm sorry to interrupt, but he wouldn't take no for an answer," his mom says with a gentle laugh. "I think he's developed a little crush."

Really kid? I force a smile at him then look over at Jordan. She glances up at me with a half-hearted grin. A sadness lingers in her eyes, and down deep I hope she's missing the feel of me against her the same way I am.

"What d'you say?" she asks.

I know what the devil on my shoulder wants me to say. Hell no, kid. Get lost. But then there's the fact that this little dude has some serious gumption, not to mention really good taste in women. What else can I say except, "Have fun."

I barely step aside before the kid jumps in my place, arms circling Jordan's waist. As I turn to leave, she keeps hold of my hand and gives it a little shake. I glance over my shoulder at her, strawberry lips spread in a smile, and she mouths, "Thank you for the dance."

I nod and trudge back to my friends.

Jett waits, rubbing his hands together, the warm-up to a serious barrage of taunts headed my way. "Cockblocked by an eight-year-old? Have I taught you nothing?" CJ jabs him in the ribs but he ignores it, coming back with round two. "Dude, this just isn't your summer. First, Laurel ditches you for her long-time boyfriend and now Jordan dumps you for an... ahem... younger man."

It's awesome to have a best friend who's a world-class smart-tass. I cock an eyebrow but can't muster any good comebacks. I'm a deflated balloon. Thankfully, CJ intercedes, threading her arm through Jett's, and yanks him toward the food truck. "Quit being a jerk and get us something to eat."

I follow behind, stealing glances at Jordan whose attention is still being commandeered by the kid and his endless twirling.

"Hey..." Gin jogs beside me and nudges me with her shoulder. "I'm sorry about that."

"About what?" It's best to play dumb. I'll never admit anything.

"The interruption. You two seemed pretty zoned out from everything except each other." She crinkles her nose. "In fact, I could've sworn you were about to—"

I pin her with a hard stare. She purses her lips and shrugs. "I could be wrong, though." She darts ahead of me, mumbling under her breath, "But I'm not."

As Gin trots past the vendor tables, my eyes fix on a sunflower sea glass necklace—the same one Jordan was admiring before the kid went missing and we had to initiate the search party. I recall the flower's meanings that were listed on the sales placard: Adoration. Loyalty. Unconditional love. A bloom that thrives in the sun and radiates its warmth out to everyone else. Textbook Jordan. Her face lit up when she'd looked at it— nothing expensive, just meaningful, and she deserves something to make her happy. And the necklace would have the best home, nestled there beside her heart.

"Bo! You coming?" Jett waves from the food truck parked at the field's edge as CJ bites into a crispy fried shrimp.

"I'll be right there," I yell back. "Gimme a sec."

I slide the necklace from the display model and hand it to the crafter. "Yes ma'am. I'll take this, please. And could you put it in one of your gift bags?"

CHAPTER 16

Jordan

The thundering roar of tires-meet-asphalt pounds in my ears and a stench of burning rubber swirls around us.

Last week while they were in town, Jett asked Bo to work the pits on his race, and CJ begged me to accompany him. I couldn't turn down the opportunity to experience the excitement of the track... or get some time away with Bo.

CJ and I amble toward the track, sharing popcorn from a red-and-white striped bag, as she fills me in on the particulars of competitive racing. She leans close to my ear, yelling above the noise. "So, is this your first race ever?"

"Yeah, and I didn't expect it to be so loud... or dusty," I holler back, waving my hand in front of my face to disperse the reddish-brown cloud hanging in the air.

"You'll get used to it." She laughs and reaches for another handful, her eyes landing on my new jewelry. She nods toward the chain around my neck. "I love your necklace!"

My fingers find the sunflower and lift it up, allowing the light to filter through the sea glass, giving it a hazy glow. "It's beautiful, isn't it?"

"Definitely. Did you buy it from one of the vendors at the market last week?"

"Actually, someone bought it for me."

"Oh yeah?" She purses her lips, eyes glistening. For a moment, her shared DNA with Miss Bessie dances across her features. "Someone *special?*"

I shrug. "The card wasn't signed."

After the concert ended, I found the necklace, nestled in tissue paper in a small gift bag, sitting on the seat of my Jeep—no card, no message attached. That's when I'd remembered I'd been looking at the necklace when the lady beside me started hollering for her lost son. After I'd found him, she begged me to tell her a way she could repay me, but I'd just smiled, unable to find the words to tell her that as a mother, too, the mere thought of losing a child wrecked me.

"I think it's probably from Caleb, though," I add.

CJ scrunches her nose. "Who?"

"He's the little boy who got lost. I helped find him."

She snaps her fingers in the air, the corners of her eyes relaxing again. "Oh, the kid who cut in on you and Bo!"

Her words pulverize the wall holding back the flood of memories from last weekend—the wall I'd kept intact all week. They rush in instantly, threatening to drown me. Caleb totally cut in—and just when I thought Bo was about to make a move. Kiss me, even. He'd tilted his head and leaned in so close the musk of his cologne had wrapped around me like invisible fingers pulling my body toward his. And I was ready.

Willing.

My heart somersaults, my breath hitching in my throat. Am I falling for Bo? Like *really* falling?

I can't. I shouldn't. And how would it even work anyway? He's my intern partner. I came down this summer looking for money, not love. To top it off, the end of the summer will put 400 miles between us. The reasons why this is all a terrible idea stack up like bricks in a brand-new wall, one my heart promptly dropkicks to the ground.

But it's been a week—seven days of nothing except a

hundred acres of ankle-deep plowed dirt, ten million bushels of corn pulled from the stalks, and five hundred million mosquito bites between the two of us. But not one kiss. Not one inkling of a would-be kiss. Not one comment about that night. Not one indication that what I thought was happening was actually happening anywhere except inside my own head.

Did I imagine it?

Between the racing thoughts and the revving engines on the track, my head spins, a weird disconnected feeling gripping my body. My heart skips, my cheeks flushing.

I shove the bag of popcorn into CJ's hands and motion toward the concrete building at the edge of the field. "I need to stop by the restroom. I'll catch up to you, okay?" She nods and stalks off to the stands, so I duck inside and trudge to the sinks lining the farthest wall, the one shared with the male restrooms next door. A middle-age lady rubs her hands together underneath the dryer, looking up at me with a smile, then swipes them down the front of her jeans, tucks her purse underneath her arm, and heads outside.

I twist the faucet's knob, cup my hands beneath the cold-water stream, then splash my face. The reflection in the mirror stares back at me, rosy-cheeked and dewy. So what if the whole concept of me and Bo doesn't make sense? Who cares if it's not what we had planned? He's unlike any guy I've ever known before, so good, so genuine. And if he's in—if there's any possibility he wants to see how this could progress—then so am I.

Now, I just need to find out if he wants the same things I do. It's been a week, true, but tonight could change everything. Tonight, after the race, it'll be the two of us—alone—and if anything needs to be said—or finished—then it'll be the perfect time.

I grab a paper towel from the wall dispenser, blotting my face, when a door squeaks on the other side of the wall. A metal grate between the two spaces allows the sound of voices to spill over.

"Who's that incredibly *fi-i-ine* woman that came with y'all tonight?" the first voice asks. His thick drawl spreads out like cold honey as he adds several syllables into the word "fine."

"Who?"

The first voice I didn't recognize, but the second one I do. I'd know it anywhere. Bo. I stand closer underneath the grate, straining to eavesdrop without missing a word.

"The new girl. The one in that strappy black tank top and those cutoffs." I stare down at myself. Oh my God, they're talking about me. The guy whistles and says, "She's got the curvy backroads I'd take a drive on any day!"

I grimace. Gross.

The gurgle of running water skews the next words but quiets just in time for me to hear, "She wouldn't be your type."

The first guy laughs and clicks his tongue. "I don't have a type. I love them all."

Oh, I bet he does. Question is, do they love him or are they all disgusted as I am hearing him spew his egotistical spiel? Chauvinistic jerk.

"Exactly why she's not your type, Jace."

"Uh oh, do I detect a little jealousy? You already planted that flag on Mt. St. Hottie?"

A fire broils in my gut. What did he just call me? Still... he poses an interesting question. One I want to hear Bo's answer to. Is he jealous? Interested?

"You're disgusting." Bo pushes out a hard sigh. "And no, I haven't and I don't intend to."

Wait... what? My heart drops to my toes. He doesn't intend to?

"So you're saying there's nothing going on between the two of you?"

I push up on my tip-toes, turning my ear to the grate, desperately trying not to miss a single word.

"That's what I'm saying."

"No flirting? No touchy-touch?"

"Nada."

"And you have no interest in her?"

"Nope. We work at the farm together. That's it."

All sensations in my body halt on cue as a weird numbness filters through. I had just imagined it, cooked it all up in my head. Wanted to see things that didn't really exist. But if that's so, how come everyone seems so hell-bent on seeing us together? Gin never hides her agenda, and Jett and CJ love poking fun at Bo whenever I'm around. Hell, even Claire has glanced back and forth between us with that goofy, full-tooth smile.

"Liar!" Jace yells. "I saw how y'all were hanging on each other earlier. Look me in the eye and say that."

"Third-degree, much?" Bo's voice takes on a razor-sharp edge as heavy footsteps stomp across the adjacent bathroom's tiles. The wooden door squeaks open and a sudden quiet infiltrates the space. Shit! They've gone outside. I run to the door and pry it open a sliver, and when two figures walk past on the sidewalk, I slink further behind the door, watching them through the crack. Bo stops, turning on his heels, and holds up a hand, his fingers shaped into a circle. "I have zero desire to get with Jordan. Happy?"

"Okay, geez. I get it. She doesn't... um..." Jace circles his hand in front of him as if trying to come up with the right words. "... float the boat?"

"Something like that." Bo smirks and trudges away, Jace following in line.

I ease the door shut and lean against it for support, swallowing down the knot in my throat.

He's not interested. Once again, I've managed to delude myself, falling for a guy who couldn't fathom being with me.

Bo's words ring some sickeningly familiar alarm bells in my head. I'd once overheard Weston's father telling some blonde girl in Daisy Dukes at the county fair that there was "zero going on" between us before he asked for her number with a wink. He insisted that I was a starry-eyed girl with a stupid crush, content to follow him around like a helpless puppy.

That was when I was three months pregnant and until that very moment had been entertaining dreams that we were somehow going to make everything work because... love. Only it wasn't love. At least not on his part. Just manipulation and lies to get what he wanted... until it got him everything he didn't want.

It was only two weeks later that he frankly relayed to me that the baby was my fault and my doing and that he wasn't about to be tied down when he had so many wild oats left to sow. *I'm sorry if you thought there was something more or that I was interested in long-term. I'm not.* That's what he said before jumping in his Chevy and heading out of town and into the wind.

Hopefully even an F-5 tornado won't blow that jerk back into our lives—ever.

I swore that day never to allow myself to repeat the past. Never believe in foolish things like love or relationships. Never to let my heart lead me like a mindless idiot to the very things that would cut me again and again.

My heart shatters like glass, each shard tearing into my flesh, ripping through from the inside out. I'm here. Again.

After the race ends, Jett, CJ, Bo, and I sit together on the brick wall at the edge of the field to watch the fireworks show. I glance up at them occasionally to issue a fake grin or an obligatory "yeah, sure" to whatever conversation is in progress, but my chest and back physically ache, as if Bo's words had been knives driven through my very core. And now, sitting here beside him—our thighs touching, arms grazing—is salt sprinkled on the open wounds. Pure torture. Every now and then, CJ shoots me a sympathetic smile and cocks her head, non-verbally asking if I'm okay. When it had taken me another thirty minutes to pull myself off that bathroom wall and squelch my trembling nerves,

I needed to concoct some reason for my extended absence, so monthly cramps it was. She never even questioned it, just asked if I needed an ibuprofen, which I gladly took for the headache sprouting in my brain.

Bo groans and whisper-yells to Jett, "What's he doing here?"

Jett lifts his eyes to the field's gated entrance and shrugs. I follow his gaze to a tall, blonde guy in skin-tight jeans and a black muscle shirt walking in our direction. His trucker cap sits low on his forehead, sprouts of curls smooshing out around the edges. Jace. The guy from the bathroom.

Bo nudges me with his elbow. "Don't talk to this guy. He'll hit on you."

His words take a minute to register. Is he telling me who I can and can't talk to after blatantly denouncing any interest in me earlier? What is this? An order? Because I don't take orders.

The first fireworks snake up to the sky with a red streak that bursts into a million rubies against the inky darkness. And with it, my aching hurt gains new teeth.

Jace saunters up and leans against the brick wall, propping one elbow on top. His eyes sweep down and then back up the length of my body. "Hey there, gorgeous. I'm Jace. Are you new in town?" His top lip curls like some Elvis-wannabe, and his breath stinks like a vile mix of bologna and old cigarettes. But hey, Bo's eyes are bulging from their sockets, so why not? He has zero interest in me, if I'm remembering correctly, so it shouldn't be an issue. And I'm happy to test that theory.

I flip my hair over my shoulder, the ends swishing against Bo's nose, and bat my eyelashes, barely getting through it without cracking a smile. "At the coast for the summer."

He wiggles his eyebrows up and down, a devilish grin broaching his face. "Aren't I lucky?"

What a cocky skeeze. I swallow down the rampant bile hurtling up my esophagus and try on my slinkiest, naughtiest voice. "I don't know. How lucky do you feel?"

Did that really just come out of my mouth? Has the world

gone full tilt or has Bo's confessions just knocked me for a loop? I've never been Vindictive Jordan and now, I understand why. Still, I'm the one who just kicked this boulder down the hill and now I'm going to have to hang on for dear life and ride it all the way to the finish.

"More confident with every passing minute."

I laugh and glance over my shoulder at Bo, who pins me with a hard, firm glare. His eyes bug out so much, I'm pretty sure I could send them flying right out of his head with one good slap to the back. Interesting. I guess the name of this game is the age-old I-can't-commit-but-I-don't-want-anyone-else-having-her-either. I never pegged him for that sort. What we had—what I thought we had—it'd felt so real.

For me it still does.

When Bo jabs another elbow into my ribs, I slit my eyes, fixing them on him. "What?"

No response, but his mouth nearly scrapes his shoes.

Jace jumps up onto the wall and loops his arm around my shoulder, redirecting my attention to him. I hold my breath to avoid his bologna-stench. "I haven't had a decent meal all day. When this is over, would you like to get a bite?"

Bo leans forward and throws his arm over me like a seatbelt. "We have to leave early in the morning."

I gently lift his arm and place it back on his own lap, now returning his glare. "We do have to get up early, but I have a couple hours free tonight."

Our eyes lock, neither of us blinking, the intensity building like a pressure cooker. *Say it, Bo. Say that everything I overheard was some epic lie. Say that the jealousy is eating you up at this very moment. Say that you want me to stay here with you. Say anything. Please.*

But he sighs and drops his eyes without a word. My heart sinks even lower. The bright bursts overhead splash Bo's face with greens, blues, reds, and golds, the thundering explosions like all bubbles of hope popping one by one in my chest. I can't believe I let myself start falling for him. I can't believe I'd started entertaining what-ifs with him.

After the finale, Jace hops down from the wall and then holds out his arms for me. I lean forward into them as he helps me down to my feet.

"Ready?" he asks with a wink and nods toward the parking lot. My throat tightens, possibly in an effort to control the increasing desire to vomit on his shoes.

I hold up my finger. "Go ahead. I'll be right there." As he saunters into the darkness toward the parked cars, I look back at Bo, still perched on the wall and staring out over the empty field.

"Hey," I say, softly punching his thigh. "Do you have the other room key?"

"It's in the Bronco," he says, not looking in my direction.

CJ and Jett stand a few feet away, horribly concealing the fact they're watching us with eagle eyes.

"Well, can you get it?" I step to the other side of him, ducking into his line of vision, and point to where he's parked on the far edge of the lot. "We'd like to head out."

Bo rolls his eyes and slides off the wall then stomps ahead of me. His voice peppers the night air but the words are indiscernible. I jog beside him, having to maintain a quick pace to keep up.

"What did you say?"

"I said why are you going out with him?" His voice has no inflection, his jaw chiseled like stone.

I dart in front of him and stop. He nearly plows into me, his feet kicking up a cloud of dust as they halt in the coastal sand. We stand-off, nose to nose, our chests heaving with labored breaths.

"Why not?" I ask, holding his gaze. "He asked. I'm single, right?"

Bo snorts and blinks in triple time. "If that's the case, then have a great time with Jace." He steps around me and swings open the Bronco's door then leans in across the seat, plucking the extra room key from the glovebox. He holds it in the air between us, the moonlight glinting off the metallic logo on the card, and smirks. "Your key to freedom, should you choose to accept it."

"Give me one good reason not to." There it is. The challenge. The tipping point.

Just as Bo opens his mouth, a jacked-up truck rolls up beside us and honks three times. Jace leans out the window. "Come on! Let's go already!"

I side-eye him and then look back at Bo, who reaches for my hand. My heart skips a beat. He does want me. He wants me to stay with him. He—

He presses the key into my palm, closes my fingers around it, and with a nod, turns and walks away.

Twenty minutes later, we sit across from each other in a back booth in a greasy spoon with a dead fly smashed on the window and a half-eaten waffle on the floor. The waitress with too much makeup and too little hygiene steps up to the table with a pad and pen in hand. Her gum smacks in a constant rhythm. "What'd'ya have?"

None of the options on the laminated page look appetizing despite the half-hearted attempts of fine photography of beef burgers on seeded buns. A grilled chicken option on the menu under "Other Plates" appears to be the safest option.

"I'll have the gr—"

"I'll order for both of us." He pauses and smiles across the table. "Trust me. I know what you'll like."

Doubtful. Truly doubtful.

"She'll have a burger, all the fixins, extra fries. Same as me."

I drop my eyes to the clenched fists in my lap. Bo would never have assumed to know my appetite. Bo would never have shot leering glances at the twice-our-age waitress and then checked out his own reflection in the metal napkin holder. Bo would never—

Bo would never want me.

Even when I want him.

He said so himself.

I clench my jaw, grinding my back teeth, and look across the table at Jace. I've spent the last three years of my life avoiding guys like this, yet here I am in some backwoods diner booth, trying to pretend I have the least bit interest in his latest bench press record or whatever he's currently babbling about. I voluntarily left with this guy—the exact sort of loser I loathe—just to piss off and prove wrong the exact type of guy I do want. Whenever my brain would like to quit sending me down these stupid rabbit holes, I'd be good to go.

Jace drones on while guzzling sweet tea and stuffing fries in his face. The thick gold chain around his neck, his boasting, or the mushed-up potato churning in his mouth as he talks—not sure which one is instigating the gag reflex more. I stare at my frowning reflection in the plate glass window. I'm here because Bo has zero interest in me as anything except an intern partner, and I wanted to make him pay for that comment by going out with this freak. But he didn't recant his statement, didn't beg me to stay. Nope. He handed me my key to freedom and walked away without looking back. Right now, he's probably already tucked in and asleep back at the motel while I'm the one on this date from hell.

Three years without a loser. Time to correct that record. Days since last incidence: zero.

CHAPTER 17

Bo

I put the key in her hand. I reminded her she had a choice. And she chose.

She chose him.

She chose wrong.

I couldn't watch her get in his truck. That sight would've been a stake to my heart. I did, however, sneak a peek at their taillights disappearing on the dark highway, two burning embers that fizzled to nothing in the night. After that, walking laps around the empty field on the far end of the track seemed like the best idea. A half-hour later, I trudge back to my Bronco and slide into the driver seat, staring at her empty space.

It'd been so natural with her riding shotgun, her hair flying in the breeze, her nonstop singing along with the radio. It was like she was made for that seat, how seamlessly her body curved into the leather, how her pink painted toes drummed against my dash.

I want her and her toes back where they belong.

I pull onto the main two-lane highway, heading in the same direction they'd taken earlier. A part of me wants to track them down, punch him square in his face, and carry Jordan back to her rightful place. But I won't because she chose to go with him. Why, I don't know, but my heart is slivered.

Instead, a few miles up the road, I make a right under the flashing marquis of the motel where we're staying and prepare myself for the long night ahead. Alone.

CHAPTER 18

Jordan

My eyes flutter open to a dark room. Bo and I got back into town earlier in the day, and I'd immediately retreated to the guesthouse, dropped my bag by the door, turned on the TV, and crashed on the couch. For hours, apparently. I raise up and stare out the living room windows at the star-filled night. Yep, definitely a classic Jordan stress response.

No wonder. There's nothing quite as awkward or exhausting as a long car ride with someone where the conversation is kept intentionally shallow. Like holding your breath and walking across landmines on the brink of explosion.

Especially grueling after a long night of insomnia.

I drag myself off the couch and plod to the bathroom, then switch on the tub faucet and toss in a bath bomb. In the mirror, a reflection of myself, mascara smeared and face red and splotchy, catches my attention. Ugh. No surprise this hot mess doesn't appeal to Bo.

My breath catches. Bo...

He was asleep in his bed by the time I returned to the room last night. Peacefully snoozing like he hadn't a care in the world. Like he wasn't bothered in the least by my being out with Jace.

Obviously, he means what he said: he's my friend and nothing more.

But while he dozed in that dingy motel room, sleep had eluded me. I pulled back the covers and lay stomach-down on my bed, staring at the back of Bo's head. At all the spiraled curls I'd fantasized running my fingers through. But friends don't do that sort of thing.

By the time his alarm rang a few hours later, I was fully dressed and packed, sitting in the arm chair by the door. He sat up straight in his bed, wiping the sleep from his eyes, and stared over at me with only a mumbled *good morning*.

The vapors from the lavender and melatonin bath bomb float in the bathroom's moist air, drawing me back to the present. I kneel beside the tub, dragging my fingers over the water's surface to check the temperature and help disperse the fizzing crystals. After the last 24 hours, something is needed to relax me and possibly render me unconscious until morning. Either will work but both would be appreciated.

I step into the tub and sink down, the warm water embracing me like a hug and promising to purge my brain of all the haunting thoughts while I fight the very real desire to submerge myself in the depths.

This is probably all for the best. I think that's the sort of positive self-talk I'm supposed to indulge in, given the situation. Besides, any relationship that could've formed between us would be destined to fail anyway. I have a kid that he doesn't know about. And responsibilities. And a home 400 miles away from here. Away from him.

Oh God, there are so many reasons for him to walk away from me.

I sigh. But for now, we still have to work together. I still need this grant money. This opportunity. And this is exactly why I told Mama at the beginning of summer that relationships were a no-go. Why did I let my guard down? Why didn't I maintain that rigid resolve to start and end summer the way I've always been—alone?

Just as the thoughts cycloning in my head reach a fever pitch, my phone buzzes on the decorative rattan bench beside the soaker tub. I pick it up. One new message from Mama. No doubt she feels her ears burning all the way up in the mountains and somehow taps into my nervous breakdown.

<Mama> *Feeling any better, Sassy?*

Yeah. That'd be a no.

When I'd called her earlier from Bo's Bronco while he was checking out of the motel room, there'd been just enough time to fill her in on the major details and glean one snippet of advice: just talk to him. Advice which I promptly ignored, refusing to discuss anything remotely related to Jace or the overheard conversation. What could be more humiliating than having heard Bo tell Jace he had zero interest in me? Oh I know— hearing him repeat that to my face. Ripping my fingernails out one by one would've proven a vacation, comparatively speaking.

But that's not what Mama wants—or needs—to hear. She has enough on her plate without worrying about my useless whining.

<Me> *Getting there.*

<Mama> *What does that mean? You talked to Bo?*

OMG, drop it already, Mama.

<Me> *No, that means I'm NOT going to talk to Bo. I'm soaking in a hot bath.*

<Mama> *Nice, though I don't think you're going to really feel better until you talk to him.*

<Me> *About what, Mama? About how I misread something as innocent as a dance? About how I eavesdropped on him saying he wasn't interested?*

Excuse me, zero interest. ZERO.

<Mama> *Knock it off. I mean, anyone could see how that'd trigger you.*

<Me> *I'm already living with one shrink down here. Please don't start too.*

The thought of Claire getting hold of this little fiasco? She'd be like a Labrador with a squeaky toy, and I'd be the shredded-up stuffed carcass leftover after the melee.

<Mama> *I just want you to be okay.*

My bottom lip trembles, and I clamp down on it, holding everything in. One thing as certain as Grandpa's love of bacon is Mama's love for me. I sniff my runny nose and tap out a reassurance.

<Me> *I am okay. I'm just going back to my original plan—get in, get what I need from this internship, get out, and get home where I belong.*

<Mama> *I know what you need. And so do you.*

And just like that, my guard is down and wham! She's back for Round Two.

<Me> *Stop! Give Weston a kiss for me. I'll talk to you tomorrow.*

<Mama> *Okay, goodnight. Call me if you need me. And oh yeah... TALK TO BO! Okay, done. Goodnight. Love you.*

<Me> *Love you.*

I lay back against the tub, letting the rolled edge cradle the curvature of my neck then tap on my phone's photo gallery, a slew of colorful photos populating the screen. I thumb down to those listed at the beginning of May and stare at the photo of Mama and Weston I took before pulling out of the drive. They are my reason and motivation. They need me to cut my crap and pull this off. But as I scroll up, another image catches my eye. A selfie of me and Bo in his Bronco on the farm, goofing off. Bo's eyes are crossed and stuck-out tongue folded into a taco. I'm laughing... and staring straight at him with some moony expression.

Mama told me before I left that Weston wanted his mama to be happy, and Lord knows that cute kid makes me happy. I stare again at the photo of Bo. But this guy makes me happy too. And what an awesome life it could be if both of them were major players in my future. If they—

No.

I can't think like that. Magical thoughts. Wishful daydreams about nearly impossible feats. Guys like Bo don't want girls like me. Girls with a past, with baggage. Girls who would ask so much more than they might be able to give in return. It's better this way, that nothing ever started, that nothing ever transpired. I got sidetracked and misled, and Bo wasn't aware of my growing feelings for him until the night of the fair. That dance triggered something in both of us—two very different somethings apparently.

I fell headfirst into one of Gin's romance novel scenes, and Bo... he discovered his running shoes. Classic pulling away. Trying to let me down easy.

I fiddle with my sea-glass sunflower necklace, turning it over in my fingers and allowing the light from the hanging chandelier to warm the colors. The magic of that night at the festival filters back to mind—the trill of the banjo, the tangy aroma of cocktail sauce on fried shrimp, the softness of his hand around my waist. I'd traced his jawline, ran my fingers in the stubble along his chin. For a moment, I thought he was going to kiss me. His head was tilted, eyes closed. He moved closer.

Hadn't he?

My mind spins. Did he do those things or did I imagine them? I mean, it has been a hot minute since there's been a guy in my life. Maybe I'd only been seeing what I wanted to see. Pretending he cared about me as more than a friend. Pretending the same way I always did about some mystical father figure waiting on me in the void. Pretending. Lying to myself.

I toss the phone onto the stool and grab my towel. So much for a nice, relaxing bath. My incessant over-thinking is drowning me. I slip into my robe and twist my hair into a bun as I head toward the bedroom, but three hard knocks on the door stop me in my tracks.

I glance at my phone. Nearly 11 p.m. Who in the world could it be at this hour? Before I can even peek out the window, another three knocks pound on my door.

"Jordan! Open up!"

Her voice is firm, hard-edged. So not a normal happy-go-lucky Gin tone. I dart toward the door and swing it open. "Hey. It's late. Is everything okay?"

"Not really. Can I come in?" She ticks her head to the side, eyes focused over my shoulder.

"I was just heading to bed, but I have a few minutes."

I step back and she pushes past me, marching straight to the couch. "I won't stay long. Promise."

I take a seat in the armchair opposite her, trying without success to catch her gaze. She gnaws her lip and stares at the ground.

"So... what is it?"

"It's you and Bo." She pushes out a loud breath and lifts her head, finally connecting with my stare. Her eyes are a little slitted, a little judgmental. "Okay, maybe more you than Bo."

She slaps me across the face without ever raising a hand. I figured she'd be irritated by our messing up her obvious desire to witness some sort of romance between us but geez. And why am I the one taking all this heat? My hackles rise.

"I'm not sure I understand what you're getting at."

"I heard everything was fine at the race track and then you got all—I don't know—weird."

Weird? "Bo said I was weird?"

"No. Bo won't talk about it." She slumps back on the couch cushions, crossing her arms over her chest. "CJ told me that you seemed to be having a great time and then everything suddenly changed. And then you left with Jace?" Her nose crinkles as she pronounces the "J" in Jace's name.

I shrug, getting up and walking to the kitchen for a glass of water. "He wanted to go grab a bite from a local diner. A girl has to eat, right?"

Her grunt echoes behind me, followed by a rustling and then the thumps of heavy footsteps.

"And going with him seems like something you'd normally

do?" When I don't turn around, Gin grabs my elbow and spins me to face her. Her wide eyes pin me with the million questions running through her head. Questions for which I have no good answers. She knifes her hand in the air between us. "Okay, let's completely forget that you obviously lost your mind and went out with him. The question is why. *Why* did you go out with Jace?"

I've been asking myself the same damn question since last night, so I'm not sure what to say. Because Bo hurt my feelings? Because I fell for Bo and he didn't reciprocate? Because punishing myself seemed like a better option? I take a long swig and set the glass on the counter by the sink. "He seemed nice."

She deadpans. "No, he doesn't. Jace is a smooth-talker and you know it. Just like you spotted Brice at ten paces. What gives?"

"Nothing! He took me out for a burger. I can't help it if *someone* got mad about it." Oops. Maybe a little too much attitude crept out in that "someone" reference. I can only hope Gin didn't—

"Oh, so that's it." Gin's radar is infallible. Of course she caught it. "You decided to make Bo jealous. But why?"

"You sound like a redundant two-year-old with a million questions. Why, why, why." I laugh under my breath. She has no idea how on-point my observation is. I know all about a toddler's unrelenting wonder.

"It's a valid question. You can tell me or I can go and try asking Bo again." She taps her foot, a countdown to spill the tea or else. When I hesitate, she throws her hands on her hips, turns on her heels, and stomps toward the door, calling over her shoulder, "Okay, here I go..."

Oh my gosh, this girl is maddening! I catch up to her just as her hand grips the knob. "Wait. Come here." She glances over her shoulder and drops her hand but doesn't turn around. I sigh. "You're right. Jace is a total tool and I would normally steer clear but... I felt I had something to prove. Especially after Bo insulted me."

Gin whirls around, mouth agape. "Wait. Bo insulted you? Why isn't this adding up?"

Ugh. I don't want to rehash this story. It's already run laps in my head all night. "He didn't insult me, like, outright. What he *said* was insulting. Does that make sense?"

Please let it make just enough sense to satisfy her. Please get the hint that I don't want to go there.

"Not really. Concrete examples might help."

Crap. This girl can pick up on every inflection in a chat, every small expression that even attempts to cross someone's face, but she will flat-out ignore them when it doesn't serve her purpose. I hope she'll contemplate pursuing a career with the FBI's behavioral unit or something. She could be a one-woman show, digging up all the evidence and then grilling the criminals until they break.

She rolls her hand in the air, urging me to continue.

"When I was in the bathroom at the race track, I overheard a conversation between Bo and Jace." I stop, stretching out my neck from side to side. Admitting this part out loud is like ripping off the bandages and pouring salt directly in those raw wounds. "Jace was asking about me and Bo said..."

Something rises in my throat. Words or vomit? I cough, willing it to dissipate.

But Gin isn't waiting. "Bo said..." she goads.

"He said I was just some nobody from the farm. That he had zero interest in me and didn't foresee that changing anytime soon." The truth blows out of me in a swoop. I hadn't realized how it'd been gripping me internally, pinching my shoulders up to my ears with tension. The admission gives me some physical peace before the repeated words pierce my heart like a bullet.

Her mouth drops open and she shakes her head. "This doesn't make sense. That is so *not* the way he feels."

"Maybe it is, Gin. He had no clue I was listening, so he had no reason to lie. I think maybe you're just seeing what you want to see instead of what really is." I step forward, grabbing her hand. "You're a romantic at heart and I love you for it, but I think it's time to let this one go."

She stares at me, pensive, then straightens her spine as a new determination steels the blue in her eyes. "You first."

A soft knocking on my door rouses me from sleep. I throw back the covers and sit up, peering through the bedroom's open blinds. Miss Bessie stands on the small porch, hand on her hip, twiddling her fingers as she waits.

Gin last night and Miss Bessie first thing this morning? The universe is determined to not give me a break.

I grab my robe, pulling my arms through, and shuffle to the door. When I open it, the flat expression on her face morphs into a wide smile.

"Jordan!" Her chipper voice rings out as she trails her eyes up and down my body. "I hope I didn't wake you."

"Oh no," I lie, tugging my robe together against my chest. "Just getting ready for a lazy Sunday."

"Since you don't have any plans, why don't you come over and have breakfast with me?" She thumbs over her shoulder toward her house. "I made a big batch of blueberry muffins this morning, and there's more than I could ever eat."

I narrow my eyes. "Breakfast with you and who else?" It's not that Miss Bessie isn't nice enough to invite me over just because. But mere hours after Gin storms over to confront me about the disastrous weekend her partner-in-crime is now standing on my doorstep with muffins? I'd be an idiot not to question it.

"Just me. James is working the morning shift today."

"What about Gin? Did she put you up to this?"

"I haven't seen Gin this morning." She doesn't flinch, doesn't divert her eyes, which in Miss Bessie's world means she talked to her last night instead so technically she's not lying. "Should we invite her?"

"No, I'd rather it just be us. I need a quiet morning."

"Sounds good. Get dressed and come on over." She turns and heads down the steps, waving at me over her shoulder.

Fifteen minutes later, I'm dressed in a tank top and sweat pants with my hair in a messy bun, standing in Miss Bessie's kitchen as she pulls a muffin pan full of steaming goodness from the oven. The sweet aroma with just a touch of spicy cinnamon hangs in the air, and I inhale, closing my eyes to soak it in fully. Grandma always makes fresh pastries on Sunday mornings back home, and these incite a flood of fond memories.

Miss Bessie uses tongs to grab each muffin and transfer them over to a large plastic tray then hands it to me. "Would you put these on the table? I'm going to grab a couple of my puzzle books and pencils. I do like a good crossword with my—"

Ding-dong!

Our eyes lock over the pile of muffins between us. I clutch the tray so hard I'm afraid it will shatter.

"Who's that?" I ask through clenched teeth. If Miss Bessie and Gin have staged some sort of intervention, I swear...

She shrugs with an innocent flutter of eyelashes. "Could be anyone. People stop by here all the time." She ticks her head toward the door. "Do you mind answering that for me, though? I need to grab those books."

I blow out a loud breath and set the tray on the table, mentally steeling myself for the impending storm waiting on the opposite side of Miss Bessie's front door. Probably some half-cocked plan to win Bo's affection. I fell for the cantaloupe ploy the first time. Fool me twice... eh, no.

I pad to the door and swing it wide. "Gin, why did—"

My voice stops working when a pair of blue eyes find mine. Eyes that melt me with one glance.

"Hey, Bo. Go-good morning." I stammer. It's the first time I've seen him since that cringy ride home yesterday, but standing here in the lemony sun rays, in his tattered jeans and t-shirt, he looks better than ever. My heart races.

"Hey. I have some produce for Miss Bessie. Gin asked me to bring it over." Of course she did. Now this whole muffin thing is making more sense. He narrows his eyes. "What are you doing here?"

"Miss Bessie asked me to breakfast."

He nods slowly as if the puzzle pieces are snapping into place for him too. I step back, holding the door open, and motion him in. He walks to the kitchen and sets the crate on the countertop.

Miss Bessie, who's already nabbed her books and slid into her seat as if she'd been sitting there all morning, looks up from her coffee with a sly grin as I take my place at the table. "Bo! I wasn't expecting you today." Before he can respond, she grabs the tray and lifts it up. "Have a muffin. Here, you can sit by Jordan."

He hesitates, his eyes roving between the tray, Miss Bessie, and me, but she just smiles, waving a hand, wafting the smell his way. "Now who could say no to good company *and* good food?" She winks at me as if I'm complicit in this shenanigan.

Mortified, I grab my coffee, taking a slow pull, and slide one of the crossword books in front of me. I open it to a new puzzle and pick up a pencil, concentrating hard on 1 Across.

Interfering unwantedly.

Well, isn't that ironic?

I smirk, and Bo quietly takes the seat next to mine as I scribble in the letters. M-E-D-D-L-I-N-G.

He grabs a muffin from the pile and takes a gigantic bite, half of it disappearing in an instant.

Miss Bessie clears her throat, drumming her fingers on the table. "CJ tells me that you two got to see them this weekend at Jett's race?" She sips her coffee then adds, "How'd it go?"

"Fine," Bo says while cramming the rest of the muffin into his mouth.

"Great," I say, burying my head further into my hand and staring at the next clue.

Bo's chair squeaks across the tile as he slides it back and jumps up, thanking Miss Bessie for the breakfast and telling her he has another large crate to bring in from downstairs. The words are barely out of his mouth before he disappears from the kitchen and out the front door.

Miss Bessie grabs my arm, giving it a shake until I look up at her. "So?" She stares at me, and when I don't immediately respond, she glances to the door from which Bo just exited and then back to me. An obvious hint to her line of questioning, which I conveniently act oblivious to. "What's going on between the two of y'all? Am I detecting—"

"Nothing. We're just friends."

"Sure?"

"One hundred percent."

"So you won't mind if I fix him up... on a date, I mean?" She folds her arms over her chest, a satisfied grin inching up the corners of her mouth. So confident she's going to get a reaction. Not today, Bessie.

"Why should I mind?" I sip my coffee, holding her gaze.

"Okay then." She lays her fork on the table and reaches over to grab her phone from her purse hanging on the opposite chair, then taps the screen. She slides it in front of me. "James's granddaughter is coming into town for a couple days next week, and I need someone to show her around. She's a looker, ain't she?"

I stare down at the screen. Blonde hair, not a strand out of place, professional makeup, and a sparkling tiara. She's the Spring Carnival Queen according to the white satin sash criss-crossing her pink sequined dress. It's all a far cry from my ratty cut-offs, tank top, and messy bun. She looks more like that Laurel girl he dumped anyway—all Miss Prim and Proper—and I can't compete with that.

Not that I'm competing. Hell, I'm not even in the running.

My heart thumps against my ribs, but I swallow the jealousy, keeping my voice steady, leveled. "Very pretty. She and James have the same nose."

"They do favor quite a bit, don't they? I think I will see if Bo will show her around..." She pauses, zeroing in on me, gauging my reactions. "But only if you're really sure, honey. I wouldn't want to overstep."

Says the infamous Queen of Overstepping.

"I don't have any say-so on what Bo does, so ask away." I push the phone back to her, redirecting my attention to the crossword once more.

I refuse to let her get the best of me, no matter how hard she tries.

The front door squeaks open then slams closed. Bo's heavy footfalls echo across the den's hardwood floor and into the kitchen. He sets the second crate on the granite countertop, and I look up when Miss Bessie clears her throat. She holds her phone out toward Bo but stares at me the entire time.

"Bo, come here. Take a look at James's granddaughter, Miranda. You met her briefly a couple months back at my dinner party? She's coming into town for a few days this week. Think you might take her out?" Miss Bessie flits her eyes between the two of us, her mouth spread wide in an awkward conspiratorial grin. The whole thing reeks of some weird entrapment, and the last thing I want is him thinking I'm in league with Miss Bessie's meddling. Bo glances my way with an intent stare, as if awaiting my reaction. The heat rises in my neck so I drop my gaze to the tabletop to hide the burn and pick up the pencil, going back to the crossword.

He sighs and hands back her phone. "Sure. I'll do it."

Miss Bessie clasps her hands in front of her. "You will?"

He will? The blueberries creep upward in my throat. So, he's willing to date other girls; it's just me that inspires zero interest.

"I'll get you the details," she coos.

After Bo leaves, Miss Bessie and I sit in silence for a few minutes, and though I keep my face buried in the puzzle, her laser-burn glare singes my body. I don't look up and give her any payoff, only focus on 39 Down.

Overdue; Tardy.

Miss Bessie leans in and taps her red fingernail on the clue I'm reading. "I believe the word you're looking for is delin-quent." She stands up and walks toward the sink, saying over her shoulder, "Basically, it means 'you snooze, you lose.'"

CHAPTER 19

Bo

"Why are you doing this?"

Gin's reflection comes into view in my dresser mirror as I stand in front of it, swiping my roll-on deodorant onto my armpits. She leans against the bedroom door, a scowl marring her face. Who pissed in her cornflakes?

"It's 98-degrees and 90-percent humidity outside. Sweating through my shirt wouldn't be very attractive."

She flinches as if I've just taken a swing at her and huffs out a loud breath. "Not the deodorant, you idiot. Why are you going on this date?"

I set the deodorant on my dresser and turn around, tucking my shirt into my jeans. "Because Miss Bessie asked me to show James's granddaughter around. You know this already."

"And *you* know that this is just another one of Miss Bessie's games!" Gin stomps toward me, jabbing a finger in my chest. "She didn't follow the plan."

"What plan?" I ask, rubbing my chin between my finger and thumb.

Gin's eyes widen when she realizes she's just blurted out the truth that I already knew: she and Miss Bessie where in cahoots on Sunday trying to arrange some "chance" meeting between me and Jordan and a plate full of muffins. The whole objective of this so-called-plan was pretty easy to figure out. Awkward, considering what happened at the race. If anything, though, it did manage to break the weirdness of that first interaction post-meltdown, and when Jordan and I had gone back to the farm on Monday, we both acted as if nothing had changed. Like a mutual forgetting... or avoidance. I guess what happens at the racetrack, stays at the racetrack.

Fine by me.

Gin licks her tongue over her teeth, obviously regrouping for another attack. She fixes her eyes on me, cocking her head to one side. "Be honest. Is this all payback for Jordan going out with Jace?"

Hearing his name catches me off guard. "How do you know about—" That's when I remember Gin threatening to call CJ for the low-down when I refused to talk. "Oh, CJ."

"We're worried about y'all." Insert sad puppy-dog face that totally won't work on me.

I shrug, splaying the biggest smile I can muster across my face. "Well don't. Everything is good. Jordan and I are just fine, as you have plainly witnessed at the farm this week."

"You and Jordan put on a great show, pretending everything is roses, but the tension between you two is palpable."

Gin is determined to sniff out every detail of that night and concoct some story in her mind about a ruined hook-up between me and Jordan. I could be honest, tell her that I had the best of intentions only to have my heart run over by the oversized tires on Jace's truck as he drove away with Jordan at his side. But what would that do except fuel her fire in continuing this match-up that Jordan so obviously doesn't want?

I turn my back on her and pick up my cologne, spritzing it a couple times on my shirt. Gin walks beside me, poking her head into my line of vision. "Do you think that maybe—even inadvertently—you gave Jordan the wrong impression? That you weren't interested?"

Wait, is Gin blaming me for this fiasco? I had so many hopes for this past weekend. The minutes on the clock couldn't tick away fast enough during that race, only for me to be left behind, alone, when she chose him. My jaw clenches in and out as the resentment prickles inside. "With all due respect to your totally inappropriate and none-of-your-business questions, it was Jordan who blatantly told me she wasn't interested when she got in that truck with Jace."

"I asked her about that." She purses her lips, wagging her head.

My sister knows no bounds. I grab both of her shoulders, stooping down face to face. "No, you didn't!"

"I did. You wouldn't talk so I went over there to see her." She shakes herself from my grip and props her hands on her hips. "She went out with him because you supposedly told Jace that she was just a co-worker from the farm and you had no interest. Did you say that?"

Unbelievable! That stupid jerk must've told her what I said. I should've known there was some sort of gimmick involved for her to go out with him.

"Yeah, but I said it to *deter* Jace. He's the kid who wants everyone else's toy. Jordan is more than a conquest. I thought if I said I had no interest, then he would leave her alone."

"How'd that plan work out for you?" Gin rolls her eyes then thrusts her finger toward the door. "Just go talk to her. You know she's crazy about you!"

My stomach drops. No, I don't know that. There have been moments—the dance, for instance, when she was rubbing my face—that I thought for sure she was interested. But then this weekend, she'd looked me in the eye, took our room key, and got in the truck with Jace. Even if she'd discovered what I'd said, she still didn't ask me to clarify. She didn't mention it at all, and it crushes me to know she thinks I'm capable of disrespecting her like that.

But most importantly, I can't keep going down these futile

roads because at the end of the day, we still have weeks to work with each other, and the outcome of this internship has to be our focus. For her family. And ours.

"Well, she hasn't said anything to me." I grab the tube of hair gel, squirt a small bit into my palm, then rub it through my curls. I avoid catching my own gaze in the mirror because I don't want to see in my own eyes what I already know is there. Disappointment. Regret. Longing.

"And have you said anything to her?" Gin chews the inside of her cheek, apparently waiting on some enlightened answer. When she doesn't get one, she jumps up from the bed and stomps to the door. "You both suck, you know that?"

"Sorry to ruin your life," I mumble as she disappears around the corner.

CHAPTER 20

Jordan

G in's not reading the book she has pulled to her nose. Nor is she talking to me. And considering Bo's "hot date" will be here any second, I don't know why I let Gin talk me in to coming over, but I suppose it has something to do with her never-ending plotting.

"How do I look?"

I glance up and the breath catches in my throat. Bo stands in the doorway, smoothing his plaid shirt into a pair of butt-hugging ripped jeans. His toned thigh muscles ripple under the fabric, and his shirt sleeves are rolled up below his elbows, the top button undone. The royal blue pinstripe in his shirt is a perfect match to his eyes, one of which is partly covered by a tuft of dark curls which spill over his forehead.

He's actually styled them tonight and something about it makes me want to run my fingers through them and mess them up a bit. How he usually wears it, all spiraled and wind-blown.

My heart flutters against my ribs, and I bite my tongue, so hard I half expect to taste blood. I can't say out loud what's really going through my head. That he looks hotter than any guy I've ever seen. That the thought of him going out on this date with Miranda makes my stomach turn. Instead, I wait on Gin to take the lead while I banish those dreamy-eyed and reckless thoughts from my brain.

But Gin doesn't move off her bed, only drops her book a half-inch to reveal a set of stormy eyes that shoot lightning bolts across the room at her brother. "You look stupid, as usual."

"Sisters." He rolls his eyes but there's no sarcastic smile to accompany it. His mouth flatlines, shoulders stooping.

I steel my spine and gird my tongue as if preparing for battle. A WW3 inside my body. I slide off the bed and walk over to him, conjuring up a belly laugh. *God, that sounds as fake as it feels.* "You'd miss her if she wasn't here."

"Would I? I may have to think about that one," Bo teases, raising a hopeful gaze toward Gin who rewards him with a middle finger. The shadow on his face darkens as he bites the inside of his cheek. These two play-fight all the time but never this. Never this intense. Never this serious.

I look back and forth between them. "Am I missing something here?"

Gins huffs out a breath and pulls the book closer to her face, almost touching her nose, as if to make a point. Bo frowns and threads his arms over his chest, looking in the opposite direction. They're at an impasse and here I am in the middle of their squabble.

I grab Bo's arms and pull them away from his chest then give him the spin gesture. "Seems like you wanted an opinion?"

He smiles and turns in place. "Do I clean up nice or what?"

My eyes rove over his body, tracing each ripple and curve while desperately willing my fingers to remain calm. "While I'm partial to your usual ratty jeans and cut-off T-shirt, I think this look works for a..."—the words stick on my tongue and I have to swallow hard to evict them—"...hot date. Except for this smudge of old toothpaste..." I say, reaching up to wipe a white smear from the corner of his lip, and his gaze meets mine, the blue as deep as an ocean. A place I'd love to swim. My breath struggles to keep up so I whisper instead. "You look very handsome."

My touch lingers too long on his lip. It's as if our skin has melted and fused us together, a heat still smoldering underneath. He reaches up to grab my hand, his long fingers wrapping around mine, and pulls the tip of my finger to the thickest part of his bottom lip where he puckers against it. Just a slight pucker, imperceivable to anyone but the two of us.

Didn't he? Or am I imagining it?

My hand trembles in his grip, and he lowers them down, never fully letting go. We graze each other like a whisper. And not once has he dropped his eyes from mine, the intensity building inside me like a tsunami.

He clears his throat. "Um, Jordan, could we—"

Ding dong!

"Bo! Miranda's here!" Claire calls out. Bo glances over his shoulder, breaking the bubble we'd been standing in.

I pull my fingers away and pan my hand toward the door, fighting to plant a fake smile on my face. "Your lady awaits."

He nods, forcing a grin, turns and darts down the stairs. I follow him out onto the landing that overlooks the foyer. Miranda steps inside the door, hugs Bo's mom, and then spreads her arms wide toward Bo. He steps into them as they close around his back, pulling him close. Too close. She leans forward on her wedge sandals and plants a kiss on his cheek, her lips closer to him than I'd just been. "I'm so looking forward to tonight!" she squeals.

I grimace, my stomach churning with a furious mix of bile and regret, and retreat to Gin's room. I don't want to see their happy exit. My heart might explode in bloody bits all over her lemon-yellow walls.

"Have they left yet?" Gin grumbles, scowling over the top of her book.

I shrug and Gin ticks her head toward the window. She can't possibly understand the excruciating amount of torture she's heaping on me with the request. I pad toward the glass, careful to strategically hide myself behind the pink curtains. In the driveway, Bo opens the passenger door of his Bronco—the place I'd just been yesterday at the farm—and gives Miranda a hand on the side step. She bobbles on those ridiculous shoes and giggles, playfully plopping into the seat. He slams the door and walks around to the driver side, pausing a moment before getting in to look up at Gin's window.

Does he see me, desperate and lurking in the shadows? A nagging voice urges me to throw open the window and yell for him, plead with him, to reconsider. To see what's standing in front of him. But the logic is that I'm not what Bo needs or wants. The chemistry is there but he deserves someone easier with fewer restraints. The nagging fear also lurks in from the background: I couldn't manage to keep my own father in my life and my one and only relationship had been a train wreck. Bo might love me for a minute, but he'd leave me. Like all the men in my life. No, it's better to let him go and spare myself the inevitable pain. Because unlike the others, Bo is one of the good guys and having him only to lose him in the end would ruin me. And I have to keep strong and focused. For Weston. For Mama. For our farm.

I ease back another step, and Bo gets in. His engine rumbles to life. Within seconds, they're backing out onto the main road and then accelerating away. I watch until his Bronco disappears from view then walk over to Gin's bed and lean against the canopy post.

"They're gone now. You can quit pouting and be happy again."

She drops the book to her lap, glaring at me. "How can I be happy when he's out on a date with her? It's wrong."

"She seems like an okay girl. Besides, if Bo likes her, it really doesn't matter what anyone else thinks."

Gin bookmarks her page and slams the book onto the bed then slides off the side, plastering her hands on her hips. Her eyes turn to stone, and a shiver runs through me. "I'm sorry. I thought you were smart."

Now she's mad at me too? What did I do? "What's that supposed to mean?"

"Why am I the only one who keeps it real around here?" Her voice raises to a shout before she pauses, taking a deep breath and collecting herself. She approaches me and grabs both of my arms, giving them a shake as if trying to wake me up. "It means that Bo likes you, and you like Bo, and neither one of you will admit it, and now you're both just... ruining everything."

"Gin, it's not like that betwe—"

"He's the one who bought you that necklace."

My hand gravitates to the sea glass. Bo bought it? But why?

"You know what else?" She asks, eyes blazing. "He told Jace he had no interest in you because he wanted him to leave you alone. Jace saw you as a conquest, and Bo knew if he said he was interested that Jace would never let up. But could y'all talk about any of that? No."

"I didn't know, but I'm sure he just wanted to—"

"So, you don't like him? You have no feelings for my brother? You're not battling the urge to puke right now because he's out with some beauty queen while you're stuck here with me?"

"Yes!" I scream back, the emotions exploding. "Are you happy now? It's killing me that he's out with her. It's a freaking knife in my heart." Of course I like him. I have *all* the feelings for Bo. Does she really think I'm standing here clutching my stomach for no good reason? My guts churn with the thought of them together. The picture running laps through my mind of his lips pressed to hers on Bessie's doorstep tonight. I stop, gasping for air, before continuing. "But you don't understand all the circumstances. You just see what's here in your face, and Bo has already made it perfectly clear he's looking for easy and convenient options of which I am most definitely *not* one." I jerk my arm from her clutches and dart toward the door, mumbling the truth under my breath. "And I never will be."

I barrel into the hallway, heading toward the stairs and my escape from this house. From Gin whose heart is in the right place but whose logic is making this all much harder than it needs to be. I know I'm not what Bo needs. I need no mirror held up in my face to understand that any better than I already do.

Claire emerges from her home office before I make it to the first step, planting herself directly in my path.

"I'm making tacos tonight. Will you join us?"

"Thanks," I say staring at my feet. "But I'm not feeling too well. I think I'm just going to go lie down for a bit."

I make a move to ease past her but she reaches out, plastering her hand to my forehead. "You don't feel warm. Anything hurt?"

My heart? I look up into her concerned eyes and force out a qualifying smile. "Just kinda tired."

She starts to nod before her gaze fixes on something above my shoulder. Something in the direction of Gin's bedroom. She's no doubt filling her in on my bout of jealousy-nausea with a quick game of charades. Claire purses her lips and gives me the look. The pity one. "Anything you need to talk about? I have plenty of time and two really great ears."

I shake my head. "I'll be okay. Just need a minute to myself."

"Of course, I understand." She steps forward and pulls me into a tight hug. "I know your Mama isn't here, and Lord knows I'd never try to take her place, but please know that my door is open to you anytime. You've become such a fixture around here that I feel like you're already mine."

I nod, wrenching myself from her embrace, and run down the stairs.

The roar of the ocean has done little to quiet the fury in my brain, the what-ifs streaming in a loop. What if I'd never revenge-dated Jase? What if I'd simply confronted Bo about what I'd heard? What if I'd never been exposed to some of the male species' most terrible specimens that have obliterated my confidence in them? Is that something I will ever be able to put behind me? Bo of all the guys I've known has never fit that mold, and now I feel so silly painting him with that same old paintbrush. He didn't deserve it, and now I might never get the opportunity to rectify that mistake.

I close my eyes, letting the wind wash over me.

"Jordan?"

The bass notes of Bo's voice cut through the darkness. I quickly wipe the stray tears from underneath my eyes before looking up at him. "What are you doing here?"

"Looking for you."

Why is he looking for me? Gin must have insisted he come out here to find poor, pitiful Jordan nursing her heartaches on the beach. Bo swipes his foot back and forth a few times, flattening out a mound of sand, before sitting down beside me. So close that the musk of his cologne swirls around us like a cocoon. My pulse quickens, throbbing so hard I'm positive he can hear the *thump-thump-thump* emanating from under my skin.

"Found me," I mumble, refusing to make eye contact, and instead pick up handfuls of sand, letting it sift through my fingers. "Did Gin send you? And why are you back already?"

"No one sent me—you weren't in your room when I stopped by—and it's nearly midnight." He laughs, and in my peripheral vision I catch him staring at me. His smile fades to a thin line. "How long have you been out here?"

Too long. Not long enough. And considering the waves lapping at my toes when I sat down have now pulled out to a distant low tide, I'm fairly certain my solitary minutes have accumulated without me noticing. "A couple hours, I guess."

"Just sitting here all alone?"

"I'm not alone. I have the Man in the Moon to keep me company." I point toward the shining orb and its dark lunar seas that make up the man's haunted eyes. "I'm assuming you've met Mr. Moon?"

"Well, not formally until tonight," Bo jokes.

We sit in silence for a few minutes to a backdrop of waves crashing against the earth and then rumbling back out again. Over and over, never missing a beat. In the distance, summertime heat lightning colors the sky in orangish hues and the breeze blowing in off the water increases. I rub my hands up and down my arms to curtail the chill.

"You cold?" he asks.

"Just a little chill from the night breeze. I'm okay."

"Here." He unbuttons his shirt, slides it off, then holds it out for me. "This'll keep you warm."

"But what about you?"

"I've got my T-shirt. I'm fine." I hesitate and he shakes it open, nodding toward the waiting arm holes. "Please. Take it."

I smile and pull it on. It swallows my body, and I tug it closer around me, wrapping myself in the cotton fabric and his smell. Knowing that only minutes before his skin was touching where mine is now sends another trail of chills up my back. A new feeling overtakes me, a warmth I've rarely experienced. Total trust.

A deep stirring to share one of my innermost secrets with him surfaces, and I relax my guard, allowing the words to spill out freely in the briny night air.

"You know, when I was little, I pretended the Man in the Moon was my father."

He pivots toward me on the sand. "Your father?"

I bite my lip and take a deep breath, gathering my courage. "I don't have a dad. I mean, yes, biologically I do, but I've never met him, never heard from him, nothing. Being a father was *not* on his priority list." Bo leans forward in the sand, wrapping his arms around his knees, engrossed in my revelation, so I continue. "I never thought about it too much when I was really young but when I started school… it was hard not to notice, not to wonder, when all the others showed up with a mom *and* dad to field trips and awards day ceremonies."

Bo sighs and massages the back of his neck. "Jordan... I can't imagine. I depend on my dad for so much, and he's always there." Deep lines crease his forehead as he stares at the sand. I know he's trying to empathize, put himself in my shoes, but I'm glad he can't fully understand. Because Mr. Johnson is an incredible dad to an incredible son.

I burrow deeper in Bo's shirt, hugging my arms around myself. "Pretty soon, I began considering all the whys. Why didn't he stick around? Why didn't he love us? Why wasn't I enough to make him stay?" A tear slips down my cheek and Bo reaches over, swiping it away with his thumb, then cups my chin in his hand.

He nudges me toward him, and I lift my eyes to his, shining with reflected moonlight. "You should never wonder if you're enough. Because you are."

His words create an emotional storm that swirls inside, one I try swallowing down, nostrils flaring as I fight to hold it back. A few more tears escape, dripping down my cheeks in little rivers. "My mother told me it wasn't my fault. That it was his. His bad choices. His weaknesses. But it was easier to pretend to my friends that he was out of town for 'work' and not have to explain he'd never been there to begin with. Pretty soon, I began to believe my own lies, but at the same time it was cool because my dad could be anyone I chose. So I decided... he was the Man in the Moon, spending eternity there watching over us, watching me grow up from afar because somewhere deep down he really *did* care." I exhale, feeling the weight of my story leaving me, and stare up at the glowing moon. The dark eyes look back at me from above. "Now I realize it was just my way of trying to find some sort of stability and security. I mean, what can you count on more than the moon? It's presence literally moves oceans and even when you can't see it, you know it's still there."

"True. But some people are that way too. Not every person you meet in life will be like your father. There are people who care, who want to be there for you, if you let them in."

His hand finds mine in the sand, his long fingers wrapping around mine, the skin calloused from work but the touch gentle and sweet.

"I told Mama about my theory and she thought it was a good idea. She told me I should never be afraid to tell the Man in the Moon my troubles. That from where he was sitting, nothing was too big to fix and he'd always give me perspective."

His thumb swirls circles in my palm. "Is that what you're doing out here tonight? Getting perspective?"

"Trying."

"On what?"

"Everything."

"That doesn't sound complicated at all." He laughs, a broad smile creeping over his face. The mood shifts, the air lighter than before.

"My life? Never," I joke. A breeze kicks up off the ocean and swirls a few tendrils of hair in front of my face. I pull my hand away and tuck the stray fly-aways behind my ears before blotting away the remaining tears with the cuff of his shirt. "I'm sorry. I don't know why I told you all that. I've never shared that with anyone except my mother. Until you."

"I'm glad you trust me."

I do trust him. Completely, and that's terrifying. Because he's exactly the kind of guy I've always prayed I'd find, but I'm not the easiest person to be with. His implicit goodness seeps out of him. I've glimpsed the guy behind the tough exterior, and, oh my God, is it beautiful soul-deep. He deserves so much—more than I'm probably ever capable of giving.

But I can't deny the fact that despite all that, I want him in my life. I need him. And so I'll have to strap that part down somewhere inside when it threatens to erupt because having him walk out of my life would crush me.

"So," I say, shaking away the thoughts and sitting up straighter. "I never asked. How was your date?"

"Good." To the point. Non-committal with nowhere near

enough information.

I lean over and nudge his shoulder with mine. "Is she as pretty as her picture?"

"Oh yeah. Prettier, actually. And a stellar personality. We laughed all night."

My stomach lurches. How in the hell will I watch him date her or any other girl that comes along? The thought is like a bobcat loose in my guts. I squeak out a complimentary reply. "Sounds promising that y'all have good conversation."

"To tell you the truth, I kept having to ask her to repeat herself because I was so distracted. I couldn't quit imagining a goodnight kiss."

I'm dying. I'm dying. I'm dead. Dear universe, please put me out of my freaking misery. I don't want to know the details... but then again, I *have* to know.

"Well, don't keep me in suspense. Did you get it?"

"Not yet." Bo moves in front of me, settling down on his knees. "Going out with Miranda tonight made me realize exactly where I want to be. With you."

My heart flutters, lungs frozen in place. He leans in, nose to nose, his mouth parted slightly, his breath warm against my skin. Our eyes lock for the briefest moment, and as my gaze drifts downward, I catch the slightest glimpse of a smile before he closes the gap, his thick lips meeting mine like a whisper. I close my eyes, letting the rush filter down through my body. He pulls back slightly to where our lips barely graze each other; I pant against his mouth, desperate to regain my breath. Desperate to have him connected with me again.

"Don't stop," I whisper, grabbing hold of his face, and run my fingers up to his hair, tangling them in his curls. His arms encircle me, strong and protective, pulling me in again, and I melt into him. Bo is the moon and I'm the tide, rising and falling under his magnetism.

My eyes flutter open, a few slivers of pale morning light filtering through the blinds to stripe the carpet. All the doubts, all the fears—Bo's kiss silenced them. The morning is quiet, peaceful, with only the tweeting of birds outside my window and Bo's soft breathing beside me.

I run my fingertips over his exposed abs, feeling the contact of his skin warming mine. Last night, he'd followed me back here and asked if he could stay. We spent hours cuddling on the couch, talking and kissing and eating stale Pop-Tarts while watching TV. He spilled soda on his white T-shirt, and my heart nearly exploded into a million pieces when he pulled the drenched cotton over his head and tossed it on the tile floor. I'd seen his body before but enjoying looking at it had always felt forbidden. Until last night when Bo officially became my boyfriend.

We stayed up until two then stumbled to bed, where I snuggled in next to him, still wrapped in his button-down shirt from earlier, and fell asleep on his chest.

Two lips press against the top of my head, shooting fire down my spine. Warm, tingly, exciting flames. I look up to find Bo staring back at me. "Good morning," he says, voice gravelly from sleep.

"Good morning." I prop up on my elbow and run my fingers through his curls, ruffling them so that they swirl out wildly around his face. "There. That's better."

He smiles as his gaze drops lower to my necklace. He pulls it between two fingers, examining it.

"Gin told me that you bought it for me. I'm sorry I didn't figure it out sooner, but I do love it."

"Your eyes lit up when you were looking at it. You kept saying how beautiful it was and all I could think is that you were the beautiful one." He lets go of the necklace and slides his hand up my cheek. "And since we're making confessions here... Gin told me that you overheard what I said to Jace."

Of course she did. I laugh, shaking my head. "Your sister gets around, doesn't she?"

"She learned at the foot of the master." He laughs but his mouth doesn't curl into a smile; It pinches into a tight line. "I need you to understand that I didn't mean a word of it. Jace is the type of guy who gets a bigger thrill out of making a girl into a conquest if he thinks another dude wants her. If I'd told him how I'd really felt about you, he would've been relentless. So I lied, hoping he'd drop it." Bo lowers his eyes as the muscle in his jaw flexes in and out. "Apparently that didn't work. You don't know how bad I wanted to hunt you two down and just punch him square in the teeth."

I trace the outline of his pouted lips with my finger. "I only went out with him to make you jealous. And if it makes you feel better, it was the *longest* two hours of my life."

He smirks, pushing up onto his elbows, bringing himself nose to nose with me. "And you could've spent those two hours with me in that motel room."

"Don't remind me!" I pull one hand to my forehead and fall back onto the pillows in dramatic fashion.

"It's okay. I'd much rather be in this one with you now." Bo leans over, his curls drooping onto my cheek, as he kisses me, slow and gentle. I push into him, deepening the kiss, when a repetitive thud echoes from outside.

I jerk my head away, straining to identify its source. "What's that sound?"

Bo squints toward the bedroom window and points to a shadow passing by.

Frantic knocking pounds against my front door. "Jordan! It's Gin! Answer the door."

A look of horror meets humor flashes across Bo's face as he buries his head in his hands. We should've expected this.

I shimmy out from the covers and whisper, "I'll answer it. You stay here."

He nods, sitting up in the bed, and grabs a few pillows,

stuffing them behind his back. I dash to the door before Gin kicks it down in all her way-too-early morning fanaticism.

Knocking again, more feverish this time. I swing the door open, and a blast of lemony light colors the living room. "Morning!" I say, a huge smile on my face. "What's up?"

Gin appears to have not slept more than an hour all night. Her disheveled hair loops into a messy bun; her clothes—the same ones from yesterday—are wrinkled and askew. But it's the uncharacteristic scowl on her face that worries me.

"Why are you so happy?" she grumbles.

I shrug, keeping my smile in its place. "I just am. Is that a bad thing?"

"When I tell you what I have to tell you then you won't be happy." She leans in close, whispering through gritted teeth.

My brow pinches above my nose as I try to make sense of her cryptic words. "What's wrong? And why are you whispering?"

"So Mom and Dad don't hear me." She points to the Johnson's house with one finger while holding up the other hand to block it. As if Clay and Claire are inside right now with binoculars targeted on this very spot. Even if they were, it's nowhere in earshot. But when Gin is in one of these moods, logical explanations won't work. I stand back, waving her in. She darts halfway into the den and turns back to me, knifing her hand in the air to emphasize each word of her revelation. "Bo. Did. Not. Come. Home. Last. Night."

Ah, so she's been keeping vigil. I stifle a laugh, imagining the rage seething inside her at this very moment. I point out the still-open front door. "Gin, his Bronco is right there, so he must be around here somewhere."

"Or he's over there..." She stabs a finger toward Miss Bessie's house. "...with that fake-ass beauty queen. She was so *not* part of the plan."

Now she's inadvertently admitting to her plan. Like I hadn't suspected it before. With all this meddling, maybe I should make her suffer a bit. I throw my hands in the air, painting my best nonchalant expression on my face. "Maybe he just got up early and went to the beach?"

Gin deadpans. She clenches her jaw and straightens her spine, marching toward me, on a mission and in no mood for my games. "I don't think you're understanding the gravity of this situation. He did not sleep in his bed last night. I know because I booby-trapped it and it's still intact this morning. And he had to sleep somewhere." Her words come out hard, robotic, with no inflection. This girl is not playing.

I reach out, running my hand down her arm. "I think you're getting too upset. Bo's nineteen. Pretty much a grown man who—"

"Body of a man, maybe, but brain of an idiot." Her face reddens, and for a minute, I fear her head may shoot off her body. "And you're the one who's not getting upset enough."

"What do you want me to do?"

"I want you to freaking come off it and tell him how you feel. I love my brother more than anything but he's an idiot. Unless you spell it out for him, he's never going to get it." She stomps her foot the same way Weston does when not getting his way. "I know you have feelings for him, and I know he feels the same about you. So why aren't y'all talking about it?"

I could tell her that her brother is in the next room. That we are together, happy, but a small part of me feels that I owe Gin this big dramatic finale to all her hard work. Let her revel in the burn for a moment. Feel all the frustration so the payoff is sweeter. Yeah, for her sake.

"Things tend to have a way of working out in their own time."

"No, they don't. You have to make things happen yourself. You had the perfect opportunity last night. He was practically begging you to speak up and tell him not to go, but what did you do?" Gin wags her head and helicopters her finger. "Oh Bo, do a little spin move and let me straighten your shirt and—"

She stops, the color draining from her face as she stares at me. An eerie silence envelops us.

"What's wrong?" I ask.

Gin grabs the sleeve of my shirt, examining it. "You're wearing Bo's shirt. The same one he left in last night." Her narrowed eyes find mine, a million question marks floating above her head.

"Oh... I um..." How in the hell do I explain my way out of this one? My breath turns shallow, choppy, as the anxiety ignites. I don't know if Bo wants to go public with our relationship yet. And I don't know if he prefers to be the one to tell her. "Gin..."

"Good morning, sis." Bo struts out into the main room, clad in only his ripped jeans. Gin and I both gasp at the sight for two very different reasons. Her eyes widen, jaw dropping, but Bo only grins, arching his eyebrows. "You act like you haven't seen your idiot brother before."

Gin backpedals as she swallows hard a few times. "So you... you did come home... you just... stayed..." Her eyes make a full revolution around the room, from shirtless Bo to me to the rumpled blankets on the couch and two empty glasses on the coffee table. "I'm interrupting. I should leave. I'm interrupting." She sprints to the door and runs out, letting it slam behind her. Seconds later, a knock sounds on the door, and I open it. Gin sticks her head in through the crack. "Before I go, could someone tell me exactly *what* it is I'm interrupting?"

I shake my head. "No."

She rolls her eyes but can't conceal the wide smile on her lips. "Fine."

Bo steps beside me and we watch Gin trot back to the main house, a new skip in her step. That girl loves a good romantic plot.

He wraps his arm around my shoulder, tugging me to him. "Let's make a pact to never tell her she's been right the entire time."

I raise up on my tip-toes, bringing my lips to his, pulling back only to say, "Agreed."

CHAPTER 21

Bo

I stand by the kitchen sink, draining the remaining coffee from my cup, when the French door creaks open. I glance into the next room as Jordan steps inside, dropping her bag by the door. She runs her hands down the front of her tank top, retucking it into the waistband of her jeans. Today, we have a series of meetings, the first of which features Dad teaching a class on mergers and acquisitions, so we'll have little time out in the field. Regrettable, too, because there are several little nooks and hideaways in the barns where I'd love to steal away with...

Jordan runs her fingers through her hair and looks up at me, a huge smile stretching her lips when our eyes meet. My heart swells.

My girlfriend. Mine. Only mine.

And to think, a couple months ago, I was sure this summer was going to suck.

She trots into the kitchen and loops her arms around my neck, pressing her body into mine. After being with her all yesterday and the night before that, last night seemed a hundred hours long without having her snuggled into my side. I don't know how many times I gazed out my window, looking to see if her light was on or off and wondering if she was doing the same.

I grab her hips and tug her even closer, leaning down to cover her mouth with mine. Her lips, super soft, taste like strawberries, and I want more of them.

A few giggles erupt from the other side of the room followed by a long *shhhhhhh!*

Jordan peels her mouth from mine and glances to the far side of the kitchen where Mom and Gin have come in and stand by the table, pretending not to look in our direction, though their side-eyeing betrays the ruse. I laugh as pink swirls lace Jordan's cheeks then lean down to her ear, whispering, "Don't be embarrassed. They already know."

What I don't tell her is that after I told Mom, she'd celebrated and then promptly subjected me to an hour-long birds-and-bees talk about all the precautions. Jordan might melt into a gelatinous puddle and seep through the floorboards if she knew so I leave that detail out.

Jordan squeezes my hand then walks over, making some polite small talk with my mom and sister. Mom keeps laughing and patting Jordan's arm and Gin flips through her phone, trying to determine an available date when she can drag her on another shopping excursion. I lean against the counter, taking in the scene. Laurel rarely wanted to see my family and when she did, we might as well have been at a funeral. Jordan's different, and they're different around her. It's like she is a puzzle piece whose unique edges snap precisely into place. A perfect fit.

Jordan tells them goodbye and motions toward the door. I grab my keys, trailing her outside.

"Did Gin tell them?" she asks, glancing over her shoulder.

"No, I did." I hurry past her and swing open the door of my Bronco, taking her hand and helping her climb up the sidestep. She pulls her seatbelt across her, staring at me, as I walk to the other side and slide in behind the wheel.

"*You* told them?" she finally asks. She says it like she can't fathom how I could possibly be proud of the fact. How can she not see that I'm the lucky one?

"Are you kidding me? I can't wait to tell everyone." I turn the key and the engine rumbles to life. "Have you told your mama?"

Jordan deadpans. "You mean you didn't hear her scream? I think it might have registered on the Richter scale."

"I hope it was a happy scream."

"You have no idea." Jordan laughs, and we take off toward the office, the wind whipping through the open top of the Bronco. She closes her eyes, lays her head back against the headrest, and reaches over, resting her hand on my thigh. This isn't the first time she's ridden shotgun in my car, but it is the first time doing so as my girlfriend. I look down at my leg, where her fingertips generate little points of fire on my skin. And her hand has never been there before. It feels natural. I drop one of mine from the steering wheel and twine our fingers together.

They stay that way until we pull in and park in the gravel lot. I scramble from my seat and jog around the Bronco just in time to help Jordan jump down from the side. Never have I ever been happier that I decided to put mud tires on this thing. She loops her arms around my neck as I grab her waist, lowering her onto the ground but not letting go. She looks up at me and smiles, the sunlight sparkling in her eyes when I dip my mouth to hers, pressing her gently against the back fender. For a moment, we forget where we are until the sound of clinking gravel against metal pulls us apart. Jordan wipes the corners of her swollen lips and glances over her shoulder as Patrick's truck pulls into the lot, parking on the opposite corner.

She frowns, watching him get out and waddle into the house. When the door slams behind him, she turns to me, twirling a tendril of hair. "I think we should lay low about our being a couple. At least here on the farm."

"Don't tell me you're trying to ditch me already." I nuzzle her neck, trailing a line of kisses over her jaw.

"Never." She giggles then pushes me away, ducking out of my grasp. "I just think we need to play it cool around Brice. You know he's going to go ballistic when he finds out."

I couldn't care less about Brice and his destroyed ego. As a matter of fact, I can't wait to see the soured-milk expression on his face when he realizes Jordan chose me and rejected him, time and again. I hope I have my phone on me to get a good photo of that twisted face. "Good. Let him."

I start to laugh but suppress it when Jordan's smile slips into a tight-lipped frown. "That could mean more sabotage. And that could be the difference between winning and losing this internship money." She stares at me with doe-eyes, spinning the bracelet on her arm. "And I *need* that money."

"Okay. Around here, we're 100-percent professional." I trace my finger down the side of her arm and lean in, so close our lips brush, as I whisper, "Though Brice can't be everywhere on this farm so...

Just as I go in for the full kiss, Jordan giggles and jerks away, sprinting toward the office. I catch up to her on the porch and after a quick peek to ensure no one's watching, she fists my shirt, pulling me down to plant a big one square on my lips. It's faster and rougher than usual, and every nerve ending in my body tingles. If this is what having a secret romance on the farm will be like—stealing adrenaline-charged kisses—then I'm in.

I'm all in.

She pulls back with a wink and slips in through the front door. I draw in a deep breath and follow her down the hall. Does this girl know what she does to me? The thought of sitting for an hour in this stupid meeting with Jordan a few inches away and not being able to touch her?

Kill me now.

We walk in and take a seat beside Doniella and across from Christopher and Patrick, who sits with his arm propped on the back of the chair beside him, probably the one awaiting Brice. Dad sits at the head of the table, shuffling through some papers, while Doniella keeps shooting me and Jordan awkward smiles and approving nods. Something tells me she knows.

And I can imagine who blabbed. Gin. I sigh. I hope Jordan is prepared. If Doniella is the fuse Gin lit with her gossip, then no doubt that news bomb has detonated and most of the farm knows by now.

Brice strolls in, kicking my chair on the way to his. I shoot him a nasty glare to which he smirks and simply says, "Oops."

One second into this meeting and I'm ready to kill him.

He tosses a folder on the table then flops down in his chair, swiveling back and forth, as Dad stands up and walks to the whiteboard. The marker squeaks as he writes MERGERS AND ACQUISITIONS. The first half of the meeting is slated as an introduction to the topic for the interns and the second half, pending business. Christopher, Jordan, and I grab notepads and pens from the pile in the center of the table, but Brice rolls his eyes, pulling his phone from his pocket. For the next thirty minutes, we scribble notes and ask questions while Brice swipes from video to video, without the common courtesy to mute them, blatantly ignoring Dad's annoyed scowls.

No respect. Not one ounce.

Finally, Dad retakes his seat and asks for updates on new business.

Brice slides the folder across the table to Dad and jumps to his feet. "The Goose Creek farm I'm eyeing for our new hemp ventures. The numbers you asked for are in that file. I met with the owners; they don't want to sell. Some sentimental bullshit about their family heritage or something. Blah, blah, blah. But I visited the bank, and I was right. Money talks. If we've got the cash, it's ours."

Not this again. And in front of Jordan, who's terrified of this very thing happening with her own family farm. I glance over at her, biting her knuckle, breathing accelerated. She drops her hand to the table with a thump, and everyone focuses on her. "But what about the family? They love their land; doesn't that mean anything?" she asks.

"No. Why should it?" Brice snorts. "If they loved it so much, they should've paid for it."

Jordan grimaces as if Brice just fired a bullet that struck her in the heart. The muscles in her neck flex as she glances down at her notepad, obviously trying to steel herself. "Maybe they couldn't. Maybe something happened beyond their control. Where's the humanity?"

Brice pretends to hold up a violin to his chin and push an imaginary bow across the strings. "The humanity is that we're relieving them of their burden. Now they can go do something else."

"If you truly loved farming, you'd know that what you're saying is impossible. You can't just go do something else. It's in your blood." Jordan picks up her pencil, gripping it so hard it snaps in two. "I would legit do anything to save our family farm from someone like you!"

Brice smirks and traces a finger down his cheek as if her words have stirred any sort of emotion in his cold, dark heart. "Someone like me? I'm hurt. Truly. Here I was thinking you liked me."

The room is silent except for Patrick who laughs and relaxes in his chair with a smug grin—a grin he drops when Dad shoots an icy glare across the table.

My blood boils. How dare this jackass insult Jordan, Dad, our very way of life. How dare he think he can waltz in here and take control when he has no right. The surge of anger quickly morphs into something else. A surge of pride. Of family. Jordan told me once that there'd come a time when I knew my future, and this one resonates.

I jump to my feet, capturing Brice's attention. He squares his shoulders and stiffens his backbone as if sensing my new-found fire.

"I think we should table this discussion, at least until Dad can meet with the farm owners and see if an agreement can be worked out," I say. "If not, there are plenty of other places for sale to consider. There's no need to start changing how we do business now."

"How *we* do business?" Brice thrusts an accusatory finger at Jordan. "Until she came along, I didn't even realize you gave a shit about this farm. Now she shows up and you're in the main office, trying to be the big man?"

I step back, cocking my head to the side as I look him up and down. Big mouth to cover his pitiful self. Everything he's fighting for is nothing that represents Johnson Farms. It's just a selfish power maneuver. "Jordan made me realize what really matters. Sorry to see you've never learned that lesson."

Brice grinds a fist into his other palm. "I've got a lesson for—"

"Enough!" Dad jumps to his feet, slamming the folder on the table. The *thwack* echoes through the room and everyone goes silent. "I agree with Bo. We're not changing how we do business. Not now or ever. I'll reach out in the next week, and we'll plan to revisit this topic at next month's meeting."

"Shocker." Brice waves his hands in the air. "Taking their side."

Dad sighs and props a hand on his hip. "This is not about sides, Brice. It's about maintaining our family name."

"If only it were that important to you." He threads his arms over his chest and death-glares in my direction. "You're more than willing to step all over family name when it suits your purpose."

I roll my eyes. I guess Brice thinks he's the only member of this family who counts.

The muscles in Dad's neck flex so tight I expect that at any minute he'll turn green and fling himself across the table in a fit of rage. "I suggest you drop this before I table this deal for good."

Brice smirks with an exaggerated shrug. "Then table it, Clay. Dad and I have money. Maybe we'll go buy it and compete against you."

"Then I wish you luck. You're going to need it." Dad slams his folder shut, dismisses the meeting and walks out of the room with Patrick hot on his heels, griping about Brice not getting his way.

As soon as their voices fade, Doniella beelines for me and Jordan, throwing her arms around both of our shoulders. "I have just been dying to say I'm so happy for y'all!" Her voice carries and I glance up at Brice, staring at us with slitted eyes. Doniella, not noticing, socks me in the arm with a wide grin. "All I can say is it is about time!"

"What's about time?" Brice stands up from the table, arms folded. Jordan groans and nudges Doniella in her ribs. They stare at each other for a moment as if telepathically communicating before Doniella's eyes widen and she nods slowly.

"Nothing..." She loops her arm through Jordan's, pulling her toward the door. "Come with me to the greenhouses?"

As they disappear around the corner, I train my attention on the notepads and pens, restacking them in the center and ignoring the laser beams shooting from Brice's eyeballs.

"What the hell is going on?" he growls. I ignore him, but my tactics are doing little to deter him. Instead, they make him more curious.

A flurry of footsteps sounds in the hallway then pauses outside the door. I glance up at Luis, one of the farmhands, giving me a thumbs-up. "Bo! Heard you and Jordan made it official. 'Bout damn time!"

Before I can respond, Brice gasps and darts around the table, pushing Luis out and slamming the door. He turns to me, red-faced, and I half expect smoke to come billowing out of his ears.

"Are you crazy?" He marches toward me, poking his finger onto my chest. "This is a huge conflict of interest! Do you think Clay would ever vote against her now?"

Really? He's mad because he thinks Dad won't vote for his team in the internship challenge. Like that was ever a possibility. Delusional idiot. That's like me thinking Patrick will side with me. Come on.

"Please. Like Patrick would ever vote against you. Their

votes are going to cancel the other's out. That's why there's an entire panel of voters, so try again."

"Okay, I will." He wags his finger in my face. "How about the fact that we know nothing about this chick and her history? How do we know she's not here trying to steal our company information or screw us over or something?"

His prolific use of *we*, *our*, and *us* is comical. Since when did we become a team? But as much as I want to laugh in his face, the desire to punch it is stronger. What exactly is he implying?

I step closer, pushing my chest into his. "Are you suggesting Dad didn't do his due diligence in screening applicants? Or are you talking shit about my girlfriend? You should think twice before doing either."

"And you should think twice about getting in my face."

"Whatever. You're pathetic." I turn around, going back to arranging the pads and pencils in some semblance of order. If I don't redirect my focus, I might just knock his head off his shoulders.

Brice doesn't take the hint. He moves closer, his hot breath rolling down my neck, reeking of the wad of dip tucked into his cheek. "What's pathetic is you licking the work boots of this girl. You don't have the best track record. Believe me, the farm hands love to make fun of you and some 'vacation ass' you tried to make into a girlfriend before she dumped you. And this is going to turn out the same way."

Don't react, Bo. Hold your temper. He's trying to rile you up. Resist.

My self-talk does little good. My brain feels as if its steaming inside my skull. But I refuse to let him get the best of me. So what if he's heard some mumbling about my big breakup? He's never met Laurel, doesn't know a thing about her so everything he's saying is some second-hand gossip he's absorbed like a gross mildewed sponge. And this from the guy who never had a girl want to spend time with him. Well, at least a sober one.

"You don't know what you're talking about," I say, keeping my voice level. My calm only incites his anger to the nth degree.

Brice slaps my elbow, spinning me sideways into the table. My hip catches the corner and a splinter of pain shoots down the muscle. "Are you stupid enough to take this girl at face value? Because I'm not!"

I regain my balance and step toward him again. I won't back down. But I will be petty and remind him that not so long ago Jordan told him to take a hike. Maybe he needs a refresher. "Good, then you don't date her. Problem solved."

"No, unfortunately I'm staring right at my problem. You and this girl are not coming in here and hijacking everything that's rightfully mine." The redness in Brice cheeks deepens as he screams in my face, "I won't let you. Either of you. I'll destroy you first."

I smirk, holding my hand up in his face. "What do you honestly think you can do?"

"Wait and see," he spits then storms from the room, slamming the door behind him.

CHAPTER 22

Jordan

"Mama..."

I say it as a warning. One filled with the utmost love and adoration but still... a warning. I snuck in a call with her while I'm stuck shoveling fertilizer into bags to carry over to the greenhouses. Bo's off on some impromptu errand with Gin, so while I'm alone in the barn, I'd figured it was the perfect time to call her and catch up. Maybe see if she fully recovered from the bomb I dropped on her last week when I told her that Bo and I were together.

I should've known better. Apparently, her interest in the matter has turned into 100-percent, sheer, unadulterated enthusiasm. Bo would never suspect his biggest fan is a 40-something woman from Appalachia.

"What?" Her voice crackles over the speakerphone as she expertly weaves the poutiness into her tone. I can practically imagine her poked-out lips and puppy dog stare. "I told you I had a good feeling about this summer."

Unfortunately, the Wrights have bigger things to worry about than my love life. Like our life. Our home. Our very existence as we know it.

I sigh, emptying a shovelful into the wheelbarrow. "Bo is the icing on the cake... but he's *not* the cake. I really have to focus. We need that money."

"Things will work out."

Lord, I love Mama, but she is maddening! So dismissive. So go-with-the-flow. But what happens when the flow hits a major dam? I'm afraid we're about to find out.

I prod further, refusing to let it go. "Any word from the bank? Made any headway?"

"No. Still September." Blunt. Monotone. Emotionless.

"We can't lose our farm," I whisper. Suddenly, the shovel weighs a thousand pounds, and I have to prop it against the wood-slatted wall. Even the air thickens like a hot, winter stew.

"We're not. I'm going to figure something out." And just like that, her spirit renews, her voice brightening. How can she flip between realism and optimism like flicking on a light switch? "You do your thing down there. Win that internship money like I know you will, and enjoy your time with Bo. You need that."

"We need a lot of things."

The line goes silent before I hear the odd squeaky sound of Mama sucking her tongue over her teeth, her signature move when determining how to approach a sensitive topic. I hold my breath, waiting.

"Sassy, don't get mad but I do have to ask. Have you told Bo yet?" Of all the subjects she could change it to, she picks this one? If she can ostrich about our finances, then I deserve to bury my head in the sand about this. At least for a little while longer.

"Not yet."

"You need to. He needs to know that you have someone waiting on you here at home. It's only right."

"I know."

She sighs on the other end, and I imagine her giving me that same shaming look she did when I was a kid and didn't complete my chores. I tell her I love her and will call her later then hang up.

I slip my phone in my pocket and lean against the wall,

drawing in and releasing a few deep breaths. My head spins, lightheaded from the muscles pulled tight as rubber bands in my neck. She's right. This conversation should've happened between me and Bo before now—it should've happened that night on the beach—but every time I think of going through with it, the words die on my tongue. Weston is the biggest and best part of my life, and I want to share that with Bo. I want to share everything with him. But what if Bo sees it as a deal-breaker? What if Bo changes his mind and walks away, like others before him?

My throat squeezes, my breath trapped, lungs refusing to expand. The only way I can know Bo's reaction is by telling him the truth. Something I owe him. Something I've been owing him since we got together.

I push off the wall, straightening my spine, lifting my chin. Now's the time. No more waiting. The time has come to confess.

Rushing from the stall, I slam directly into Brice's chest. He stands like a brick wall in the threshold. I backpedal and stare up at his face, smug and cocky. A 20-lb bag of fertilizer rests on his shoulder.

I clench my jaw, regaining my composure. After his blatant declaration of war on me and Bo at the meeting this past week, he's been popping up everywhere we go. Lurking. Lingering. My mind reels, rewinding to the conversation I just finished with Mama. Did he hear? Could he have been listening? No. I was alone in the stall, and I'd checked the main room. No one was there, and I would've heard him come in. Right?

I swallow hard, eyeing him up and down. "Are you spying on me?"

"Self-important, much?" He snorts and nods toward the bag he's gripping in place. "I'm loading fertilizer, but I'm sure you know all about it. Looks like you've already been hauling plenty around here."

Any opportunity to make a so-called joke about my running some scheme on the Johnson family. I honestly believe this dipshit has convinced himself that for me, the internship is secondary to ruining his life. It's bizarre.

"So funny. As usual," I snark and shove past him, heading toward the barn entrance. He can insinuate what he wants. If he was bringing anything of value to the table, then he'd have more to focus on than me and Bo. Like putting together a lucrative land deal that Clay would actually consider.

As I round the corner, Bo trots across the grass path, yelling my name. His jeans hug his thighs, and I let my gaze linger too long on how the denim molds to every contour, his muscles flexing and relaxing with each step. My heart drums in my chest, warring with excitement and dread. How can he be mine? And how will he take the news I have to share with him?

I steel my spine as he approaches. The best way is to get it done. Don't hesitate. "Hey Bo, I have something to tell you. Can we go—"

"Me first." A toothy grin spreads his lips, piquing my interest. "Dad got a private dining room at that nice restaurant on the pier this evening for Mom's birthday."

It's Claire's birthday? How come no one said anything until now? "I didn't know it was her birthday."

Bo waves his hand. "She hates making a fuss. Always says no presents, but she does love going out to eat and ordering a nice, big piece of caramel poundcake. We'll leave a bit early to get ready so I'll pick you up around 5:30?"

I nod. "Great."

He leans in, pressing his lips to mine and for one glorious moment erasing every shred of worry and doubt swirling in my brain. He pulls back with a wink and turns to go but stops abruptly. "Oh yeah... you wanted to tell me something?"

Panic grips me. Now is not the time. I refuse to bring up such a heavy topic that'll dampen the mood for tonight's dinner, especially when I can't begin to fathom how he'll respond. Claire deserves all eyes on her for her special day. There'll be plenty of time later to sit down and explain to Bo that I come as a two-for-one package deal. What will a few hours hurt? I smile, shaking my head, and throw my hands in the air. "I forgot. I'll let you know if I think of it."

Balloon bouquets and streamers adorn every corner of the private dining room. The door swings wide as the waiter shuts off the lights and pushes in a rolling cart. On top, a large pound-cake topped with sparkler candles fizzles and pops in a flurry of light. Claire gasps, steepling her hands in front of her mouth, as they transfer it to the table in front of her.

Clay stands up, humming aloud and pretending to tune his vocal cords. As we all begin singing the Happy Birthday chorus, I glance around the table, taking in the collective scene. Bo and Gin clap and smile at Claire, so much love and admiration in their eyes. But the one who draws my attention the most is Clay. His eyes never leave Claire as he sings to her, head angled in her direction, a huge grin peeking through every note he sings. So rugged and tough on the farm yet so gentle and mild when it comes to her. He looks at her the way she's currently looking at her poundcake. Like it's the best gift he's ever received.

She blows out the candles, extinguishing them in one breath, and the waiter flicks the lights back on. Misty-eyed, Claire blows everyone a kiss and then stares up at Clay, who bends down to press his lips to hers. Bo and Gin groan in unison, but I can't stop staring at them, at their example of what true love should look like. Devotion and admiration and joy.

I wish Mama could find it, experience it. My stomach flutters. My biggest fear is I robbed her of that opportunity. That she gave up searching for it because of me.

"Happy birthday, my beautiful bride. You make 39 look so good!"

She laughs and they kiss again as the waiter begins slicing the cake and passing it around the table. That's when it hits me.

If Claire is just turning 39 then that means she was only 19 years old when she got pregnant and gave birth. I never realized before that she had been a teen mom like me. I glance back and forth between her and Bo, imagining what it will be like when the same scenario repeats with me and Weston in the future. Is it too much to hope my life will turn out as happy as Claire's?

I nudge Bo in the ribs and he turns to me, forking in a huge sliver of cake. "I didn't realize your mom was our age when she had you."

He finishes chewing and takes a swig of tea, then says, "Yeah, can you imagine? Being our age and tied down with a kid already?" He saucers his eyes and sticks out his tongue. Gin mirrors him. My breath catches in my chest. He might as well have taken his fork and stabbed it in my heart.

I swallow down the tiny bite of cake in my mouth along with his flippant words. It sticks like a rock in my chest, refusing to budge. "I don't know. Your mom did a beautiful job with it." I force a smile and reach over to squeeze his hand. "Obviously."

"That's mom. Not me." He laughs, holding up his arms in an "x" across his chest.

"Right?" Gin laughs, licking a dollop of frosting from her finger.

"So, y'all don't ever want kids?" I try to maintain a nonchalance about the line of questioning, but my own voice rings loud and clear in my ears. Tense and terrified.

Bo shrugs. "One day."

Gin snaps her fingers in the air. "But *not* today!"

They smile, returning to their cake and conversation, but I can barely hear them. The sounds around me fade to a distant buzz, as if there's some sort of barrier between me and them. The blood pumps through my veins like speeding cars on a highway, and my fingers begin to shake. My breaths come faster, like I've just completed a marathon, and a hollow ache grips my stomach. I drop my fork to my plate. That cake will have to wait.

I don't think I could get it past my esophagus before my body expelled it with force.

I yank my phone from my pocket and mumble something to Bo about an incoming call from Mama, and then I bolt for the side door, which exits onto the pier. The cool ocean breeze hits me in the face, a welcome relief from the panicked heat rising in my cheeks and neck, and I walk to the farthest edge, overlooking the Atlantic. The dark waves pound the shoreline, and above me, the moon and a million pin-dots of light blanket the sky.

Any hope I have of Bo understanding—accepting—my situation? Dead in the water. I close my eyes, gripping the wooden rail, and look up to my old friend. My perspective-giver. Tonight, though, he's silent yet screaming. Straightforward but convoluted. Precise but imperfect.

Because there's no easy answer to this. No absolutes. I turn around and look back into the windows of the dining room at the four Johnsons laughing and talking at the table, one happy unit, and for the first time I'm transplanted squarely into my mama's shoes.

I'm on the outside looking in at everything I want and everything that is so far out of my reach. This is why Mama cries herself to sleep at night. This is why she gave up.

Maybe it will be my destiny too.

CHAPTER 23

Bo

I glance up at Brice across the truck bed. I've never minded working the fields of late corn when they come in, shucking and silking hundreds of ears for the market, except when it requires my playing nice with him—and working in the same space for extended periods of time. The smug expression currently spanning his face makes me want to take this ear of corn and shove it straight up—

Jordan's phone buzzes in her pocket. She lays the ear she's working on the tailgate and pulls off her gloves, tossing them beside it.

"I'm just going to duck over here and take this call," she says with a small smile.

Small smiles seem to be all I've been getting these past couple days. Qualifier ones. Smiles that say something's not quite right even though she's trying to pretend they are. It started after Mom's birthday party when I found her out on the pier, tears in her eyes. I asked her what was wrong. Begged her to tell me. But she swore it was just a sudden attack of homesickness after talking to her mama.

She wouldn't look me in the eye when she explained, though, and Jordan always looks me in the eye.

I swallow hard. Unless she's lying.

But about what?

I watch her walk over to the barn and lean against the doorway, glancing over her shoulders a few times to make sure no one's there. Probably her mama again. I swear they've talked more in the last two days than in the eight weeks she been down here.

I pick up another ear of corn, using my knife to shear off the end then pull down the papery shucks. That's when hot breath scorches my ear.

"You're not curious who's on the other end of that line?"

I turn around to face Brice, hovering by my shoulder, tongue rubbing over his front teeth.

I shake my head, refocusing on brushing the silken strands from the kernels. "Nope."

"Even if it could be her boyfriend back home?"

I lift my eyes, peeking at Jordan, who seems to sense my renewed attention. Her eyes meet mine briefly and there it is again. Small smile.

No. Jordan's going through something right now—something she isn't sharing with me just yet—but I refuse to let Brice plant crazy ideas in my head. Of course, he's pulling out all the stops. He told me point-blank that he would ruin us.

"Okay, whatever."

Brice clicks his tongue and jumps onto the tailgate, pulling off his gloves to examine his nails. "The other day I overheard Jordan on the phone with her Mama, who wanted to know if she'd 'told you' yet." He tweaks his fingers in the air as he quotes the phrase.

"Told me what?"

He puckers his lips and bugs his eyes out in one of those I-told-you-so sneers. "That's the million-dollar question, ain't it? Her mama warned her that she needed to be honest and tell you about the person waiting on her at home." He leans forward and pats me on shoulder. "Now who might that be?"

I shirk his touch and step to the other side of the fender, putting space between us. My boiling blood can't be trusted to keep me from exploding on him. "Why would I ever believe you?" I snap.

Brice slides off the tailgate, his boots stirring up a cloud of dust, and motions for Christopher to join him. Before walking away, he once again steps into my space, leveling his eyes with mine. "Don't have to. I'm not telling you because I like you. I'm telling you because I don't want you being stupid and getting our farm wrapped up in some scheme."

As they trudge back to the fields, I make note of Brice's confident swagger. Just another one of his ploys.

He, too, has probably noticed Jordan's distant, far-off gaze and is trying to use it against her. Against us. He even warned me that our relationship would end like my previous one—funny since he didn't know one thing about Laurel except that she was a girl I dated that'd been cheating. Of course, he wants to rip open those old wounds and hope they fester out all over Jordan. Jerk. How stupid does he think I am? Jordan's got something weighing on her, but it's not about us.

We're solid. A brick wall.

Right?

Jordan walks up behind me, threading her arm through mine, and lays her head on my shoulder. I inhale the sweet scent of her shampoo and smile. This is more like it.

"What's going on?" I ask, glancing over at her.

She catches my gaze but drops it just as quickly, snuggling into my arm. "Nothing."

Jordan and I walk up the beach, the evening's humidity heavy like a wet blanket. A squadron of pelicans fly above us in a line, casting long, loping shadows on the sand. She hasn't talked much, at least not anything beyond the usual chatting.

After we got home from the farm this afternoon, I took it upon myself to single-handedly pull her out of whatever funk she's been wading in the last few days. It's time for Unshakeable Jordan to make a comeback. We strolled to the pier and ordered cheeseburgers and Cokes and sat at one of the restaurant's picnic tables, talking about the corn harvest and how the thick shucks point to a colder winter coming. But while she was eager to describe the coloring of the fuzzy caterpillar she'd found under the silks of one ear of corn, she expertly diverted any questions about her family back home and the sudden rash of urgent phone calls.

Now, strolling in the surf after dinner, she's clamming up again.

I chew the inside of my cheek, letting my thoughts ebb and flow in sync with the tide. Brice made his wild accusations to draw on my insecurities, but as I glance over at Jordan, soft and serene as the ocean breeze tousles her hair, there's nothing to indicate she's anything like Laurel. That girl was an expert at disguise, hiding her true intent and snapping on whatever façade she thought would keep me from asking questions. Jordan is the opposite. Her feelings, her every emotion, rides proudly on her shoulders without reserve. There's no wondering whether or not she's upset. The only question is why.

Tonight, I intend to find out.

We approach the part of the shore where it bends into the St. Helena Sound, a part only accessible by trekking up and over a massive dune. Jordan goes first, her feet slipping in the sand, and I give her a boost before climbing up behind her.

But as I reach the top, Jordan stretches out her arm, stopping me in my tracks. She ticks her head to something just beyond the bend. I search the horizon to get a better view of what's captured her attention. A small congregation of people stand on the sand, just inches from where the ocean laps the beach's edge. In the center, a couple holds hands along with someone I suspect is a minister as the sun sets behind them, casting the scene in an orange halo. Beside the woman, a little girl sways from side to side, clutching a tiny bouquet of flowers.

Jordan remains motionless as if frozen in the moment. I clasp her hand in mine as she bites her lower lip.

"I always wanted that for Mama," she whispers, leaning close, her voice quivering. "A guy to love her and be with her... and accept me." Her arm muscles tense as if she's internally fighting to keep standing. "But she always found those 'not today' guys."

Not today. She spits out the phrase with a scowl etched on her face, and the memory strikes me like a lightning bolt. It's the same verbiage Gin and I used when Jordan made a comment about Mom being a young mother like her own. Oh shit. I never meant for it to come off as an insult. Is that the reason she bolted from the dining room and lingered on the pier until I convinced her to rejoin us?

My stomach knots. I'm an idiot. She trusted me that night on the beach, telling me how she always felt like a liability instead of an asset when it came to her mama's personal life. How she'd wished for a man who could love them enough to be there. To actually give a shit. And then I go and say something stupid, basically making fun of her pain to her face.

I tighten my grip on her fingers, pulling her away from the scene, and we amble down the dune and back toward the pier. She doesn't say anything at first, just stares out over the waves as we walk hand-in-hand. Finally, I muster the courage to break the silence. "I understand now why you've been upset the last few days," I say. Jordan turns to me with curious eyes, as I continue. "I know what I said at my mom's party was insensitive. And I didn't mean it."

She tries to give me one of her qualifier smiles but it fades as quickly as it begins to appear. "You did, but it's okay. You were just being honest."

"But I wasn't. I was just making a stupid joke, and it wasn't funny. You've confided in me, and I never should've been so flippant."

The wind whips a few tendrils of her hair across her face, and Jordan pushes them back, tucking them behind her ear. Her bottom lip quivers. "Mama never got her happy ending because of me. Her 'baggage,' according to so many guys. They wouldn't even give her a chance. She always told me that I was wrong for feeling like it was my fault—that it was their own hang-ups—but then..." Jordan's cheeks tinge pink and her chest heaves up and down as if she's having trouble taking a deep breath.

My pulse accelerates. "What?"

She pans her hand in my direction. "Here's the nicest, most upstanding guy I know saying exactly what I always feared." Her voice cracks, small whimpers creeping out between the words. Her eyes wander back to me. Vulnerable. Hurt.

My heart splinters in my chest as her words punch me in the chest. How did I not realize?

"I didn't know what I was talking about. I've never been in that position, and I don't think anyone could say what they would or wouldn't do until they've experienced it." I pull her to my chest, wrapping my arms around her, wanting to cocoon her. Protect her from the visceral pain etched on her face. "But one thing I do know. You shouldn't blame yourself for anything because any guy who gave up having you in his life—in any capacity—royally screwed up because you are the most amazing person. I am better because of you."

Her whimpers increase to full sobs, and she brings her hands to her face, burying herself even further into my chest. The tears wet the front of my shirt. I lead her to the jetty, and we sit on the rounded boulders, the ocean gurgling up and over our toes.

When she finally looks up at me through swollen, red-rimmed eyes, the ghost of something else still dances in her features.

I run my hand down her soaked cheek, cupping her chin. "Is there something else wrong? Something I should know about?"

She pinches her eyes closed. Something lurks, something

threatening to pour out of her just like the thousand tears, but she struggles against it. She holds it back.

Maybe if she realizes that I know something's up, then she'll let me in. "You've just been talking to your mama a lot more lately so I thought that..." I blow out a loud breath. "I don't know."

Jordan straightens her spine and palms both sides of my face. She brings her lips to mine, soft at first then pressing harder. We linger after the kiss, and her mouth grazes against mine as she says, "There's just a lot of dynamics... things I can't really explain right now. But I will. Because I need to. Because you deserve to know everything."

She pulls back and stares into my eyes. I don't know the details, don't know what she needs to divulge, but Brice is wrong. There's no malice or contempt in her eyes; she's not planning some get-rich-quick scheme to take down our farm. But there *is* something there. Sadness. Worry. Conflict.

"Tonight, though, will you hold me?" she asks. "I just need to feel you beside me."

I nod, pulling her against me and running my hands through her hair. I will hold her tonight without questions, without discussion, but tomorrow we talk. Tomorrow, we figure everything out.

CHAPTER 24

Jordan

I slip from the covers and tiptoe into the kitchen. The red electronic numbers on the microwave clock reads 11:12 a.m. A little too late for breakfast but plenty of time for coffee. God knows I'm going to need it to get through what I have to do today.

When I do, there'll be no more nights like the one that we just shared.

Nights filled with cuddling on the couch, watching movies. Talking about nothing special into the wee hours of the morning. Snuggling together as we fall asleep in each other's arms.

I asked him to hold me last night, no questions asked, and he did. He did it so well.

But now the sun is hanging high in the sky, and my borrowed time is running out.

I open the coffee canister and measure out four scoops of crystals then fill the tank of the coffee maker with water. With the push of a few buttons and a whir of steam, the carafe begins to fill.

I walk to the den and sit on the couch, looking out the window over the pool and patio, a flood of memories from this summer filtering through. My first day here I swore I'd keep my focus on the internship and off Farmer Johnson's hot son. So much for that. He was only hot then; now he's so much more.

I sigh. He's everything I've ever wanted.

It's our Sunday off work. We might not have a work schedule for the day, but a timetable does exist. A part of me wants to forget it, slide back into place in my bed, resting my head on his chest. He's still sleeping, not even knowing I've left. It would be easy to return to my happy place. Enjoy a few more moments of the feel of his skin. But I can't. The other part of me—the logical side—screams that it will only prolong the hurt ripping through my insides right now.

When he wakes up and steps out of the bedroom, then I'll tell him it's time to talk. Time to know everything I've been holding back.

The coffeepot beeps, and I push myself off the couch and walk back into the kitchen. I grab a mug from the shelf, pour some coffee and stir in a sugar packet.

The steam curls up from the cup and into my face.

You can do this, Jordan. You can be strong. You've done it before. You can do it again.

I grab the mug and head toward the bedroom just as the door swings open and Bo, pulling on his shirt, dashes into the living area.

"I got a text from Luis, and I have to run out to the farm. I'll be back this afternoon."

Before I can open my mouth, he's out the door, his footsteps pounding each step. A few seconds later his Bronco rumbles to life and peels out of the sandy driveway.

Weird, to say the least, and totally inconvenient. Screwing up the courage to tell Bo about my life—all of my life—requires more gumption than anything else I've done. Because he has come to mean more to me than any guy, outside of Grandpa, that I've known.

I walk into the bedroom, staring at the indention in the pillow where his head was just lying. Maybe it isn't the right time to tell him. Maybe this is the universe's way of thwarting my plans. I sip the coffee but it meets my stomach with a slash of pain. No. No more stringing this along. Now is the time.

Right now.

An hour later, after grabbing a quick shower and getting ready, I slide behind the wheel of my Jeep and pull out onto the main road, pressing the gas pedal to the floor. If I don't hurry, my nerves will win and I'll back out. The beach houses and then the moss-laden oaks pass by the side windows in a blur as I make my way to the farm. Bo said Luis texted him, and he's generally working in the barn, so I take the gravel path heading out behind the field to the barn's entrance. One of the farm trucks sits catty-cornered out front, but Bo's Bronco isn't there.

I get out of my Jeep and walk into the barn, discovering Luis in one of the back stalls. When I step into the room, my boots thump against the wood floor, and he looks up with a grin.

"Jordan! What are you doing here today? Your day off, right?"

"Yeah, but I was looking for Bo."

He furrows his brows. "It's Bo's day off too."

"He had to come in." Okay, confusing. Bo specifically said Luis had texted him. So why is he standing here, staring at me like I have three heads? "Wait, I thought he said it was you who texted him and called him in?"

Luis shrugs, propping himself against his shovel. "Wasn't me. The only other person out here today is Walter. Ain't nobody else around."

I nod and walk to the entrance, running the morning's events through my mind. He did say Luis, right? Or did I just assume? No, I'm positive he said he texted him. My brain hurts from trying to make all the irregular pieces form some semblance of truth. Walter pulls up on the ATV and hops off, nodding in my direction.

I nod back, but then stop him and ask, "Have you seen Bo by any chance?"

He points across the field toward the office. "I did see his Bronco up by the main house just a bit ago."

I pat him on the shoulder. "Awesome. Thanks."

The ATV Walter left behind still has the key in the ignition. I jump on it and head the back way to the office, around the fields, and park by the greenhouses. The Bronco sits in his usual place in the gravel lot out front, but there's another vehicle, a sedan I've never seen before, parked beside it. Weird. If it's some kind of meeting, why wouldn't Clay or Patrick be here? And why did he run out of the apartment this morning like he was headed to a five-alarm fire?

I stalk up the side of the house, peering in a few of the windows, but inside is dark and empty. Spying isn't exactly my forte but now my interest in piqued. As I near the front, mumbled voices drift through the air. It's impossible to make out the words, but one of the voices is deeper like Bo's; the other is higher-pitched. Female. Not Gin, Doniella, or Claire. I'd recognize their voices anywhere. But this one I have heard before, though I can't put my finger on it.

That is until I peek around the corner of the house. At the far end of the porch on the opposite side, Bo sits beside a brown-haired girl about our age. When she turns to him and I catch her side profile, my breath hitches.

That's why it seemed familiar but not recognizable.

Because I've only seen and heard her once before.

Laurel.

The entire scene morphs into a movie reel, one where someone has enabled slow motion. My heart drums in my ears as I watch it unfold. She strokes his cheek. He grabs her hand and pats it. They're talking again, the words inaudible. She leans in, closer, closer, closer, until her lips pucker against his face. They pull apart, but it's short-lived, because Bo then reaches out, wrapping an arm around her shoulders, tugging her to him.

My head spins. Why hasn't he told me he's still communicating with her? How could he tell me he wanted to be with me if he still wants to be with her? We're nothing alike. Nothing! And here I've been torturing myself about not being straightforward with him while he's been blatantly lying to me. It was delusional to think Bo would be different than any other guy I've ever known. My throat tightens. They're all cut from the same cloth. Cheaters. Liars.

I slink back behind the wall and pad softly through the grass until I'm sure my footsteps won't be heard. I jump on the waiting ATV and drive as fast as I can back to the barn and my Jeep, tears pouring and blowing in the breeze.

Hey! You've reached the voicemail of Sheryl Wright at Wright Family Farm. I'm sorry I missed your call, but if you'll leave your name and number, I'll get back to you soon.

"Hey Mama. It's me."

Deep breath. Hold back the waterworks. If Mama hears the tears... I swallow hard. No. She won't hear them because I can be strong.

I start again. "Today is just... one of those days where I need to hear your voice. I miss you and Weston and I just feel stupid and... I'm sorry, I shouldn't be leaving all this on your voicemail. I know you're probably out on the tractor or in the barn. I just... I just don't know...." My voice breaks and so does the dam holding back the flood of emotions. I panic and end the call before the first sobs can be recorded.

I wipe my eyes, stomping my foot in the sand, sending a glittering spiral of dust into the air. I'm a terrible daughter. Here Mama is having to look after Grandma and Grandpa, take care of the farm, and keep up with a rambunctious three-year-old and all I can do is call and leave bumbling voice messages to stress her out even more. I can't throw my romantic burdens on her shoulders.

I blink away the lingering tears, sniff my nose, and clear my throat then dial her number again. Voicemail. *Beep*.

"Hey Mama, it's me again. I just wanted to call and tell you to disregard that last message. I was having a moment, but it's over now. I'm good, so please don't worry. Love y'all. Bye."

Pointless. I might as well have covered myself in Saran wrap. She'll see right through that ill-rehearsed spiel.

"Your face looks longer than a basset hound's ears." I startle at the sound of Miss Bessie's voice, unaware that anyone has been watching me. She stands in her backyard, staring at me across the grassy expanse. "I thought young love was supposed to make you happy, not... whatever this is."

I trudge in her direction, stepping over the seashell-borders Gin has pieced together around the Johnson's flowerbeds. The truth bubbles inside me, and I need someone to listen, to comfort me. Someone to put their arms around me and tell me it's going to be okay. Mama's not answering, and I can't talk to Claire or Gin about this. "Sorry, Miss Bessie," I mumble.

Her smile drops as she meets me halfway, wrapping her arms around me. I fold myself into her, soaking in her warmth. How could this be happening again? How could I have put myself in this position? And how could Bo have lied to me, misled me about what we had?

Miss Bessie loops her arm in mine and ushers me toward her patio swing. We sit side by side, as she brushes away the strands of hair stuck to my wet cheeks. "Talk to me, child. What's going on?"

I take a deep breath, finding my words amongst the million thoughts swirling in my head. "Did you ever have a pretty big secret—not a lie, just something you didn't divulge when you probably should have—and just when you're about to tell someone, you find out they're keeping their own secret? A secret so big it breaks your heart?"

Miss Bessie brings a closed fist to her mouth then pulls me to her chest, hugging tight, as she leans her head on mine. For a moment, I close my eyes and pretend it's Mama. Mama whose hugs fix everything. Mama who always knows exactly what to say.

"Shhhh," she coos. "Tell me all about it."

Talk to him. No-holds-barred, open honesty. Tell Bo the true story of all my responsibilities and ask him point blank why he was kissing Laurel and lying to me about it. That's what Miss Bessie said.

She let me clean up my face, gave me a piece of her home-made pound cake, and spent an hour doling out advice. And for the first time all summer, I got to pull out my phone and show someone photos of Weston eating his birthday cake last fall and riding on the tractor with Grandpa. It felt good to be a hundred percent myself, no hiding, no secrets.

I walk across the lawn as Bo pulls up in his Bronco and hops out, a huge grin on his face. My heart sinks. I didn't put that smile there, but I can guess who did. A lump rises in my throat but I push it down.

"Mom called. She has dinner ready." He reaches for my hand, and reluctantly, I take his, though I keep my fingers squeezed tight together. The thought of Laurel's hand being where mine is now sours my stomach. My phone rings, and, grateful for the interruption, I yank my hand away and pull it from my pocket.

Mama. Finally.

"I'll be right there. I'm just going to take this," I say, waving my phone in the air. He nods and heads inside while I take a seat on the steps. "Hello?"

"Sassy, are you okay? Do I need to come down there and kick somebody's ass?"

Typical response from Mama when her little girl is hurting. I'm actually surprised she isn't halfway here already, ready to wage war with whoever made me cry.

"It's just been one of those days, and I missed you and Weston." The emotions surge upwards again, but I can't succumb when everyone's waiting on me inside. "I'm just sitting down to dinner though. Can I call you back tonight?"

"Of course you can, but before you go..." Her voice trails off before I hear her call out to someone else. "Weston, come here... it's Mama."

Giggles fill the speaker along with a loud rustling noise and I know he's hijacked the phone from his Mimi's hands. "Hey Ma-ma!"

The melodic tenor of his voice sweeps away all my worries in a heartbeat. I clutch the phone closer to my head, wishing I could snuggle him instead of this cold, hard plastic. "Hey baby."

"Tell Mama that we're about to take our bath and go to bed!" Mama's voice bleeds through in the background.

"I go to bed!" Weston squeals. "Night!"

"Oh, Weston. I miss you. I love you so much. I can't wait to see you again."

Mama takes the phone, tells me to call her back later, and the line cuts. I sit, looking out on the sandy roadside dunes and wishing instead for the rolling Blue Ridge hills. What I wouldn't give to breathe in that clean mountain air and lay my head in Mama's lap. Edisto is beautiful but nothing compares to home when your heart is hurting.

Two loud thuds on the porch startle me, and I turn just in time to see Bo's arm withdrawing from a crack in the front screen door, his two muddy boots tossed onto the planks. The screen door slams shut as he retreats inside. Claire must've reminded him about her "no work boots in the house" rule.

I stand up, mustering every bit of strength, and walk inside to the dining room. The rest of the family waits at the table, and I quickly slide into my seat.

"Sorry about that. My mama called," I explain, unrolling my napkin and laying it across my lap.

Claire nods with a smile, but Bo grunts, grabbing his fork and spearing a carrot, which he shoves into his mouth, followed by another. The fork tines hit the plate with a sharp grating sound that sets my teeth on edge. He, however, doesn't seem to notice and only levels a hard stare in my direction, his eyes not moving and barely blinking.

I can't return the favor, so I stare at my plate. If I look at Bo, I'll definitely regurgitate everything I've already eaten today on Claire's lovely flowered China. Seeing his hands reminds me of him holding hers. His shoulders remind me of her hugs. His lips...

I clutch my napkin, bringing it to my mouth.

"Are you two having a fight or something because it's pretty frigid down here on this side of the table. And I'm sort of afraid I'm going to get impaled by a flying broccoli spear or a baby carrot here in a couple seconds," Gin pipes up, breaking the awkward silence. When no one responds, she darts her eyes between the two of us and then mumbles, "Oh-kay."

Claire clears her throat, picking up with Gin's failed attempt. "So... Jordan, how was your day, dear? Did you enjoy your time off?"

I finish chewing a sliver of grilled chicken, but before I can answer, Bo blurts out, "Oh, I think she had plenty of *other* things to do today." He shoots me a hard glare. "Things to do, *people* to talk to."

I narrow my eyes. I'm not sure what he's insinuating, but it's awfully bold to pull shit with me when I saw his extracurricular activities this afternoon. "I'm sure you had just as much on your schedule. Any interesting *meetings* you want to share?"

Claire holds out both of her hands like stop signs, waving them back and forth. "I'm sensing there's some friction tonight, and maybe we should consider discussing it openly?" When no one responds to her gesture, she cocks her head to the side, trying again. "This kind of emotion is not good to hold in while we're eating—not good for our mental health or our digestion."

I blow out a loud breath and push away my plate. "I agree. As a matter of fact, I'm not very hungry, so I think I'll just skip supper tonight and go on back to the guest house."

Bo rolls his eyes as he pulverizes a carrot into orange mush on his plate. "Yeah, because it's much easier to run away and hide than admit the truth."

Claire clears her throat, a panic rising in her face, pupils dilated. "I think we need to pause. Things can be said in the heat of passion that aren't meant. You can't recover a word after it's spoken, so let's make sure—"

Gin tosses down her fork, slamming her empty fist on the table. The glasses and dishes rattle. "What truth?"

Exactly, Gin.

My chair slides back so quickly it nearly turns over as I stand up, palm pressed to my chest. "Truth? You want to talk to me about truth? *Sorry Jordan, Luis called. He needs me at the farm.*" I repeat the excuse he gave me earlier in my best pathetic-lying-cheater voice, wagging my head back and forth. Juvenile, maybe, but the rage bubbles out of me. I place both hands on the table, leaning over the top toward him. "Seems legit until I go to the farm and the guys spill the beans that you're really up at the main house. With who? Laurel."

Gin gasps, fire flicking in her cheeks. "Laurel? She's back and you're seeing her?" She shakes her head, mumbling under her breath, "Dumbass."

I glance at Gin, confirming her accusation. "Oh yeah, she's back. And just like that—" I pause, snapping my fingers in the air—"your brother's right back with her."

Bo jumps to his feet, this time being the one to slam a fist on the table. Claire's glass topples, over, spilling tea and ice cubes across the top, but no one moves to wipe it up. "I am not!"

I steeple my hands in front of my face, blowing air out and taking it back in, attempting to keep myself from going full-blown bitch. "You didn't hold her hand, hug her, and *kiss* her this afternoon? I just imagined all of that?"

Bo's eyes saucer and a deep blush colors his cheeks. "I didn't kiss her." He retakes his seat, glancing up from under his dark lashes. "She kissed me."

My heart stops. It freaking short-circuits. Because even if I know what I saw earlier, until he just admitted it, I was holding on to some misguided hope that I'd been wrong. That I misunderstood. I hadn't. The tears want to fall, and I struggle to hold them in. "Well, that makes it all fine then."

I slump back into my chair, defeated. A deafening silence descends on the table, everyone frozen in shock, their mouths hanging open as their eyes bounce between me and Bo like ping pong balls in a championship match.

"Why are you getting all holier-than-thou when you have a little secret of your own?" Bo leans forward on his elbows, laser focusing on me. His voice is hard like steel, but slow and calm. Too calm. "You thought you were pulling one over on me, too, but surprise, surprise. I already figured out your secret. I know all about it."

"What secret?" Gin asks.

"Not what. Who." When he says the last part, his jaw flexes in and out.

"Who?" Gin's voice grows more frantic.

Bo sits back in his chair, folding his arms over his chest with a satisfied smirk. "Weston. Jordan's boyfriend back home."

I blow out a loud breath, palming my forehead. "That couldn't be further from the truth."

"I heard you on the phone just a minute ago. *Goodnight Weston. I love you. I miss you. Can't wait to see you.*" Now it's his turn to use the mocking voice, but he doesn't know how misguided he is. He's jumped to the wrong conclusion. "Who else would you say that to besides a secret boyfriend?"

My stomach wads into a ball, and I'm grateful for not eating a bite of the supper. My voice quivers as I say, "This is not the way I wanted to tell you."

"Oh my God, so you admit it? I can't believe this is happening to me again!" Bo jumps up, turning and slapping the dining room wall with all his might. A few of Claire's collectible bells tinkle on their shelves. He looks back at me, and for the first time ever, tears gather in his eyes. "I thought you were different. You and I were on a different wavelength. You made me believe... but no." He balls up a fist and grinds it into his forehead, his bicep flexing so hard his whole arm trembles, then walks back to the table and leans over it. "Just tell me to my face, Jordan. Admit—right here, right now—that Weston is your boyfriend from back home."

My muscles weigh a million pounds, pulling me down, collapsing me. Bo already hates me now, so finally revealing my secret should be easy. It's not. Because once he finds out, he'll never want to talk to me again. "Bo... Weston is *not* my boyfriend." He rolls his eyes and tries to look away, but I reach across the table, cupping his chin, making him hear the next words off my tongue. "He's my son."

CHAPTER 25

Bo

The floor moves beneath me and my legs threaten to follow suit. I sit down hard, grabbing the sides of my chair to make sure I don't go limp and roll off the side.

A son. Jordan has a kid. Why hasn't she told me before now? Did she not think that was a significant fact I deserved to know?

My breath comes out in quick spurts, my head getting dizzy. I tighten the grip on my chair.

Mom stands at the head of the table. "I think it's prudent we all take a moment and breathe. We've put a lot of... information... on the table tonight, and I think we need to take some time to unpack it." Her voice struggles to maintain that cool, calm, and collected therapist tone until everyone, including Dad, begins pushing back their chairs. "No one leaves!" she snaps, her voice's sudden razor-sharp edge stopping everyone in their tracks. Like obedient soldiers we all sink back to our seats. Her tight smile returns after a few deep breaths.

"Let's just take this in order of how these revelations came to light, shall we?" Mom takes three long inhales and exhales then turns to me. "Care to explain about the Laurel situation?"

Not really. The truth is that Laurel should have never been here. I didn't ask her to come; I'd left no open invitation for when she's in town. But I also couldn't take the chance that my ignoring her would lead to her barging in here and upsetting Jordan. Especially when she threatened to do just that.

"I got a text from Laurel saying she was at the farm and wanted to talk with me and that if I didn't come meet her, then she was coming here to the house. I never invited her, and I hadn't heard from her since that day at the pool until this morning. I never wanted her showing up here and upsetting Jordan." I look over at Jordan as I speak her name, and she glances up. The hard edge evaporates, leaving only the softness I've come to know these past few months. "I thought I could handle things and she'd go away."

Mom squints her eyes as if weighing my explanations, nodding as she makes the pieces connect. At least for the most part. She bites her lip, then asks, "My question is how, instead, did you two become affectionate?"

The thought of Jordan seeing us and thinking I was cheating on her twists my guts. "We didn't." I look at Jordan when I say those two words. She needs to hear them. She deserves to. "Not in the way Jordan thinks." Mom massages her chin between her thumb and forefinger, lifting her eyebrows to encourage me to elaborate. "Laurel has come to stay with her grandmother down here and wants to get back together, but I told her no." I shift my focus to Jordan, speaking the next part directly to her. "Because I'm with you and want to be with you." I turn back to Mom, pleading the rest of my case. "Yeah, I grabbed her hand and hugged her because as much as I hate what she did to me, I still want to be the nice guy and let her down easy. She kissed me on the cheek; I didn't kiss her back. And shortly after, she left."

Jordan blows out a loud breath and drops her head into her hands. "I'm sorry," she mumbles from between her fingers.

"I didn't tell you because you'd already been so upset lately, and I never wanted you to feel insecure with me."

Dad and Gin sit silently, mouth agape as if shellshocked. But mom leans her head back against her chair, staring up at the ceiling. It's what she often does while conducting her own forensic investigation in her brain. "Can I ask a question?" This time, she levels her gaze on Jordan, who sits up straighter under the scrutiny, swallowing hard and wiping away the moisture from her face. "Why were you at the farm if you didn't have to go in today? Were you following Bo? Did you not trust him?"

"No, it's not that." She shakes her head. "I went looking for him because I wanted to tell him about Weston."

Huh? That seems... convenient. Obviously, mom agrees. She slides off her glasses, biting on the arm. "I'm not sure I follow."

"Last night, I promised Bo that I would tell him everything about my life back home. Things I hadn't told him before; things he deserved to know. I was ready to talk first thing this morning but then he ran out so suddenly. I'd already screwed up the courage to tell him, and I didn't want to lose it, so I went looking for him."

So, all of that is plausible. The flurry of phone conversations, Brice's overheard information, Jordan's reluctance—it all makes sense now. All except for one thing. And it's the most important issue of all because I've made decisions, put my heart on the line, without having all the facts. "Why haven't you told me before?" I ask.

Jordan's bottom lip trembles and shame colors her cheeks as she stares down at the table. "Because I'm selfish. And a coward."

"No, you aren't." Gin reaches over and grabs Jordan's hand. They exchange genuine smiles, the kind absent from Jordan's face the past few days. "Help us understand things through your eyes."

Jordan sighs and stands up, walking over to the windows overlooking the patio. She keeps her back to us, but her face reflects in the glass. Her eyes clamp shut and remain shut as she begins sharing her story. "Growing up, people talked about Mama because I didn't have a father. Those same people judged me when I got pregnant. *Look at her. She's just like her whore mama.* I noticed it all—the whispers, the stares, the religious tracts left in our mailbox." She pivots on her heels and walks back to the table, turning her eyes on me. "I told you about the way I grew up. And that's not an excuse— I don't make excuses—it's just when you're young and gullible and desperate for stability, you're all too willing to believe the smooth talk. You think it's love, but it's manipulation."

An image of Jordan, years younger, naïve and trusting, knits together in my mind. And right beside her, a Brice-like figure, calculating, controlling, lying. No wonder she loathed Brice from the beginning. She'd already been burned by someone like him in her past. And it changed her life forever.

Mom steps around the table to Jordan, pulling her into a side hug. "I definitely understand that, but not all men are slick opportunists. There are plenty of decent ones who would care about you and your son."

Jordan huffs out a breath and pulls away, padding back to the windows. "When Weston was 18 months old, a friend set me up with this 'great' guy. Over dinner, I told him about Weston. Afterward, we went to the movies, he excused himself to the bathroom, and never came back."

Gin covers her mouth with her hand, glancing at Mom with saucered eyes. Mom grimaces but does her best to tuck it away, doing her classic therapist move to wash the emotion from her face. My stomach drops as I imagine her sitting in the theater seat, glancing back to the door when five minutes passed. 10 minutes. More. How her shoulders must have slumped as she collapsed back in her seat when realizing. I frown as if second-hand sensing her pain.

Jordan grinds her fingers into a fist that she slams against her thigh. "I was humiliated, but not surprised." She turns around, jaw steeled, the blue of her eyes dulled. "I'd seen it before. When I was in elementary school, Mama dated a guy. I really wanted him to be my father, but one day, they got into a huge argument and he said he didn't want to deal with her baggage AKA me. After that, she quit trying."

Mom and Dad exchange glances as Jordan retakes her seat at the table and reaches across, grabbing my hand. I don't push her away but I don't pull her in, either. I just let my hand lie on hers, limp. Not because I don't have any feelings for her but because I have too many feelings all at once, bouncing off each other, colliding and combusting like a nuclear reaction.

"I know I should've told you sooner—that night on the beach—but I couldn't. I was afraid, selfish, because I didn't want to lose you. You mean so much to me." She slips her hand from mine, dropping it to her lap. "I don't expect you to understand. There's no way you could. I just need you to not hate me for stealing these moments with you. For allowing me to have this time we've shared to last in my memories for the rest of my life. Because to me, there will never be another Bo Johnson."

The sound of my name, stated in her voice, breaks me. I don't hate her. Not in the least. And even though I understand her hesitancy in telling me about her son, I honestly don't know what this means for us. I'm not sure I know myself well enough to make a decision. I should tell her, but I can't. It's as if my mouth and brain have quit communicating, leaving only a void.

Mom nods in my direction. "Do you have anything to say right now?"

"I... I..." The words won't come. They refuse to move.

"It's okay. Really." Jordan offers me a half-smile, doing her best to ease my anxiety when she's standing there, her entire life stripped naked in front of us.

Without warning, Mom breaks down, tears free-falling down her face as she rushes to Jordan, yanking her to her chest. She waves at Dad to take over the conversation.

A heavy silence descends on the room, the only sound the intermittent sobs alternating between Mom and Jordan. Dad gnaws his fingernails as he stares at the small puddle on the tablecloth left behind from the ice of Mom's spilled drink.

Finally, he slides his chair back, stands up, leveling his eyes on Jordan whom Mom releases from her grip, and clears his throat. "Thank you for confiding in us and trusting us with your story. It obviously hasn't been an easy road, but it's one that has molded and shaped you into a fine young woman, a hell of a farmer, and I'm sure a wonderful mother. With that being said, I think it might be best to take some time and absorb everything. And Bo..." He walks to my chair and presses his fingers into my shoulder. "You need to step back and assess where you are with this. This situation isn't one to play around with. It's serious."

"Thanks, Clay, Claire, Gin..." Jordan takes turns looking at each of them before turning to me. Her eyes search me, probably looking for any signs of reaction on my part, but my body feels rigid. Foreign. She continues, "And Bo for letting me explain. I'm sorry for any hurt I've caused, but please know that I'm a realist and there will never be any resentment on my part if you were to end my internship journey tonight or..." Her jaw flexes as storm clouds roll across her face. "...never speak to me again. I mean, what guy would ever want to pick up the slack and take on another's responsibility?"

Her question stabs me in the chest, slicing between my ribs, filleting my own history like a gutted fish. She means it in a rhetorical sense, but for me, her question needs an answer. It has an answer. One I rarely talk about.

"My dad." I stand up and stare at the very sort of man Jordan believes can't exist in real life. A man very real to me. The man who accepted, loved, and raised another man's son. "He adopted me and chose to be my father."

CHAPTER 26

Jordan

Bo's taillights disappear down the road, two orange orbs dissolving into the darkness. Quickly. Yet painstakingly slow.

He left without another word. He dropped the bomb of his paternity then simply stood up, turned, and walked out the door. By the time I could unglue my feet from the floor to run after him, his foot was stomping the gas pedal. The engine, growling from the acceleration, stopped me in my tracks. A warning to keep my distance.

For his sake.

For mine.

Now, I stand at the end of the Johnson's driveway, enshrouded in the inky blackness of night, staring down the desolate highway. A place where he used to be but isn't anymore.

The summertime humidity pricks my skin with sweat beads that morph into ice chips as stray breezes creep in off the ocean. I close my eyes and conjure up the memory of his arms around me, how the strength in his muscles pressed into the softness of my skin, how the heat lingered in the touchpoints between us. The images, though, are vapor, misty remembrances dancing like ghosts then fading to oblivion when I try to focus on them.

Tiptoeing on the verge of vivid sight before hiding themselves again.

I almost had everything I've ever wanted. But only almost.

My eyes burn, the salt from the air mixing with my tears as I amble toward the beach, the sand shifting and sliding beneath my feet.

I've lost him.

But did I ever really have him?

Or have I been fooling myself this entire time? Playing a masochistic game of hope in a hopeless situation. Setting myself up for the inevitable fall. Convincing myself to chance the improbable.

There was never any question how my life would turn out. At least not at the beginning of summer. But then Bo...

He'd changed everything. He made me believe. He made me hope.

I muffle a sob in my throat.

I've played this moment repeatedly in my head over the last few days, the concocted images always brimming with drama, punctuated with screams, laced with accusations, flooded by tears. But they've all proven false. Instead, he was silent, struggling, almost as if an invisible hand was pulling him away.

I had prepared myself for his anger. For his loathing. For his grief.

I hadn't expected the silence, so heavy, so thick that it pulls me into the void, compressing me, squeezing my organs. Our once-consuming, radiant, joy-inducing romance has morphed into a black hole of dense emotions, so painful that neither of us can identify the sludge we're now standing in.

So we're quiet. Silent.

It's the most painful sound in the universe. An absence. An empty hole. A bottomless pit.

One I'll never be able to crawl out of.

But the silence has followed me here, the ocean so calm that it feels dead, lifeless. No crashing surf. No salty spray as it meets with earth. It's as if the water is holding its breath, waiting for something.

Above, the stars blaze brighter in the absence of the glowing moon but their light is still too faint to highlight the waves slowly rolling to shore.

Bo had become my constant, my new moon, but now staring up into the void, the truth sinks in: both of them have left me, sequestered me in the darkness. Alone.

Playtime is over and reality slinks back in. I am truly my mama's daughter, and it's time to accept that.

Maybe it is where I've always been meant to be.

CHAPTER 27

Bo

I lay back on the slatted boards, staring up at the hazy rash of stars twinkling from the Milky Way. Way out here on the dock, away from the town center, even the faintest light is easily visible. The water gurgles underneath the dock, giving it the slightest sway, and the tall arms the shrimp boats creak in the breeze.

There's no better place on the island to stretch out under the stars and think than on the docks at the Ramsey shrimping company. I can't begin to count the nights Jett and I came out here to talk about whatever was usually on his mind. Racing, his mom, and last year, CJ. I was always the advice-giver, but tonight, I'm the one in need.

That's why when I excused myself from the table and left everyone sitting there a couple hours ago, the first thing I did was get in my Bronco and text him. He was out of town, a couple counties over, but dropped everything, jumped in his Challenger, and headed my way.

He still doesn't know what's wrong. Jordan's news isn't something I could drop on him unexpectedly. Honestly, I'm not sure I can even verbalize it. The incessant questions run through my brain with no detour. Can I handle a kid? Do I even want to?

What if he hates me? What if he likes me? What if I meet him and then Jordan and I don't work out? What if I refuse to meet him? How could I not like him if he's like his mom? But what if he's like his father? And who the hell is his father? Where is he?

My head spins, the faintest stars blurring in and out of focus, as heavy footsteps thump against the wooden boards. Jett sits down and then lays back beside me. He swivels his head, staring. "Never thought I'd see the day where you needed my advice. This must be pretty huge." He laughs but stops when I don't join in. In my periphery, I watch his eyes search my face, waiting on some kind of reaction, but I haven't been able to muster much of anything since the truth came out.

After a long beat, I finally ask, "Are there any dealbreakers in a relationship for you?"

Jett raises up on one elbow, peering down at me. "What happened? Jordan didn't cheat on you, did she? She doesn't seem the type."

I shake my head. "No... nothing like that. I found out something about her. Something I didn't know when we first got together. She—"

Jett slaps his hand over my mouth. "Before you tell me anything else, I have to ask. Does knowing what you know now change how you feel about her?"

Valid question. I close my eyes, conjuring up an image of Jordan. Do I feel different about her now? Does she feel like a changed person somehow, now that I know everything? I swallow hard.

The answer is no.

She's still the same Jordan—the same one I held just last night. The new doubts, the new insecurities, really don't have anything to do with her at all. They're all centered on me.

I snap my eyes open and look over at him. "Absolutely not. I still think she's amazing. But now... I don't know if *I'm* good enough. Or prepared enough. Or too much of an idiot?"

Jett shakes his head. "Well, now you've really lost me."

"Jordan has a kid. A three-year-old boy, Weston."

Cue the audible gasp from Jett. "Woah. Damn," He mumbles, his mouth dropping open as he lowers back down to the dock and stares up at the night sky, not moving. Like he's letting it register. After a silent pause, he sits up, cross-legged. "Why didn't she tell you before?"

I pick up a tiny shell laying on the dock and roll it between my fingers. "People in the past haven't been the nicest about it."

"I can imagine." He removes his baseball cap and runs fingers through his hair. "How did she tell you?"

"That's a complicated story." I sit up, too, and let my legs dangle off the side of the dock as I recap the events of the last few days. He gives me his undivided attention, his reactions dancing over his face, but none so much as when I relay what happened at the end of our confrontation tonight. "That's when I just blurted it out. I told her about my dad."

Jett's mouth drops open, and he grabs my shoulder. "You told her that? But you don't tell anyone."

"I told you."

"Yeah, but I've been your best friend forever."

"I don't know why I told her. I just..."

Jett furrows his brows, chewing the inside of his cheek. "Hmmm."

"What?"

He shrugs. "I think it says a lot that you reacted that way. She shared something; you shared something. You didn't leave her hanging. You met her where she was."

Good point. When I thought Jordan had a secret boyfriend, the anger swirled in me like a tornado. But when I found out the that she had a kid, the shock of finding out was no more paramount than the feeling of relief that it wasn't another guy. And then she began recalling the stories of those guys in her life before me—losers—and how they'd skewed her expectations. My mom shared her pain, the proof etched on her face as she pulled Jordan to her. And then he stood up.

My dad.

And for the first time, I fully understood how freaking awesome he is.

How lucky I am.

How without him, my mom could've been in Jordan's exact position, and I would've been Weston. Would we have survived without him? Sure, my mom and Jordan both have backbones of steel. But would our life have been missing an integral piece in a man who stepped up and did the things he didn't have to do but wanted to do? I'm not sure there's a way to measure all he's given me, and I make a mental note to tell him more often how much I appreciate him. For being that man. For being my dad.

And Jett understands this as much as I do.

"My dad. Your stepmom, Jenniston. We got lucky. I just don't know if I'm capable or ready for all of this," I say. Making that admission is hard but honest.

He nods. "Dad dated a few people on and off before Jenniston. None of them really cared anything about me—it's like they tolerated me instead. I never got to know them and when they showed up, they just sucked up my dad's time and ignored me. But Jenniston was different. She tried to get to know me. She considered us a package deal. Looking back, I'm glad she was in it for the long haul because I got really attached to her."

I turn to face Jett head-on, leveling my eyes with his. I need his input. I need his perspective. "What do I do?"

He puffs up his cheeks, holding his breath before blowing it out slowly. His head tilts back to the wooden railing as he stares up at the sky. "It's tough. Kids change things. They get attached, and they don't need adults coming in and out of their life." He leans forward again, meeting my gaze and not looking away. "If you're really committed to Jordan, I say go for it. Meet the kid. Get to know him. Get to know them as a unit. But if this is a summer thing, it's probably time to step away before anyone really gets hurt."

I sigh. "So, you're telling me this decision is all on me?"

Jett hunches his shoulders, lifting both hands. "You'll make the right choice. I mean, look who your best friend is. You got that one right!"

The sand shifts under my bare feet as I trek through the access point and over the small dune, scanning the beach for one particular figure. She sits, back to me, and stares up at the dark sky. There was never any doubt where she'd be. I'd sought perspective from my best friend; she'd turned to her pseudo-father figure. The one who'd consistently been there for her.

But that was before me.

I walk over and sit down on the sand. Our fingers linger inches apart but make no move to join. There are things that need to be said, decisions to be discussed.

Jordan presses her lips together, flattening them into an invisible line before she turns to me, her eyes pinned to the sand, evading mine. A torrent of "I'm sorrys" and "I should haves" stream from her mouth like a wide-open faucet.

I hold up my hand. "I don't want to hear your apologies. I'm done with them." She freezes for a beat then lifts her eyes to mine, her mouth creasing into a deep frown. I straighten my spine, sinking my shoulders and lifting my chin higher. There's going to be no more of this tonight. I point to the phone in her lap. "Call your Mama. Put it on speaker."

She hesitates, her face pinching in confusion, before she reaches for it and dials the number. Her mama answers on the second ring.

"Hey Sassy. What's up?" Dark notes color her tone. Suspicion. Anticipation. And none of it positive.

"I don't know actually." Jordan's voice breaks as if the emotional dam she's tried to rebuild since supper is holier than Swiss cheese. "There's someone here who wants to speak to you."

"Oh-kay?" she mumbles.

I take Jordan's phone and hold it up between us, angling it at my face. The time has come for me to set this whole situation straight. "Ms. Wright? This is Bo Johnson. I'm... I mean, we... um, I'm..." Jordan appears on the verge of a breakdown so I offer her a reassuring smile. I hope my next words still fit into her plans. "I'm Jordan's boyfriend."

A long exhale sounds on the other end. She chuckles. "I might have heard you mentioned once or twice."

The admission sends chills rocketing through me. Jordan had given up on guys, given up on finding something real. But she broke her own rules when we got together. She saw something in me that cut right through her fear. She saw my potential before I saw it myself.

"I was wondering if you had some free time this weekend?" I ask.

"I think so." She states it plainly but a question lingers behind the scenes.

"Good. I wanted to take an opportunity to meet you, and the grandparents, and... Weston." Jordan steeples her fingers in front of her mouth. I reach out, running my fingers down her arm. Our held gaze is an impenetrable rope, tying us together, pulling us closer. "I'd like to get to know all of you."

A few sniffles bleed through the line. Like mother, like daughter. She clears her throat and says, "Well, I think that would be lovely, Bo. We'd love to have y'all here."

"Thank you, ma'am. See y'all soon."

I hand the phone back to Jordan. She pulls it to her face, her movements slow and measured, as if she's stunned by my request. "I'm gonna have to call you back," she mumbles into the phone, then ends the call before any reply. It falls to the sand between us, but Jordan makes no move to retrieve it.

She stares at me, chest heaving, before getting to her knees and lunging forward, circling her arms around my neck. In the next moment, her lips find mine, moving like a whisper at first but growing stronger as she palms both sides of my face and tugs me closer. I wrap my arms around her, running my fingers under the hem of her shirt and molding them into her soft skin.

I'd imagined this kiss while I was driving back from the dock, hoping that the barrier standing between us lately would dissolve, transporting us back to that first kiss on this very beach, under this same moon.

But this one is so much better. Freer. Uninhibited. Because this time, there is nothing between us but honesty, every secret dissolved.

She pulls back, her lips still grazing mine as she pants against my mouth. "What do you want to know?" she asks. "I'm an open book. Ask me anything."

A million questions parade through my brain, but only one deserves my full attention in this moment. "We'll get to all that. Right now, I only have one." I pick up her phone from the sand and hand it to her. "Can I see a picture of Weston?"

A huge smile creases her face as she opens her photo gallery.

CHAPTER 28

Jordan

"Omg, he's precious!" Gin sits on my comforter, swiping through the photos of Weston in my phone. It's felt amazing the last few days being able to show him off after so many weeks of hiding. She pauses on one of me holding Weston in our backyard while he points at the chickens and traces a finger over his hair. "He looks so much like you, except for his curls. It's strange, but they sort of look like Bo's."

"I know." I smile, staring down at the photo. One of the first things I noticed about Bo, beside his deep blue eyes, was his head full of spiraled curls. They reminded me of Weston's, though something about Bo's made me want to run my hands through them. They still do.

Gin bites her lip, drumming her fingers on her leg. She glances between me and the photo. "Can I ask something personal?"

"Better than anyone I know." I quip, almost laughing out loud. Gin requesting permission to get personal? Since when did she learn boundaries? I look down at her eager eyes. "Go ahead."

"Does Weston look anything like his father?"

So much for the boundaries. The hair prickles on my neck just having him mentioned. He has no part in my or Weston's future and if I could discover a way to time-travel backwards to successfully rub people out of existence, he'd be number one on my list. My nose crinkles as I'm forced to talk about him. It's like swallowing pickle juice. Times ten. "That is a person of whom we do not speak." Gin's eyes saucer and she shrinks back, pulling an imaginary zipper over her lips. I sit down beside her on the bed, patting her thigh. "But no, thank God."

She shoots me a grin then hesitates, lips puckering as if another question rears its head, but then thinks better of it and pinches her mouth closed. I'm sure she's dying to ask me more but thankfully, she's holding off. As I fold a few outfits and load them into my duffel, Gin swipes to a photo of my family—one of us standing in front of the farm's sign. "Are you nervous?"

"About going home?" I ask. She nods, biting her bottom lip. Maybe she's wondering more about how Bo will be received. No problem there, though. I half expect Mama to have laid out a red carpet. "No way. I'm excited to introduce Bo to everyone, and they are chomping at the bit to meet him." Then it dawns on me. Maybe she's asking because Bo has confided in her. "Why? Do you think he's nervous?"

"He says not... but he's lying." When I frown, Gin immediately waves her hands, adding, "In a good way, obviously. He wants Weston to like him."

"He will. Weston loves everyone." An image of Bo, Weston in his arms as they stroll through the mountain meadows, forms in my thoughts. I clutch the shirt I'm folding to my chest as I imagine them laughing while the wind tousles their curls. "Not that it's hard to love Bo," I add.

This has become a usual occurrence over the last few days. One minute I'm totally normal, the next I'm off in la-la-land, daydreaming about everything Bo.

"How can something be so cute and so gross at the same time?" She sticks her tongue out and pokes a finger toward the back of her throat. "And speaking of gross... I can't believe y'all are leaving me alone to work with Brice this weekend. You know he's going to be giving me the third-degree every chance he gets."

Ugh. Nothing like mentioning Brice to pull me out of all my Bo-inspired fantasies. The past days of Brice's sabotage have paled in comparison to the ire in his eyes since he discovered Bo is going home with me to meet my kid. After Bo confessed about his own adoption, the loathing Brice angled at Bo finally took shape. It's why he keeps mentioning things about family and blood. It's like he believes Bo should be punished for not sharing DNA with the Johnsons or that Clay is somehow incompetent because he had the audacity to take Bo as his own. I grit my teeth and throw the last of my clothes into the bag, yanking the zipper shut. More irrefutable proof that Brice is a total jerk. But why has he declared war on me too?

I hoist the bag onto my shoulder and grab my keys from the nightstand. "I don't understand why Brice is so dead-set on hating me."

"Because you are the triple-threat to him." Gin stands up and walks with me to the door, waiting on the landing while I lock up. "You aren't captivated by his supposed charms, you're smarter than he is when it comes to the farm, and you're influencing Bo to actually want to stay and work there. That's everything he considers fatal flaws and you bring all three to the table."

I roll my eyes. If demonstrating my skills on the farm and encouraging Bo are deadly sins according to Brice, then I guess our rivalry is a sealed deal. I don't pander, and I refuse to take a dive for anyone.

Gin and I walk down the stairs, and then she hugs me. "Have fun. Drive safe!"

"Will do. Good luck at work," I say with a laugh. Gin scowls, giving me a thumbs down.

I turn and skip to my Jeep where Bo leans against the fender waiting on me.

Bo spent the first part of the trip nervously chattering, but now, several miles out, he's silent, staring out the window as he picks the skin around his nails. Every time I ask if he's okay, he shrugs it off and insists he's just taking in the scenery. I glance out the side windows of the rolling hills and exposed rock ledges, so different from the flat, sandy coast. Still, there's no doubting the anxiety descending on his shoulders right now. Impressing adults is so much easier than impressing children. A three-year-old has no filter—they either like you or hate you, and no matter what the verdict, everyone's going to know.

I reach over and grab his hand as we turn onto our road. "Don't be nervous. My family is pretty chill, even if we aren't as open with our feelings as yours. They're going to adore you."

"I hope so." He darts his eyes in my direction but then fixes them back on his lap.

"It's Weston, isn't it?"

Bo throws his head back on the headrest, raking his fingers through his curls. "What if he hates me?"

I slow down and turn on to our gravel driveway. A cloud of dust kicks up around us as our farmhouse comes into view. My heart flip-flops. "He's not going to hate you." I laugh, tightening my grip on his hand. He squeezes my fingers in return. "Weston's nothing if not his mama's boy. I happen to think you're the best, and he will too."

Bo lets down his guard and smiles wide, but it evaporates when we pull up in the yard and find everyone sitting at the picnic table, awaiting our arrival. His face blanches, all color fading from his cheeks. And for the first time since we left Edisto, my stomach crimps too. My two worlds are on the brink of merging, and I need this to go smoothly. For Bo to fall in love with my family and them, with him. Because all of these people I want in my life for the long haul.

Mama speed walks toward the Jeep with a huge grin on her

face. Weston, snuggled in her arms, yells for me and waves his hands in the air. I unlatch my seatbelt and scramble out of the door, my feet no sooner hitting the dirt than I take off toward them. Weston extends his arms to me, and I scoop him up, pulling him to my chest. The sweet cottony scent of his baby shampoo swirls around us as I press my lips to his forehead. He squeals as Mama steps up and wraps her arms around both of us. The flutters are gone, my heart swelling ten times its original size.

God, I've missed this.

Mama steps back, her eyes locking on mine and then traveling to someone over my shoulder. Bo. Though his face has regained some of its color, his wide eyes and trembling hands suggest that at any moment, he might pass out and fall backwards into the driveway. I hold back a laugh. I've seen him go head-to-head with Brice all summer, never batting an eye, and now faced with three generations of Wrights, he's about to succumb to the pressure.

Still holding Weston, I walk over to Bo, Mama trailing on my heels.

"Mama, this is Bo. Bo, my mama."

Bo sticks out his hand, but Mama grabs it and pulls him in to an embrace. "No need to be formal around here," she says. "Especially when I've done nothing but hear about you for the last two months." She releases her grip and gives him a wink. He laughs, the blush rising in his cheeks as his gaze ping-pongs between me and the squirming child in my arms.

I swallow hard. "And this is Weston."

CHAPTER 29

Bo

Two large ice-blue eyes fixate on me. And they're not the only ones. It's as if the collective group of Wrights are all holding their breath, waiting to see how this first meeting goes. My breath catches. If he hates me or starts crying, what will they do? Kick me out? Tell me to go home?

I stoop to Weston's level and give him a little wave. "Hey, Weston."

His face scrunches up, nose crinkled. "Who are you?" His voice still has that babyishness, but I can just make out the words.

"I'm Bo." I enunciate the B so he can understand how to pronounce my name. The last thing I want him thinking is that my name is No or Go. Both of those would be bad.

My pulse races in the silent pause, where he continues to look me up and down. Then, his tiny lips spread into the biggest smile as he yells, "Hey, Bo!" and returns my wave.

Thank you, God. A wave of relief washes over me.

Weston begins kicking hard and flapping his arms, and Jordan struggles to keep control over his wiggling body. "Down! Down!" he insists.

She lowers the squirming kid to the ground and as soon as his bare feet hit the grass, they take off toward a field adjacent to the house. He stops midway and turns around. "Bo! Bo! Come see moo-moo! Come here!"

I glance over at Jordan, who grabs my hand and squeezes it. "Told you so."

Weston doesn't hate me. He's actually motioning me to follow him. I nod and smile at Jordan and her mama, ten thousand pounds lifting off my shoulders, and take off in his direction. He turns and runs, his legs toddling fast as he points to the cow grazing by the wooden fence. I catch up to him beside the gate where he turns to me and lifts his arms in the air. My mouth drops open. He wants me to pick him up. Panic rushes through me; I've never spent too much time around kids, only helped Gin a few times when she babysat on the island. And I never toted them around. I smile down at the set of eager eyes looking up at me, his arms shaking as if trying to drive home the idea that he wants to be picked up. I stoop down, grabbing hold under his arms, and lift him to my hip. One arm circles my neck while the other points to a cow, meandering toward the fence. She greets us with a deep bellow.

"My moo-moo! See her? She's my cow!"

I reach out and pat the cow's head and Weston follows suit. "What's your cow's name?"

"Mabel."

"I see introductions have been arranged." Jordan's voice surprises me and I whirl around, a little too fast. Weston's fingers clench my neck, but instead of screaming, he squeals with laughter. Jordan runs her fingers through Weston's curls, then holds out her hands. "Want to come with me and we'll show Bo our favorite spots on the farm?"

"No!" Weston yelps, grabbing me harder and pulling back from her. "I go with Bo!"

Jordan and her mama exchange curious glances, and Sheryl shakes her head. "Well that only took a minute for Weston to be enamored. The mother-son resemblance is strong." She chuckles and steps away, wandering down the fence line toward the open fields in the distance.

Jordan blushes and grabs my free hand, leaning in to whisper, "She's not wrong. I pretty much fell for you the first time you climbed in my Jeep and ate one of my barbecue sandwiches."

That first day at the market delivered this beautiful girl to my doorstep, but I was too scared to even consider it after that shitshow with Laurel. Now I look over at this girl beside me, holding my hand, gazing at me as if I hung that moon she loves so much, and I can hardly believe how far we've come in two months. Who knew that barbecue sandwich was just a beginning to all this?

I nudge her shoulder with mine. "You think we can get Grandma to fix a few more of those sandwiches?"

Jordan laughs and nods. "I think we can convince her."

For the rest of the afternoon, we walk hand-in-hand, Weston in my arms, over the farm's rolling acreage. Jordan and her mom show me the old barn and the grassy meadow filled with Bobwhites, the mountainous vistas robbing my breath. Now I understand Jordan's love of this land, her commitment to saving this special place. It should never be spoiled by the development creeping into the area. It should remain pure, natural.

Like her.

At supper, Grandma serves her barbecue over rice, and as Jordan promised, Grandpa grumbles over his skinny portions and steals every opportunity to sneak more when Grandma's back is turned. I sit at their table, watching them laugh and joke, and never once feel like a visitor. It feels like home.

I wipe my mouth and lay my napkin on the table, then look over at Jordan, airplaning food into Weston's mouth.

My heart somersaults.

They feel like home.

While Weston zooms his die-cast tractor over the rug in his room, I sneak to mine on a mission to change out of my button-down, rechecking that the baby-gate at the top of the stairs is locked in tight on my trek through the hallway. Jordan wanted to catch-up with her mama for a while and I volunteered to watch Weston and play with his favorite farm set, but the stagnant heat is getting to me.

I yank off the shirt, tossing it on the foot of my bed, then tug at the hem of my undershirt, peeling it off my skin and leaving behind a sweaty slick on my abdomen. The humidity of a Southern July night in conjunction with no A/C is like sitting in a sauna. Jordan's grandma keeps saying the mountain air is cooler because it's closer to Heaven but I'm thinking I took a wrong turn somewhere because tonight, it's Hell. I raise the bedroom's large window that overlooks the front yard, a gust of wind sweeping through the space. It only makes me hotter if that's possible. The air is a thick, wet blanket.

I dig through my duffel bag, searching for a cotton T-shirt, when a whining metal door catches my attention from outside. Footsteps pad across the wooden-slatted floor below, and the creak of dueling rocking chairs commences. I press my face against the screen, focusing on the amber rays flooding over the yard from the front porch light.

"Oh Sassy, it's so good to have you home, though I suspect we've been missing you more than you have us. Weston excluded from that, of course."

"I have missed y'all terribly—missed home—but I will admit this summer has been better than I ever imagined."

Jordan is having a good summer. With me. That's all I need to know. I smile and pull on the new T-shirt, heading back to Weston's room.

"No doubt in part to a well-built, dark-haired, blue-eyed hunk?" Jordan's mama's voice, louder than before, now contains a new edge. I stop in my tracks and glance back at the open window. It would be a total Gin move to spy on them and their private conversation, and I don't want to be that kind of snoop. But they are talking about me.

"Shhhh!" Jordan's laugh peppers the night air, the blush in her cheeks bleeding through into the tone. It makes me want to hear more, and so reluctantly and against my better judgement, I backpedal to the screen, squatting down and leaning as close as possible without pushing through and plummeting to the ground below.

"Okay, I admit it—he's gorgeous, but Bo..." she starts again, her voice hushed to normal tone, "...he's so much more than that. He's... everything... he's my—"

"Your man in the moon?"

"No. Better."

Chill bumps spill down my arms. Better. I'm better than her ideal man. Me.

"I'm loving that smile on your face, and I know he's behind it so I have to tell you that I am a fan of Bo Johnson. Though obviously not his biggest fan as that role seems to have been taken already."

Jordan giggles and takes a drink, her ice clinking against the glass. She smacks her lips and I imagine the dewy drops of sweet tea lingering on them. "He is pretty damn great."

They fall silent, the night returning to a melody of crickets chattering in the field and the whistle of wind through the gables, but the lull in conversation isn't easy—it's pregnant with weight. Heavy.

Sheryl sighs and clicks her tongue.

"What is it?" Jordan's rocker pauses and her voice drops an octave. "Come on, I can tell there's something weighing on you."

A glass slams on the side table with a loud bang. "Shit, Sassy, I don't want to screw up this wonderful evening."

"Tell me." A near-frantic pleading edges forward in Jordan's tone.

"Well, there's been a man sniffing around here, asking questions about how much we'd sell the place for."

"But our farm's not for sale."

"Of course it's not." Another sigh, this one longer and more pronounced. "At least not yet."

Not yet? I swallow hard. Losing this land would kill Jordan.

"What?" The squeak of the rocking chair quells suddenly. "Y'all wouldn't—"

"No. Not by choice. But we haven't been current on the mortgage in quite some time, and old Gerald at the bank is getting... antsy... especially as more interest presents itself."

"Can the bank do that?"

The tremble in her voice slashes through me because I know the answer to that question, and it's one she doesn't want to hear. They can. They will. They often do. In fact, a few of Johnson Farms' acquisitions came at the expense of other farmers who couldn't find a way to make ends meet. Never the hostile takeovers Brice wants, but we often bought up farms in financial distress in agreement with the owners.

"Foreclosure is absolutely within their power, but I've met with Gerald, told him about what we have cooking and he seemed willing to give us the benefit of the doubt. For the time being. Maybe that's one of the few perks of working with a small-town lender. It's hard for them to stomp on your dreams when they have to see you in Sunday church."

I sigh. Let's hope the "Power of the Pew" will be enough to dissuade this Gerald from moving forward on anything else.

"I'm going to fix this. We're going to do something to turn this around for our family." Jordan's voice turns stony and hard in an instant. In one fell swoop, she ties her anxieties into a bundle and trades them for a strong, determined mandate. She will fight until the bitter end, that's apparent. "Is there anything else?" Another awkward pause. "Oh shit, what?"

Sheryl clears her throat as another gust of wind blows through, stirring up the oversized metal windchimes on the porch's corner and sending out a flurry of foreboding bass notes. "Guess who's back in town?"

My heart races. I don't even need Sheryl to expand on the who—I know it in my gut just by the way she almost whispers the question into the night air. My single greatest fear hangs among the stars, hovering in the air like a monster ready to pounce. Jordan's ex. I know virtually nothing of him, but he is Weston's father and that's a connection far beyond what we've shared so far.

I turn my ear toward the screen, desperate to hear Jordan's response and willing my pounding pulse to quit its assault on my ear drums.

"What? Please tell me you're joking."

Please, I repeat in my head.

"He's called a few times over the summer, even came by twice, looking for you."

Jordan's feet drop hard on the porch floor, her abandoned rocking chair flailing backwards into the siding with a *thwack*. "He had the nerve to step foot on our property?"

"Oh, he didn't stay long, but I did have to hide the key to Pa's gun safe."

Clomp. Clomp. Clomp. Jordan paces the floor below, back and forth, her steps becoming increasingly heavy. "Did he... see Weston?"

"No. Didn't even ask about him."

"So why is he slinking around now? After all this time?"

"I don't know. He wouldn't say. Just kept asking for you." The second rocking chair bumps against the siding as Sheryl stands up. I imagine her approaching a fragile Jordan with fire blazing in her eyes. "There was no reason worrying you with it before, but now that you're back in town... you know how quickly word spreads in this place. I reckon he'll be bringing his ass back on over here as soon as he hears, unless you settle it first."

Jordan lets out a muffled grunt. "I can't believe—"

"Bo!"

I freeze in place, not moving, not even breathing, and the voices below go quiet. Do they know I've been listening in on their private conversation? I ease to standing and tiptoe toward my bedroom door, running smack dab into Weston, who's barreling around the corner with a stuffed Holstein in his chubby grip. "Bo, Bo, Bo! See my cow! Moo! Moo!"

I sweep him into my arms and head back to his room in a silent sprint, hoping I don't meet Jordan or Sheryl darting up the stairs on my way. When we're safely back on his rug, I crouch down and say through ragged breaths, "That's an awesome cow, dude!"

The box fan Jordan brought me last night before bed hums in the pre-dawn silence, a monotonous whirring punctuated by the bird calls beginning to increase outside my window as the sun's rising nears. At least the breeze helps cut the humidity.

Someone's up in the house already, though there's been no noise, just the nutty smell of brewing coffee floating up from downstairs. Probably Grandma. She and Grandpa were in bed asleep not long after sundown last night.

I, on the other hand, got maybe thirty minutes. Every time I closed my eyes, it proved useless. I'd come here worried about Weston hating me only to discover that the kid and I got along great. But it was idiotic thinking to assume the worst of it was over. I hadn't anticipated Jordan's ex landing back in the picture.

She hadn't really said anything about him. Nothing substantial at least. But she shares a kid with this dude so that has to mean something was there between them, at least at some point in the past. I scour my brain, trying to remember the discussion at the dinner table the night I found out about Weston. She thought it'd been love but it was manipulation. Yeah, that's what she said. But if he manipulated her once, could he again? I mean, Jordan is smart, but when it comes to the heart...

I glance at my phone. 5:52 a.m. Today's a shipment day at the market so Gin would have to report early. She is probably there or in route right now. I turn over, propping myself up on my elbow, and call her.

She answers on the second ring, sobbing. A male voice echoes in the background. My mind races. What's wrong?

"Gin? Are you okay? And who's with you?"

She sniffles a few times, hiccups, then takes a deep breath. "That's just Brice making fun of me. We're working the shipment this morning, and while I had a few minutes I wanted to finish reading the black moment in my book." As she says this, renewed sobbing bleeds through the line and Brice's jeers become clearer as he fake boo-hoo-hoos in the distance. She yells at him to shut up then continues, "The couple just broke up. And after all they've been through!"

I shake my head. Only Gin and her romantic fantasy worlds could be in this much uproar before daybreak. "You do realize that these are fictional characters, right?"

"Not to me!" She sighs then pauses, sniffling. "How are the mountains? I'm sure you're having a much better time there than I am here, being stuck working the market with Brice." She growls the last part under her breath.

"It's beautiful up here. The Wrights are great. Grandma's food is amazing. Weston is super cute…"

I don't know how to bring up the subject of Jordan's ex, and as the silence builds, I can almost feel her ears perking, her internal radar going berserk behind the scenes.

"But?" she finally asks.

"I overheard a conversation between Jordan and her mama, and it has me worried."

Gin snorts. "*You* were eavesdropping?"

"It was an accident, and then I just didn't stop."

"Taking a page from my book, I see." She giggles, but when I don't join in, she cuts it abruptly. "Really, though. Why are you worried?"

"Jordan's ex is back in town and apparently he's anxious to talk to her."

"Jordan's ex is back?" She yells it so loud into the phone, I'm not sure if I'm hearing her through the line or if her voice has sent sound waves echoing through the atmosphere from Edisto.

"Shhhh!" I hiss, shifting my eyes to the closed door as if at any moment, Jordan will spring through and magically know I'm lamenting her ex's grand return.

"Sorry," Gin's voice lowers to a loud whisper. "What does he want?"

"I don't know. What if he wants them to get back together?" The words sour on my tongue and shoot a vile bubbling into my gut.

"Then he's too late. She has you."

I'd kill for just a fraction of the easy matter-of-fact attitude she has. But what if I'm not enough? She was with this guy long before I was in the picture. The same way Laurel was with her boyfriend.

"Yeah, but she has history with this guy."

"Bad history from what I can tell. And who wants history when you have a future? You could be her future." I grunt and fall back on my pillow, staring at the ceiling. Gin groans into the phone as if she's talking to the stupidest person alive. "Look, why don't you just ask her?"

"Then she'll know I was eavesdropping. Why hasn't she told me?"

"Maybe because this ex means absolutely nothing to her and she doesn't want to freak you out. Isn't that the same thing that happened with you and Laurel?"

Touché.

"I guess. But Laurel and I didn't have a kid involved in that rigmarole."

"Do you trust Jordan?"

"I do, it's just—" A knot builds in my throat. It's just... I've been hit by the infidelity train before. Losing Laurel pissed me off; losing Jordan would wreck me.

Gin blows out a deep breath into the phone. "I get it. You've already been burned once and you want no repeat performances."

"Pretty much," I mumble.

"Okay, I'm going to say something really shocking here, so stay with me. Ready?" I nod as if the message will be telepathically conveyed across the distance. "Jordan is not Laurel." She says each word singularly and with emphasis, as if trying to drive the message home through my thick skull.

Simple and to the point. And very, very accurate. "No, she's not. You're right."

"Aren't I always?" The usual sunshine returns to Gin's voice. "No one blames you for being nervous, but don't jump to conclusions and sabotage a good thing. Jordan *isn't* hung up on her ex. From the little she's actually said, I'm pretty sure she hates him. I mean, has she ever even mentioned his name? Nope. Nothing says distance and avoidance more than that."

"Good point." They're all excellent points, and this is exactly why I called Gin in the first place. She can be a total pain in the butt sometimes but she has an uncanny ability to whittle down to the core of things and give me some perspective. "So, what should I do?"

"Trust yourself. Trust Jordan. Everything's going to be fine."

CHAPTER 30

Jordan

My fingers grip the leather-bound steering wheel so tight the knuckles whiten. The country music station Mama switched the radio to drones on in the background, blurring with the whirring of the tires on the two-lane highway. If only the static could somehow block out the incessant thoughts in my head.

Like why is he back in town? What does he want that's so urgent? And why now?

These are all burning questions for which I have no answers and no further clarity despite my uber-short phone call with him last night. It repeats on a loop in my brain.

What do you want? That's the first thing that popped out of my mouth when I heard his voice again, like a terrible ghost from the past.

I need to discuss something with you—in person, he'd said. *I can come over.*

No. I'll meet you in town.

I don't want him around Bo. I don't want Bo thinking that there is a possibility that anything is ever going to happen with this jerk again. This visit has solidified my feelings in ways I never expected. This thing between us is the real deal, a palpable energy so intense it's like a magnet pulling us together. For the first time, I'm beginning to think I've finally had a real taste of love—the romantic, made-in-the-movies kind that makes you feel all trippy and clumsy and completely wonderful.

Of course, the snake would slither back into the picture now.

The parking space in front of Hometown Diner is vacant so I roll into it and cut the engine but don't make any moves to get out. The idea of what lurks inside crushes my nerves into a malfunctioning pile of mush. What if he wants to fight me for custody? What if he wants to get back together? What if he's really an alien who conned me into our fake relationship with mind control and that fully explains my stupidity for trusting him in the first place? What if, what if, what if?

In my periphery, Mama stares at me, chewing her fingernail. The white part is now totally gone, the quick raw and red. "You don't reckon—"

"I don't know anything more than you, Mama, except he's not getting his filthy hands on Weston," I say, not turning to look at her, but instead scanning the row of plate-glass windows until I spot him in the second booth from the back. He sips a soda through a straw and scrolls through his phone, calm as can be.

Jerk.

"Then what else—" She furrows her brows, a deep frown creasing her face. "Unless—"

"I don't know what he wants, but there's only one way to find out."

We hop out of the Jeep and Mama flanks my side as we push through the glass door. The little bell on the handle tinkles over the murmuring voices, and he looks up, our eyes meeting. My stomach liquifies and runs down into my toes as my heart thunders against my chest, instigating the teensiest bit of light-headedness.

"I'll be at the counter in case you need me," Mama whispers in my ear before taking a seat near the cash register.

His booth is only ten steps or so further but walking over the grimy tiles without Mama behind me feels more like slogging through cold peanut butter.

"You brought reinforcements?" He laughs, running a hand through his dirty blonde mullet and leaning into the aisle, gazing past me toward the counter.

"My mama always has my back. More than I can say for some people." My voice flexes strong and firm, not wavering and puny the way I imagined it would. The pinch in my shoulders relaxes as I slide into the opposite side of the booth. I've got this; I'm stronger than I know. "What do you want?"

He smirks, an obvious look of amusement inscribed on his face, and sits back, folding his arms over his chest. "No hello, how ya been?"

The fires of Hell lick my skin, the urge to hurdle the table like a bobcat and claw his eyes out an enticing fantasy. I grit my teeth. After all he's done—after all these years—does he honestly think I care? I lean forward, clenching the edge of the table. "I don't give a damn how you've been, and I'm not much for useless small talk so cut the crap."

"The naïve little girl I left has become a vicious woman, I see."

That's what happens when a Mama has to protect her baby from a threat. I guess he didn't realize that the mess he left behind would regroup and gain a little gumption along the way.

"A woman who has zero interest in your stupid games... or anything else you might have in mind."

His jaw drops open as he rolls his eyes, raising his hand like a stop sign. "Cool your jets. I don't have any interest in getting back with you."

Maybe he thinks that will hurt my feelings—that explains the smug expression dancing on his face—but instead it's a much-needed shot of relief. I blow out a deep breath and sink back against the plastic seat. "That makes two of us."

The bell on the door rings out again as a middle-aged man

walks in, grabs a menu, and sits at the small booth catty-cornered from us. He glances over, darting his eyes between the two of us. My cheeks burn as I realize what a spectacle we must be, arguing in front of everyone in this small-town diner. The man issues me a curt smile and picks up his cell phone, hiding his face behind it.

Across the table, a gruff cough draws my attention back to Jerk Boy and for a moment, I catch a glimpse of Weston's nose, the small bump on its ridge, and wonder again how my sweet kid came from this... this person.

He leans forward, elbows on the table, and steeples his fingers against his chin. "How's the baby? Is it healthy?"

It. He calls Weston "it" as if he's not a real person, an inno-cent child he'd helped create. I swallow down the bile and fix my hard gaze on his. "Perfectly healthy and I'm a damn good mama so don't think you're going to crawl back in here after three years and—"

"Woah! Please tell me there's an exit ramp on your rant highway between here and Crazytown." He shakes his head and spirals a finger beside his temple. "I don't want to see the baby. In fact, that's why I'm here."

I nibble my thumb nail, trying to make sense of the words coming from his mouth. He doesn't want me. He doesn't want Weston. Nothing's changed from the last few years from what I can tell. So why is he here now, urgently asking me to make sure there's no contact? I should think my silence and lack of interest in tracking him down all these years would speak to my intentions. Watching him disappear without a trace sure spoke to his.

"What exactly do you mean?"

"I need you to sign this." He retrieves a manilla folder from the seat beside him, pulls out a stapled collection of papers, and hands it to me. I scan the first page with its complicated legal jargon. "It relinquishes all my rights and obligations to the child. I don't want this... situation... ever coming to light." He sighs and sucks the remaining soda from his nearly empty glass. "I'm getting married next month and she doesn't know."

Now I see. Hiding the sins of his past behind a legal divide is what this is all about. He can't gamble that I'll continue not to make waves for him going forward because if I do, New Girl will find out. And then she'd see him for the lying, no-good cow patty he really is.

"You're getting married?" A low-pitched laugh works its way up from my belly as I shake my head. "Poor girl. She's gonna need a lot of those thoughts and prayers everyone likes to dole out." I flip through the remaining pages to the last one, which requires a few initials and a dated signature. One little document between his claims on Weston and my eternal peace of mind? I'm totally on board to kick this loser to the curb. Weston has plenty of valid and respectable people to look up to. "I'm totally on board with signing this and getting every trace of you removed from our lives, but I do need a lawyer to look it over first."

He slaps his hand on the table, rattling the salt and pepper shakers. I glance over my shoulder at Mama, who's now glowering in our direction, one foot on the stool and one on the tiled floor like she's ready to swoop in at any minute. I shoot her a nod and a smile, calling off the waiting dogs.

"A lawyer?" he growls in a loud whisper. "You angling for some sort of financial settlement?"

Of course his pea-brain would go there. Weston was always a burden to him, an obligation he wanted to flush down the toilet. Not a blessing like he is to me. I stare across the table at the guy who I'd once thought I'd loved and smirk. Now that I've had a taste of something so real, so genuine with Bo... those old feelings were vapor. Just childish infatuation with an older guy's charms.

I lean across the table, my face inches from his, and pinch his chin between my thumb and forefinger. To the casual diners in the restaurant, it might even look happy or flirty, but to him, grimacing in pain under the pressure of my grip, it's anything but. "I don't want your money. I want to ensure that once I do sign this and you walk out that you can never walk in again."

He shakes free, his jaw clenching in and out. "Sounds good to me."

"I'll get this reviewed, signed, and in the mail to your lawyer." I smile and tuck the paperwork into my purse. "I wish I could say it'd been nice to see you again but... it hasn't."

"I wish I had more to offer but... I don't." He leans across the table and closes his hand over mine. It's sweaty and clammy and the mere touch of his skin sends a rush of fire—the deadly sort—through me.

I snatch my fingers from his grip and wipe them on a napkin, meeting his solemn gaze with a sardonic smile. "And you never did. But don't worry about it. I already got the only good thing that'll ever come from you."

I slide out of the booth and turn my back on him for the final time. If I never see his face again, it'll be too soon. Mama throws a few dollars on the counter for her coffee and trails me out the door.

As soon as we're in the Jeep and the engine revs to life, Mama's questions pour out like flood water. I explain the conversation, and she pulls the documents from my purse, scanning through them, before she turns her eyes back on me. No smile, no frown.

Just concern.

"How do you feel about all this?"

How do I feel? I haven't really taken the time to digest it fully but as the yellow dotted lines disappear below us, an easy relief begins to take hold. One I haven't felt in a very long time. Most people might be sad or even angry that their child's father bailed but not me. Because he had never been a father. Because he was never the best choice for Weston. And now, with him expunged from our future completely, the possibilities suddenly seem limitless.

"Relieved actually. Weston deserves better—I deserve better —and maybe we can actually get it now."

Mama shoots me a broad, toothy grin, pinching her shoulders to her ears and rubbing her palms together. "Maybe you already have?"

I shrug, unable to stop the upturn in my lips. "I guess we'll see."

The ball is definitely in Bo's court now. I know he has feelings for me, and he's great with Weston. He's everything I could hope for in a guy. But he's just finding his way into adulthood— like me—and it'd be unfair to strap him with so many expectations off the bat. I won't push for hard and fast commitments; I won't saddle him with my responsibilities. But I will let him know that I'm there for him and eager to pursue whatever level of relationship he desires. He'll make his own decisions—in his own time and place.

Weston's eyes keep closing and then popping back open as he desperately fights sleep. After supper, Grandma and Grandpa went to bed and Mama walked out to the pasture to check on Mabel, so the three of us settled into the rocking chairs on the porch to watch the dusk crawl in, complete with the pinpricks of lightning bugs on the horizon and the trill of tree frogs harmonizing in the distance.

Weston refuses to sit on my lap, instead crawling into Bo's and curling himself into a ball. His little fingers fiddle with the hem of Bo's T-shirt, rubbing the cotton the way he usually does his blanket as he drifts to sleep. Bo pats Weston's back, the rhythmic thumping working slumber magic. His head lays limp against Bo's chest, the smallest line of drool ribboning from the corner of his mouth.

I watch them, my heart swelling against my ribs. When Bo

readjusts in the rocking chair, Weston stirs briefly but then closes his eyes once again.

"I can take him," I offer.

"No way. This is my buddy. We're hanging out."

You're killing me, Bo! I want to scream it from the top of my lungs because watching him with Weston here on this rickety porch with that easy grin on his face, I see in real-time the sort of life I want. He makes it so damn vivid, but despite that, reality creeps in around the edges, harassing me, taunting me, that this isn't promised. Life is sinking sand so many times and what's here today can be gone tomorrow just as quickly. I'm so attached to him—to this—that it scares me and thrills me all at the same time. For once, I just want to let the worry go and embrace it and really, truly believe that this time things will be different. Happy endings do happen for some people.

My stomach twists. But do they happen for me?

I sigh. To be determined.

Mama ambles toward the porch, her figure taking shape against the darkening sky as she steps near the porch light. She scuffs the bottoms of her boots on the mat then walks up the steps to stand beside us, panning her hand toward the fields. "Nice evening for a walk around the property if I do say so myself. Now give me that boy." She leans downs and scoops Weston from Bo's arms, snuggling him to her chest. He doesn't even rouse with the movement. "Mimi's gonna get him tucked in and then I'm gonna go check my eyelids for holes. Probably won't hear a thing the rest of the night." She winks at Bo then disappears with Weston through the screen door.

If I've ever seen a conspiratorial glance, this would be it.

I cock my eyebrow at him. "What was *that* all about?" Bo, an impish grin on his face, holds out his hand. I take it as he leads me down the steps and toward the far pasture. "No really. Tell me."

"So suspicious." He clicks his tongue with a *tsk tsk tsk*, mocking me for my constant inquiries. I know this look on him, and he has something planned. "It's our last night here, every-one's tucked in, and it's a beautiful evening. Your mama is right. What better way to spend the night than soaking up this place you love so much with a nice walk out to your favorite spot?"

Okay, so he has a point. And since everyone else in the house is already asleep or on their way there shortly, there is no reason to feel bad about sneaking away with him for a little alone time. I cuddle in close to his side as we stroll along the edge of the wooden fence down toward the old barn. The breeze rolls like gentle waves over our skin, the blowing air cooling the drops of sweat down the back of my neck. Around a bend and just past the barn's lean-to, Bo pulls me off the path to a waiting blanket, spread on the ground, surrounded by a collec-tion of lanterns, their flames casting pirouetting shadows over the tall grass.

I clasp my hand over my mouth, mumbling through my fingers, "What is all this?"

"A little surprise your mama helped me cook up." Bo smiles, the bright white of his teeth standing out against the darkening sky, as he looks pretty proud of himself. He grabs both of my hands and pulls me to the edge of the grasses and wildflowers in the meadow. "I've been told that just after sunset is the perfect time to hear the last calls of—"

Bobwhite!

A lone voice rises up from the field, and with the remaining bits of light slowly fading into the inky blackness, probably one of the last of the evening. My heart jumps. Almost like a sign.

"My old friends," I say, my voice wavering. How sweet of him to remember these things that are so precious to me, so mean-ingful. No guy has ever given that much effort.

"Them... and him." He tips my head up to the sky and the Southeastern horizon where the moon glows a luminescent amber. "Your favorites."

Once upon a time they were my favorites. My soft spots. My hope for the future. Now, things look a bit different. I turn my eyes back to his and run my fingers over his cheek. "No, my favorite is right here."

He inhales deeply before leaning in to crush his lips to mine. It's the first time since we been here that we've had any alone time, and as his mouth captures mine, I realize exactly what I've been missing the last couple days. The quick pecks on the cheek in front of my family were nothing like this. A new fire stirs in my belly as I wrap my arms around his shoulders, pulling him in deeper. The aching need rips at me.

Bo responds positively, running his fingers through my hair, pressing harder into our kiss. Our bodies move in sync, perfect rhythm, until he suddenly pulls away, cheeks flushed.

"Sorry," he mumbles, standing back hands on his hips as he pants hard. He glances over his shoulder toward the house. "We should probably take a minute and relax."

"I'm perfectly relaxed, but if *you* can't take the heat…" I tease, wagging my finger in his face.

"Oh, I can handle it just fine… but not right now." He holds up his finger, telling me to wait, and he runs back to the blanket and rifles through a bag sitting on the corner. Grandma's large brown photo album is in his hands when he trots back. "I perused this today while you were out. I want to show you something." He flips to the middle and turns the page toward me, pointing at an aged sepia photo of a little girl standing with a bundle of grapes.

What in the world is so special about it? "A picture of my grandma as a little girl?"

"Yes!" He belts it out as if he's just exposed a colossal secret and I've missed the boat. "A photo of your grandma as a little girl in her family's vineyard. Did you know they had a vineyard?"

I shake my head. Grandma was born into a farming family, but I'd never known them. She was the youngest of twelve children and by the time I'd come along, most of her original family had either moved off or was buried in the family plot. "Okay, so?"

Bo's mouth drops open. "So? This is the answer. What better place to carry on that legacy, to focus on the farm's expansion and also celebrate your roots?"

A vineyard? My mind whirls. That certainly presents some awesome possibilities and we do have the land available. But what about the equipment? The infrastructure? The general know-how? I slit my eyes. "What all are you thinking?"

"Acres of vineyards. Tastings and tours. Maybe even have a little café featuring some of grandma's recipes. Al fresco dining on a terrace overlooking the mountain view. Then..."

I giggle. The light has never sparked in Bo's eyes the way it does now—like pure excitement and adrenaline and inspiration all rolled together. "There's more?"

"The *best* part." He grabs my hand and pulls me to the edge of the field, at that perfect and precise spot where the hills ramble downward to a sloping meadow, unveiling the undulating rounded Appalachian peaks. The nearby brook gurgles over the smoothed rocks in a soothing melody. "Right here in your favorite spot, we'll build a beautiful, rustic arbor with doors that open to reveal that." He pans his hands wide, framing the mountain vista. "A wedding venue, Jordan. Can you imagine how many people would want to host their dream wedding here? But that's not it..."

The happy notes in his voice trill upwards with excitement as he pulls me backwards and spins me around to face our old barn.

He's got to be kidding me. "The barn?" I ask, one eyebrow peaked into my forehead.

"Totally refurbished as an event space. Wedding in the meadow and reception here in a state-of-the-art facility." Bo pushes the big doors open and struts inside. The moon glow filters in, casting the entire place in romantic ambiance. "String up lights, put in rustic flooring..." He circles in place, hands on his hips, as he scans the interior. He stops when his gaze finally meets mine. "What? What's wrong?"

How do I tell him that his ideas are pure gold but they can

never happen? How can I burst his balloon? It dawns on me that he doesn't fully understand the depth of our desperation. "I love all of your ideas but we don't have the capital to make this work. We're flat-out broke."

Bo strides toward me and grips my shoulders. "I called Dad. He knows people who invest in these sorts of things."

"In tiny farms like this?"

"Absolutely. Because they understand that it won't be tiny for long, and they'll make their money back plus some. It's just good business." He squats, coming eye level with me. "And the only thing 'tiny' about this farm is the current budget. The people who live here, the acreage, the grit and love for the land, the natural resources—those are all huge."

Damn, he could sell oceanfront property in Nebraska with that smile. My heart drums in my ears. Could this really be the answer we've been searching for?

"And this old barn?" I say, staring into its expanse. There's a roof that needs work and lots of cleaning to do, but it's structurally sound. "We can really make it shine again?"

"Everyone will want to hold events here." Bo steps behind me, pressing himself against my back, and sweeps his hand in front of me. "Can you imagine?"

"And when it's all done, would you come back here and dance with me?" I turn and thread my arms behind his neck, pulling him nose to nose. "Like we did at Edisto?"

"Why wait?" He pulls his cell phone from his pocket and taps the screen a few times before the folksy melody we'd danced to that night streams through the speaker.

"Is that—"

"Yep." He looks down at his feet, a blush overtaking his cheeks that's barely visible in the moonlight. "I downloaded it that night so I could re-live the memory. Of course, my ending was a little different than what happened in reality."

How could I forget the intervening kid and the look on Bo's face when all he could do was give in? I didn't want his fingers to pull away that night any more than I want him letting go of me right now. I press closer to this body, feeling all of the bumps and bulges meet mine.

"Why re-live an old memory when you can make a new one?" I whisper.

Bo darts his eyes up with a new intensity I haven't seen before. My heart butterflies against my ribs, a lightheadedness making everything around us go slightly fuzzy, except for his face, which remains crystal clear. And oh, so close.

He circles his arms around me, allowing his fingertips to slip under my shirt and skim across the skin above the waist of my shorts. I shudder, a stream of chill bumps spilling down my spine, and lean forward, capturing his lips once again. He kisses me harder this time, with more determination, and I reach down, grabbing the hem of his T-shirt and hitch it up, silently begging him to remove it. He steps back, wrenches the shirt from his body, and tosses it to the barn floor.

I tease him, playing peekaboo and tugging down the straps of my tank top on each shoulder before finally grabbing the edge to pull it over my head. Bo watches me toss it on top of his and then travels his eyes up and down the length of my body. When he swallows hard and runs his hand up the back of his neck, my nerves light up like sticks of dynamite because I know his thoughts are walking hand-in-hand with mine.

He strides toward me, his steps firm and deliberate, then cups my face in his hands. No words, only a deep eye contact that reaches inside and pulls me to him like an unseen force field. I don't fight it. I don't want to.

My body collides with his, the once-tender touches now brisk and hungry. I reach behind my back and unsnap my bra, letting it fall down my arms to the ground between us. A low moan escapes Bo's lips as he backs me into the barn door, the scratchy wood on my back a stark contrast to the hot moisture of his lips trailing up and down my neck. His hands roam, leaving no skin untouched, setting every inch of me on fire.

I pop the button and tug the zipper down on his jeans, allowing them to fall lower on his hips, but just as I begin pushing them further, Bo jumps back. I gasp from the sudden lack of his touch as he bends forward, hands on his thighs, panting for air.

"Jordan, I—" he says between deep breaths. "I can't start something because I'm going to want to finish it, so—"

"So start it already." I close the space between us and grab his hands. They tremble against mine. "And finish it. I'm ready if you are."

He pulls out his wallet, removing a silver disc, then tosses it onto the pile of clothes. He puts his hand on the small of my back and tugs me toward him, so close his smell—a hint of vanilla and oak—swirls around me. His lips graze mine as he leans in closer, stopping one last time for him to ask again, "You sure?"

"As long as I have you, I'm sure of everything."

The words no sooner leave my tongue than I feel his against it, probing, tasting, taking me in. I twist my fingers in his curls as he lifts me off the ground, wrapping my legs around his waist as if I weigh no more than a feather, then carries me to the blanket. The flickering lanterns dance in the breeze, and a million stars blaze overhead in milky rashes. Bo steps out of his jeans, leaving them in a crumpled pile, and I pull my lips away from his to fully take in the view. The golden beams highlight the contours of his body, the ripple of his abs, the solid muscles of his arms—my eyes sink further still—the physical proof of his own need.

My breath gets stuck in the airways, my lungs threatening to explode. Can he be this wonderful? Could this sort of life really be mine?

He hooks his thumbs in the waistband of my shorts and pushes them away; they puddle around my ankles. My cheeks turn to fire as I stare down at myself, a flood of self-conscious-ness washing over me as I suddenly feel exposed, vulnerable. Bo strokes my jawline, letting his fingers run down the slope of my shoulders, over the side of my breast, and down my hip.

"You are so damn beautiful," he whispers.

I crush my lips to his, grabbing hold of his arms and pulling us both down onto the blanket. We move in sync, skin on skin, every nerve ending exploding and tingling under his touch. And here in my mountain home under a full moon, our bodies rise and fall together, pushing and pulling, ebbing and flowing, like the Atlantic's tides, our two worlds fusing in one exquisite moment.

Later, while the rest of the house is silently sleeping, I lie in my bed re-living the night's events, his fingers kneading into my skin, his lips moving against mine. The ghostly caresses still dance across my body. I grab my phone from the nightstand and thumb through the photos of our weekend—candid shots of Mama being her goofy self, selfies of me and Bo, in-the-moment captures of Bo entertaining Weston—and pause on the last one taken. My heart swells. Mama had insisted we pose by the fence then grabbed my phone and snapped it. Bo props against the wooden rail, one arm draped around my shoulders, the other hoisting Weston on his hip. We face the camera with toothy smiles—all except Weston, who's staring straight at Bo, wide eyes and a grin to match. It's taken that kid zero-point-two seconds to get attached.

I laugh under my breath. He is his mama's kid. I just hope we both don't end up hurt by all of this in the end.

A gentle rapping on my door pulls my attention away, and I shut off the phone and put it on the table. "Come in."

Bo pushes it open, peeking around the edge. His curls are wet, matted to his head, like he just got out of a shower. "I saw your lamp on, so I just wanted to tell you goodnight."

"'Night," I whisper, but as he starts to close the door, my need to be close to him boils over. "Stay with me."

He stops in the doorway, frowning, and shakes his head. "I shouldn't. It's your grandparents' house, and I don't want to be disrespectful."

Typical Bo. Always a gentleman.

"My grandparents only want me to be happy. And you make me happy."

He smirks and ticks his head toward the staircase. "I don't know. Your grandpa has a lot of firearms in that case in the—"

He stops short when I deadpan, not buying into his excuses. "They don't come up here. They live totally on the bottom floor. It's just me, Mama, and Weston up here, and Mama knows everything. And Weston is too young to understand." I flip back the covers and pat the pillow beside me. "Promise I won't try anything. See? Pajamas and everything." I pan my hand up and down, showcasing my tank top and plaid cotton shorts. When he hesitates still, I give him the puppy dog eyes. "Please?"

He runs a hand through his hair, mussing it up, then steps in the room and pushes the door almost closed. "You can talk me into anything."

"I'll keep that in mind for future reference," I quip, pulling the sheet over him as he settles in beside me, giving the bed an instant warmth that it didn't have before. I lay my head on his chest, trailing my fingers down his arm. "And don't pretend you don't want to be here."

He wraps his arm around me and snuggles closer to my side. "Oh, I definitely want to be here."

I press a kiss to his chest and close my eyes, mumbling a quiet prayer to the heavens. Please let him mean it. Please let him mean it for always.

My eyes flutter open to pale rays of light slivering the room. They dance across the walls, cut by the rippling sheers that billow out in front of my open window. The breeze this morning isn't humid for once, but light with a hint of coolness. Pleasant, like a fresh beginning.

I sigh and reach for Bo's hand but find a much smaller one instead. I spring up in bed and stare down beside me. Sometime during the night, Weston had apparently crawled in between us and is now snuggled into Bo's side, snoozing away. Both Weston's and Bo's chocolate curls spill onto the cotton pillow, mingling together, and Bo wraps a protective arm around him.

I bite my lip, stifling a would-be sob in my throat. They look so natural, so peaceful, and I can't help thinking that this is the way things should always be. My heart flip-flops in my chest, the sensation both exhilarating and scary. This is what I want for Weston—the same thing I always wanted for myself—a strong role model to be there for all the moments, big and little, that would come along. Someone to read the bedtime story or hold a little hand crossing the street or simply listen to whatever tale was being spun.

I had that for a little while—a man who stood in the gap and did the things he didn't have to do. But then, just like that, he was gone.

The floor creaks in the hallway and I look up. Mama stands at the threshold, staring in the ajar door, a hand clasped over her mouth. I pull back the covers and slip out unnoticed, tiptoeing beside her. I try to smile, but a huge teardrop spills down my cheek.

Mama brushes my hair back from my face with a knowing expression. She's no stranger to this very scenario.

"Don't go crossing bridges. Some of them do stay," she whispers.

"Yeah, but some don't." I glance back at them, still snuggled in the bed. "And what if he doesn't?"

CHAPTER 31

Bo

Mom stares at me over the top of her glasses, doing that weird thing she does with her mouth—like she's swishing non-existent mouthwash—while she's constructing a full analysis in her head. She lowers her gaze to my hands, and I know she's looking to see if I'm fidgeting. I still my fingers, forcing them to freeze in place, but my pinky betrays me with the slightest tremble. Her eyes narrow, zeroing in. Damn.

"Are you apprehensive about something?"

I shake my head. Apprehensive isn't the right word. More like curious. I know how I feel after this trip to Jordan's home. My headspace is clearer than ever before. It's Jordan's perspective I'm unsure of.

She barely spoke to me, let alone glanced in my direction, on the way back. Not like she was mad, but maybe... sad? Logically, it was probably about having to leave her family yet again, but something about the way she kept side-eyeing me told me there was more to the silence. What I wouldn't give for a crystal ball with a direct connection to her brain. But at least I know someone who's been in her shoes and can shed some light.

I sit forward in my chair, elbows on my knees. "I've been thinking."

Mom cocks her head to one side. "About?"

"My biological father. And Dad."

She sighs, scooting back in her chair, and steeples her hands to her chin. For a moment, she closes her eyes, and my stomach drops. Maybe I shouldn't be asking her this, making her relive her own past hurts. But something in me has to know how her story unfolded, so I can have some insight into what it must have been like to be in her situation. To get some perspective on what Jordan might be thinking.

"I knew this day was coming. And with you and Jordan being together, I figured it would be sooner than later." She removes her glasses and lays them on her desk, then walks around extending her hand to me. I take it, and she leads me to the couch on the far wall where we sit on each end, backs against the arms, facing each other. "What do you want to know?"

I swallow hard. The hardest question comes first. I'm diving straight into the deep end. "If my biological dad hadn't died, would you have preferred to raise me with him?"

Mom had never hidden the fact from me that Clay Johnson is my adopted father, but that information had never really affected me because the "adopted" part always seemed so irrelevant. He is my father in every single way. The only man who I've ever known in that role. My biological dad never even knew I existed. When I turned fourteen, Mom told me all I ever really wanted to know about the situation. They had been dating for nearly a year when he was killed in a motorcycle accident. About a week after his passing, Mom was lethargic and vomiting and my grandmother insisted she go to the doctor. That's when she found out about me. She didn't meet Dad until I was eight months old, but he'd accepted us both, and within two years' time, they were married with Gin as well. A happy family of four.

But through it all, she had to have thought of him. At least sometimes. And if she had, did that also mean Jordan had given that sort of thought to Weston's father? I don't know.

Mom bites her bottom lip between her teeth, eyes turned

toward the ceiling. Another of her usual mannerisms when she's searching for the right words and doing her best to be mom and not therapist.

Finally, she blows out a loud breath and says, "Everyone's circumstances are different. Paths are different, and once a way has been chosen, there's really no going back and re-choosing. Sometimes we don't choose our paths; sometimes they choose us. I never wanted your biological father to die so tragically, and I hate that he never knew about you. Would he have been a good father? I don't know, but I'd like to think so. But that wasn't in the cards for us—Clay was. And not for one minute have I ever regretted marrying him and having him adopt you. You've always been as much his as mine."

I smile. She's right. There's no less of a connection between me and Dad just because our DNA doesn't match. My bond with him is as strong as the one I have with Mom. That leads me to my next question.

"How did you know Dad was the one? Was it something he said or did?"

Mom throws her head back laughing. "What didn't your father do? He was wonderful in every way. He loved you from day one, carting you around on his hip, pushing cars across the floor, walking you through the fields to check on the crops. And at the same time, he loved me so well. Still does." She reaches her arm across the back of the couch, twiddling her fingers. I slip my hand into hers. "But in the end, I really think you chose him. The first time you met him, you put your little arms in the air, wanting him to pick you up. It's like you just knew."

My heart drums against my ribs, remembering Weston doing the same thing to me, motioning me to follow him, lifting his arms in the air. Could it be that he knew I was there for all the right reasons? That there was a future to be had?

I steel my stomach and ask my final question—the one I'd been turning over in my mind for days. "Do you think I can do this?"

She squeezes my fingers and leans forward, capturing my gaze. "As a therapist, I'd tell you that if we all sit around waiting for the perfect time to do something or when we think we're 'ready,' then we'll be waiting forever. You can be informed. You can prepare. You can make commitments. But until the rubber hits the road and 'life' happens, you can't make predictions about the future. You can only live the present to your absolute best abilities and then take things as they come." She scoots closer to me and pulls her hand to my face, tweaking my chin. "My advice as your mom is much simpler. I want you to be happy, no matter what that looks like. Just be happy."

I stand outside her door, gathering the courage to knock. Now that I'm absolutely certain of how I want this thing between us to go, I only need to find out her take. My stomach crimps. What if she's changed her mind?

I lift my hand, knocking three times. Footsteps sound behind the door before it swings open. Jordan stands there in a ratty tank top and athletic shorts, hair in a loose ponytail, and I swear she's never been so beautiful. "Hey," she says with a tight smile, panning her hand toward the room. "Want to come in?"

I walk in and she closes the door behind me with a soft click. She follows me to the couch where we sit side by side. Jordan pulls her legs up, wrapping her arms around them. What I really want to do is slide over beside her and stay there all night. But the look in her eyes tells me we need to have a chat first.

She bites her bottom lip between her teeth then looks over at me, eyes rounded. "You didn't talk much on the way back."

"Neither did you."

Seems like we both had 400 miles worth of thinking to do.

"I'm not going to lie…" She jumps to her feet and walks to the island between the den and kitchen, grabbing the edge of the granite counter so hard her knuckles whiten. "After I saw you with Weston—how well you two got along—well, it got me worried." She drops her head, the loose strands from her pony-tail falling around her face, blocking me from seeing her expression. What could I have done this weekend that worried her? Some misstep with Weston?

"Worried?" I ask.

"That this won't last." I can barely discern the words coming from her mouth as her face is still veiled by a fringe of hair. This trip brought nothing but positives for me, but Jordan's tone is hesitant, unsure. "Weston's biological father didn't stay—neither did mine—and they had actual blood ties. You don't have that, so what would keep you around?"

What is it with the blood ties? Why is that the only accepted definition of family? What about chosen family, found family? Somehow that feels more, not less.

I push myself off the couch and walk to her, grabbing her shoulders and gently massaging them. "Are you kidding me?" I spin her around to face me, brushing the strands of hair from her face. Our eyes connect, hers darting back and forth, searching mine. Searching me. "*You* will keep me around. Weston will. This relationship we've built. It might not be a blood connection, but it's a *real* one. I don't want y'all because I have to or because I'm supposed to. I want y'all because I *choose* to want you—and I'll keep choosing y'all."

She pushes forward, crashing her lips to mine. They move slowly at first, then faster. I run my fingers up her back, letting them roam further, tugging at her ponytail, cupping her jaw to keep her close. Now this is how I expected tonight to go. But just as I move my hands to the buttons on her blouse, she pulls back, eyes narrowed.

"How do you know it'll work? How do you know this is something you want to keep pursuing for the long haul?"

I shake my head. This girl. She can't fathom how anyone would intentionally pick her and actually stick by her. So many in her life have done her wrong. I won't be one of them. "Not to go all Claire-the-therapist on you, but no one knows the future. We can only make our educated, heartfelt choices and see them through. But I've had a phenomenal example to rely on. They don't make them better than my dad, and I want to be just like him."

Jordan smiles, one that finally reaches her eyes. They pinch up at the corners, her lashes fluttering in rhythm with her quick blinking. She loops her arm through mine and pulls me to the couch. I settle onto the cushion and pull her down to me. She draws her legs up beside her and lays her head on my shoulder. We laugh and talk about the trip, peruse the photos on Jordan's phone, and snuggle together, watching TV.

After a while, Jordan picks up the remote and mutes the program. "Can I ask you a personal question?"

I nod, pressing a kiss to her forehead. Nothing is too personal for us to discuss. For her, I'm an open book.

Light from the candle we lit, which sits on the table, dances over her face, splashing fingers of warm amber across her skin. "Do you ever wish your biological father had been in the picture?"

My heart somersaults. Why is she asking about biological fathers? I'm sure she does want to know more about mine but is it mine that's on her mind? Or is it Weston's? I haven't yet had the guts to ask her about what I overheard despite Gin urging me to. But still, one thing Gin said did give me some relief. Jordan had picked me already, and, on top of that, she didn't seem too happy when her mama brought up the subject. No, on this I'll have to trust her; if Weston's bio dad was still a factor, she would've told me by now.

Of course, she could also be thinking of her own absentee father and the fact she never had anyone to step into that gap and accept the position. I can't imagine how different my life would've been without Clay. I don't want Weston to grow up with that sense of loss.

I sigh. "My biological father died before I was born. Before he ever knew I existed. Do I wish I could've known him? Yes. But the one thing I do know is that for whatever reason, Clay Johnson was meant to be my father. And he's been a damn good one. Who knows how my life would've turned out without him?"

Jordan nods and lays her head against my chest, unmuting the TV. She doesn't have to worry about any of that anymore.

CHAPTER 32

Jordan

I meander through the greenhouse, fertilizing and watering the new sprouts, all while my mind wanders back to our trip home and the deeper connection we'd discovered there among the mountains. It has only sweetened our days back here on Johnson Farms in the countdown to the finale of the internship. That money is within reach now, and it's the only thing able to tear my thoughts away from Bo.

Well, mostly.

The few days after returning to Edisto have been magical. Bo's family asked a million questions, and Claire thumbed through the photos taken at our farm—the ones of the three of us posing together. Gin came over and we stayed up late talking like sisters would. Clay and Bo yammered on and on about the possibilities a vineyard had for success in the Upstate and the best prospective investors who had not only deep pockets but also sharp business acumen. Bo and I spent evenings on the beach, talking and kissing and letting the ocean bubble up and over our toes.

To make things better, Brice and Patrick have been out of town for a few days for something they called "personal business." One can only hope they are off getting some sort of exorcism for the terrible demons they both house inside. No matter the reason, no one seems to miss them.

Bo steps behind me as a I repot a few of the seedlings into larger quarters. He nuzzles his face into my neck, trailing a line of kisses from my collarbone to my chin. "I'm supposed to go meet with Jett this afternoon, but I'll see you after dinner?"

I smile and find his lips with mine. "I'm looking forward to it."

He gives me a wink and saunters to the door, letting it slam shut behind him. I scoop another helping of fertilizer pellets into my watering can and then fill it to the brim with water, stirring as it fills in order to incorporate. The contents swirl into a bright blue. I'm carrying the hose back to the holder on the wall when the door opens again, heavy footsteps crunching over the pea-gravel.

"Back so soon? I thought—"

My words die on my tongue when I glance over my shoulder. It's not Bo.

"Hello, Jordan," Brice says with a sneer.

"Oh good. You're back." I roll my eyes, refocusing on the plants, patting the soil tight around the roots before adding water. "To what do I owe this pleasure?"

He steps beside me, leaning on the wooden table with his arms crossed over his chest. "Pleasure is all mine. At least today." When I don't react, he levels a hard glare in my direction and grabs my arm, spinning me to face him directly. "I want you gone. I want you nowhere near Johnson Farms or Bo ever again."

I snort. Does he really think I'm gullible enough to follow his demands? I'm not here for him or because of him. He has no pull over me.

"And what makes you think I give a damn about your whims?"

"This." Brice reaches into his back pocket and pulls out an envelope stuffed with folded papers. He slips them out and unfurls them in front of me. Some sort of legal paperwork.

"What is this?" I ask, grabbing hold of the corner, though he won't allow me to pull it from his grasp. I lean in closer, squinting to read the small, typed print. My stomach drops when I note a familiar address at the top along with other key terms like *default*, *pending sale*, and *deed*. My fingers fill with lead and drop from the paper back to my side. I stare up at Brice whose top lip curls into an evil grin.

"It's not hard to access property tax records. They're out there on the internet for all to see." He re-folds the paperwork and stuffs it back in his pocket. "If you thought you were going to slink in here and screw up Johnson Farms, maybe you should've cleaned up your own messes first."

My hands tremble, pulse racing ninety miles a minute. So what if he hates me? What does that have to do with my family? He doesn't even know them. "Why the hell do you care about my family's property?" My voice comes out like a growl.

"I don't. It's just a means to an end." He shrugs and rubs his hands together as if this insanity actually makes sense. My mind reels. What does that paperwork mean? That Brice owns our property now? That he stole it out from under us? My vision blurs in and out and I reach back, groping for the stool. I finally find it and shuffle backward to sit down on the edge. "Bo's not a Johnson by blood. And if you ran off with him tomorrow, that little hillbilly-hick spawn you have would never be a Johnson either. I'm sick and tired of bastards taking over our family fortune." My blood boils in the veins. How dare this jerk call Bo —and Weston—bastards. They are a credit to what he'll ever hope to be. I slide off the edge of my stool but Brice leans forward over me, nearly bending me backward. The sadistic glow in his eyes turns them like soot. "Hope you enjoyed playing with Bo for a hot minute because it's over now. Unless you don't mind seeing Grandma and Grandpa's sad faces as their farmhouse burns to the ground."

I gasp at the visual, lunging toward Brice, my hand clutching at his throat. "You asshole. Don't you dare lay a finger on—"

"Uh-uh-uh." He pushes me back, that same infuriating grin on his lips, and wags a finger in my face. "Relax. I might be able to arrange a negotiation."

I slit my eyes, trying to regulate my breathing. "What does that mean?"

"Well... I have something you want, and you have something I want."

Every unholy, disgusting vision runs through my head. "If you think for one second that I'm going to sleep with you—"

"Woah, don't flatter yourself. Brice Johnson doesn't do... left-overs." He crinkles his nose, swiping his hands through the air as if brushing me away. "What I mean is I have your deed, and you have the power to eliminate yourself, and consequently Bo, from any influence in Johnson Farms."

"I don't understand."

Brice blows out a loud breath and knifes his hands in front of me like I'm a two-year-old he's lecturing. "Let's make this simple. I'm not interested in running off half-cocked into this stupid vineyard idea Bo hatched out of his ass. If you cease to exist in our world, that goes away. Secondly, the only thing standing between me and being named the next CEO is Bo. Clay was this close—" He pauses, holding up his finger and thumb an inch apart. "—to naming me for the position before Bo's 'last chance summer'. He was never going to stay here... *before* you. But now, he's up in farm business all the time. If you leave, then I'm positive Bo will too."

I hold up both hands like stop signs, shaking my head. "I'm not jeopardizing Bo's future. Don't even ask that. Besides, you don't know. Bo may just want to succeed his father. I don't make his decisions." I scoff at his logic. He may force my hands by threatening my family's land but that has no bearing on Bo's future. He decides his path. It's always been his choice and not mine.

Brice laughs—the horror-movie, sadistic sort—then walks over and grabs both of my shoulders, stooping to my eye level.

"Let me be clear. I'll get rid of him in one way or another. Either he leaves Johnson Farms after you break his heart or I can always arrange a little accident. Farming is a tough industry. Long hours, hard work with heavy, dangerous equipment. Accidents happen all too frequently. I'd hate for Johnson Farms to endure something like that."

My breath catches in my throat, my lungs refusing to inhale. I knew Brice was a pig-headed jerk but I never took him for an unhinged maniac. My bottom lip trembles as I process his words. Hurt Bo—kill him even—in a farm accident? How would he even do it? The tractor? The plows? I gulp, shoving him away from me, then plunge my finger against his nose, screaming through gritted teeth, "Don't you dare hurt him!"

Unaffected, Brice shoves his hands in his pockets, smiling again. "There's a price to pay if you play with me."

"I'll go to Clay. Or the police."

"Go ahead. I'll burn down your—excuse me, *my*—house and destroy the land."

I grind my fingers into fists, squeezing so hard my nails cut crescents into the skin of my palms. He might have me over a barrel but there's something he hasn't thought of. "You act like my leaving could solve everything, but it won't be that easy. Bo will come after me."

"You really did buy into all those white picket fences, didn't you?" He slaps a hand over his forehead, laughing out loud. "Bo won't run after you... not if you make the reason you're leaving good enough. Make him feel the rejection. Maybe a 'reunion' with your baby-daddy? That should do it."

My heart drops. After everything that happened with Laurel, Bo thinking that I'd left him to reunite with another guy would destroy him. His trust, his self-worth were so damaged from that entire debacle, it is a miracle he put his faith in me. But Brice doesn't care about anything like that. He wants Bo to hurt, mentally, physically, emotionally. And I just want to cushion him from any pain. I stare up into Brice's dark eyes. "You'd love that, wouldn't you? To see him hurt?"

"Don't make me out to be the bad guy here. I'm concerned about my future... and yours." He lifts his hands up as if totally innocent. "I mean, you don't have to do what I'm saying, but then you and your kid and your mama better start looking for a new house. Maybe you could check Grandma and Grandpa into one of those retirement homes in the city. I hear those are nice. Of course, you'd have to find a way to afford that since, you know, you wouldn't exactly have money or credit. Perhaps a nice mountain cave?"

Fury wraps my spine like a venomous snake. "You play with people's lives like they're chess pieces," I spit at him. "Pathetic, piece of—"

"No, you play with people's lives, Jordan! You set all of this in motion." Brice is screaming now, shoving a finger in my face. "Now I'm holding all the cards and asking how much you're willing to wager. How much do you love your family? How much do you love Bo? If you leave—permanently—then everything can go back like it was. Like this summer never happened. If you don't, a lot of lives will fall apart." His nostrils flare, jaw locked tight. "Don't cross me, Jordan. I'm warning you."

We face off in a silent stare down until my phone rings, and I glance down at the screen. Why is Mama calling me now? Has he done something already?

I step away from Brice and turn my back to him before answering. "Mama?"

A few noises crackle on the line followed by her heavy breaths. I've heard her like this before, picking and choosing her words. Bad news. "Sassy... I don't want you to worry... everything's stable now... but your grandpa... he's had another heart attack."

Pain grips my chest, like I'm experiencing his from across the distance. "What? How is he?"

"He's in the hospital. They're doing an angioplasty and

putting in a stent tomorrow morning. Doctors say that he should do well with that procedure, but he can't keep getting stressed out."

"Why is Grandpa stressed?" I glance over my shoulder at Brice, who stands staring in my direction, eyes slitted. I swear, if he's the cause of this, I will tear him from limb to limb.

"That's the other reason I'm calling." A garbled sound, like muffled sobs or extra breaths bleed through the line. "We got a visit from Gerald at the bank. Some big moneybags came in and put a bid on our place—a motivated buyer as they called it—and after fourteen months of delinquency, they're tired of giving us extensions. They've accepted the bid and the paperwork is being processed. We have to be out in thirty days."

Thirty days. And I know exactly who Mr. Moneybags is that created this storm. Who put Grandpa in the hospital. Who's threatened to do the same to Bo. Or worse.

My stomach grips. And only I can stop him.

I whisper into the phone, "I'm coming home now, and we're going to figure this out. I just need to pack up my things, and then I'll hit the road."

"You bringing Bo with you?"

My heart splinters into a million pieces. No. I have to leave him behind. For everyone's sake. "No, it'll just be me."

We hang up, and I clutch the phone in my hand, trying to hold onto some fragment of myself, something that connects me to the people I love most, while I feel as though I'm drowning in a vat of murky water.

"What happened to Grandpa?"

His voice stirs the bile rising in my esophagus. I spin around, glaring at him. "He had a heart attack because you..." I can't bring myself to finish the sentence. Give any credence to his devious plot.

Brice strides toward me, reaching out to rub my shoulder. I shirk his condescending touch as he lowers his voice, saying, "I told you innocent people would end up hurt. It's already starting.

But you can end this by ending things with Bo and leaving. Now." It's a warning. One he's already making good on. And I can't allow my family to hurt anymore. I can't allow Bo to be put in jeopardy because of me.

I stare into his eyes, unfeeling, emotionless, hard. "I guess I don't have a choice, do I?"

He smirks, proud of himself. "Good girl."

I stand in the doorway of the Johnsons' guesthouse, staring back in at the place that'd morphed into my home for the summer. The couch where Bo and I had sat, planning our market event. The kitchen table where Gin strong-armed me into shopping for that embarrassingly tiny bikini. The bedroom where Bo and I had spent many nights, snuggling and talking. All memories to be locked in the past the moment the door shuts behind me. I readjust the strap of the duffle bag on my shoulder and set my suitcase at my feet, still staring inside. I don't want to turn around, don't want to leave, because I know it will all be final. Be over.

But I have to. Mama needs me at home, and Bo needs me to leave, whether he knows it or not. I won't let him continue being Brice's victim. If letting him go—letting us go—is what it takes to keep him safe, to let him have a life, then it's what I'll do.

My feelings don't matter. I'll put them away, lock them in a lockbox in my mind, and only bring them out when I'm alone and can wallow in my sadness. Like Mama.

I sigh, gathering my things, and pull the door shut. It closes with a click, and I trudge down the steps to my Jeep. A quick glance at the main house reveals no one outside, no one watching at the windows. Relief. Now I can pack up and leave without any of those big scenes. I can't face them and muster the courage to lie and tell them I'm perfectly okay driving out of their lives forever. God, I can't face Bo and rip his heart out when mine is already skewered and spit-roasted. I'll have to send him a letter. Or call. Anything but face him.

I open the door and am loading my bags into the back seat when her voice comes out of the blue. I glance back at Claire, walking from Miss Bessie's house, eyebrows scrunched together into a line.

"Jordan? What's going on?" When I don't answer, she jogs toward me and grabs my arm. "Where are you going? You still have another week."

Oh God, oh God. I don't want to do this.

"I... I have to leave. Grandpa had a heart attack and..."

She gasps, pulling her hand over her mouth. "I'm so sorry. Is he okay?"

I nod, pushing my driver seat back into place and pulling the keys from my pocket. "I need to get home. I should've never left."

"Oh honey. You couldn't have prevented this, but I understand your need to be with your family now. Here, let me call Bo. He can drive you—" She begins pulling her phone from her pocket but I reach out, blocking her. She looks up at me with curious eyes.

"No! I'm good. I can do this."

She cocks her head to the side, sympathy pooling in her eyes. She thinks I'm just trying to be strong. She has no clue the battle ripping me to shreds below the surface.

"Jordan, you're a mess. Please—"

"I need to leave now. There's no more time." I hop into my Jeep and slam the door. As the engine rumbles to life, I roll the window down partway because I can't leave without at least telling her some semblance of how I feel. "I just want to say thank you for everything this summer. Y'all have been incredible, and I promise I'll never forget any of you."

"Forget us? It sounds as if you'll never see us again." Her arms drop to her sides as she narrows her eyes, searching my face. They slice through me, and I can't let her see the truth. I look away, staring out my windshield. "You will see us again, right?" She says each word slowly, carefully as if I'm a grenade she might accidentally detonate. I don't answer, and she steps forward, palming my window. Her breaths come heavy and in spurts as she processes the scene. "Jordan! Bo's in love with you. We *all* love you. Whatever else is going on…"

I'm breaking, piece by piece. My courage slips. "Claire… I can't. I have to go. I'm sorry." I don't dare look at her, only shift to first gear and slam my foot against the gas. The Jeep's tires spin against the sand, throwing up a cloud of glittery dust, as I peel out of the drive and swerve onto the main road. Not letting up. As the Jeep goes faster, so do my tears, welling in my lashes, blurring the images of this place I'm leaving behind.

The roar of the engine fades to background static as Claire's voice repeats in my head.

Bo's in love with you.

A knife twists in my guts. My greatest wish now my biggest fear.

My phone rings in the cupholder, and I glance down at it. Bo. Claire must've called him. It goes to voicemail, and then begins ringing again. And again. And again.

This time a beep sounds and the red fuel light illuminates on my dash.

Shit. I cannot deal with this right now, but I have to stop and fill up the tank. There's not another station on the way out for a good thirty miles.

A few minutes up the road, I pull off at the tiny convenience store in front of a pump on the far side, hoping the grove of palm trees at the corner will block me from anyone who might be driving by. My phone rings again, and I ignore it, jumping out to start pumping my gas.

The pump turns on, whirring as the fuel pours into my tank. Five gallons. Ten. Fourteen. Almost there. I stare hard at the pump, willing the last gallon to fill faster. It clicks off and I grab the handle just as Bo's Bronco comes flying past. He squeals his brakes and U-turns in the road, pulling into the lot.

Damn.

He jumps out and sprints in my direction. My heart pounds. I can't do this. I can't. Over his shoulder, I spot Jett in the passenger seat, staring at us. At least Bo will have a friend to pick up the pieces of the unholy hell I'm about to unleash.

I hold my breath as he throws his arms around me, wrapping me into the biggest, warmest hug. I fight any reaction, keeping my body rigid, mentally sending ice down my spine. *You have to do this, Jordan. You have no choice.*

He pulls back, his eyes round. "Mom just called and told me. How's Grandpa?"

"They say he'll recover, but things have to change." I keep it monotone. Robotic almost.

"He won't be pleased about no bacon." Bo smiles at his joke but it dissolves when I don't reciprocate.

"There are going to be more changes than that." I take a deep breath, pulling my hands from his. "I'm about to drive off this island, and I'm never coming back here. Ever."

He exhales. Sharp, quick. Like someone punched him in the stomach. "What?"

"Grandpa's heart attack was a sign. That's where I'm supposed to be. That's where I belong." My throat tightens as I conjure up the next lie. "All of this was just... just a summertime thing."

"All of this?" He flicks his finger between us. "Or me and you?"

I cross my arms over my chest, closing him off. Holding me in. "Bo, please—I feel bad enough."

He steps back, mouth dropped open, as he shakes his head. "*You* feel bad? Did you even have real feelings for me?"

Of course, I did. I do. I always will. But I can't tell him that.

You have to lie, Jordan. Lie! Break his heart to save his life, his future. Say that one thing that will tear him apart and sting him so badly that he'll never want to see you again.

My internal dialogue rages. My brain kicking my heart's ass. *Do it!*

"I did care for you... but not that way." The lie tastes bitter as poison on my lips. It's killing me. "I'm in love with Weston's father. I always have been, and now he wants us to be together."

"No, no, no!" Bo yells, raking his fingers through his curls and scrunching them against his scalp. He shakes his head, breath coming faster. "I don't believe you. If all this is true, then why would you introduce me to Weston?"

"To make my ex jealous. And it worked." I stare at my feet. Seeing the torment etched in his face and not collapsing in pain is impossible. "He was coming by all summer looking for me and when he heard about us being in town, he asked me to meet him. And I did. He realized that he still loved me... and Weston." I bite my lip, hiding the reality that Weston's father doesn't want him or me. Never did. I inhale the briny air, willing the oxygen to strengthen me. "I can't deny him a real family. I can't deny it for myself."

Bo squats down, propping his head in one hand. "I never thought... you never said..."

This can't keep on. The harm is already done. Now I have to end his suffering. "I guess you were my back-up plan."

"Your back-up plan?" He springs to his feet, a fire lit in his eyes, turning them almost purple. I look back to the asphalt.

"Weston has a chance for a real family," I say. "You know how important this is to me. If you care about me—if you ever cared about me—then you won't interfere."

He steps closer, so close I could raise my head and press my lips to his. Torture. "Why won't you look at me?" The words are soft, his voice quivering.

Damn you, Brice! I hope you burn in Hell!

I lift my eyes, meeting his in a stony glare. A brick wall.

"This ends now, Bo. Don't ever call me again. I don't want to talk to you. I don't want you messing up anything for me." He opens his mouth for a rebuttal, but I shut it down before the words can leave his mouth. "Better yet, go call Laurel. Maybe she'll finally bump you to her number one choice."

His mouth snaps closed. He doesn't respond. He doesn't have to. It's in his eyes, the burning blue turned dark and tumultuous as the ocean. They lock in on mine as if we're in a staring contest; neither one blinks. His boots grind in the sand as he backpedals, legs dragging in the slightest way that seems as if they'll give out on him at any moment. Jett jumps out and runs to Bo, grabbing his shoulders and steadying him. They exchange a few words and then Jett shoots a death glare at me over his shoulder.

I've done the job. I've completed the task. Bo's life is safe. My family's farm is safe.

My future is over.

My stomach churns because I always knew this would be my lot in life, to follow a loveless existence like Mama. I just never thought fate would be so cruel as to give me a small taste of the euphoria of being head over heels only to rip it from my clutches. The wound is open, raw, and bleeding. And now I've given Bo one to match.

Jett settles Bo in the passenger seat and then jogs to the other side, jumping in behind the wheel. The engine rumbles to life and the Bronco spins tires as it exits the gravel lot, spitting rocks and sand out behind it. Bo doesn't turn around. He never looks back.

As I'm going to get back in my Jeep, my gurgling stomach explodes and I hit all fours, heaving up the contents beside the gas pump.

CHAPTER 33

Bo

The tears won't stop. They flood down my face and drench my shirt. I don't even care that the group of kids building sandcastles beside me keep looking over as if I've lost my mind.

Yeah, give it ten years, kid, and you'll get it. Getting dumped sucks. When Laurel did it, though, I just got mad. But Jordan? She's ripped my freaking guts out.

I stare out at the whitecaps dotting the horizon as purplish-black storm clouds roll in. When Mom called me in a panic, she said something with Jordan was "off." Something strange about the way she kept diverting her eyes and gritting her teeth like she was holding back something. Mom thought she was worried sick about Grandpa. She missed that Jordan was about to use that situation to toss me to the curb.

But why? Everything had been perfect just hours ago in the greenhouse. We kissed—she was kissing me as much as I was kissing her. There was no hesitancy, no questioning.

Of course, I never saw the Laurel situation coming either. I pick up a broken fragment of shell and chuck it into the incoming wave. It splashes then sinks from sight. Maybe I'll never learn my lesson.

My phone dings. Probably Jett checking up on me for the

fiftieth time. After the Jordan fiasco, he drove us back to the Ramsey's practice track where he had to finish training, but he begged me to stay. I refocus on the ocean water, crashing in and then pulling back out in rhythm. I needed a place that felt bigger than the heartache annihilating my insides. I needed a place to wash away the pain.

I pick up my phone and stare down at the screen.

<Brice>: *Meet Me. Behind Market. 10 minutes.*

Yeah, that'll be a no. As if this day could get worse. I tap out a quick response.

<Me>: *Now is not the time.*

The phone dings back almost immediately.

<Brice>: *If you still care anything about Jordan, now is definitely the time. 10 minutes.*

My heart stalls in my chest. *If you still care.* How does Brice know anything about what's happened with Jordan? Random puzzle pieces of this screwed-up scenario pile into my brain with no rhyme or reason; none of them fit in a way to make sense.

I get up, brushing off the sand, and run to my Bronco. It fires to life and I pull out of the beach access lot, speeding toward the market, the hundreds of visitors in their flashy bathing suits and multi-colored umbrellas blurring into a rainbowed haze through the windows.

My mind races. One minute, Jordan's happy. We're happy. But Brice wasn't around, and now, just as he returns, Jordan is telling me we're over, that she never cared for me like that. Even though we solidified so much while on our trip. I mean, that night outside the barn was the statement of how we felt. Right? Then again, I did overhear that part about Weston's father being in town, and Jordan did admit to seeing him. But when?

I make a left into the market's lot and tear around to the back where Brice's truck is parked under the large oaks. He leans against the fender, chewing on a long blade of seagrass. I pull up and slide out of my seat, running up to him, chest to chest. He did something. That smug gloat on his face confirms it.

"What do you know?" I growl.

He rolls his eyes and pushes me back. "Woah, bro. Hostility —keep it in check."

"Cut the shit. Jordan breaks up with me and then you just happen to text me about her? There are no coincidences when it comes to you."

He smiles and tips his visor at me, the blade of grass still pinched between his teeth. It bounces on his lips as he says, "Well, Bo... that might be the nicest thing you've ever said to me. It's time you gave credit to those who really get things done around here."

Is that an admission? Fire consumes me. I lunge at him again, my fingers curling around a clump of his shirt. "What did you do to Jordan? If you touched her, I'll—"

He grasps my hand, squeezing my knuckles and breaking my grip on his shirt. He flings my arm down. "You sure are overprotective of some chick who just dumped you."

"How'd you know about that?"

"I know about a lot of things. And now, so will you." He pinches his lips together and shrugs, pulling out a large manilla envelope from the seat of his truck. "For instance, I bet you didn't know your girlfriend—excuse me, *ex-girlfriend*—hadn't been so faithful." He tosses a few photos on the hood in front of me. Photos of Jordan sitting in a diner with another guy, his hand holding onto hers. Photos of her leaned across the table like she's whispering or maybe even about to—my stomach churns —kiss him?

I want to look away, but I can't. The photos are like a magnet, and I'm the masochistic idiot that keeps staring at them, committing every detail to memory—ones that will haunt me tonight as I try to sleep.

This must be Weston's father. The photos are recent, too, because Jordan is wearing the sea glass necklace I bought her that night at our market event.

The reality sinks in me like a boulder. She wasn't lying. She went to see him while I was in her hometown, at her farmhouse, babysitting Weston. She really was going back to him, that piece of shit who'd abandoned her and stayed MIA for years. How is he the better option over me?

And how does Brice know about any of this? And why does he care? Is all this just a ploy to get me here and gloat, revel in my torture?

I run my fingers over the glossy 4x6 prints, wishing I could mash my thumb into the guy's face and rub him out of existence. "Where did you get these?"

"When you went galivanting off to her farm, I was concerned. We have a big operation here, and we can't just let anyone into that. No one knows anything about this girl, who she is, what kind of people they really are. So, I hired a private investigator to keep tabs. I have to say... I never expected this... but it does work out perfectly."

He must've laid these photos out for Jordan too. That had to be why she ran. "Did you threaten to expose her with these photos? Is this why she left?"

He triggers his finger in my direction with a tongue click as he shakes his head. "Oh no. She doesn't even know I have those. I'm just enjoying the look on your face as you digest my 'I told you so.'" Brice rifles back through the folder and pulls out a collection of stapled papers. Some official-looking documents with stamps and seals. "She was persuaded by this."

I pull the document from his hands and flip through the papers. Lots of legal jargon about Jordan's grandparents' farm. "I don't understand," I mutter, continuing to read through the paperwork.

"Jordan and her family are more than a year delinquent on their mortgage payments. Extension after extension but nada. That's not the kind of liability Johnson Farms need to associate with. It's just not good business, and the bank agrees too." He snatches the paperwork from my grip and slides it back into his folder. "So, when someone comes in with a generous cash offer, a small-town lender suddenly doesn't feel as much generosity and grace as before." He smirks and lifts his hand, rubbing his finger and thumb together. "Money talks."

My mouth becomes a desert. "Are you saying—"

He tosses the folder into his front seat and then leans back against his truck, cracking his knuckles. "I bought their property. I am the new owner of Wright Family Farm."

Shit. Jordan must be having a conniption right now. Maybe her feelings for me were never to the extent of mine, but I know she did care about me in some capacity. She trusted me enough to confide in me about their financial issues, and I sat there, so naïve, and told her we'd solve them. Because my love for her could conquer anything in front of us.

I pause, a load of bricks dropping into my stomach. *My love for her.* My internal thoughts stitched it together before I could ever realize it on my own. I'm in love with Jordan. I love her, and I never told her. And now I'll never get the chance. Because even if it wasn't for her ex-boyfriend slinking back into the picture with all the pretty promises history says he'll surely break, how could she ever see past the fact that a member of my own family —idiotic and devious as he may be—was the one to mastermind the ultimate injury and steal her family land?

That's why she wouldn't look at me. It wasn't just about her choosing Weston's father. She can deny it all she wants, but we had love between us. Going back to him is all about her own father issues clouding her judgement. Maybe I could have talked her out of that nonsense, but this? This is unforgivable.

With jaw locked, I step forward, my chest bucking against Brice's. "You're not going to get away with this. Once Dad catches wind, he'll—"

"He'll do what? I'm the land owner. He can't do shit." The infuriating smirk reappears and he pretends to buff his nails on his shirt. "But I can. I hear there's a growing market for condominiums with an Appalachian view. What do you think about the name Brice Meadows? The Cliffs at Bricewood, maybe?"

"You threatened Jordan's farm, didn't you?"

"I don't make petty threats, Bo. I make deals. You, me, Jordan... we all have our price. Jordan wants a life with her baby-daddy on their farm. Her perfect little family, and I can give her that as long as she stays away... permanently. Which as it turns out, wasn't such a hard decision for her. She'd do anything to save her farm—she's said so before—and she was already looking for a way to break things off with you. Even I couldn't script something that perfect. Afraid you just got dumped for a better guy." He snorts. "Again."

We all have our price. Is he admitting that he's some sort of sadistic monster, that his currency is all about inflicting pain on people and sitting back to enjoy? "I don't get what's in it for you. You have no interest in that land."

"Ding ding ding. Way to go, Bo. Maybe you aren't as dense as I always thought." He thumps my forehead, and I swipe at him, knocking his hand away, as he laughs. "How can I put this simply? Jordan wants her farm. You want to protect Jordan. I want Johnson Farms. Everything stands to work out to everyone's benefit except for one little thing standing in the way."

"What?"

"You." He levels a hard gaze on me, bugging out his eyes. "Jordan's family can have their farm back, when I'm instated as the future head of Johnson Farms. That can happen once you submit your resignation and your denial of any place in the company going forward." He reaches back into his truck and comes out with yet another set of legal papers. "I've taken the liberty of having the paperwork drawn up. All you need to do is sign on the dotted line." He flips to the last page and hands it to me, then pulls a pen from his shirt pocket.

I flip back to the front and read the first line.

I, Beauregard Johnson, do hereby resign from Johnson Farms, effective immediately.

I look up from the papers. "And if I don't?"

He pinches one shoulder to his jaw. "If you don't sign... if you attempt to contact Jordan... if you even think about taking this to anyone else, I'll make good on my promise. That broken-down farmhouse, barn, fields, everything will be razed before sunset to make way for my condo development. It'd be a shame for the Wrights to find themselves homeless with no money and no credit. Child Protective Services would probably swoop in and take the kid away too."

Nausea churns inside me like violent waves. Jordan has already lost her farm, her beloved land. But to lose Weston? To have him ripped from her arms? It'd kill her.

And I can't let that happen. Because I love her. No matter who she's with.

Brice snatches the paperwork from my grip, leaning back in the window of his truck. "Of course, if you're bitter and you want to ruin Jordan's life..."

"No!" He stops and glances back at me, an evil grin ticking up the corner of his lips. I have no choice. Brice swore he'd find a way to exact revenge and he did. "I'll sign it. Just give them back their farm."

He holds out the papers and I grab them, flipping to the last page. I lay them on the hood of my Bronco and click the pen, letting it hover over the signature line. I'm letting my inheritance be stolen, so she can have hers. She deserves it. She's always known what she wanted with zero hesitancy. I want her to be happy, no matter what. I press the pen to the page, the ink flowing out, steady and sure, as I sign my name.

No sooner do I put down the last stroke than Brice grabs the papers, clutching them like a trophy. He slaps me on the shoulder. "Think of it this way too. Signing this repays Clay for all he did for you. A man so committed to honoring family who's been faced with the prospect of leaving his farm to someone he isn't even related to? He didn't want you to know how that was killing him inside. Now that weight is lifted too."

I drop my head, defeated. Maybe Brice is right. Maybe everyone would be better off if I just disappeared. Maybe too many people have spent too many years trying to pretend that I wasn't the outsider just looking in.

Brice walks around and gets in his truck. It cranks with a loud roar. He calls my name through the window, and I look back over my shoulder at him.

"Remember, if you open your mouth to anyone or make any attempt to contact Jordan, I'll make her pay." He backs up, his tires crunching gravel, but pauses before pulling out to say one last thing. "Pleasure negotiating with you."

CHAPTER 34

Jordan

I stand in the hallway at the bottom of the staircase, peeking into my grandparents' room through the cracked door. Grandpa lies in the bed while Grandma sits beside him in the armchair she's pulled to the bedside, reading a book aloud. His procedure went well this morning, and we were allowed to bring him home. Grandma has refused to leave his side all day, always fussing over something—fluffing his pillows, bringing him a cold water, standing over him while he sleeps, two fingers pressed to his neck.

This is what I want. A love that withstands the pressures. One that perseveres.

I really thought Bo and I had a chance, a future. Until in a blink, it's gone, and I'm left with nothing but memories. I think of Mama, twenty years ago, standing in this same house and feeling exactly the way I do now.

"Psst. Psst! Sassy!" I turn and look up to where Mama is standing on the second-floor landing at the top of the steps. She motions me to join her. I pad up the stairs, slowly so as not to instigate any loud creaking to disturb the grandparents. She points to Weston's room, the door pulled almost shut, lights off, and whispers, "I just checked on Weston. Tuckered out already."

I smile. It was nice being able to give him a bath, read him a story, and tuck him in tonight. Those were the things I longed for in Edisto, and being able to do them again tonight did bring a measure of joy. A bright spot in an ocean of gray.

I kiss Mama's cheek and walk to my room. Slipping into bed and pulling the covers over my head doesn't seem like a bad idea. Though, if the dreams continue tonight—the ones of Bo being hurt by farm equipment—there'll be no rest.

Mama pads behind me, all the way to my bed, where she flips open the cover on my suitcase. "I thought maybe we could unpack your clothes and talk."

She doesn't understand that her request is impossible. At least if she wants me to maintain some semblance of sanity. "I don't want to talk," I mumble, re-zipping the suitcase and laying it on the chair in the corner.

Mama cocks her head to the side, staring at me. Her eyes laser through the hard shell I've tried to build around me and cuts right to the quick. The red, raw, bleeding wound. She sighs and sits down on the bed, patting the empty space beside her. I consider bolting for the door. I could outrun her, go sleep in my Jeep and lock all the doors. But, then again, what's the point? She already knows how I feel. She's been here too.

I trudge to the bed and sit beside her, as eager to discuss this as I'd be to have a tooth pulled. She turns to me and strokes my cheek. "It's okay, Sassy."

"Mama..." I start, but just calling her name pulls the plug on the flood of emotions I've been holding back. They rush forth all at once, in buckets of tears and a snotty nose and some incoherent babble.

She doesn't fall apart. She remains my rock. "I know." She pulls me to her, running her fingers down the length of my hair. She smells like the sweet honey glaze on the cornbread and the musty earthiness of the barn. I burrow in closer to her, hiding myself in her arms. "You loved him," she whispers.

There it is. The one feeling that's been stirring in my heart that I never had the courage to speak out load to Bo. And now he'll never hear it. At least not from me. "I do love him," I admit.

She doesn't say another word, just holds me closer until I've cried so much her blouse is soaked. Then comes the guilt, crashing down on top of me, and I sit back, wiping away the wetness from my cheeks, swallowing down everything else. She's never spewed her sadness on me, and I shouldn't do this to her.

She squeezes my hand. "Let it out. There's no shame in just letting it out."

"But you never do. At least not in front of me. You hold it in and..." I stop short of finishing the sentence—the one where I admit to hearing her very real despair alive and well in her bedroom at night. She thinks the pain is hers alone, but it's not. And it's never been.

"And?"

"And cry at night into your pillow. I've heard you... so many times."

She grimaces and looks down at her lap. "I'm sorry you've heard that."

"No, Mama. I'm sorry. You're the best woman I've ever known and you deserve so much." I bite my tongue, trying not to confess the real problem because admitting it hurts so damn much. "You could've had it without me being in the way."

A flash of anger glints in Mama's eyes but is quickly replaced with something else. Shame? "Have I ever made you feel that way?"

I shake my head. Absolutely not. Mama has poured every ounce of herself into me, Weston, and this farm without one complaint. Not one snivel, not one meltdown. But the tears at night—the ones she'd thought she'd hid so well—told the true story. "No, but I know it anyway."

She sighs, turning her body on the bed to square herself in front of me. "Let me put it this way. Do you regret Weston?"

"Never."

"Because he's your baby?"

"Of course, I just…"

"You're still my baby no matter how grown-up you are." She palms both sides of my face, staring into my eyes. "You, Jordan Sassafras Wright, are my biggest accomplishment. That I could bring someone so loving, so tender, so wonderful into the world? That, in turn, you would create that precious baby boy with a smile that could buckle the knees of the world's meanest hearts? It feels almost divine."

How does she do it? Make her sacrifice seem so poetic? So inspired? I know she understands the pain tearing through me right now because she's been here. She's loved someone and had that taken away, yet here she is so strong and resilient in the face of so much adversity. The tears pour again as I scoot closer on the bed and lay my head on her shoulder.

"How do you do it? Live without love once you've had it?" I ask through the sobs. "I feel like there's a hole punched in my chest."

It's a question I've wanted to ask her for a long time but never really had a reason to before. That's changed.

She wraps an arm around me, running her hand up and down my back with a deep sigh. "It hurts now, and it will for a long time. Maybe that ache won't ever fully go away. It'll rear its head when you think of the what-ifs or wonder how the path could've worked out differently. You just have to hold on tight to the pain and see it through. But on the other side, you'll discover the true beauty of love. Even the shadows left behind can bring something positive… sweet memories, life lessons, resilience. And in time, you'll have the opportunity to love again."

Bo awakened something in me this summer. Something special I'd only felt with him. No matter how hard I try, the thought of sharing that with someone else seems impossible. And not just impossible, but revolting. I only want Bo.

"I can't imagine loving anyone else." I push up on my elbow, and she looks down at me. "And what about you?"

Mama narrows her eyes, fidgeting with her hair, obviously uncomfortable with my pointed question. "What about me?"

"When will you take another shot at love? When is it *your* turn?"

She smiles and leans in, planting a kiss on my forehead. "Love will find its way to me when it's time. Just like it found its way to you this summer."

CHAPTER 35

Bo

The clanging of hurried footsteps on the metal stairs rouses me from sleep. I check my watch—2 p.m.—then pull the drawstrings of my hoodie tighter, pinching the fabric into a peep hole around my face. I told Jett I needed some downtime to be alone and he readily offered his apartment at the track, but I should've figured he'd come rushing out here to check on me today. He's sulked out here a million times but the minute I, the even-tempered one, needs a mental getaway, everyone panics.

The key grinds in the lock and the door creaks open, allowing a sliver of blinding daylight to cut through the otherwise pitch-dark room. Muscles rigid, I lay still, not even taking a breath. I don't want to talk about it. I just want to be alone. Why can't Jett let me suffer here in silence, marinating in my own crap? Why can't he—

"Bo?"

Shit. Her voice isn't what I'm expecting. I sit up in the bed and glance over my shoulder toward the door at her shape silhouetted against the light. Laurel.

"What the hell are you doing here?"

She steps inside and flips the wall switch, bathing the room in a fluorescent glare. I squint my eyes tight, temporarily blinded, but hear her footsteps pad closer. The edge of the mattress depresses and as my vision filters back to normal, she's there, perched on the quilt, hands folded in her lap and bottom lip bit between her teeth, a set of doe eyes trained on me. "I really needed to see you."

Wow. I just got dumped by a girl going back to her ex only to be visited by the other girl who'd used me to cheat on her boyfriend. No thanks. "I don't have the time or the interest." I lay back against my pillow, turning over on my side, facing away from her and her sudden need to talk it over with me. Speaking of which...

"How'd you even find me?" I grumble.

"I brought her." Gin's voice sounds from the doorway and I jerk to sitting, finding her leaned against the doorframe.

"You?" I glance between the two of them, standing within spitting distance of each other and no WWE-style throwdown in sight. Something's up. "What is this, some sort of intervention?

"Jett told CJ where you were, and she told me. I was going to let you have your privacy for a few days but then..." Gin sighs and walks over to the bed, sitting down a mere foot from Laurel. "You really need to hear what she has to say."

Since when has she been a Laurel fan? What about those beady, lying eyes she warned me against?

I thread my arms over my chest and glare at both of them. "Five minutes."

"That should do it," Gin says and nods a go-ahead to Laurel, who reaches into her purse and pulls out her cell phone. She drums her nails nervously over the screen, the clicking noise interrupting the silence.

She inhales deeply and then forges eye contact once again, her expression heavy. Nervous. "I was at the bonfire last night, and I overheard a guy showboating about how he was about to take over Johnson Farms and was going to be 'freaking rich.' Needless to say, it got my attention."

Brice. Of course he'd be bragging about his victories, trying to use it for leverage with the female crowd. No girl in her right mind would want him just for him. I throw my hands up. "You're not telling me anything I don't know. I resigned from the farm—for good. The farm *will* be his one day."

"It doesn't have to be." Her timid voice sets off a series of explosions in my chest. Because she's wrong. It does have to be that way or else Jordan's family will pay the price. And as much as she ripped my heart out with that business about giving her ex another shot, I refuse to be the person Brice uses as a conduit to hurt her.

I jump to my feet, uncinching my hood and pulling it down. They need to see the determination in my eyes when I tell them to drop whatever they're planning to do on this crazy mission. "Yes, it does! I can't stay or—"

"Or what?" Laurel's eyes widen as she leans forward, almost as if trying to draw it out of me.

I whirl around and face the wall. Brice made it perfectly clear the price Jordan would pay for my talking. "Nothing."

Footsteps cross the wooden floor and a hand reaches from behind, gripping my shoulder. "Or he'll make good on his threats to evict Jordan and her family from their land?" Laurel asks.

My heart sinks to my toes. I turn to face her, my lungs fighting my ribs for room to expand. "How did you know about that?"

"He used your love against you." Her lips pinch together and for a minute before she gains a second wind, straightening her spine and running her tongue over her teeth. "He knew you would sacrifice for her, but what he didn't know is that when he bragged about his exploits, I'd be within earshot." She pushes her cell phone into my hands and smiles. "Someone once told me I'm pretty good at playing people so last night, I decided to play the player."

She nods toward the phone screen and presses the triangle play button. After a momentary flutter of static and erratic movement, the picture straightens out to reveal a sea of bodies, all captured from the chest down in a dusky haze, lit up by the orange bonfire flames and the waning sunset. One body stands particularly close, drink in one hand, college ring on his finger. Brice.

"Damn girl. That ass is fine in those little shorts." His words slur together. Tipsy as usual. "I'm Brice Johnson. Local legend."

He reaches his free hand toward her but she swats it away with a coy giggle. "Nice to meet you, Brice, but don't be getting all handsy now." Laurel's voice carries its usual Southern twang but punched up a few levels. Extra syrupy with long, loopy vowels. Just Brice's taste.

He holds up the red plastic cup in his other hand. "One cup of my Island Punch and you'll be begging me to put my hands all over you."

Another giggle from Laurel. Only this time, she reaches out and strokes his arm. "That sounds like some damn good punch."

"Made by yours truly. Gimme a sec. I'll get you a taste."

"I'll be waiting," she calls after him. The camera angle follows his trek over the sand to a table where the punch is being ladled out of a large cooler. While waiting on the drink, Brice flirts with another partygoer in a white bikini, taking the opportunity to run his hand up her thigh and over her butt. She gives him the finger before running back to her group of friends, but he just waves her off, grabs the drink, and heads back toward Laurel, who whispers, *"Jerk. I'm gonna nail your ass to the wall."*

The camera shifts again, back to the original position, and I'm guessing Laurel's attempting to disguise what she's doing. Brice never seems to catch on. He adjusts his belt and points to the jetty. "Why don't we slip over here by the rocks... get to know each other a little better."

Through Gin's fake puking sounds beside me, the video shows Laurel trailing after him toward the jetty. "Okay, but not far. You might try to take advantage of me."

Brice plops onto a large boulder and pats the one beside him.

As Laurel sits down, he leans in close, his polo shirt nearly blocking out the full screen. "Take advantage of you? Of course not. I'm a total gentleman." He laughs and then adds in a gravelly voice, "Unless you don't want me to be."

They sit for a moment in silence, the waves lapping the shore in a wash of background noise, before Brice asks, "Where you from?"

"Virginia. And I already know you're from here. Heard you're some big shot. Own a farm or something?"

"You heard right."

"Did you start it yourself or is it more like a family thing?"

"It's a family thing that I stole back from the thieves who tried to take it from us."

I look up, exchanging a glance with Gin, who rolls her eyes and sticks out her tongue.

"Thieves? Ooh, that sounds exciting and... a little dangerous." Laurel's flirty response draws me back to the recorded scene. She walks her fingers over his knee, then relaxes her hand on his thigh, giving it the slightest squeeze. "I love it when guys don't mind going after what they want... no matter what it takes."

"Oh really? Well sit back and listen to the master." Brice kicks back, crossing one leg over the other. Laurel repositions the phone so we get a clear shot of his smug face as he recounts the unfair horrors he suffered at our hands and the fact that I wasn't fit to run anything.

"Bo never really seemed to care until this summer when his girlfriend came along and then suddenly, they're gung-ho, constructing vision boards and shit. Like they had any right! He's not even a Johnson by blood, dammit, and then there she is with a bastard kid in the mix. My dad and I knew it was up to me to make sure Johnson Farms remained in true Johnson hands."

My blood boils in the veins of my neck, the way he talked trash about Weston, how he called him a bastard. The same exact way he feels about me.

"So, you..." Laurel playful taps Brice on the chest, "...took it upon yourself to set things straight, amiright? How'd you do it?"

Brice wedges his cup in the sand and sits forward, elbows on knees, and sweeps his hands out in front of him. "Get this... my dumb cousin Gin was in the market reading one of those sappy romance books one day, crying her fool eyes out because the couple had split up. She kept blabbering about how the girl was forced to choose between her love and her family and that when she left the dude, he basically went berserk and got all depressed and shit."

"Your plan was to break them up?" The question lingers in the air between them as Brice reclines against the rock again, a devilish smile creeping over his face and up to his eyes.

"Yep. A little manipulation. A little blackmail." He shrugs, shaking his head. "Turns out his little farm whore hadn't been paying the rent for over a year, so I went to the bank and purchased it out from underneath them. Money talks." He gloats, wobbling his head back and forth, while rubbing his fingers together.

"Sneaky sneaky."

"Yep. I told her to leave or I'd burn the property to the ground in front of them. I may have also threatened to arrange a little farming accident for ol' Bo if I'm remembering correctly. A little extra motivation never hurts." He picks up his cup and tips it back, but nothing comes out. He's already downed another. He stares into the empty depths, then crushes the cup in his fist and tosses it out on the sand. "The deal was that if she successfully left and ended all communications, then I'd consider giving them a good deal on the buy-back. With interest, of course."

My heart drums in my ears. Oh my God. He had forced Jordan's hand by outright threatening their farm... and my life.

"You really are a powerhouse," Laurel whispers in a slinky tone, stroking his ego. "One question, though. How did that get the other guy out of the farm?"

"Simple. He's one of those marshmallow types—all heart-on-his-sleeve, no brain, beta male. I simply told him he had to resign from the farm and deny his inheritance or I'd wreck his long-lost girlfriend's future." Brice one-two punches the night air as if he's a boxer who just scored the TKO. "He caved like the bitch I always knew he was."

Screw him.

"You should teach a course on how to *really* get things done in business."

"Maybe. But I'd much rather talk about how I get things done in the bedroom... or wherever you like it."

Brice leans in and for a brief moment, his gaze lands on the phone and his eyes pierce the screen, lasering directly into mine. That's when I know. I will find a way to take this asshole down, and then I really will stare into his eyes and let him know that I am Bo Johnson and I'm not taking his shit anymore. Jordan had the strength to fight for her family, and now I'll fight for mine. And I'll fight for her.

Laurel's arm sweeps in front of the camera, partially blocking the view as she tries to divert his attention from the phone. "So much for the gentleman, I see."

Brice laughs and trails his finger up Laurel's skin. "I'll be on my best behavior... as long as you aren't."

"You are too much!" She giggles and stands up, brushing the sand from her shorts. "First, though, I need to go to the ladies' room. Is it up by—"

"By the pier. And hurry back. I'll be waiting for my prize." He winks and puckers his lips as if sending a kiss through the air. Total sleaze.

Laurel leans down, wrapping her arm around his neck in a quick hug, and lifts the camera behind his back so that it focuses solely on her face. A smile crooks up the corner of her mouth. "Oh, I can't wait to give you *everything* you deserve."

My wallowing in self-pity has morphed into stewing in a pit of flames. I hand the phone back to Laurel and clench my fists, the anger threatening to spew out like lava. "So, Brice orchestrated all of this? Every last detail."

Gin walks around the bed and grabs my arm. "Yep, and I didn't want to tell you before because, well, there was no point then. But I did ask Jordan about her ex after y'all got back. She told me that she did meet up with him because he wanted to legally take himself out of the picture. He relinquished all rights to Weston." My heart drums against my ribs as she continues. "My guess is that she made up that crap about going back to him because she knew that was the only way you wouldn't chase her down. She was banking on the fact that you'd respect her wishes about Weston's future. That, and she probably knew bringing another guy into the picture would dredge up bad memories." She darts her eyes over to Laurel who drops her gaze to the floor. "She did what she had to. But Brice messed up. He saw Jordan as your weakness. But she's not... she's your strength." A wicked smile spans her face as she threads her arms over her chest. "And we're going to beat Brice at his own game."

My brain is on overload, the circuits feeling fried. "How can you be sure?"

Gin pulls her latest romance book from her bag and holds it up. "Because that dipshit plotted the black moment for y'all, but he's no romance guru. Everyone knows that after the point of hopelessness comes the best part of any true love story."

Now she's talking in riddles and comparing my life to one of her books? "What does that even mean?"

"We get revenge on the jerk... and then reconciliation for you and Jordan."

"But if he owns Jordan's family's land—"

Gin shakes her head, running her tongue along her bottom lip "I don't think he does."

He's been lying? But I saw the paperwork myself. No doubt Jordan did too. "You think he's bluffing?"

"No. I just think he's a male chauvinist idiot."

Gin hunches over her corner desk in the farmhouse, rifling through a slew of papers in the plastic tray and mumbling a string of nonsensical syllables under her breath. She hasn't expounded on her mysterious theory of how all this is going to come together, not even in the ten minutes of silence when we were alone together after dropping Laurel off at her family's place. Gin insisted she not come with us to the office because if Brice caught us together, the whole plan might blow up. However, she's yet to let me in on this plan, and my nerves flicker like sparklers under my skin. Jordan's farm is riding on this. My place here at the farm. Our future.

"Yes!" Gin pulls a packet of paperwork from the bunch and hoists it in the air like a trophy. Her maniacal laugh echoes against the wood paneling. She hands it to me, and I scan the front page. It's the same paperwork Brice had shoved in my face. The sale agreement, now with Brice's signature and Patrick as co-signatory.

"Is this the signed contract on the land?"

A glint sparks in her eyes as she nods. "Mmm-hmm."

My stomach fills with lead blocks. "Then it's over. He owns it. He wins."

"Nnn-nnn," Gin sing-songs while shaking her head, a grin inching over her face.

I glance back down at the document. It's official with signatures and everything. "What am I missing?"

"Oh, just Brice being his usual, predictable, nasty self." She snatches the paperwork out of my grip and points to the bottom line with Brice's and Patrick's scrawl. "It's signed, it's sealed, but it *ain't* delivered."

"You mean..." I jab my finger at the legalese, the pieces falling into position in my brain. "The bank doesn't have this?"

"The jackass put this in *my* work folder. He feels scanning and emailing his own business documents is beneath him... I

believe he called it 'woman's work.' He thought I'd be too stupid
to do anything except follow his orders." She plunges her thumb
to her chest. "Well, this woman is about to work one over on his
sorry ass. You would think such an intricate part of his plan he'd
handle himself, but there's no accounting for jerkish behavior,
now is there?"

The lead wall in my gut crumbles, a wave of easy breath
filling my lungs. I grab Gin's shoulders and give her a shake.
"You're a genius."

"I know." She smirks then narrows her eyes. "Now go call
Dad."

When the front door of the farmhouse opens, Dad nods at me
and I slip into the small bathroom adjoining the boardroom and
stand in the darkness, out of sight of those coming in for dad's
impromptu meeting. My stomach clenches tight. I've never been
one for confrontation and no doubt this one is going to be
nuclear.

In the two days since Gin's discovery of the unfiled paperwork, it's taken every ounce of strength not to pick up the
phone and call Jordan. To tell her that help is on the way. But
taking any chances before the deals were done, the loose ends
wrapped, wasn't a risk I was willing to take.

"Clay, what in the hell is going on?" Patrick busts into the
room, yanking off his cap and tossing it on the table. He flops
into the chair at the far end and rears back, throwing his dirty
boots up on the edge. "We didn't have a meeting on the docket
today, and I got a million things to do. I was—"

"Whatever it is, I'm sure it can wait." Dad's voice is calm,
measured. Almost relieved. "This is more important." He looks
up and gestures to the door. "Brice, Gin, Doniella. Please come
in and have a seat."

They walk in and find their places at the table, Gin inconspicuously gazing toward the bathroom for a quick minute, a huge grin on her face. Brice settles into the chair beside Patrick and glares at Gin across the table. "What's she doing here?"

Gin's smile creases downward and her eyes narrow. "Oh, I've just been catching up on my shredding and paperwork and filing. You know, all that 'woman's work' you guys don't want to handle."

Brice eyes a basket full of paper shreds on the middle of the table. "You think you might could actually clean up after yourself?"

Dad walks over and closes the door then retakes his seat at the head of the table. "She," he says, pointing at Gin, "is my daughter and a part of Johnson Farms. She has every right to be here."

"If your kids are included in this, then where's Bo?" Brice glances at Patrick and they snicker. "Oh yeah... sorry. Forgot. We won't talk about that."

Dad's fingers clench the pen in his hand. "No, Brice. We absolutely need to talk about that. Bo's unexpected departure from the farm has caused me to reassess a few things. Hence our meeting here today."

Patrick drops his feet and leans forward, elbows on the table, lips flatlined. "You want to cut to the chase here?"

"As you all know, this summer has been a time of soul-searching for me. A time to contemplate the future of Johnson Farms and whose hands it will be left in after my time as CEO comes to an end. This isn't something to be taken lightly. The management of a generations-old company is contingent—"

Patrick waves his hand in the air. "Yeah, yeah, yeah. We don't care about your speeches. Let's just get down to business and set right a whole lot of wrongs."

"I couldn't have said it better myself, Patrick, because that's exactly what I'm determined to do. Right the wrongs that have been committed here." Dad stands up, cracks his knuckles, and then walks around the room to stand behind Patrick and Brice.

"Johnson Farms was founded on the premise of family, and going forward, this farm will honor that commitment. So, without any more useless speeches or bravado, I want to officially name the successor of Johnson Farms as..." Brice's spine straightens as he pulls his shoulders back. Patrick reaches over and pats him on the arm. "My son, Beauregard Johnson, who will be appointed as co-owner with his very capable sister, Ginny Johnson." Dad's face erupts in a toothy smile as he extends his arm toward the head of the table where Gin stands up and I walk out of the shadows to meet her. "Meet the future of Johnson Farms."

It takes a full minute for the revelation to register on Brice and Patrick's faces. First, their eyes widen, then their jaws drop, and as the look at each other, reddish swirls rise from their necks into their cheeks. Brice jumps to his feet, pounding a closed fist on the table. "This is bullshit! He resigned. He's not even a *real* Johnson! And she's a girl."

Gin rolls her eyes and throws her hands on her hips. "You figured that all out on your own, did ya?"

"About that resignation..." Dad says, walking toward us and pointing at the bin on the table. "If you care to take a closer look at the bowl of shredded paper, you'll find Bo's letter among the scraps. I would never accept his resignation, especially when it was coerced by the despicable actions of someone who claims to have the farm's best interests at heart." He turns and sets his glare on Brice. "Yes, I know all about your little blackmail attempts. That won't fly with me."

"Fine. Don't say I didn't warn you." Brice stampedes around the table, thrusting his chest into mine and pushing closer nose-to-nose. "Your little girlfriend's farm is going down, and you'll be the reason why!"

I don't back down. I don't even blink. I hone my eyes in on his, locking in like steel. Dad clears his throat and Brice glares in his direction. "If you take a second look at those paper shreds, you'll see what's left of your so-called trump card. A signed offer on real estate is really no good unless it's in the hands of the bankers and yours... well, it isn't."

He whirls around, his gaze connecting with Patrick's, before both sets of eyes fix on the table and the pile of scraps. In unison, they dive toward the bin, pulling out shreds and examining them. "Thief! You can't steal my private property and shred it!"

"We didn't steal anything," Gin says, leaning in over Brice's shoulder. "You gave it to me, dumbass. Once again, your ego is definitely bigger than your pea-brain."

"Fine. Who cares?" Brice swipes the bin off the table. It hits the wall, sending papers shreds flying in all directions. "This changes nothing. I'll call the bank today and finalize it!"

Dad slides the landline phone across the table. "Use the farm phone. Do it now. I dare you."

"You dare us?" Patrick yells, all of his restraint now evaporated. "You dare us?" His eyes bulge from their sockets, veins pulsating like blue rivers down his neck. "You two stole your positions here and you—" his attention turns on me— "you never belonged here. You're just some whore's son Clay pretends is his. You have no rights here. You never did and you never will!"

My bottom lip trembles and I do my best to control it. Dad has never made me feel as if I didn't belong, and I'm pretty sure he's been protecting me from this vitriol all along. The weird comments, the hatred hurled at me for no good reason, the passive aggressiveness. Dad has stood in the gap all along and knocked it down before I'd even felt it. He knew, but he never wanted me to.

Warm fingers grip mine and squeeze hard. Dad stands shoulder-to-shoulder beside me, an impenetrable wall. "I've got you, son," he whispers.

Across the room, Brice holds the receiver to his ear, a smug grin etched on his mouth. "Gerald Smith, please. It's urgent." He paces back and forth until there's an apparent answer on the line. "Gerald, Brice Johnson here. I was just informed that my signed paperwork on the land deal was not submitted so if you can send me another copy, I'll get that signed and back to you within a few minutes. I'm very motivated to move forward on this." His face scrunches into a deep scowl. "What do you mean it's no longer up for bids? We discussed—what? When? But how could they—I see." Brice drops the receiver back into its cradle and runs a hand through his hair.

"What is it?" Patrick grabs Brice by the shoulders, bringing him face to face.

"The property is no longer eligible for purchase." His eyes shift over Patrick's shoulder to Dad. "All liens against it have been satisfied." Patrick drops his head and Brice pushes past him, rushing toward us. "I guess you think you're pretty smart, don't you, Clay? So smart that you'd take the farm started by *our* family—not his—and throw away its legacy on common gutter trash? Some fatherless bastard that could've come from anywhere or anyone and his equally stupid sister? Is that what you want for Johnson Farms?"

Dad steels himself and steps forward, the toe of his boot butting against Brice's. Gin steps behind him and grabs my hand.

"As a matter of fact, these two are exactly what I want for Johnson Farms. I have never seen more dedication to this farm and this family than I have from these two right here. And I have never seen such deceit and perversion as I've seen from you two. Bo may not share my DNA but he is more Johnson than either of you will ever be." Dad jabs his finger toward the door. "Now get out. You're both fired."

Brice's nostrils flare, the muscles in his jaw pulsing in and out. "You can't do this. We'll fight you in court!"

Dad laughs and folds his arms. "Good luck with that. I am the owner of Johnson Farms. I decide its direction."

Brice stomps his foot, yelling, "We'll see about that!" before marching out. Seconds later, the front door slams so hard, the picture frames rattle on the wall.

Dad walks over and holds the door open for Patrick. He

stops in front of him, shoulders slumped. "Clay, you need to take time and re-think this. I thought we were family."

The f-word. Patrick knows it's Dad's weakness. Family is always his obligation, and Patrick's banking on using guilt to coerce him into reversing his decision.

But Dad doesn't flinch. He doesn't even bat an eye. "After this summer, I've discovered that your and my definitions of family are two very different things, and I like mine better." The door squeaks open wider. "Good-bye, Patrick."

A couple hours later, Dad drives and I sit beside him in the passenger seat, staring over at the man who has dedicated his life to family, those blood-related and those not, with equal love and protection. He doesn't care about blood tests and DNA swabs or biological ties. He only cares about the true bonds—the real ones—forged through our relationships with each other.

I hope one day I can be the kind of man he's exemplified to me.

He glances over from the driver's seat, a smile on his lips. "Everything okay?"

I nod, trying to put together the words in my head so they don't jumble coming off my tongue. He needs to hear what I have to say. Because even though I know deep down that he's aware, he still needs to hear it spoken aloud. "I don't know if I've ever really said thank you for all you've done for me."

"Bo—"

I hold up a hand, shaking my head. "Let me finish. Now more than ever, I realize how scared you must have been, how much of yourself you had to give, to take me in and be the dad you didn't have to be. You had no obligations to me, yet you accepted me—loved me—like a true father should."

He reaches over and pats my shoulder, his fingers gripping me tight, and I notice the redness blooming under his eyes, his bottom lip trembling. Mine begins to shake as well but I muster up the strength to hold it firm, so I can finish what I have to say.

"Maybe we don't share blood, but you *chose* me, and that was the best gift of all. I am a Johnson and I am your son no matter what anyone says, and I hope that I can always live up to your example."

CHAPTER 36

Jordan

We're seated on the floor beside a heap of flattened cardboard, masking tape, and memories collected over more than four decades in this house. My heart breaks with every item bubble-wrapped and stashed in a box. The sound of a car door slamming floats in through the open window, and Mama looks at me, brows furrowed. I shrug. I'm not expecting anyone. She sighs and gets up, brushing off her jeans, and walks to the double windows overlooking the front yard.

She blows out a loud breath and turns around, hands on hips. "Here comes that damn Gerald from the bank. Why can't he just leave us in peace?"

When Gerald sold our farm out from under us, he might as well have declared war on Mama. She is taking a defensive stand where he is concerned, and the man has a lot of gumption—or maybe just a death wish—to come within ten feet of Sheryl Wright. Especially when she is standing there at the front screen with a scowl on her face and a boxcutter in her back pocket.

The porch floorboards squeak as he makes his way across them to knock on the door. Mama pops around the corner so quickly, he jumps and shuffles backwards a few steps. When she doesn't say a word of greeting, he asks to come in. Mama unlocks the door and swings it open, not moving from her post. He gives her a faint smile and then smooshes himself in the small space between her and the wall to enter the living area.

"Afternoon, Sheryl." He nods at her then turns to me. "Jordan." He holds a green folder with paperwork, which he hands to Mama. "I wanted to stop by today and bring you this."

She snatches it from his grip without looking inside. She exhales so hard the front flip of Gerald's hair lifts with the breeze. "More paperwork?"

"No ma'am. That is the deed to this property." His voice wavers as he points to the folder in Mama's hand. "The Wrights now own it, free and clear."

What did he just say? I stand up, glancing between Gerald and Mama. Is this some sort of sick joke on Brice's part? Or did he make good on his promise to restore the farm to us since I left Bo? No. Brice could never be trusted to do the right thing, only the wrong one.

Mama flips through the paperwork with narrowed eyes that sweep back and forth down the pages. She closes the folder and lifts her gaze to Gerald. "I don't think I understand. We're preparing to pack up and move. A couple days ago you were selling us off to the highest bidder."

"That deal was never finalized."

My breath catches in my throat. Never finalized? That means... no Brice? I race to Mama's side.

"The agreement was never signed and before it was, some last-minute funding came through to satisfy the liens."

Mama cocks her head to one side like she's having trouble making sense of what Gerald's saying. To tell the truth, we both are. None of this makes any sense. Brice had the sale agreement in hand. I saw his signature in ink. How does all that get negated?

Mama grunts. "What kind of funding? A loan? 'Cause I haven't agreed to any terms."

Gerald shakes his head, kneading the cuff of his button-down shirt. "No ma'am. A private investment."

"Somebody paid off our loan?" Mama scratches her head and stares at the floor. I know she's running a list of people through her head, searching for any potential matches. "Now who in the hell would do that?"

Gerald, looking skittish as ever, chews the inside of his cheek. "I'm not at liberty to say, ma'am."

"Look, I ain't playing with you." Mama reaches forward, fisting the collar of his shirt. His eyes bug out and he backpedals a few steps, his back slamming into the wall beside the door. "I'm gonna ask you one last time... who paid off our farm?"

"I did." Another voice—one I recognize immediately— chimes in from the front porch. We all swivel on our heels to find Clay standing at the screen door, his hand on the latch. "May I come in?"

This time I'm the one manhandling Gerald, grabbing his shirt and pulling him away from the door. I stand on the other side of the screen from Clay, rubbing my eyes. I can't believe he's here. But I'm so damn glad he is. And he's the one who paid off our loan. But how did he pull that off? How did he outwit Brice's conniving?

I open the screen door and grab his hand, pulling him into the living room. "I can't believe you're here." The giddy words fall off my tongue like melted butter, but my stomach drops when he walks in and the door slams. There's no one behind him.

I gulp down an uncomfortable bubble of air lodged in my chest. Clay may have saved the day but the damage I've had to inflict on Bo remains. I can understand why coming here would be the least palatable thing on his to-do list. I wouldn't want to see me either.

"Hey Jordan." Clay pulls me into a side hug before focusing his gaze on Mama. A smile spreads his lips. "Hey Sheryl."

Mama steps forward, shaking her head, and wraps her arms

around Clay. She leans back, a toothy grin on her face. "Lord have mercy. Clayton Johnson, you haven't changed in twenty years."

My mind reels. Twenty years? "Wait. You two know each other?"

"Remember the girl from Ag Camp I told you about? The Dolly Parton aficionado?"

"That was my mama?" Memories from that night around the firepit flood my brain. He said they'd been on an internship together. Gin joked about her being his girlfriend but he said no, they never dated. He said she had big dreams of Nashville but that something must've happened to derail those. I swallow hard. Now I know that I was the hurdle on the road to her dreams. That's why this summer meant so much to her. That's why she pushed this as my saving grace. I look up at them. "So that's how I landed the internship this year."

Clay holds up his hand. "Hold on just a minute. Your mama sent me an email, got your name in front of me, but you won it all by yourself, Jordan." He grabs my shoulder, crouching to my eye level. "And you proved yourself time and again. Let's get that clear."

In the moment of heavy silence that follows, Gerald, who's been scooting toward the door, excuses himself and heads to his car. Mama pads to the window and watches him go, the heels of her boots thumping the hardwoods as she drums her fingers against her thigh. I'm familiar with that particular staccato of her steps. She's stewing on the inside and on the verge of exploding... just as soon as she works out exactly what she wants to say.

She spins on her heel and walks back across the room, stopping in front of Clay, eyeing him up and down as if he's on the stand in municipal court.

"I suppose I should say thank you for coming to our rescue with this generous offer—and I do thank you—but I'm sorry Clay, I have to ask, what is your angle here? And why in the hell did someone from Johnson Farms try to steal our home in the first place?"

Damn, Mama. Put the man on the spot why don't you?

But Clay doesn't balk. He remains calm, holding up a finger. "First of all, that land grab had nothing to do with Johnson Farms. Brice and his father Patrick have fostered some old animosities about my inheriting the farm over them. They especially didn't want Bo inheriting it from me since..."

"Since he wasn't blood." I finish the sentence for him. Brice had made his motivations all too clear.

Mama scowls. "All of this because Bo isn't biologically yours? What difference does that make?"

I deadpan. "Come on, Mama. You have seen how nasty people can be about unwed mothers and their kids. For some, the only thing that matters is some match in the double-helix. Not character. Not integrity."

"You're right," Clay says, exhaling as walks over to the couch and sits down, head in his hands. "I did my best to shield Bo from all that, but I couldn't. Not in the long run."

Mama and I join Clay on the couch and he relays the events of the last few days since I left Edisto. How Brice once again made a spectacle of showing off the land sale agreement only to never officially submit it. How Bo and Gin, with—surprise, surprise—help from Laurel, uncovered the whole plan and brought it to his attention. How they arranged their own little surprise for Brice and sent him and Patrick packing. How Christopher wasn't punished for Brice's actions but instead awarded the internship money. How now that our farm is stable, they want to talk further about partnering on that vineyard.

I smile. Even Gin in all her enthusiasm for happy endings couldn't have tied up this story's ending in any prettier bow. My stomach gripes. Except for that part about me and Bo. That's a freaking tragedy.

"I do have one question, though." Clay turns to me. "What did Brice say to you? To make you leave the way you did?"

"He told me I had to leave—tell Bo I was going back to my ex—and cut all communication or he'd have our house and farm burned to the ground and build condos on the land. He also said..." I stop as the tears begin flowing down my cheeks. The other threat has spurred nightmares ever since the words were uttered. "He said he'd arrange a 'farm accident' for Bo. Hurt him."

Mama gasps, getting up off the couch, and crouches in front of me, pulling me into her arms. "Why didn't you tell me?" she whispers into my hair.

"Because he said if I said a word, he'd follow through on his promises. He had the paperwork for the land sale. I saw it with my own eyes, and I know what kind of person Brice is. I couldn't hurt us. And I couldn't let him hurt Bo." I can barely get the last words out as all the terrible scenarios I'd imagined parade through my brain.

Mama jumps to her feet, fire swirling in her cheeks. "Son of a bitch, punk kid, crooked weasel." She grinds a fist into her other palm. "He should be in politics instead of agriculture with all his shady backstabbing."

"Well, the future's open if he so chooses. He and Patrick have both been fired and banned from all Johnson Farms land." Clay stands up, a proud smile on his face. "And today I officially named Bo and Gin as co-successors of the farm."

A mix of pride and joy circulate through me. I cannot think of two more deserving people. And Bo worried so much this summer that he'd never find his way. I told him a time would come when everything became clear. Even if he hates me now, at least he'll remember those words. "Please tell them congratulations," I say.

Clay trains his eyes on me. "I'm sure Bo would rather hear it from you."

"No, he wouldn't." I stare down at my bare feet, trying to squash the ugly memories cropping up in my brain. "I had to say horrible things to him... I had to hurt him so he wouldn't follow me. I had to make him hate me."

"I don't know what was said between you two—Bo didn't care to share the specifics of that—but he must still care about you an awful lot if he was willing to resign the farm in order to protect you and Weston and this family." Clay picks up my phone from the coffee table and hands it to me. "I just think you'll never know until you try."

Mama smiles and nods her head toward the door. "Go call him, Sassy."

I take my phone and walk out onto the front porch, dialing Bo. His phone rings five times and goes to voicemail. I hang up without leaving a message but immediately call back. Voicemail. Call again. And again. And again. Voicemail each time. I grab hold of the porch post, my head spinning, feeling stuffed with cotton.

He took one look at that Caller ID and didn't answer. He really does hate me now. I walk beside the window and peek in. Mama and Clay sit on the couch, iced teas in hand as they catch-up after a twenty-year absence, laughing and talking. I can't go back in there. I can't admit that I've royally screwed up everything.

Instead, I walk down the porch steps and amble toward my favorite spot in the field. The place where the Bobwhites call. The place where Bo and I...

I'm breaking, fracturing. Feeling like a million broken pieces that somehow keep moving as one, fooling everyone that I'm surviving while little by little, I'm withering to nothing.

The moon, a pale orange, glows in the Southeastern sky, hanging just above the treetops as a mirror image to the pinks and purples swirling around the sunset. I sit down in front of the barn, looking out over the rolling vista before lifting my head to greet Mr. Moon.

"I really blew it this time, didn't I? If only you could give me the perfect advice I'll need to fix this." The burning crescent hangs there, silent. Watching. "I had to drive him away. I said the most awful things, when all I really wanted to say... all I've wanted to say all summer is..." I pause, cupping my hands around my mouth. The moon may not respond but he—and this universe—are damn well going to hear me shout it from the top of my lungs. "I love you, Bo. God, I love you so much!"

A covey of birds takes flight from the meadow, their flapping wings creating a long *woosh*. But beyond that, another sound. Faint but familiar.

"I love you too."

My breath catches in my throat and chill bumps race down my body. Please, please don't let me be hallucinating.

I twist sideways in the grass and spot him immediately as he steps forward from the shadows of the barn. A pale glow glints across his features and just like that night on the beach, he becomes the moon and I am the tide, rising to meet him. Magnetic.

"You're here," I say, getting up and ambling toward him, my body feeling as if it's floating, my toes dragging the ground.

He walks toward me, one hand extended. "There's nowhere else I want to be."

I slide my hand into his, his fingers closing around mine. "I'm so sorry for everything I said. I didn't mean it. I didn't mean a word of it. I had to make you hate me. I had to make you think it was over, but your face..." I clamp my eyes shut and bury my head against his chest, the shame burning like flames in my body when I recall his reaction. "Oh my God, I can still see your face and it's killing me. I wanted to curl up and die. The hurt on your face—I don't ever want to be the person that hurts you."

He cups my chin in his hands, prying my face away from his body and forcing me to look at him. His blue eyes sparkle again, no longer dark and stormy as they last were. "It's okay. Brice did his best to prove your claims—that you'd gone back to your ex—he even manufactured some photos as proof, and looking at them..." He grinds his teeth, nostrils flaring as he recollects himself. "The thought of you with someone else tore me up. It made me realize that I don't want another guy touching you. Or holding you. Or loving you. I want it to be me." He gingerly swipes a few stray hairs from my face, leaning down close so that our lips are a whisper apart. "Because I want to touch you, and hold you, and kiss you. Because you are without a doubt my Miss Wright, and I love you."

"I love you more." I jump into his arms and he scoops me up, wrapping my legs around his waist. He crushes his lips into mine, fast and hungry, and I run my fingers through his curls, tugging him closer. When he comes up for air, I lean my forehead against his, eyes closed. The musky scent of his shampoo mingles with the sweet honeysuckle floating in the twilight air. His long lashes tickle against my skin as they flutter open. I lean closer, my lips nearly touching his ear. "Is this for real? Is this too good to be true? Promise me we'll never be apart like that again."

Bo sets me on my feet, and I raise my gaze to his, steady and strong. He doesn't flinch one iota. "My feelings for you are one hundred percent real, and, I'm here to stay. Brice's antics didn't work, and I'm not your father who'll up and disappear or any of those other guys who couldn't bother to stick around. I'm going to be right here to love you and to fight for you... and Weston." He kisses me again, longer this time, only pulling back to reassure me once more. "I'm not going anywhere."

CHAPTER 37

Bo

Ting. Ting. Ting.

Dad taps his fork against his wine glass, then slides his chair back, standing up at the head of the table. I reach down and grab Jordan's hand, which rests on my thigh. Three months have passed since that night we reunited under the rising moon but holding her hand still never gets old. And after tonight, I'll have plenty more opportunities to do so. Because tomorrow, I'm moving to the Upstate.

Dad clears his throat and everyone hushes, turning eyes on him. "Tonight, we officially kick-off the collaboration between Johnson Farms and Wright Family Farm, with the Wrights bringing their operation under the Johnson umbrella." He opens a folder on the table and pulls out a collection of papers. "With a few signatures, everything will be finalized." He pulls a pen from his pocket, clicks it on, and scribbles his name on the line. Then, he looks to the other end of the table and holds up the pen. "Sheryl?"

She smiles, winks at Jordan, then stands up and walks beside Dad. In a matter of seconds, her name is added to the paperwork. The notary steps forward, having them initial several places as he fills out the necessary documents and embosses his seal on them.

After some intense planning and a strict contract negotiation that brought Wright Family Farm into a financial partnership with our farm without compromising the ownership of their property, Dad, Sheryl, and Jordan's Grandpa reached an agreement that will bind our two families for the foreseeable future. At least on the business side of things. Relationship-wise, Jordan and I are already set.

Weston wiggles in his booster seat, coloring a picture of a crab on his kiddie menu in long red smears. Jordan laughs, fluffing his curls with her fingers. My heart swells. Starting tomorrow, this becomes my everyday life.

Because the vineyards were my concept, Dad appointed me the lead on the collaboration, reporting back to him. He needed an on-site manager who could relocate to the Upstate to monitor progress and who also had a deep understanding of the concept. Check and check. It took me about one minute to say yes when he asked me.

Spending every day working with Jordan? Yes, please! After the last few months of on again-off again separation, tomorrow can't come quick enough.

I glance across the table at Mom and Gin, heads bent together as they chat and laugh. I'll miss them, though. And Dad. I stare past them, out the wide windows overlooking the pier and the Atlantic. The waves roll in, crashing into the sand and dissolving into a fizzle of white foam. And I'll miss that.

The memory of Jordan on the first day I met her, pulling off the road underneath the Piggly Wiggly sign when her eyes first glimpsed the ocean springs forward. She'd been so entranced, so taken by something I'd been taking for granted. She made me remember how special this place is.

Weston giggles and Jordan pulls him into her lap, bouncing him on her knee.

She also showed me love like I'd never known. Love that gets its ass kicked and keeps fighting the fight. I'll follow her anywhere.

The notary packs up his toolkit and steps away from the table. Dad and Sheryl shake hands and Mom snaps a couple of photos with her phone.

"Here's to Quail Valley Vineyards!" Dad raises a glass and we all follow his example.

Jordan looks at me underneath a flutter of long lashes. "Looks like we're official."

"We've *been* official." I joke, leaning in to kiss her cheek. "Now we're just in business together."

Weston catches me and grins, wrapping his chubby arms around my neck and Jordan's, smooshing all three of us together, then throws his head back laughing as if he's playing an epic game.

She chews her cheek, narrowing her eyes. "Does this make you my boss?"

I bring my lips to her ear, grazing her skin as I whisper, "Why? You want me to boss you around?"

She cocks one eyebrow into her forehead. "You, Bo, are—"

"I need to potty!" Weston yells, hopping down from Jordan's lap and dancing around, holding himself. She'd been working on his potty training since returning home and the one thing she told me is consistency is key, so if the kid's gotta go, he's gotta go now.

"I'll take him," Gin says, getting up and trotting around the table. She holds out her arms, and Weston practically jumps into them. A few visits with Gin and he's in love already. And the way her cheeks round, the deepest dimple peeking out when he's around, I can tell the feeling is mutual. They begin walking to the door, but Gin stops, glancing over her shoulder. "Y'all should go out for a quick walk on the beach. It's a nice evening and you won't get the chance to do it again for a while."

They disappear out the private dining room's door, headed for the restrooms, and I take a moment to study the other people in the room. Dad, Mom, and Sheryl sit together, laughing and talking, glasses of wine in hand. In the corner, Doniella and Luis lean close, watching a video on her phone.

Then I feel her gaze on me. I turn, finding Jordan eyeing me up and down. "What is it?"

"Maybe we should sneak out for a quick walk. A one-for-the-road?"

I nod and stand up, holding out my hand. Jordan slips hers into mine and we wander out the glass French door onto the pier. She closes her eyes, absorbing the moment, the whir of the ocean water spiraling around the pier's wooden legs.

I wrap my arms around her, tugging her to my chest. "What are you thinking?"

She sighs, opening her eyes. The waning sunset casts long dark shadows across us. "Is it going to be strange not being here?"

I've thought about it a million times, waking up in the mountains instead of at the coast. Different, yes. But waking up in the same locale as her? Perfection. That's when I think of something I'd forgotten to tell Jordan. A past moment a few months ago when I came to this very pier, contemplating the way she was stealing my heart in all the right ways. It was the same night I emailed her favorite band and asked them to perform at our fateful market event, the one where our dance almost led to the most perfect first kiss. And even though we didn't kiss that night, in my head, it's all turned out so differently. Her lips on mine, mine on hers.

"Bo?"

Her voice snaps me out of my daydream, and I stare down at her, eyes rounded and full lips parted as she watches me.

"I want to show you something," I say, grabbing her fingers and pulling her toward the steps. We amble down the flight to the underside of the pier and the famous carved leg where people for generations have inscribed their names on the historical record of Edisto.

She runs her fingers over the scratched letters, studying them.

"There's always going to be a part of us here, even if we're away." I grab her hand and lift it up and to the left. To my name. To hers.

"Is this me?" She covers her mouth with her hand, eyes saucering. "How did that get there?"

"I put it there. Back in June. Because I already knew..." I stop short, swallowing back the words.

She smiles. "You knew what?"

"That you were going to leave your mark on Edisto, the same way you already had on me. I was too scared to tell you then that I was falling for you." I cup her chin, bringing her lips to mine. They are soft and full, moving against mine, until I pull back slightly to add, "But I'm not scared anymore. Now I want it all."

She kisses me again then fixes her eyes on the ocean. Her bottom lip tugs down as she darts her gaze back to me. "Aren't you going to miss this? Being home?"

I run my fingers through her hair, holding my hand at the back of her head. "As long as I have you, I am home."

Jordan purses her lips and loops her arms around my neck. "Those sweet words. If I didn't know any better, I might think—"

"Bo! Jordan! They're serving dessert!"

I scowl. Gin. I swear my sister was born with a radar built in to her brain.

Jordan pops up on her tiptoes, quickly pecking my lips, then skips over to the stairs. She stops on the third one and holds out her hand, a huge smile spreading her lips. "Coming?"

The girl standing in front of me is not who I expected to be mine when summer first started, but it turns out she is everything I needed. Looking back, I'm glad fate intervened to slaughter my heart and then put it back together in the most exquisite way. A million times better than it started. Because when it comes to Jordan, I've found more than love. I've found direction, meaning.

I trot to the steps and slip my fingers in hers.

I've found family.

The End

Acknowledgments

Wow! Writing the acknowledgements for this book hits different after the utter ups and downs from 2020 until now. There were dark times I thought I might give up this authoring gig, but I love storytelling too much to give up my passion, and it is because of you, **Dear Readers**, that I push on! So for those of you who read, review, and support me in your own ways, I just want to say thank you for always believing in me, even when I've struggled to believe in myself. I hope you embrace this story of Bo and Jordan in the same way you did Jett and CJ and Gage and Rayne.

To God: *Farmers who wait for perfect weather never plant. If they watch every cloud, they never harvest. (Ecclesiastes 11:4)* This is the perfect verse for this book and for life. Thank you for helping me realize that there will never be a perfect time. There is just time and all we can do is step out on faith and do our best to make it our own version of perfect.

To Jena: My ride or die! You have been with me since the beginning of this author career and become a dear friend, cover designer (I mean, y'all...true artistry right there!), and fellow writer. I couldn't do it without you! Love you big time!

Some lovely friends, both writerly and non-writerly, who've been a light in the darkness: Every time you've touched base with me, every time you've recommended one of my books, every time you've created a Tiktok or reel or social media post, every time you've reviewed, and every time you sent me messages out of the blue just to check on me, the status of my next book, or to tell me how my writing affected you personally, please know that I cherish every single one of those experiences. I could write a million lines telling you how much it all means to me but the crux of it is that I appreciate you, I'm grateful for you, and I love you all.

To my children: Quit growing up so fast! When this author portion of my career began you were just "babies" but now you're all "grown-up" teens and tweens. It has been the joy of my life to be your mother. In all three of you, I see glimpses of me and your Daddy expertly blended and mix-matched into the most awesome humans I've ever known. You make me proud. Always.

To my husband: Love of my life, best friend, better half, #1 supporter—those are just a few of the words I use to describe you. We just hit 20 years together—20!—and I've loved ever minute of it. Let's go out and do 20 (30, 40, 50...) more! You have my heart forever.

And lastly to The Person Of Whom We Do Not Speak: You know who you are. You have been the biggest stumbling block in my career. But like all stumbling blocks, you may have tripped me up for a second, but I've sure enjoyed kicking you and your influence to the curb and running it over with my own gumption. I'd like to say I can kindly tell you that I hope all your dreams come true, but I can't. Unlike you, the lies don't fall so easily off my tongue. The truth is that for you, my "grace" ran out a long time ago. And in the spirit of that old Southern saying, "If you can't say something nice, then don't say anything at all," I'll just leave you with this: If anyone deserves to reap what they have sown, it is you.

About the Author

Brandy Woods Snow is an author and journalist born, raised, and currently living in beautiful Upstate South Carolina. She earned a BA in English/Writing from Clemson University and worked in corporate communications and the media for nearly two decades before pursuing her true passion of writing novels brimming with Southern culture, twisted family dynamics, young love, and deep-diving emotions. When Brandy's not writing, reading, spending time with her husband or driving carpool for her three kids, she enjoys kayaking, family hikes, yelling "Go Tigers!" as loud as she can, playing the piano and taking "naked" Jeep Wrangler cruises on country roads.

www.BrandyWSnow.com
Romantic at heart, Southern to the core.

Also by Brandy Woods Snow

Meant To Be Broken

The first book in the *Carolina Clay* series

As Much As I Ever Could

The first book in the *Edisto Summers* series

As Long As I Have You

The second book in the Edisto Summers series

As Fast As We Can Go (Coming Soon!)

The third book in the Edisto Summers series

Printed in Great Britain
by Amazon

87708357R00235